No Heart to Kill

Creative Texts Publishers products are available at special discounts for bulk purchase for sale promotions, premiums, fund-raising, and educational needs. For details, write Creative Texts Publishers, PO Box 50, Barto, PA 19504, or visit www.creativetexts.com

No Heart to Kill
by C.W. Wells
Published by Creative Texts Publishers
PO Box 50
Barto, PA 19504
www.creativetexts.com

Copyright 2023 by C. W. Wells
All rights reserved

Cover photos used by license.
Design copyright 2023 Creative Texts Publishers, LLC

This book or parts thereof may not be reproduced in any form, stored in a retrieval system, or transmitted in any form by any means—electronic, mechanical, photocopy, recording, or otherwise—without prior written permission of the publisher, except as provided by United States of America copyright law.

The following is a work of fiction. Any resemblance to actual names, persons, businesses, and incidents is strictly coincidental. Locations are used only in the general sense and do not represent the real place in actuality.

ISBN: 978-1-64738-101-1

NO HEART TO KILL

by C.W. Wells

CREATIVE TEXTS PUBLISHERS

Barto, PA

In memory of my brother, Mason

TABLE OF CONTENTS

One	1
Two	14
Three	22
Four	34
Five	40
Six	48
Seven	54
Eight	63
Nine	70
Ten	79
Eleven	88
Twelve	91
Thirteen	99
Fourteen	111
Fifteen	122
Sixteen	129
Seventeen	141
Eighteen	151
Nineteen	166
Twenty	180
Twenty-One	192
Twenty-Two	202
Twenty-Three	210
Twenty-Four	217

Twenty-Five..222
Epilogue..223

One

Clay Moorhead coached high school football for 36 years. He'd won six state championships, made men out of boys, been lionized in Caton, Texas, and yet found himself on a furnace-like summer morning in the sights of a high-powered, Bergara B-14 Ridge SG/Gray Bolt action rifle.

He had purchased his sleek bass boat after the town's boosters had slipped him the biggest payout of his career to honor his nearly four decades as one of the most celebrated high school coaches in Texas. Moorhead never fought the weight of his golden handcuffs. Over the years, boosters had bought Moorhead new pickups, built an addition on his home and a swimming pool in his backyard, helped pay for his kids' college tuition, and covered his trips to Vegas, where he sat in Aria with a toothpick dancing in his mouth chatting up the ladies and making himself a fixture at the poker table. With booster money in his pocket and his wife at home, he took special care in being able to pay for fresh companionship. While he championed honor and integrity to generations of players, after a few bourbons and several hands of poker, he conveniently forgot the lessons he preached, sleeping with women young enough to be his daughter.

With a Panther baseball cap pulled low on his forehead and thick wraparound sunglasses shielding his eyes, Moorhead sat in his Skeeter TZX bass boat on an empty lake and lazily raised his rod to cast when the .308 round hurtled from the Bergara's graphite black cerakoted barrel and exploded in the center of his chest. The round struck with a blunt thud, the echoing rifle shot rippling across Twin Mesa Reservoir.

A few hours later, a bass fisherman spotted Moorhead's boat drifting in the middle of the lake. He found Moorhead splayed on the Skeeter's deck in a coagulated pool of blood. When Billy Pax, the County Sheriff arrived, he cursed and wiped the sweat off his brow with the back of his hand. Then he turned to the distraught fisherman and asked with a grunt, "How are we going to find a coach in late July?"

Gale McClanahan was repairing fences in the blinding sun when he spotted a gleaming black pickup bouncing toward him in a swirl of dust on one of the ranch's narrow dirt tracks. Gale placed his pliers on top of a fence post and pulled off his leather work gloves. He tilted his stained Stetson back and felt trickles of sweat run from his temples. Since rescuing his family's ranch from foreclosure two years before, Gale had found the work demanding and endless. Broken machinery, torn fences, sick cattle . . . the list went on and on. But given what he'd been through, he never uttered a single complaint.

Gale didn't recognize the pickup and wondered why anyone would be in such a hurry. He folded his arms across his chest and watched the vehicle pull up alongside his truck. Gale's bruised and battered dust-covered F-150 stood in stark contrast to the top-of-the-line pickup. Gale noticed a dealership plate on the vehicle as two men climbed out of the truck. He didn't recognize them. The oldest had that soft look – a fleshy neck and thick waist – as if he sat in an office all day and told people what to do. With a nod, Gale said, "How can I help you?"

The older man stepped forward and shook Gale's hand. "Bart Waters." Waters was in his sixties and gave Gale a sugary smile. "This is my business associate, Dean Spivey." The other man, two decades younger, nodded and clasped Gale's hand. Waters stood over six feet, had pale blue eyes, and thin gray lips. Spivey was short and stocky with a blunt nose, sharp eyes, and a helmet of black hair.

"We need to speak with you, Gale," Waters said.

Gale cocked his head, his mind beginning to race. "Okay."

"Can we go under that shade tree?" Waters asked. "It's hot as hell."

They walked slowly toward a lone live oak that sat several yards from the fence line. The West Texas plains spread out before them, vast and empty. Waters began in a slow, easy, confident drawl, as if he'd rehearsed what he was about to say.

"No doubt you heard about Clay Moorhead?" Waters asked.

Gale nodded. He had coached against Moorhead and never liked him. On those Friday nights, when the Kinney Lions had battled Caton, Gale sensed something about Moorhead that had made him uneasy. Moorhead's teams were well coached and highly disciplined, but his brash swagger had clouded Gale's respect for the man. For that reason, Gale had always taken special gratification in beating Caton.

While Moorhead had celebrated himself as the best high school football coach in West Texas, most of Gale's coaching brethren understood that Gale McClanahan had quietly surpassed him as a legend. Gale's teams had won seven state championships before he'd found himself leading the San Antonio Lone Stars and turning around the worst team in professional football. After one season, where Gale and his family had nearly been destroyed by a ruthless owner, he walked away from the League with a hefty settlement and rescued his family's ranch from foreclosure. He hadn't coached since.

"A tragedy," Waters continued. Waters and Spivey shook their heads mournfully. "Clay was a good man, but he left us with a problem."

Moorhead had been murdered. It was an odd way they seemed to put blame on a dead man, Gale thought.

"Clay had a great run. It's terrible to see it end the way it did. But life moves on," Waters said, his eyes boring into Gale's. Waters paused before saying, "We have sixty-three boys who don't have a coach. Practice begins in less than a week. We got one of our most promising teams ever, and we'd hate to see a championship season spoiled because of Clay's death."

Spivey looked at Gale. "We need you, Coach McClanahan."

"That's right," Waters echoed. "We'll do whatever it takes to sign you on."

Gale said, "I'm not looking to coach. I'm done with that. I have a ranch to take care of, a business to run."

"We understand," Waters said, pressing. "It'll only be for one season until we can properly find us a coach. But we haven't got time to diddle around."

Gale felt a vague sense of unease. "Why not name one of Moorhead's assistants?" Gale asked. He didn't like the way Waters spoke or the flashy Caton High Championship rings on both men's fingers. Gale didn't believe in bringing attention to himself nor did he respect anyone who did.

"They're not ready. Besides, we got the best football coach in Texas, some would argue in the country, standing right in front of us."

In the two years since Gale had walked away from the Lone Stars, he had received several pro coaching offers. Colleges had called, too, looking for McClanahan to use his magic to turn their programs around. He didn't bite. He'd promised himself after nearly losing his family that he'd spend the rest of his days overseeing his parents' ranch. There were moments when his heart tugged to coach, but he'd made a promise to himself and, more importantly, to Marybeth that family would come first.

"I'm sorry, I can't help you," Gale said.

Waters' eyes clouded for a moment before he fell into a feigned look of understanding. "We know what you went through in San Antonio. We don't blame you for being gun shy."

Gale's eyes hardened.

Waters continued as he stared for an instant at the dirt track leading to the fence line. "But I have my reasons for driving over an hour and nearly breaking an axle to speak with you. And I'm a man who doesn't take no easily."

"I've known Bart my whole life, Coach McClanahan," Spivey said, smiling thinly. "When he wants a deal to happen, it's gonna get done."

"I wouldn't own the largest string of car dealerships in West Texas if I weren't a man of persuasion, Gale," Waters said. "I want you to be the next coach of the Caton Panthers. Those boys need a coach like you. You stood up to Vernon Voss and brought him down, and you took the worst team in the League and won. And it's a fact that college and pro teams have come calling."

Waters kicked dirt with his boot and looked away, his eyes narrowing and finally settling on Gale. "Clay was loud and brash. He told people he was the best high school coach there ever was, but I knew better. I'm looking at the best right here and now, and his name ain't Clay Moorhead. What's it going to take?"

Gale said, "I gave you my answer. Thanks, but no thanks."

"Dean, don't you think he'll want to hear our offer first?" Waters asked.

"I do."

"We'll pay you one hundred thousand dollars for five month's work. Hell, we'll even rent you a big ole house with a pool, give you a new truck," Waters pointed at Gale's beat up pickup, "and make sure the missus is taken care of."

"I told you 'no'. I gave you my answer and I got reasons for it."

Waters shook his head in mock disbelief and looked at Spivey. "I think he means it."

"I think he does," Spivey said.

"And here we drove all the way to Kinney." Waters turned to Gale. "I'm going to leave this conversation where it is, but I want you to consider my offer. We have impressionable young men who need a coach to mold their character. And we're offering you the prospect of a championship team. Let that settle in Coach McClanahan. You think about my offer when you're out here in this ungodly heat fixing fences."

"It's time for me to get back to work," Gale said.

"Think about it. I'm going to be following up," Waters promised. "And Gale . . ."

Gale gave Waters a hard look. Spivey shifted on his feet, as if he were standing on hot coals, waiting for Waters to continue.

"We're going to get this done," Waters said, smiling. "I'm not sure you know who you're dealing with."

"I'm not interested," Gale said, his patience running out. "It's time for you both to move on."

Waters smiled. "You'll be hearing from me," he said, as he and Spivey turned to go. "Remember those players. They lost their coach, son. Clay was murdered." Waters paused, letting the word *murdered* sink in. "They need someone to depend on, Gale."

Gale's six-year-old daughter had picked up the habit of walking around the house, her toy cell phone pressed to her ear, mimicking her mother, Marybeth. Tilly was taking great joy in reprimanding an imaginary spam caller. "How did you get my number?" Tilly asked, holding the phone close, ignoring Gale when he entered the kitchen. "I'm very busy. I have things to do. Please don't call me again!" Tilly pushed the end call button on the toy cell and smiled at Gale. "These people keep calling. It's a nuisance, Daddy. I needed to tell them to stop." She emphasized the word *nuisance,* exactly how Marybeth did.

Gale smiled and looked at Marybeth who turned from the kitchen sink and rolled her eyes. Tilly wandered out of the kitchen. Gale hated cell phones and thought it was a bad idea to buy Tilly the toy. But Tilly had prevailed. Gale found it hard to say no to his daughter. He knew it was a weakness that in Tilly's teenage years would come back to bite him.

Without asking, Marybeth poured Gale a large glass of water. He was soaked in sweat and his face and clothes were covered in dirt. She scrunched her nose and handed him the glass. "You're a mess," she said. "Go shower and get cleaned up."

Gale took a sip and said, "Two boosters from Caton showed up and asked me to coach the team."

Marybeth took the folded dish towel in her hand and set it on the counter. Her stare penetrated Gale.

"Caton?"

"They want me to coach the high school now that Clay Moorhead's gone."

Marybeth surveyed the kitchen for a moment before responding. They had spent thousands of dollars renovating Gale's family ranch house, including a significant remodeling of the kitchen. Marybeth had worked with a designer to get each detail right. Stainless steel appliances, soapstone counters, Shaker cabinetry, and hickory floors had made the kitchen pop. While Marybeth had retained her job as an elementary school teacher and they had otherwise remained frugal, after the multi-million-dollar settlement from the Lone Stars, Gale had urged Marybeth to splurge a bit. It was the least he could do.

"I'm not moving to Caton," Marybeth said.

Gale had to keep himself from smiling. "Me neither." Two years before he'd been enticed into signing a contract with the Lone Stars. The decision had nearly destroyed his marriage. "I told them to find someone else."

"Good. Is that it?"

"That's it."

"What did they offer you?"

"Nothing that would make me take the job."

"It's awful about Clay."

"I'm still trying to figure out why someone would kill him."

"You always had a bad feeling about that man."

"I can't explain it."

"Something was going on."

Gale nodded. "Something. "

"Were they good men, Gale?"

Gale frowned. "Gave me a hard sell."

"Figures." Marybeth smiled, her eyes crinkling. Much of the time she was all business like most everyone who grew up in the oil patch, but when she gave Gale that easy smile, he was reminded of all the reasons he'd fallen in love. He walked across the kitchen and kissed Marybeth lightly on the lips before she could shoo him away.

"I love you Gale McClanahan, but you stink." She held her nose. "Go take a shower. And use soap," she called to him as he turned to leave.

Waters pulled onto State Highway 349 for the drive to Caton. Spivey looked out the passenger window at the flat, desolate landscape, dotted with cattle grazing and frozen oil derricks under an unforgiving sun. Spivey turned and said, "Where do we go now, Bart?"

Waters set his jaw and glanced at Spivey. "You don't think this is over, do you, Dean?"

"You think?"

"We'll get him."

"I'm not so sure. . ."

"I didn't figure the easy way would work, but it was worth the trip to size the man up. We've got cards to play yet."

"Seems a tough nut to me."

Waters shook his head and tapped his forefinger on the steering wheel. "Oh, he'll coach."

Spivey leaned back in the pickup's plush leather seat. He was chief bean counter as CFO for Waters' array of car dealerships, oil and gas interests, and "other" businesses. "You offered him 100K and he practically spit at us."

"Clearly, McClanahan doesn't care about money or he'd be coaching in the League."

"What does he care about?"

Waters drawled, "His family and his reputation."

Spivey nodded and looked out the passenger side window.

As if to himself, Waters added, "That's right. I figured the easy way wouldn't work."

Spivey turned. "Avery's still pissed, Bart."

Llyod Avery had been Moorhead's longtime assistant. After Moorhead's death, Avery had assumed he'd be given the head coaching job. Waters said, "Lloyd needs to know his limitations. McClanahan's a winner, and a choirboy to boot."

Spivey gave Waters a knowing look.

Waters continued. "McClanahan will make people forget Clay. The sooner people stop thinking about him the better. We have too much at stake."

"You seem certain."

Waters paused and tapped his finger again on the wheel, his expression fixed. "More certain now than I was before."

"You know, I can't stop thinking about Clay getting shot."

"Whoever pulled that trigger might have done us a favor," Waters said, looking straight ahead at the long strip of empty road.

Gale's ribs hadn't healed. Nearly two years earlier, they'd been shattered by one of Vernon Voss' henchmen who'd kicked Gale so violently that he still experienced dull pain every time he breathed hard. When Gale had played for Atlanta as a backup safety, he'd sprinted downfield on a kickoff against Chicago and been blindsided. He'd woken up in a hospital room after suffering a broken jaw and the worst concussion of his career. He was no stranger to pain but driving fence posts and stretching wire fencing had left his ribs so sore he was unable to sleep.

Marybeth lay curled on the other side of the bed, her breaths even and deep. Gale turned and looked at her in the faint light of a half-moon coming through the lace curtains. Since walking away from the Lone Stars, they'd rediscovered common ground and had made an even deeper commitment to one another. Revitalizing his parents' ranch had given them both purpose but had especially consumed Gale as he worked tirelessly to rebuild the herd and make the business profitable.

That said, there were days when he missed coaching. He missed the players, his assistant coaches, the teamwork and sacrifice, the thrill of winning. Coaching in the League had brought him the satisfaction of knowing that he could win at the game's highest level, but Gale's proudest moments were the seven state championships leading the Kinney High School Lions.

Gale turned from Marybeth and stared at the bedroom ceiling. He couldn't shake the feeling that the two men, Spivey and Waters, weren't done with him. And Moorhead. . . why would someone kill a high school football coach? Gale had heard the grisly details about Moorhead being struck by a round from a high-powered rifle. When Gale was fourteen, his father had taken him elk hunting in New Mexico. They'd spent an early morning in November fighting off the cold waiting for the herd to venture forth from the tree line. Gale remembered his father's subtle nod when a bull emerged from a stand of aspens, condensation pouring out of the elk's nostrils. Gale's hands shook as he sighted the elk and fought off the agonizing feeling that he was about to kill. His father had put his hand on Gale's arm to calm him as they crouched behind an outcropping of boulders. Gale hated himself for what he was about to do. Yet, he'd steadied the pounding of his heart and squeezed the trigger.

Gale never hunted again. He remembered fighting off the tears as he knelt next to the slain elk. Blood stained the bull's chest where Gale had shot him flush through the heart. His father had marveled. Gale's first kill had been a shot so clean that it would have been the envy of a seasoned hunter. As Gale bit his lip and hid the terrible feeling of taking the elk's life, he made the vow he would keep. He had no heart to kill.

A few years before he coached the Lone Stars, the Kinney Lions had beaten Caton on the road in overtime to advance to the next round of the playoffs. The Lions had benefited from a bad pass interference call and won in the final minute. Clay Moorhead had gone ballistic, tearing up the sideline. When the game had ended, Gale did what he always did. Before his players had lined up to shake hands, Gale had jogged to midfield to shake hands with the opposing head coach. Moorhead had spotted Gale coming and had yelled in a deep drawl, "How much did you pay the refs, McClanahan? Get your players the hell out of here."

Gale had been stunned. He'd stared hard at Moorhead, who had turned his back and walked toward the locker room. One of Moorhead's young assistants had witnessed the interaction and said, "That's just Clay. He'll be alright. He'll probably call you in the morning to apologize."

The call never came.

Gale turned on his side and closed his eyes to the sound of Marybeth's steady breathing. He was tired and sore but on the edge from the conversation with Spivey and Waters. He knew they weren't done. If it had been on different terms, he might have accepted the opportunity. He missed coaching. But he wanted no part of the two men from Caton.

Gale sipped his coffee and spotted Jack Engle walk through the Pump and Drill Diner door. Engle walked slowly with a subtle limp and nodded to the scattered oil field workers, ranchers, and merchants eating breakfast in the early morning. Engle had shredded his ACL years before playing for Dallas.

Engle came over to the table and sat down. Without hesitation the waitress brought him a cup of coffee and refilled Gale's. "You two having a serious meeting?" Janet asked, smiling broadly. She was in her late-twenties, eight months pregnant, and had been one of Engle and Gale's former students. "I'm not in trouble, am I? Detention?"

Gale grinned. Engle, the retired principal of Kinney High School, gave Janet a stern look before breaking into a soft smile. "You were one of my favorites. Never had any trouble with you." He looked at her protruding stomach. "But I'll say this. Looks like you're in trouble now."

Janet laughed and rubbed her belly with her free hand, her cheeks rosy and full. "Can't wait. Nothing like carrying a baby in the middle of summer. God, it's been hot. Breakfast?"

Gale and Engle both gave her a look of commiseration. Then Gale said, "Just coffee."

Engle's wife, Barbara, had planned a long-awaited trip across the country for her and Jack to visit places they'd never seen. She had dreams of touring New England at the height of autumn. They'd be gone for over a month. While it was true Engle had struggled with retirement, Gale knew Engle wasn't sure what to think of spending weeks in a car hopping from one tourist spot to another. He didn't much like crossing county lines.

Gale turned to Engle after Janet walked back toward the counter and told him about Spivey and Waters. When Gale finished, Engle nodded and took a sip.

"I first met Clay Moorhead years ago when he came to Caton." Engle paused and shook his head. Engle had been Kinney's football coach for thirty years before handing the job over to Gale. "We were at a coaching convention in El Paso. He spent the whole time at the bar. Wasn't interested in what anyone had to say. He had all the answers. He had a wife and young kids, but that didn't stop him from staying out all night."

Gale leaned back and continued listening.

Engle said, "I heard rumors over the years of womanizing, but that doesn't ordinarily get a man killed. He must have riled up the wrong person. There must have been something else. A coach like Clay Moorhead can do most whatever he wants in a town like Caton . . . *if he delivers*. That's why I never took money from boosters. I kept 'em at arm's length. I never wanted to be owned or fall into the trap of thinking I was untouchable."

Gale nodded knowingly. The year before he had coached the Lone Stars, Kinney boosters had approached him about a special services contract. He had politely declined.

"I don't think those men are done with me, Jack," Gale said, putting his elbows on the table. He had a fresh scar running across the back of his hand. He'd cut it a few months earlier stretching barbed wire. "I got a premonition."

Engle looked at Gale. "There'd be only one reason to take that job."

Gale's eyes narrowed.

"We were in the business of educating," Engle said. "Those kids need a coach who can turn the culture around. Clay preached honor and integrity, but from what I heard and saw, never lived it." He looked over at Janet, smiled, and raised his cup for a refill before turning back to Gale.

Gale had known Jack Engle since he was a boy. Engle had been his high school football coach and had given Gale the opportunity to be head coach when everyone in Kinney, Texas thought he was too young. Engle had been a mentor and father figure and had served as Gale's offensive coordinator in San Antonio when Gale had found himself desperate and alone. There was no man he trusted more, especially now that his father was gone, killed along with his mother in a head-on collision. Gale wasn't all that surprised that Engle sensed he missed football.

"I never liked Caton," Gale said as Janet refilled their cups.

"It's a strange town. Their priorities are upside down. Chances are, if you took that job, you'd have a fight on your hands."

Gale nodded.

Engle paused. "But you could do a lot of good."

"With the culture they have, I'd make some serious enemies."

"I know," Engle said, breaking into a smile, holding his coffee cup in both hands. "That's why you'd be the perfect man for the job."

Gale noticed the red double cab pickup parked next to the metal corrugated storage shed when he pulled up to the house in the late afternoon. He'd been in town meeting with his attorney, Grayson Wallace, a legendary character who'd negotiated his multi-million-dollar settlement with the League. Gale hoped to buy an additional 500 acres of property abutting the ranch. They'd been discussing the offer.

Gale climbed out of his truck and was greeted by Tilly, who sat in the grass under a shade tree frantically trying to finish a popsicle before it melted.

Before Gale could ask about the red pickup, Tilly belted out, "A boy is in the house with Momma."

"A boy?" Gale asked.

"That's what I said, Daddy. A boy. Didn't you hear me the first time?"

Gale suppressed a smile. Til was becoming more and more like her mother. Marybeth's mannerisms were not lost on their daughter. Frequently,

Gale would become preoccupied in thought, only to discover that to Marybeth's displeasure, she had to repeat herself. Til had caught on.

"What does he want?" Gale asked.

"I don't know. Momma's giving him cake."

Gale went into the house and found a teenager sitting in the cream-colored living room with an empty plate on his lap. The boy sat on the plush couch that Marybeth had purchased in Midland. Marybeth gave Gale a cautious smile and said, "Eben has come to see you, Gale. He's had two pieces of cake, and I suspect he wants more."

The teenager gave a sheepish grin and stood up. He was tall and rangy. A quarterback, Gale guessed. He shook Gale's hand and introduced himself. "Eben Daly."

Gale didn't recognize the kid. He wasn't from Kinney. Gale gestured for Daly to sit. "More cake?" Gale asked with a smile sitting down across from him.

Daly shook his head. Gale and Marybeth were no strangers to teenagers. When Gale was teaching math and coaching, Kinney High School students were always coming over to their house. Over the years, Marybeth had served more team meals than she could remember.

Daly looked nervously at Gale. Gale had found since he turned the Lone Stars around and been honored as Coach of the Year, that people treated him like a celebrity. He disliked it and tried hard to put them at ease.

Daly said, "I came to ask you if you'd coach us, sir. You heard about Coach Moorhead. We don't have anyone, Mr. McClanahan. Practices start next week. I'm the team captain, and I think you can save our season."

Gale leaned back in his chair. He glanced at Marybeth, who was sitting across from him, listening intently. "Did you come on your own, or were you sent?"

"I heard Mr. Waters and Mr. Spivey spoke with you. I heard you said, 'no'," the boy said. "I came to see if you would change your mind."

"Don't you think I should be taken at my word?"

The teenager shrugged and said softly, "My dad knows people from Kinney, and they all talk about how important you were to their kids. Everyone saw what you did for the Lone Stars."

Marybeth looked at Gale. Gale could see her expression softening.

"I have a ranch to oversee. I gave up coaching."

"Yes sir, I know," said the teenager. "We had a team meeting last night. Only the players. We don't know what to do. There's a lot of pressure to win. The whole town thinks we got the best team in a long time. But Coach Moorhead's *mur* . . ." he cut short the word, ". . .*passing* has got everyone panicked and upset. My father's the Baptist preacher. He said that God has a plan. We think you are part of that plan." His voice began to tremble. "Sir, we got no one right now. You'd save us, Mr. McClanahan."

Gale studied Daly. He wondered if Waters and Spivey had coached him, given him a game plan, patted him on the back with a "*go git him,*" and sent Daly to Kinney. After the Lone Stars, Gale was more wary of people. He was done being played.

Gale decided to be direct. "Did Waters and Spivey send you?"

The teenager shook his head. "No sir. Honest."

Gale caught Marybeth's eye. Her brow was furrowed, but he couldn't tell which camp she was in.

Daly added, "Please?"

Gale leaned back. "I don't make spur of the moment decisions. I learned that the hard way." Marybeth looked at him knowingly.

Gale thought of Waters offering a house with a pool, a new truck, 100 grand. Gale shifted in his chair. "I'm sorry, son, but I can't help you. I appreciate you coming to see me, but you go back to Caton and tell Bart Waters to find another coach."

Daly's face fell. "You won't coach?"

"Sorry." Gale felt a pit in his stomach.

After Daly left, Gale turned to Marybeth. "What are you thinking?" he asked.

"They need you, Gale."

"I don't want to go to Caton."

"I know," Marybeth said, wrapping her arms around him and resting her chin on his shoulder. "It's for the better. But I hated that."

"I hated it, too," Gale sighed, holding her tight.

The call came the next morning. Gale and Mason Hayes were patching a leaking stock tank as several Longhorns grazed nearby in the rising heat. Gale could see Mateo Santos, his other ranch hand, in the distance digging an irrigation ditch with a trencher. Expert horsemen with expansive skillsets, Hayes and Santos worked seamlessly together tending to the herd and daily maintenance of the ranch.

The plains spread out around them, painted in muted tones under the glaring sun. Gale pulled the phone out of his back pocket. He didn't recognize the number but took the call. Gale recognized Bart Water's gravelly voice. He looked over at Hayes, who had a weathered, sun-beaten face. Hayes wiped his forehead and kept working to patch the crack in the stock tank.

"Have you considered my offer?" Waters asked.

"Did you send the kid?" Gale questioned bluntly.

"No."

"Who did?"

Waters paused as if he were expecting the question. "He came on his own, Coach McClanahan. He's a stand-up boy. The team needs a coach. I'm not suggesting he didn't know about our meeting on your property. News spreads fast in a town like Caton, but I didn't ask him to see you."

"Did Spivey?"

"Dean didn't say anything."

Gale turned away from Hayes and said, "I'm not accepting your offer."

Waters went silent for a few moments. "That's a shame," he said finally, as if he were suddenly weary. "If that boy didn't convince you, maybe something else I got will. Meet me in Midland at Wall Street Bar and Grill at 5:30."

"Midland?"

"That's what I said."

"I'm not interested."

"Oh, you'll be interested, Gale. You be there. Understand?"

"If I'm not."

"I'd hate seeing you hurt."

"Is that a threat?"

"It is what it is. 5:30."

"If I don't show?"

Waters' voice turned to ice. "You love your family, Gale?"

Gale stayed silent. His pulse quickened.

Waters said, "If you love your wife, you'll be there. Wall Street Bar and Grill. I'll be waiting for you."

Waters hung up. Gale stared at his cell and shoved it in his back pocket. Mason Hayes looked over at him and said, "What was that all about?"

Gale kicked at the dirt, his mind racing. "I'm not sure, but it looks like I'm gonna have to find out. It's possible I'm headed into trouble."

Hayes shook his head, tipped his hat back, and pointed his caulking gun toward the sky, like a cowboy with a six shooter. "It won't be the first time."

Two

Gale's eyes took a moment to adjust when he entered the dim, dark-paneled, crowded bar. He focused and finally spotted Waters sitting in the back at a corner table. After hesitating, Gale made his way through a maze of people celebrating the end of the workday. Waters' eyes blinked with recognition when he saw Gale approaching, and he smiled and pointed at the empty chair across from him. A glass of bourbon rested on the table. Gale reluctantly sat down.

"What'll you have?" Waters asked.

"I'm not here to socialize," Gale said.

Waters leaned in, his smile vanishing. He took a sip of bourbon and scratched his chin before speaking. "I gave you a hell of an offer, Gale, and you looked a gift horse in the mouth. But I'm a generous man. That offer still stands. If you know what's good for you, take it. Don't ask questions. Don't refuse. Don't be stubborn or prideful. You agree to coach, and everyone profits."

Gale's fist tightened, and he felt the urge to reach across the table and grab Waters' throat.

Waters held up his hands as if to say, "I tried." Waters' expression darkened, and he leaned back and pulled a folded letter from his front pocket before tossing it on the table in front of Gale. "Read it."

Gale stared at the letter. His thoughts spun. He slowly reached over and picked up the envelope.

"I warned you," Waters said, watching Gale unfold the letter and begin reading.

After a few moments, everything began to blur. When Gale finally finished reading, he looked up at Waters with fresh hatred.

"You should have taken the deal," Waters said calmly, as if he were speaking to a wayward son. "It would have saved heartache."

"What is this?" Gale asked.

Waters tapped his finger on the table and sipped his drink. "Things aren't always what they seem, Gale. Marybeth's mother was a party girl. She liked to drink. She liked men. She wasn't always a good girl."

Gale glanced again at the letter which was written in a woman's hand. Gale recognized Marybeth's mother's handwriting from Christmas and birthday cards she'd sent her daughter over the years – the large, distinct letters and rounded curves. The way she signed her name. He looked up and set the letter on the table.

"Marybeth's father was on the road, driving around Oklahoma selling drill equipment. I guess one night, her momma's loneliness was too much. A few drinks, conversation, an empty bed, and nature took its course. Your wife was conceived."

Gale's heart sank. He thought about Marybeth's mother. Delilah had been the Kinney High School homecoming queen whose big ambitions all fell short. She'd always resented Gale because Delilah had hopes for her daughter becoming a doctor and practicing in a place like Houston or Dallas. Instead, Marybeth had married Gale, stayed in Kinney, and had become a special ed teacher. A few years earlier, Marybeth's mother and father had moved to Colorado. Gale remembered when Marybeth and Gale had been dating as teenagers. Gale had gone over to Marybeth's house, which sat on three acres outside of Kinney. When no one had answered the door, Gale had walked around to the back and seen Delilah passed out face down on a recliner. Her bikini lay clumped beside her on the patio. An empty bottle of wine sat on the wrought iron outdoor table and a glass had shattered on the cement. It was a little before noon. Despite Delilah's drinking, Marybeth's mother was taut and tanned, a striking woman in her early forties. Gale stood transfixed, staring at the small of Delilah's back and her sensual curves. He struggled to look away.

A party girl.

Gale's dread built as Waters continued.

Waters said, "Before he died, the Senator gave me his letters, a whole stack of 'em, and told me to burn 'em. I was his executor if that tells you anything about the man." Waters flashed a smile. "Marybeth's mother wrote him that love note after finding out she was with child. Delilah knew the Senator was the father. She needed him to know that he was responsible. Maybe she was hedging her bets."

Waters paused.

"But it doesn't end there. Years later, Delilah found herself in the middle of a pyramid scheme. Seems she and one of her . . . let's call him . . . *friends* . . . were trying to bilk some little old ladies, promising all sorts of things." Waters stopped and let his words linger. "She got caught and had to call in a big favor from H.W. You wouldn't want that to get out, would you? Spoil your good wife's family name?"

Waters set his glass on the table. "We wouldn't want these secrets exposed, would we, Gale? Marybeth McClanahan, the illegitimate daughter of the Honorable State Senator H.W. Owen. If you care about your wife and family, you coach Caton High School. Understand? You win, too." Waters slowly reached for the letter, folded it carefully, and placed it in his shirt pocket. "What's it going to be?"

Gale looked down at the table and after a few seconds raised his head. If the truth came out, it would devastate Marybeth. For years she'd been conflicted about her relationship with her parents. She clung to the delicate hope that her mother would come to accept her decision to marry Gale and raise her daughter in Kinney. Marybeth wished her mother had the same sweet disposition as her father, who kept silent for fear of Delilah's wrath.

"If this ever comes out," Gale said, his face flushed with anger.

"I'll take that as a 'yes.' Glad we could strike a deal, Coach." Waters stood up and laid a 20-dollar bill on the table. "I'm real sorry we needed this additional meeting to come to terms. You had your chance." Waters smiled, his sharp teeth flashing. "Welcome to the Caton High School Panthers."

After meeting with Waters, Gale made the drive home. The sun hung over the horizon like a drop of blood.

It was all surreal. The woman Gale had married was the daughter of one of the most notorious state politicians in Texas. Owen had held an iron fist over his district for years and had chaired the State Affairs Committee, which, rumor had it, helped him siphon thousands of dollars to line his own pocket. For a time, he'd presided over the powerful Transportation Committee, which, along with the Texas Railroad Commission, had a grip on the oil and gas industry, whose coffers had proved even more lucrative. Owen eventually had been indicted only to have the legal proceedings dropped. Gale had met Owen once when the State Senator had come to celebrate the opening of Kinney's new high school and could easily detect whiskey on his breath. He'd given a blustery speech and left shortly afterwards. Marybeth had turned to Gale with disgust. She'd detested Owen's self-serving politics.

Gale wondered what he was going to say to Marybeth. She'd be surprised and angry when she heard the news that he'd accepted the Caton job. He thought about manipulating the conversation, telling her he was doing the right thing solely because of the players. But he dropped the notion. It wasn't true. He figured if anyone could handle the truth, it was his wife.

When he entered the house, Tilly sat next to Marybeth in her pajamas while Marybeth read to her. Gale could tell Marybeth was trying to read his expression as she set the book down. Tilly climbed on her mother's lap as Marybeth held her tightly.

"How did it go?" Marybeth asked, smiling. Her eyes were radiant, and her hair was clasped in a ponytail. "What did he offer you now?"

Gale shook his head.

Marybeth studied her husband's face. She frowned. "What's the matter, Gale?"

Gale sat down across from her and Tilly and took a deep breath. "Can we talk?"

Marybeth's face grew pale. She rose off the couch and said, "Til, it's bedtime."

"But you didn't finish the story," Tilly protested, a look of disappointment washing across her face.

"Tomorrow," Marybeth snapped. "Now kiss your father and say goodnight."

A few minutes later, Marybeth returned to the living room and shook her head in disbelief. "You took it, didn't you?"

"I did."

"I thought we put that to bed," her voice rising.

"I didn't do it for the money, to be a hero, or because I missed the game."

"I'm listening."

"I wish you'd trust me on this one." Gale took a deep breath and leaned forward. He said softly, "Things aren't what they seem."

"What are you talking about?" Marybeth sat down across from him, her face softening with his tone.

Gale swallowed and looked away for an instant. "Your mother, Marybeth."

"My mother?"

"He has some dirt on her."

"Tell me."

Gale focused on his wife. "You're not your father's birth child."

Marybeth sat back, as if what he'd told her had failed to register. Then her eyes began searching Gale's in bewilderment. "What are you talking about, Gale McClanahan?"

"She fooled around."

"What?" Marybeth shook her head in disbelief.

Gale took a deep breath and recounted the conversation with Waters. He left out the part about Delilah's involvement in a pyramid scheme. He felt it would be too much. After a few minutes, Gale finished with "that's why I took the job, Marybeth, to protect you and your family. Maybe it was paternalistic, but I didn't want you to get hurt."

Tears streaked down Marybeth's face. She wiped them away with the back of her hand. She put her head down and started to sob, and then she looked at Gale, her jaw clenching, her mascara smeared across her cheeks, her hands balling into fists, and choked, "*I always knew my mother was rotten.*"

Gale sat back. He'd rarely heard Marybeth speak ill of Delilah, even though her mother had treated her as a failure and Gale as a near pariah. Gale always had the sense Marybeth's dad had a soft spot for both of them but didn't dare show it for fear of his wife. Gale instinctively liked him. He was a sweet, kindly man.

"My poor father," Marybeth moaned. "He can't ever know, Gale."

"I know." Marybeth's father had been struggling with a heart condition. If the secret got out, it could kill him, Gale realized.

Gale climbed out of his chair and slid next to her. He pulled her close as she buried her face in his chest.

"H.W. Owen's daughter. Jesus Christ," Marybeth said between sobs. "I feel so much shame."

Gale kept silent and held her tight.

"Can you still love me?" she asked.

"More than ever."

Two days later, *The Kinney Gazette* ran the story online about the new coach of the Caton High School Panthers. Gale closed his laptop, knowing people in town wouldn't be happy. Gale McClanahan was a member of the Kinney High School Athletic Hall of Fame, one of a handful of graduates to have played in the League. One of the winningest high school coaches in the state. Some people in Kinney would think he'd crossed a sacred line. They'd say that since he coached the Lone Stars he'd changed, and in a way, they didn't know how right they were. He didn't much care what people thought anymore. His skin had toughened, grown thicker. Even Marybeth had commented that he had a harder edge. Never one to suffer fools, he was even less inclined to do so now. Gale had to admit, having several million dollars in the bank made it easier. He took special satisfaction that he'd earned every penny of the Lone Stars' payout. In fact, he could have sought and received far more if he'd decided to be vindictive.

Gale knew it wouldn't take long before his cell phone chimed and the texts and emails packed his inbox. He'd kept his decision to coach Caton to Marybeth, Jack Engle, and Engle's wife, Barbara. The one person he didn't tell, and probably should have, was Grayson Wallace. Wallace had been instrumental in helping Gale in San Antonio, and his law office was perched above Main Street in a brick building built at the turn of the last century. Wallace was perhaps Kinney High School's most ardent fan. After games, he'd send long emails to Gale critiquing Gale's coaching decisions, and over the years, Gale had answered nearly every one of them. Gale pursed his lips when he saw Wallace's incoming call and braced himself. He pictured Wallace in his dusty, paneled office cluttered with thick law journals, a glass of whiskey resting on his oak desk.

"Traitor," Wallace said when Gale answered. "How could you do it, Brutus?"

Gale gave a half-smile. Wallace had been a classics major at Vanderbilt and read Shakespeare for pleasure. He was the most learned man Gale knew.

Wallace continued, his deep baritone rising. *"'Judge me you gods! Wrong mine enemies? And if not so, how should I wrong a brother?'"*

"It's only for a season, Grayson," Gale broke in.

"One too many."

"Caton needs a coach. I can set things straight," Gale said.

"After 30 years of Clay Moorhead?" Wallace asked with a prosecutorial tone. "We'll see. And Marybeth?"

"She's okay."

"'Okay?' That tells me what I already knew." Wallace paused for a few moments. "How much did they offer you?"

"Not your business, Grayson."

"Well, you should have told me, Gale. I could have dissuaded you. I know more than I should about Caton."

Gale leaned back in the kitchen chair. Wallace's ability to sniff out rumor and gossip were legendary. "What do you know?"

"It's a snake pit. Rattlers. Cottonmouths. Maybe a viper or two. Enough asps to kill Cleopatra ten times over. Beneath that football program lies a veritable river of treachery and deceit."

"I get it. Tell me about Bart Waters?"

"Ah, Bart. I fought Waters in court eight years ago over oil and gas rights on a property north of Ozona. His attorney was a lackey. Waters made one of several dubious claims against my client."

"Did you win?"

Wallace grunted. "The wretched insurance company forced us to settle out of court. Undoubtedly, I would have prevailed. Waters has been a power broker in Caton for years. Been married a few times and accused of tax evasion even more often. The charges were dropped every time. Somehow, the US Attorney always got cold feet. That's not all. At one of his used car dealerships, there were accusations he rigged odometers. I heard he blamed it on a rogue manager and quietly paid off irate customers. To boil it down for you, he's a small-town crook."

"What else?" Gale asked.

"Clay Moorhead called me a few days before he was murdered."

"Moorhead?"

"When in distress, people know that I'll lend an ear. I can be a useful man for scoundrels like Clay and suckers like you."

Gale took the shot as his due.

"What did he want?" Gale asked.

"He said that he might need my help. There wasn't his usual bravado."

"Was he specific?"

"He left it at that."

"Have you told the sheriff's office?"

Wallace hesitated. After a pause, he said, "Of course."

"What did they say?"

"They thanked me."

"That was it?"

"Yes."

"Nothing else, Grayson?"

"I asked them if they had a motive, were close to finding the killer."

"And . . ."

"They said they had no leads."

"How's that?"

"I'm not sure," Wallace said, "but there's something fishy in the state of Caton. I wish you had told me about coaching Caton High School. I could have saved you from trouble, Gale. Waters and his cronies don't play fair, and I suspect they're not going to play fair with you. You may be no better off down there than you were in San Antonio."

For an instant, Gale wondered if he should tell Wallace about Marybeth's mother. He dismissed the thought. Despite his brilliance as a lawyer, Wallace sometimes abandoned discretion to his close circle of friends after a few bourbons. "What's your theory on Moorhead?" Gale asked.

Wallace sighed. "Who knows what a man like Clay Moorhead was doing?"

"Enough to be shot."

Wallace sighed. "Whatever he was doing, we may never know. The wagons have circled."

"Practice starts in a few days," Gale said.

"Have you met the coaching staff?"

"Not yet."

"The principal?"

"No."

Wallace paused. "You want my advice?"

Gale asked, "Do I have a choice?"

"You better win, Gale. The town of Caton doesn't take losing kindly."

"At this point, do you think I'm a stranger to pressure, Grayson?"

"I think you're walking into an ugly situation. Maybe worse than you know."

Gale asked, "How can it get worse? A man was murdered."

"I don't know, Brutus, but my instinct tells me it can."

Three

Caton High School sat two miles from town and was built in the 1970's. The high school rested on the edge of an abandoned oil field next to deserted railroad tracks once owned decades before by Rock Island. The high school had seen better days. The pavement was cracked in front of the main entrance, the beige painted bricks looked pale and worn, and the classroom windows were small and covered with dust. The trim was peeling around the entrance doors when Gale walked into the building and was greeted by an overweight security officer glancing up from his phone. On the wall, painted in Panther blue and gold in large letters was the school's motto, *Fair Play*. Gale noted with irony how Caton High's academic building stood in stark contrast to the School's stadium, which rested behind the high school like a gleaming fortress. Clay Moorhead Stadium had been built a few years before. It was a multi-million-dollar, state-of-the-art facility that seated 10,000 fans. Gale shook his head. The stadium made the high school look even shabbier. The town wasn't afraid to show its priorities, Gale thought.

The security officer escorted Gale down the empty hallway, where Gale found the principal, Myron Bellwether, sitting in his cramped and sparse office. Bellwether had a nervous tick, his left eye twitching up and down. He was slight, sporting metal-rimmed glasses and a bright red bow tie. A scarred desk sat in the corner with stacks of paper and folders sitting on top and a laptop pushed to the side. A couple of diplomas hung on a stark, white-washed cinder block wall. Bellwether and Gale sat across from one another in folding chairs. Between them sat a cheap, laminated wood coffee table and a few dusty Caton High yearbooks.

Bellwether had a habit of nervously glancing at his phone, which rested in front of him on the coffee table as if he were bracing for an email from an angry parent, a text from an upset teacher, or worse, a call from a Caton booster.

Bellwether leaned forward and said without conviction in a squeaky voice, "It's a shame what happened to Coach Moorhead. Left us all upset.

All wondering why." Bellwether frowned and rubbed his hands together, his one eye fluttering up and down. Gale tried hard to look away from Bellwether's tic. Bellwether said nervously as if the office was bugged, "If Mr. Waters says you're the right person to coach, then I'm not going to quibble. I admit, I don't know much about football. I was a music major. He paused and added, "I play the clarinet." He shifted in his seat. "I'm sure Mr. Waters has the best interest of the School at heart, so I'll just stay out of it."

"You're the principal. How can you stay out of it?" Gale asked.

Bellwether furtively glanced at his phone before answering. He said meekly, "You'll have my full support, Coach McClanahan. I'm sure everything will be fine."

Gale was used to Jack Engle's staunch support. Engle was a rock, a school administrator who'd stood up to anyone betraying Kinney High School's mission. "And if it isn't?" Gale questioned.

Bellwether's voice fell into a whisper. "Then I'll have trouble. I suspect we both will."

Gale stared at the timid man across from him.

Bellwether hesitated and swept the room with nervous eyes, his one eye going up and down like a piston. He lowered his voice again making certain no one could overhear. "Please, I don't want problems. I learned my lesson. Just do what they say and everything will be fine," Bellwether said.

"What do you mean, you learned your lesson?" Gale asked.

Bellwether rocked forward and put his head down, then looked up. Bellwether's lip quivered. "I moved my family from Missouri to take this position," he trembled. "My wife didn't want to come, but I didn't have a job. Mr. Waters and Mr. Spivey told me they'd take care of me, give me all the support I needed."

"And?" Gale was beginning to feel a surge of sympathy.

Bellwether stared into space before he replied. "Last year, I tried to form a committee to meet about the football program. I thought I could help. The boys on the team are under awful pressure. All the time. Incessant. *Win, win, win.* That's all they hear. They hate playing. I know it. Coach Moorhead drove them hard. He did what he wanted, all with the support of the boosters." He hesitated. "You need to do what they tell you, Coach McClanahan."

"If I don't?"

Bellwether leaned forward. "There'll be threats, recriminations. *Things happen here.*"

"What kind of things?"

For an instant, Bellwether closed his eyes and took a deep breath. "I've said enough."

Gale studied Bellwether's face. He asked, "Why was Clay Moorhead murdered?"

Bellwether stared at Gale, the blood draining from his face.

Gale sat back in his chair. "Do you know?"

"Of course not."

"What was Clay doing to have someone kill him?"

"I don't know."

"A high school football coach gets shot fishing in broad daylight?" Gale questioned.

"He was a complicated man. Maybe he made enemies," Bellwether stuttered.

"Who?"

"I don't know. I stayed away from him. He called me derogatory names and told me if I stepped foot in his locker room, he'd run me out of town."

"Wait a minute. He called you derogatory names?"

"Yes. I'd rather not say." Bellwether's face flushed with embarrassment.

"What else?"

Bellwether's mouth twisted. He picked at his thumbnail. "Nothing else."

"Are you sure?"

"Yes." Bellwether again glanced at his phone.

Gale said, "Look. I'm not Clay Moorhead, and I'm not here to make your life more difficult. I'll do what's best for the players. Understand?"

Bellwether gave a half-nod. His eye twitch began to slow.

"You're welcome anytime around the team," Gale said, reassuringly.

"Mr. Waters isn't going to like that."

"I don't care," Gale said. "If anyone gives you trouble, you let me know."

"I don't want trouble."

"I know. You've made that clear."

Bellwether's eye began to twitch faster, and he picked harder at his thumb. He said, his high voice rising, "I've had enough trouble. You can't imagine. I just want to protect my family."

Gale shook his head. He thought about Waters leaning back and dropping Marybeth's mother's letter on the table, the menacing expression, and the threat, *Do you love your family, Gale?* Gale felt for Bellwether. He wondered what Bellwether knew about Clay Moorhead's murder. The smell of fear permeated the office. After a few moments, Gale lifted himself from his chair. It was time. He needed to meet the coaching staff.

The coaches' conference room was empty when Gale arrived. Gale had wandered around the deserted stadium complex until he found the room where the meeting was to be held. He stood in a sparkling room with new carpeting, a large screen TV mounted on the wall, a small kitchen area with a sink, microwave, coffee maker, and a stainless-steel bar refrigerator. He set his laptop and notepad on the large, hardwood table surrounded by a dozen swivel chairs. Half a dozen large action shots of Caton High football players hung on the walls in silver metal frames along with a large, framed photograph of a beaming Clay Moorhead, standing at midfield after winning a state title, surrounded by euphoric players and fans.

Out of curiosity, Gale opened the refrigerator door. It was stocked with bottled water, Coke, and half a dozen bottles of beer. Gale shook his head at the discrepancy between Caton's decrepit high school and Myron Bellwether's cinderblock office. While Kinney High School had erected an impressive football stadium a decade before, the town had built a state-of-the-art high school to match. When an overzealous School Board member wanted to spend taxpayer money on an indoor football training center, Gale and Jack Engle had managed to dissuade him. Gale enjoyed impressive facilities, but he'd thought building an indoor practice field for the Lions was excessive considering the desperate need for better teacher salaries and the pressing issues of the town. Gale was old school. He didn't like artificial turf (he still had turf scars on his elbows from college and the League) and believed that pampering teenagers led to entitlement. In a small, West Texas town like Kinney, sitting in the middle of the oil patch, Gale had wanted his players to earn everything they got. He felt it was a worthwhile life lesson for people who were going to have to find a way to make it in this part of the country.

Gale closed the refrigerator door and turned when Clay Moorhead's assistants entered the room. A few nodded, but no one shook Gale's hand as they found chairs around the table. No banter or smiles. It felt like the hushed atmosphere of a funeral, not the beginning of football season where energy and excitement hung in the air. It was a far cry from the easy smiles and spirited conversation his coaching staff displayed at Kinney High School. An uneasy silence permeated the room as Gale sat in the lone chair remaining at the head of the table.

Gale wondered if the somberness the coaches displayed came because of Moorhead's death. They had every right to be troubled, but Gale sensed more unease than sorrow as they entered the conference room. "I'm sorry about Coach Moorhead," Gale began.

A few men nodded, but one of the assistants at the far end of the table stared at him stonily. Gale recognized him. Lloyd Avery was one of Clay Moorhead's longtime coaches and had overseen the offense for years. He had frying pan hands, hard eyes, thick black hair, and a cleft chin. Gale noticed a large Rolex on Avery's wrist. Gale remembered he'd played at Texas Tech, and for a few years in the late '90s, had started at center for Denver. When

Gale had heard that Moorhead had died, he'd assumed Avery would take Moorhead's place.

"We had a good thing going with Clay," Avery said, breaking the silence. "Now that he's gone, there's a lot of uncertainty."

Gale stayed silent.

"No disrespect. But we're worried a new coach is going to mess with us, Coach McClanahan. We don't want anyone breaking from the Caton way." Avery paused and gave a half smile. "We punt here, Coach. We don't go for it on fourth down from our one yard-line."

The other coaches broke into smiles. Since coaching the Lone Stars, Gale had become infamous for being a disciple of the renowned economist, David Romer, who wrote a controversial scholarly paper about punting hurting a team's chances of winning.

"What's the Caton way, Coach?" Gale asked.

"Clay's way."

Gale leaned back. He noticed the other coaches nodding.

Avery went on. "With all due respect, we don't need a white knight riding into town telling us what to do. You've inherited a great staff. Let us show you how we do things here."

"If you're worried about me messing things up, why didn't any of you take the job?" Gale asked, smiling thinly.

Avery shook his head. "Who wants to follow in the footsteps of a legend?" His eyes swept the room. The other coaches stayed silent.

Gale noticed Avery's eyes sharpened when he spoke. A hint of resentment? Gale wondered if Avery had coveted the head coaching position. Knowing a little something about him, he felt like it could hardly be otherwise.

Avery continued. "That said, none of us wants what we've built pissed away."

Gale studied the coaches' expressions. "What makes you think I'll mess it up?"

Avery smiled and looked around the room. "We're just sharing our concerns. We want to get 'em on the table. And we don't want anything or anyone disrupting the good systems we got in place, especially not someone who's only here a year."

Another assistant with a shaved head, sunken cheeks, and a hook nose broke in. It was Buck Marshall. Gale had played against him in high school. A bruising linebacker, Marshall had gone on to play at Arizona State. "Hell, let's talk about *the real world.*" Marshall's hard edge stood in contrast to Avery's more subtle approach. He caught Gale by surprise. "Everyone in this room serves at Bart Waters' pleasure. Waters has one simple provision."

"You know what that is?" Avery asked, tapping his index finger on the table.

"You tell me," Gale said.

"We win." Avery leaned back and gave a knowing look to the coaches around the table.

"That's right," Marshall said while Avery and the coaches listened on. "Luckily, with Coach Moorhead, we've never had any trouble winning. With a happy Waters, our bread gets buttered."

"Now you think you'll have trouble?" Gale asked.

Marshall's eyes clouded. "We just want to make sure we're clear with you, Coach." His tone was confrontational.

"Now Buck, let's remember that Mr. Waters thinks Coach McClanahan can deliver." Avery continued, "It can all be good, Coach. You do what all of us have been doing for years, win games our way and make Bart Waters and the town of Caton proud."

"That's right," Marshall echoed.

Gale felt all eyes fall upon him. He realized there was no going back to his family and his ranch. Marybeth's mother and H.W. Owen had seen to that. "I said I would coach, and that's what I'm going to do."

"Under Caton's terms," Avery said, giving Gale an uneasy smile.

"I've won everywhere I've been," Gale said through gritted teeth.

Avery pursed his lips. "You'll see soon enough that our way works. It has for years."

Gale resisted the temptation to ask how many state championships they had won, or how many times over the years the Kinney Lions, under Gale's direction, had beaten the Panthers.

"I've put together a pre-season practice schedule," Gale said, shifting the conversation. He tried to rationalize that coaching Caton was only for a season. It wasn't a life sentence. He could offer no resistance, do it the Caton way, and get out of town. But Gale shook off the thought. He'd learned from his father to do things the right way and for the right reasons. He'd made the Atlanta roster not on talent, but on toughness and desire. He'd fought Vernon Voss and won. Gale peered around the room and took a deep breath. He felt a dull ache in his side from the broken ribs he'd suffered two years before. He had another fight on his hands.

"We already have a pre-season practice schedule," Avery said, cutting him off, sliding a folder across the table to Gale. "We've used the same schedule for years. No need to change. Clay believed in consistency."

"Consistency?" Gale asked.

"That's right," Marshall echoed.

"The boys know what to expect," Avery said.

Gale opened the folder. He shook his head. "It says practices begin at noon and go to 3 p.m."

"That's right," Avery said. "We do what's best for the team."

"That's against state regulations." In the height of a West Texas summer, pre-season practices were held early in the morning and late in the afternoon to avoid an unmerciful sun and scorching temperatures. A three-hour practice was unheard of.

"What regulations?" Marshall asked. The coaches began to smile.

"A boy could die at that time of day," Gale shot back.

"Don't you worry, Coach. We give 'em plenty of water. We got the misters running at full force."

Gale looked at the schedule again. He said with alarm, "Full pads the first day?"

"Always," Avery said. "We hit here in Caton. We make men out of these boys."

"No one hits on the first day of practice anymore," Gale said. "The State Athletic Commission will have our heads."

Avery laughed. "Hell, those state boys know better than to show up in Caton."

"I see you really have the interest of the boys at heart all right," Gale said dryly.

"Caton men will take care of Caton boys. You do what Clay did," Marshall said, "and things will be good."

"I don't see anything good here."

"Clay knew what he was doing," Avery said, resting his elbows on the table and looking hard at Gale. "He taught us well, Coach."

"We start practice at 6 a.m.," Gale said bluntly. He noticed Avery and Marshall shoot looks at each other.

Avery shifted in his seat. "That ain't going to work," he warned.

"Why?"

"Some of us need our beauty rest," Avery said. "Especially Buck here."

"That's right," Marshall said.

Gale's jaw tightened. "6 a.m. It's not negotiable."

"This is what we were talking about, Coach," Avery said, glancing at Marshall, who was shaking his head. "That's not the Caton Way."

"Let's call it the McClanahan way then," Gale said, sliding his chair away from the table.

Gale walked out from under the stadium into the blinding sun and felt heat rise from the pavement. Before opening the door to his pickup, he took a minute to try to shrug the tension out of his shoulders. Then, as he opened the door, he heard a voice call out. It was a woman standing next to a silver

Camry. She wore sunglasses and a soft blue, light cotton sundress. She was a few years younger than Gale and had dirty blonde hair cut above her shoulders. She had high cheekbones and wore dangling rectangular amber earrings. Gale thought her pretty.

"Coach McClanahan?" she asked.

Gale blinked his eyes. They stung from the heat. He noticed the beginning of a headache.

She said, "You have a moment? I'm Katie Tuck. The school counselor and assistant principal."

Gale nodded.

"Can we get out of the sun?" she asked, brushing a wisp of hair away from her eyes.

"That's a good idea." The temperature had already risen past a hundred.

"But not here. Can I buy you lunch?" she smiled.

"Lunch?"

"Yes. I need to know if you're as advertised."

"How's that?" Gale asked, feeling a trickle of sweat running down his back.

"I'll tell you. But let's get indoors. I can't stand outside in this furnace much longer."

Gale followed Tuck to a farmhouse sitting in an overgrown field about five miles outside of Caton that had been converted into a vegan cafe. The cafe was as out of place as a restaurant could be in West Texas. The menu was written on a blackboard above the counter in swervy pastels and the walls were painted a startling pink. Framed posters celebrated Earth Day and organic farmers. The specials of the day were vegan burritos and Chana Masala wraps. Gale wondered what a Chana Masala wrap was.

They sat in the back of the restaurant and sipped cold tea. People were starting to drift in for lunch. The tiny restaurant was slowly filling up.

"How's the chicken fried steak?" Gale asked, smiling.

"Welcome to the Happy Longhorn."

Gale studied the café menu. "A cattle rancher's nightmare."

Tuck smiled. "I have nothing against a burger," she said. "I put my hankering for a chicken Caesar salad aside today so we could talk. I figured we'd have more privacy here. The place is popular, but not for the people who'd wonder why we're having lunch."

Gale sat back, waiting for more.

"Myron Bellwether said he met with you." Tuck's expression softened. "He said you seemed kind. And he also thinks you might be the type to stir up trouble."

"I'm not sure another man has ever called me kind."

She took a sip of tea. Gale noticed she wasn't wearing a wedding band. She had long, delicate fingers and clear blue eyes. "Kindness is something Myron rarely experiences. So he notices. I've felt bad for him. They push him around, make him do things he hates. Poor man."

"So why lunch?"

"Clay Moorhead's death was awful. I don't wish that upon anyone, not even Clay. But it presents an opportunity."

"Opportunity?"

"To change things."

"How so?"

Tuck pursed her lips then said in hushed tones, "Clay's death wasn't a surprise."

Gale leaned back.

Tuck continued. "If you had told me a year ago someone would kill Clay, I would have said, 'he had it coming.' The man was a narcissist and a sociopath. Vile. I wasn't surprised that someone did him in. He manipulated everything and everyone to get what he wanted. Far from being just about football, for Clay, football was just a means to an end. What he really wanted was to live like some feudal lord."

The waitress came over to the table. She wore her green hair spiked along with a nose ring and multiple ear piercings. One arm was tattooed in a floral pattern from wrist to shoulder. She asked, "Ready to order?'

"The quinoa bowl, please," Tuck answered.

"What's quinoa?" Gale asked, perplexed.

"It's good," the waitress said reassuringly.

Gale squinted at the blackboard. In the last few months, it had dawned on him that he needed glasses. Marybeth had caught him squinting at the TV and had admonished him for not seeing the eye doctor. He turned to the waitress, wondering if the nose ring and all the piercings hurt. "I guess I'll have the burrito."

"You'll love it," the waitress said. "Anything else?"

Tuck looked at Gale. He shook his head. "That's it," Tuck said.

Tuck carefully unfurled the paper napkin holding her utensils and placed the napkin on her lap. She went on. "Here's the background you need. Bart Waters runs the town and has been School Board president for years. He has a sycophant, Dean Spivey, waiting to take over. Caton's a backwater. No one cares about anything but football. Waters hands out pieces of candy like a new ambulance or fire truck, maybe helps fund a little league field and a new park. As long as he makes these civic bribes, no one crosses him. The principal position has been a revolving door. No wonder. It's all about football."

Gale thought about the meeting he'd just had with Clay Moorhead's coaches.

"No one says anything. People in town don't seem to care as long as the football team wins. Waters knows that. The losers are the kids." Tuck's cheeks flushed with anger.

"None of this tells me why someone decided to kill Moorhead," Gale said.

"True. But my guess is that someone had a score to settle. Someone wanted to take the bastard down."

"Or," Gale said, "Moorhead knew too much. He was getting too big for his britches."

Tuck reflected for a moment. Her blue eyes clouded. "Maybe. But it doesn't matter anymore. Clay's dead. That's where you come in." She paused. "I know what happened in San Antonio. When I heard they hired you to coach the Panthers, I knew they'd found a coach who could turn things around, maybe cause some good trouble. Frankly, I was shocked Bart Waters approached you. You don't seem like Waters' type."

Gale shrugged.

"But it makes sense. He's controlled everyone for a long time, including Clay. He thinks he can control you. He wants to win because he knows that's the key to controlling Caton. The town will forgive just about anything, even stealing from the till, for a trip each year to Dallas. Waters clearly thinks you can deliver a state championship."

Tuck fell back into a whisper. "Those boys are under the worst kind of pressure. I can't tell you how many of those players have slipped into my office over the years, and when I shut the door, broken down sobbing because they hated playing for Clay Moorhead. It's staggering. And then I'd see them the next day, walking in the hallway wearing their Caton football jerseys acting as if they ruled the world. But it's all a façade. The truth is that Caton High School football is malignant. The cancer needs to be cut out."

"That's where I come in?"

"Yes. That's where you come in, Coach." For a moment, Tuck studied Gale. "I know why you took this job."

"Do you?"

"For the kids."

"Why do you say that?" Gale asked. Gale could only wish Tuck's words were true.

"Myron Bellwether may be seen as a lightweight, a tool. But if people dug deeper, and saw beyond the glasses, bow tie, and eye tic, they'd see he's a perceptive human being who cares deeply about his students. But of course, he's powerless to stop what's going on. He told me this morning, after his experience in Caton, he thought he'd just met a football coach who cared more about his players than winning."

"My teams have won seven state championships," Gale said with an ironic smile.

"True. But you're not an asshole."

"You just met me."

"I can tell."

"How?"

"You didn't walk out of here when you saw the menu. Plus, Myron's right. You have kind eyes. There's nothing demonic about you, Coach McClanahan and that makes you a unicorn in Caton football circles."

"A unicorn. How about that? My daughter will be pleased."

Tuck smiled, then continued. "Clay Moorhead was a bad man." She hesitated, carefully choosing her words. "He hit on me the first time I met him. I was new to town, fresh out of grad school with a counseling degree. We were at a faculty and staff barbeque and his wife was sitting in a lawn chair by the pool. He moved in close, put his hands on my hips, and told me that if I went out with him, we'd have fun. I'd never have to worry about anyone messing with me. I'd be Clay's girl. He never even took his toothpick out of his mouth."

"What did you say?"

"I was shocked. I pulled away without a word and left the party." She took a sip of tea and went on, her voice cracking. "A year earlier, I'd lost my husband, Mark. He was killed in a motorcycle accident."

"Oh, I'm so sorry."

"I did nothing, but what I really wanted to do was kick Moorhead in the balls."

Gale smiled.

"Castrate him. Instead, I went to Waters."

"What did he say?"

"He laughed it off, told me Clay was kidding. He told me I needed to have a sense of humor."

"And?"

"A few days later the principal before Bellwether wrote me up. He put a letter in my file saying I didn't inform a family about a meeting I had with their daughter. The mom and dad said I told the student she should be taking antidepressants. He said the student's parents were outraged."

"Did you?" Gale asked.

"Are you kidding? Of course not. The girl came into my office to ask if I had a tampon."

"You got set up?"

Tuck nodded. "Guess who the parents were?"

Gale had a guess but didn't say anything.

"Dean and Audrey Spivey."

Gale nodded. "Why stay? Why not move to another district? Counselors and assistant principals are hard to come by."

"I don't run from fights," Tuck said, her voice steely. "And from what I understand, you don't either. Which is why you are about to eat a tofu and sprouts burrito."

Four

Three days later, Gale stood in the early morning in an empty locker room with growing anger. He'd communicated with players and coaches that practice would begin after a 6:00 a.m. organizational team meeting. It was now 6:15. After a few more minutes, he sent Lloyd Avery a text.

There was no reply.

Gale walked to his pickup and slid into the cab. He googled Avery's home address, turned on his GPS, and pulled away from the parking lot. Ten minutes later, he parked his dusty truck in front of a large, white two-story home with a well-manicured front lawn. Sprinklers whirred in the early morning, drenching the grass and flower beds. Gale knew that even small towns in West Texas had water restrictions. He wondered how many gallons Avery had wasted keeping his fescue-seeded lawn looking like a well-cared-for fairway.

Gale noticed no cars were parked in the driveway. Gale climbed out of his pickup and rang Avery's doorbell. When he sensed no movement in the house, he pushed the buzzer again. Finally, Gale turned and climbed into his pickup. Either Avery slept like a dead man, or the house was empty.

Shortly before noon, Gale met Avery outside the locker room. Avery was wearing a Caton High School T-shirt and shorts.

"We were supposed to start at 6 am," Gale said, trying to control his anger.

"You didn't get the message?" Avery said sarcastically.

"No."

"We practice at noon. We told you that, Coach."

Gale stared at Avery. One of Avery's knees had a large, purple scar scissored across it. In addition, he had a three-inch scar running along his Adam's apple. The surgeon had gone through the front of Avery's neck to repair a career-ending herniated disk. If you played in the League long enough, surgery was inevitable. Gale noticed Avery had scratch marks on his face, as if someone had dug fingernails into his cheek and bridge of his nose.

Gale hadn't noticed them a few days before when the coaches had met. Gale said, "I'm not putting those kids on the field in the middle of the day."

"I thought we explained that."

Gale stayed silent.

"Those boys are used to practicing in the heat. Hell, they won't respect you if you don't push 'em, Coach. They're used to Clay Moorhead. They're going to think you're runnin' some kind of country club."

Gale thought of the practices he had led over the years, the discipline and toughness his teams demonstrated. He thought back to the Lone Stars, coaching at the highest level. Even with pro football players, he didn't have them practicing in the mid-day summer sun. It was a recipe for disaster. He recalled a rookie offensive tackle for Arizona who had died from heat stroke a few years earlier during training camp.

"Well, as I recall, my country club boys whipped your Caton boys often enough. We'll start this evening."

"You don't want them to think you're soft, do you, Coach?" Avery gave Gale a sugary smile.

"Soft?" Gale's eyes hardened.

Gale could tell that Avery was carefully considering his next words. He forced a smile. "Mr. Waters ain't going to like this."

Gale dismissed the threat. "We start with a team meeting today at 5 p.m. Understand? I'm telling the players to go home."

Avery slowly nodded.

"Make sure the coaches get the word," Gale said, through gritted teeth.

"Will do, Coach McClanahan," Avery said, shaking his head, and slowly moving past him down the hallway. "But I'll expect you'll be hearing from Mr. Waters."

Ephraim Hernandez sat on the trash-covered berm next to Home Depot alongside a half dozen other undocumented migrants with sunburned skin and dirt-covered hands, hoping someone would swing by in a flatbed or a pickup truck and give him work. What else could he do? He hadn't any idea where or how to look for Maria. In the early morning, the heat was already building, and the parking lot was filling with contractors hoping to get a jump on the day. He knew what all migrants knew, that despite the official posturing of immigration authorities, Del Rio, Texas needed the labor. It was a cat and mouse game that he'd played before, but this time, instead of the constant fear of capture, Ephraim was torn between an infinite sadness and a burning fury. His hatred for the man with the scar was so deep that he wondered if God would forgive him.

He drank coffee from a large Styrofoam cup he'd bought at the 7-Eleven across the street and rubbed his eyes. It was always this way. If he was lucky, a truck would pull up and the men in the cab would give the order to climb in back. Ephraim would try to doze as the vehicle grinded its way to the work site. And for the rest of the day, he would try without success to put away the thought of Maria and the terrible, aching feeling in his heart.

Gale found the players sitting in full pads on the gymnasium bleachers in nervous anticipation. There was a buzz in the gym. A new coach who'd coached in the League and unlike Clay Moorhead, had a flat stomach and no snuff tucked between his lip and gum. Gale shot a look at Lloyd Avery and Buck Marshall, who ignored him. Gale caught Avery leaning against the gym's concrete block wall and smiling at the other assistants. Gale glanced at the coaches. They seemed to be waiting for what would come next.

Gale noticed the teenager who'd come to his house. Eben Daly sat in front. He was biting his lip. He and his teammates seemed to sense that a drama was playing out before them.

Gale surveyed the players. *Full pads*. He said, "Go back to the locker room and take your equipment off. We're going in helmets and shorts. Understand?"

The players began to shoot each other glances. Gale realized that Avery and the other assistants were about to object, so Gale cut them off. "Go!" he said to the players.

Hesitantly, the team rose and started clumping down the aluminum bleachers. When they had streamed out of the gym, Gale turned to the coaches, his ears hot. "I said no pads."

Avery shrugged and said, "I guess they didn't get the memo, Coach."

Gale felt blood rush up the back of his neck. "From now on they'd better."

"Whatever you say," Avery said, dismissively. He turned to the other coaches, his square jaw jutting out. "Welcome to Caton Country Club, boys."

Thirty minutes later the players circled around Gale on the practice field while the assistants hung together a few yards away. Gale eyed the team. Each year, he started the first day of practice with a spirited game of dodgeball. He wanted players to bond. He had other tricks up his sleeve, especially when pre-season dragged on. He recalled during training camp with Atlanta when the grind of double sessions had hit the players hard. Injuries had started to pile up. Contusions, broken fingers, torn nails, pulled hamstrings, swollen knees, and aching ribs. One day, instead of practice, the coaching staff sensed the players' exhaustion and had several large tubs of ice cream sandwiches delivered. Gale remembered how he and his teammates had sat in the cavernous, tiered team room feeling the delicious rush of air conditioning eating ice cream sandwiches while the movie *Old School* flickered on the screen.

NO HEART TO KILL

Gale always cultivated leadership in his quarterbacks, so he pulled Eben Daly, the preacher's son, aside and spoke to him softly. The teenager shot an uncertain look toward Avery, but then broke into a smile and trotted toward the far side of the practice field.

An instant later, Daly shouted, "Freshman and sophomores on this end of the field, juniors and seniors on the other."

The players looked confused. One kid, with a buzz cut and a build like a defensive end spoke up. "What are we doing coach?"

"You ever heard of dodgeball?" Gale asked.

The kid smiled and the other players began to grin. The assistant coaches looked dismayed. Gale noticed Avery stepping toward him. Gale said, "The team that wins gets bragging rights, boys, and no sprints."

The players smiled, and a murmur swept through the team. "Really?" the kid who had spoken up asked.

"Hell, yes," Gale said.

As the players trotted to their respective ends of the field, Avery said, "What are you doing, Coach?"

"What does it look like?"

"You tell me."

"It's called team building."

"These boys are used to a firm hand. Clay pushed them hard." Avery reached into his pocket, pulled a toothpick out, and stuck it in his mouth. "When these boys go home tonight and tell their daddies they played dodgeball during football practice, you're going to hear about it, Coach. Their fathers all played for Clay. They all practiced in the middle of the day. They wore full pads and hit." Avery shook his head and his sharp teeth flashed through a half smile. "They're going to think the new head coach is some kind of puss. Are you a puss, Coach McClanahan?"

Gale turned and faced Avery. He wanted to take him down. Besides being one of the best football players in the history of Kinney High School, Gale had been a state wrestling champion. While Avery had at least seventy-five pounds on Gale, all it might take was a double shot to the legs and Gale might stand a chance.

Gale sensed Avery read something in his expression. "Besides," Avery said. "You're making us look bad."

"Look bad?"

Avery spat. "But have it your way. You're the head coach."

"Thanks for the vote of confidence."

"Anytime, Coach." He made the word sound like an epithet.

Gale turned away. Avery walked over to Buck Marshall and shook his head. Soon the players were playing a ferocious game of dodgeball. Gale spotted smiles and heard laughter. He wondered what their fathers would say.

If Avery was right, Gale could expect his phone to ring. *Hell, dodgeball? Coach Moorhead would be rolling in his grave. What are you doin', Coach?*

But there's a new sheriff in town, Gale thought. *Clay Moorhead's dead, and I'm going to do it my way.*

When he arrived home in the darkness, Gale found Marybeth sitting in one of their new overstuffed chairs with her feet propped up on a matching ottoman. Her computer rested on her lap, and she looked up when the front door opened. At times, it startled Gale when he walked into the renovated house. He'd grown up in the home, a one-story dwelling with dark, boxy rooms, narrow hallways, and a cramped kitchen. Marybeth had designed the new floor plan and made sure the house had plenty of natural light and open space. They had built an addition; a spacious living room that flowed to a slate patio. Gale wondered what his parents would've thought about the work Marybeth and Gale had done to the house.

"How did it go?" Marybeth asked, failing to look up from her computer. Since discovering the truth about her mother, Marybeth had fallen into dark moods, undoubtedly still trying to come to terms with her mother's past. Her question seemed perfunctory. Gale figured it would take a while before Marybeth came out if it. He'd give her all the time she needed. Hell, even he was struggling. He'd tried hard to erase the thought of Marybeth's mother and H.W. Owen conceiving his wife, but the shock hadn't worn off. Like him, Marybeth needed some time. She was the most sensible, honest person he'd ever known. When they'd first had one another under a swath of stars on a pile of blankets in the back of Gale's pickup, Gale knew he never wanted to be with another woman.

"We played dodgeball."

"Dodgeball?" she asked, raising her eyebrows. "I'm sure that went over well in Caton."

"Sure did."

Marybeth shook her head and looked up from her laptop. "There's a plate for you in the fridge. Chicken."

Gale hesitated, and said, "One of the assistants called me a puss."

"That's offensive, Gale. I hate that word," she said with disgust. "I can see you've made some fine new friends."

Gale nodded.

For a moment Marybeth looked away, then changed the subject. "You forgot to take out the garbage this morning."

"Sorry . . ."

"The plate is in the refrigerator," Marybeth said and turned her attention back to her computer.

Gale nodded and turned to the kitchen. He loved his wife, and he knew that if he gave her time and space, she would return to him stronger and more determined than ever.

Five

Three days later, people lined the field watching the Caton High School Panthers' evening practice. Gale noticed Bart Waters and Dean Spivey standing alone at the far end of the practice field in the fading twilight with arms crossed and jaws set. After three running plays, Gale had changed Lloyd Avery's play, and Eben Daly had thrown a 30-yard strike downfield. Daly excitedly raised his hand in the air and high fived the players around him. He was clearly enjoying the offensive freedom Gale was granting him. Daly was a natural athlete. Big, strong, and agile. He had a quick release and could throw the ball on a line. Nevertheless, when Gale changed the play, Avery's eyes had darkened and he had turned his back. Even after the play worked, he wasn't excited.

From when he had started until he was killed, Clay Moorhead had run a blunt, Power I offense. For that reason, Gale believed Moorhead would have been even more successful if he'd shown more creativity. Gale always felt confident about game planning against Caton High School. Moorhead believed in power football, sending the running back into the hole behind a burly offensive line. The times Kinney had lost, it wasn't because of Moorhead's strategy, it was because Caton had bigger, stronger, more talented players. Gale's team simply wore down in the fourth quarter. "Give me Tornado, 42 Zip," Gale said to Avery after the offense ran another running play.

"Hell, that's not our sequence, Coach," Avery shot back, scowling.

"Run it," Gale said.

Avery rolled his eyes. "We haven't run that play in ten years."

Gale felt his ears grow hot. "Then why have it in the playbook?"

Avery shook his head and walked away.

A few seconds later, Daly took the snap and threw a perfectly arced ball to the wideout sprinting down the sideline. Gale heard a wave of chatter ripple through the crowd. Daly slapped his hands together after the completion and grinned at Gale. Then Gale heard Avery say to Daly, "Don't get too excited son. You may never run that play again."

Gale felt his face flush with anger. He turned to Daly. "Let's keep the momentum going, Eben. Lightning Strike 71 Zip."

"What the hell are you doin'?" Avery snapped. "You're showing me up, Coach."

Daly nervously glanced from one coach to the other. "You heard me, Eben." Gale had had enough of Avery. He said to Daly. "I want the fade right over the receiver's left shoulder. If you miss, miss out of the end zone."

Daly called the play and broke the huddle. A few seconds later, he threw a perfectly completed ball for a touchdown.

"There you go," Gale shouted, clapping his hands together as the starting offense high fived each other. "Can you do that under pressure, Eben?" he asked, his eyes boring into Daly's.

Daly nodded. Gale could tell the quarterback's adrenaline was flowing. Two years before, Gale had helped Matt Abruzzi, an undrafted free agent, become an accomplished quarterback in the League. He'd driven Abruzzi hard but had allowed him to play with abandon.

Gale decided to end practice on a high note. He shouted for the kids to circle up. He spotted Lloyd Avery spit and turn his back to the team. Avery started cutting toward Spivey and Waters. Marshall followed. Gale set his jaw and said to the boys kneeling around him. "Tomorrow, 6 a.m. Get some sleep. Don't be playing video games all night."

The players huddled around him and grinned.

As the kids walked across the field to the locker room carrying their shoulder pads and helmets, Marshall and Avery continued to huddle with Spivey and Waters. Avery's face was red as he spoke and Waters seemed to look past him toward Gale, who was following the players. A few seconds later, Gale saw Waters coming toward him.

"You got a second, Coach?" Waters asked with a sugary smile.

Gale stopped and faced Waters. "A second."

"How come you got Lloyd all in a tizzy?"

"I think the better question is why the offensive coordinator gets in a tizzy when we score a touchdown."

"Heck, you've coached against Caton enough to know we're a power football team, Coach McClanahan. Lloyd thinks you're making him look bad."

Gale studied Waters and kept silent.

"Coach Avery is a respected offensive coordinator. Lloyd and Buck have been running their sides of the ball for years."

"They're not the head coach."

"Do me a favor, son." Waters smiled thinly. "Keep Lloyd happy."

Gale breathed slowly trying to quell his rising anger. "Anything else?"

"All you got to do is listen to your assistants and win. It's real simple."

Gale moved past Waters and headed toward the stadium.

"One more thing," Waters said.

Gale turned.

"I heard you told Bellwether to come around the team anytime he likes."

Gale stared expressionless.

"I don't want that boy anywhere near my football team. Understand, son? He's everything that football ain't."

"What does that mean?" Gale asked with barely contained disgust.

"Softer than shit."

Gale looked at Waters' flabby waistline. He felt his spine stiffen. "Anything else?"

"Like I said, you let Marshall and Avery do their jobs."

"What if I don't think I can do that and win at the same time?"

Waters shook his head slowly back and forth. "You do what I say if you know what's good for you. You listen to Buck and Lloyd. They're good men, Coach McClanahan. Figure it out. That way, we can keep our little secret to ourselves, right?"

The next morning, Gale didn't know whether to feel irritated or relieved. The players had begun to stretch on the practice field, and Marshall and Avery were nowhere to be seen. Gale looked over at the other assistant coaches who returned his stare with a shrug. Gale wondered if Marshall and Avery had made the decision to boycott practice. He was about to blow his whistle to bring the team together when Marshall and Avery emerged from under the stadium and walked slowly onto the field. Avery shot Gale a glance and started eyeing the laminated practice plan. Marshall followed and stood next to him with a blank face and crossed arms.

Gale took a deep breath and confronted them.

"Practice started at 6 a.m.," Gale said.

Marshall scowled. Gale noticed he had a welt below his eye and his fingernails were caked with dirt. Avery's eyes were bloodshot.

"I ask the players to be on time," Gale said, "and the coaches."

"Sorry, Coach," Avery said. "Buck and I got lost coming to practice."

Gale set his jaw and eyed both men. He turned toward the players, ignoring Marshall and Avery. He shouted, "Let's go. Everyone circle up. We have a lot of work to do, boys. We scrimmage in three days."

The call came in the early afternoon. Gale was making the drive home to check on Mason Hayes and Mateo Santos, who'd been wrestling with a faulty transmission on one of the ranches' flatbeds.

Gale's old pickup didn't have Bluetooth, so when the cell started chiming, he put the call on speaker phone. It was Grayson Wallace.

"How's Benedict Arnold?" Wallace asked, his voice booming out of Gale's tinny cell.

"Feeling Caton's love and admiration."

"I suspected as much."

"I have two coaches who don't like my play calling."

"I feel their pain," Wallace said.

Gale laughed. "If I had followed your advice, Grayson, I would have been fired from Kinney years ago. You're a good lawyer but leave football to me."

"I will now. I root against Caton. That said, as you know, I have a penchant for sticking my nose where it doesn't belong. I called a friend of mine who's a judge in Del Rio."

"Tell me more," Gale said.

Wallace paused dramatically. "I called him about Clay Moorhead. He said they have no leads. The sheriff's office has been uninterested, to say the least, and the case has gone cold. Even the state authorities are downplaying Clay's death."

"Clay was killed less than a month ago. The story's been on every front page in Texas. Hell, how can it go cold?"

"Someone's killing the investigation. I even heard they're pushing a theory that a stray round killed Clay."

"Pretty accurate stray."

"Someone target shooting near the reservoir. It wouldn't be the first time."

Gale knew how far a high-powered round could carry. There was no shortage of gun enthusiasts in Texas. Nevertheless, Gale made a sound that expressed his incredulity.

"Far-fetched, I know."

"Why do you think Waters wanted me to coach so bad?" Gale asked. "I've been thinking about that. Why not find someone who's as dirty as he is? Someone who's sympatico?"

Wallace paused. "Ah, the million-dollar question, but I have a theory. Waters needed someone who has a clean image. Someone who would make people forget Clay Moorhead and think Waters was on the up and up. A paragon of civic virtue."

Gale grunted. "How flattering."

"He trades a legendary coach with questionable ethics for a legendary coach who drinks milk and helps old ladies cross the street."

"In my defense, I nearly killed a man," Gale said.

"Waters doesn't know that."

"What else doesn't he know, Grayson?" Gale's eyes swept the empty plains and road ahead. He passed an oil derrick pumping under the summer sky.

"Maybe that he's got a bigger problem on his hands."

"Other than Moorhead getting shot by a stray bullet," Gale snorted. "What's that?"

"Gale McClanahan."

Gale shook his head. "I've got two assistant coaches who hate my guts."

"What else is new?"

Gale sighed. "Grayson. I keep going back to *how* Clay died. If it was a murder, it was a statement. A headline. Why not a drug overdose, or have him die in a car accident?"

"All good questions."

"I don't get it."

"Whoever killed him doesn't share your sense of imagination."

Gale said with disgust, "Well, it sure as hell wasn't an errant round."

"This is true."

"Waters?"

"Bart's conniving and devious. He wouldn't have used a rifle."

"What are you saying?"

"Whoever killed Clay had an agenda and didn't mind using brute force."

Gale tapped his finger on the wheel. He thought about Myron Bellwether's fear and Katie Tuck's anger. He thought about Waters and Spivey, arms crossed, stonily watching practice as if they were judge and jury. *Executioner, too?* He thought about Marshall and Avery telling him there was only the Caton Way. He woke from his reverie when he heard Wallace say, "Be careful, Gale. There's someone out there who most likely enjoyed killing Moorhead."

"I haven't done anything yet to deserve getting shot."

"Give it time, my boy," Wallace sighed. "Something tells me you're just the sort to poke the serpent with a stick. And when you do, don't go fishing."

Nearly everything about Lloyd Avery's play calling cut against Gale's coaching philosophy. The scrimmage against Sheridan was winding down, and Gale kicked the turf in disgust as Avery called the fullback's number again. Eben Daly's body language showed how bored he was watching the running back pile into yet another tangle of bodies. Gale knew that if the Panthers were going to make a run in the playoffs, they'd be facing teams as big and rugged as theirs. They would need Daly's athletic ability and more imaginative play calling to give them separation.

Gale reached his limit when he heard Avery call another run play on third and four. He said into his headset, "Scratch that. Give me 23, Red

Lightning." The pass play was designed to send the tight end ten yards up the middle into the seam. Gale had noticed the tight end had been left open nearly the entire scrimmage.

"What did you say?" Avery said into his headset, turning toward Gale.

Gale repeated the play.

A receiver stood impatiently next to Avery waiting for a decision before he sprinted out to tell Daly the call.

"I already called the play," Avery grunted. "Go!" He shouted at the receiver to deliver the play to Daly. The kid sprinted toward the huddle.

Gale stepped toward Avery and placed his hand over his microphone so the other coaches couldn't hear.

"Nobody's covering the tight end."

"Let's stick with what we do best, Coach," Avery responded with a hard stare.

Once again, Gale fought the urge to grab Avery by the throat. He took a deep breath. Even for a scrimmage, the stadium was filled on a Friday night, and Gale wanted to avoid a confrontation with Avery in front of the whole town.

"We'll talk," Gale said in disgust.

"Can't wait."

A few seconds later, the Panther's running back was dragged down for a one-yard loss.

When the scrimmage ended, Gale was following the players toward the locker room when he saw Marybeth and Tilly with Jack and Barbara Engle walking to the stadium exit. Marybeth held Tilly's hand, gave Gale an uncertain smile and a wave, and Jack Engle shot Gale a knowing look and shook his head. Barbara, pretty as ever with her short silver hair and clear skin, rolled her eyes. In the morning, the Engles would be hitting the road for their trip across America. The realization gave Gale a pit in his stomach. As a friend and mentor, Gale relied on Engle. His absence loomed large.

As Gale went under the stands to the locker room, he spotted Dean Spivey in the empty corridor by the entrance door jabbing his finger at Myron Bellwether. Bellwether, wearing a white dress shirt and bow tie, looked stricken by Spivey's onslaught.

When Spivey turned and saw Gale, he pulled his finger out of Bellwether's face and whispered to the principal, "I warned you, Myron."

Bellwether's face was ashen, and his eyes betrayed his fear.

"The players are waiting for you, Coach," Spivey said, turning to Gale and pointing at the locker room door.

"They can wait," Gale shot back. "What's going on?"

Spivey smiled thinly. "Mr. Bellwether and I were just having a little conversation. Isn't that right, Myron?"

Bellwether's head jerked up and down.

"You can move on now," Spivey warned Gale. "This isn't your business."

"Leave him alone," Gale said.

"You're sticking your nose where it shouldn't go, Coach McClanahan. Go coach the team."

Gale noticed that Bellwether began to shrink even more at his intervention. But Gale couldn't abide bullies, so he approached Spivey.

Spivey pulled back a few steps and for a moment eyed Bellwether before turning to Gale. "Okay. Have it your way." He turned to Bellwether. "Just remember what I said, Myron."

When Spivey had left, Gale said, "You okay?"

Bellwether shoulders sagged.

"What was that about?"

Bellwether hesitated, then said meekly, "Nothing."

Gale shook his head and reached for the locker room door. "I told you I'd have your back. If you want to get pushed around, fine."

Bellwether leaned his shoulder against the concrete wall and closed his eyes for an instant. "We caught Mr. Spivey's son with a stash of opiates. I called Mr. Spivey and told him I had to call the sheriff, and he told me he'd ruin me if I did."

Gale noted the irony. Spivey was one of the town's biggest boosters, but his son didn't play football. Instead, he did drugs.

"I have to call the authorities. It's the law."

Gale nodded.

"I called the sheriff, and he laughed at me. Laughed! He said it couldn't be true."

"What?"

"He told me to forget about it for my own good," Bellwether choked.

"The hell? What's going on here?"

Bellwether's eyes grew lost. "I don't know."

"What did you find?"

Bellwether stammered. "The boy had a freezer bag full of powder. It's locked in my desk drawer."

Gale shook his head. The bag could be anything. Or a mixture. But one thing he knew for certain. No matter what the contents were, it could be deadly.

"What am I going to do?" Bellwether asked feebly, his lip quivering.

"Kick him out of school."

Bellwether's eyes grew big. "Waters will never have it."

Gale turned away for a moment and then back to Bellwether. "I need to speak to the team, and then I'll meet you in your office."

"What for?"

"I need to see what Spivey's kid was trying to sell. Then we'll go from there."

"You don't understand."

"The boy needs to be taught a lesson. He could kill someone."

Twenty minutes later, Gale entered Bellwether's office. He found Myron Bellwether, bewildered, sitting in a battered folding chair in a trashed office. The scuffed coffee table was smashed into pieces and Bellwether's metal desk had been overturned and bludgeoned. The drawers had been forced open and files lay scattered on the linoleum floor. Bellwether's laptop had been hurled against the wall and lay in pieces.

Gale looked at the mess and turned to Bellwether. "You okay?"

Bellwether said weakly, "They took it."

"They?" Gale asked. "You mean Spivey?"

When Bellwether didn't answer, Gale shook his head. He thought again of Spivey jabbing his finger in Bellwether's face, bullying him, and felt his jaw clench. "Let's get your office cleaned up."

"What about the drugs?"

"There's nothing we can do. They're gone."

When Gale finally turned onto the ranch after midnight and made the half-mile drive to the house, he noticed Marybeth had left on the porch light, but the rest of the house was dark. When he entered the living room, he kicked off his shoes and crept silently upstairs. After he washed his face and brushed his teeth, he entered the darkened bedroom.

"Gale?" Marybeth murmured.

"Go back to sleep," Gale whispered.

"You're home late."

"I had trouble."

"Trouble?" Marybeth turned slowly to him in the darkness as he slid under the sheets.

"I'll tell you in the morning."

"Oh, Gale," she said, too tired to keep her eyes open. "What now?" she asked before falling back asleep.

Gale closed his eyes. He was bone tired. His only solace was Marybeth, who had draped her long, smooth leg across his and pushed up against him.

Six

 Bart Waters had grown up in Caton the son of a dirt-poor, abusive alcoholic. His father had bounced from job to job in the oil fields before killing himself after discovering Waters' mother had been with another man. Waters was fifteen years old when his father died.
 When he turned seventeen, Waters started selling used cars. It didn't take long for Waters' prospects to take off. He was a natural on the lot, big and imposing, a wheeler dealer with a rubbery smile and a firm handshake. Soon, Waters purchased his own lot, and a few years later, when the town's only car dealership tumbled onto the market after a decade of decline, Waters mortgaged everything and bought it. In time, Waters found himself snapping up car dealerships across West Texas.
 He'd been a fixture at Rotary and one of McClendon County's rising stars. It didn't take long before H.W. Owen, a newly minted state senator, and Waters struck up a friendship. They had much in common. They were womanizers, opportunistic, ambitious, and unscrupulous. Waters with his power and influence soon had a vice grip on the town of Caton. As School Board President and Head of Town Council, he found ways through bribes, kickbacks, and "pay to play" schemes to siphon funds from nearly every contract the school district and town signed. When speculation about fracking hit West Texas, Waters began purchasing large tracts of land. Soon, he was negotiating favorable oil and gas leases with the help of Owen, who used his political clout and sharp elbows to ensure a generous cut from every leased well. Despite H.W. Owen's death, Waters was now completely entrenched, with enough legitimate fronts to mask the fact that he was a de facto don of a West Texas mafia. He saw himself in just this way. A Vito Corleone of the oil patch. And as long as the Caton Panthers won, no one seemed interested in crossing him. Football was the glue that held his empire together. For years, Clay Moorhead had seen to that.
 It was Texas after all.

Lloyd Avery sat across from Waters as Waters gazed out his office window toward the lot watching Buck Marshall close a deal with a dirt-poor couple on a pre-owned compact. Framed photos of Caton's championship teams hung on the walls, and a large photo of Waters and Moorhead hugging after the team had won the state championship rested prominently behind Waters' desk. The woman, barely twenty with stringy hair and acne-covered cheeks, wore torn jeans and held a crying infant in her arms, while her boyfriend, rail thin with stubble on his chin, wore a greasy baseball cap, a stained t-shirt, and skin-tight Wranglers. He kept nodding as Marshall snowed them.

Avery formed a cruel smile as he and Waters watched the scene. "That's the one with the bad transmission, Bart."

"Did you fix it?" Waters asked, putting his boots up on his oak desk.

Avery slowly shook his head. "Hell, no."

"How long before they're back?"

"A few weeks. I'll be sure to explain to them that they drove it too hard."

Waters grinned. "It's amazing what bad drivers we have around these parts."

"How's our boy from Kinney?" Waters asked.

Avery frowned. "Do gooders bring problems, Bart."

"This one provides excellent cover. Besides, I own him."

"McClanahan's got me and Buck worried."

"I know he does, but like I said, I own him."

"What about Spivey's kid?"

Waters frowned. "Dean got careless, but he swears he's got it under control."

"You buying it?"

"I don't know, but I can tell you one thing. I'm not going to have some snot-nosed teenager screwing up my operation."

His operation, Avery thought with disgust. Avery and Marshall took all the risk and did the dirty work, and Waters sat fat and happy, Avery thought. Spivey, too. Avery detested Spivey and always had. He looked out the window and watched Buck Marshall close the deal. Marshall shook the boyfriend's hand and started walking the couple into the dealership.

"What's got you worried about McClanahan?" Waters asked.

"He was in Bellwether's office last night."

"So?"

"I don't trust him."

Waters slid his boots onto the carpeted floor and stood up. He turned his back to Avery and looked out at the car lot. "All McClanahan knows is a punk teenager was selling drugs and a daddy was trying to protect his boy."

"The boy had thousands of dollars' worth of fentanyl. It wasn't some kid peddling weed to his buddies."

Waters turned to Avery. "Send McClanahan a message."

Avery shook his head. "I don't think it'll work."

"Screw with him, Lloyd. And make sure Bellwether doesn't talk."

"We already sent that message."

"How?"

"Myron woke up to a surprise this morning."

Waters formed a half smile.

"There's one less pet in the neighborhood. We left it hanging from a tree."

"Good," Waters said. "That will keep his mouth shut."

"Yup."

"And if it doesn't, that old boy might get strung up, too." Waters paused and flashed his sharp teeth. "His bow tie would make a good noose for that scrawny neck."

Gale walked out of Clay Moorhead Stadium into the blinding sun. He'd just put the team through a brief late afternoon workout in shorts and t-shirts after the scrimmage the night before. It was a Saturday ritual bringing the players in for treatment, film, a light lift, then a stretch and a few laps around the field. He'd managed to avoid a confrontation with Avery, who'd kept mostly to himself and then had huddled with Marshall during the team meeting. After practice, Gale had spent a half hour running passing drills with Eben Daly and a group of receivers, who, the previous evening against Sheridan, rarely touched the ball. After the drills, one of the boys had asked Gale about coaching the Lone Stars, and Gale had told the kids a story about McCann Foster, one of the toughest players he'd ever coached. Gale sensed the kids were curious about him, and excited to play for someone who'd coached in the League.

Gale had tossed and turned the night before. He'd never really fallen asleep. He'd lay awake thinking about Dean Spivey poking his finger in Myron Bellwether's face. He angrily thought about Spivey's kid peddling potentially lethal drugs around school and worried about his players and the other students who could be harmed. He kept flashing to his own daughter, who would someday be a vulnerable teenager.

He climbed into his stifling pickup for the drive home to Caton when his cell rang. He didn't recognize the number but took the call. He heard Katie Tuck say angrily, "Did you hear what happened to Myron?"

Twenty minutes later, Gale found himself driving Tuck to Bellwether's house.

When they arrived, they were met at the door by Bellwether's wife, a small, mousy woman with flaxen hair. Her eyes were red, as if she'd been crying, and her face was ashen. "Myron's not here," she said. "Did you hear what happened?"

"We heard," Tuck answered. "How's your daughter?"

Bellwether's wife looked away and began to softly cry. "It's terrible, Katie. The way those men treat Myron. The way we live waiting for them to hurt us. They killed my daughter's cat. What else will they destroy?"

Tuck looked away as Gale pursed his lips.

Bellwether's wife said, "Myron's a gentle man. He's scared. We're scared. There's no end to this. We never should have come to Caton. I knew it. And now it's playing true."

"I'm sorry," Tuck said. "Is there anything we can do?"

"Nothing," Bellwether's wife said, wiping her tears away and stepping back into the house. "Nothing at all. The damage has already been done. If I could only convince Myron that we need to leave, job or no job."

"Do you always look this fierce?" Gale asked a few minutes later as they drove to Dean Spivey's house. Tuck ignored him and stared out the passenger side window as they drove down Main Street with its small row of battered brick buildings and store fronts shimmering in the late afternoon heat. When they passed the old McClendon County Courthouse, Tuck said, "Turn here."

Gale soon realized they were driving into the same neighborhood as Lloyd Avery's house. In the cactus and scrub of West Texas, the handful of spacious homes, manicured lawns, and shade trees felt like an unnatural oasis. As they were driving down a leafy street, Tuck pointed and said, "This one."

Gale pulled up to a sprawling two-story house with box hedges in front, live oaks, and flower beds filled with begonias. A silver Porsche was parked in the driveway next to a dark green Range Rover. "Are you sure this is a good idea?"

"No, but I'm doing it anyway." Tuck looked at him. Her hair was pulled into a ponytail, but her look of sheer determination revealed her to be every bit the school counselor and administrator on a mission.

Tuck pursed her lips. "I keep thinking about Myron's little girl and the cat."

Once again, Gale thought about Tilly and said, "Right. Let's go."

After they rang the doorbell, a small Hispanic woman cautiously opened the front door. "Yes?" she questioned in a near whisper.

"Is Mr. Spivey in?" Tuck asked.

The woman nervously glanced at them. Before she could answer, Spivey came to the door. He looked irritated, and as usual; his jet-black hair looked as if it had been sprayed into place.

"Where's your son?" Gale asked.

"None of your business," Spivey shot back. The small woman drifted away, shrinking into the spacious living room with its grand piano in the corner and plush sofa and chairs.

"I think it is," Tuck said. "I also know there's a little girl who's heartbroken because her pet was murdered."

Spivey scowled.

Gale heard a woman's voice in the background say, "Who is it, Dean?"

Spivey snapped his head around and yelled, "No one, Audrey. Let me handle this."

"Handle what?" she asked from the other room.

Spivey stepped angrily outside and shut the door. "What do you want?"

Gale noticed that Spivey had bags under his eyes that matched his own.

"We need to speak to your son," Tuck said.

"That's not going to happen."

"Why not?" Gale asked.

"Because no one speaks to Johnny without my permission."

"Where'd he get the drugs?" Gale asked bluntly.

"What are you talking about, McClanahan?"

"Where?"

"You got wrong information. Understand?"

Out of the corner of his eye, Gale could see that Tuck's face was flushed. Her eyes were sending out daggers.

She pointed at Spivey. "I swear Dean, if that shit kills any of my students, I'll be your worst nightmare."

Spivey broke into a half smile. "You're pretty when you're angry. Did you know that?"

"You're vile."

"You know how Ms. Tuck's husband died, Coach McClanahan?"

Tuck's eyes continued to bore into Spivey's, but the blood drained from her face.

"Out joy riding on his Harley after a few drinks and a good screw. Isn't that right, Katie? That could have been you on the back of the bike, hugging him tight. Instead, it was the poke bunny he preferred to you."

"Shut up," Gale said.

He turned back to Gale. "They'd been shacked up in a motel north of Rozelle."

Gale had heard enough. He grabbed Spivey by the collar and shoved him against the door. First Bellwether and now Tuck.

"Gale," Tuck said sharply. "No."

Spivey's eyes bulged, and he tried to wiggle free, but Gale held him suspended off the ground like a plastic-haired scarecrow.

Tuck said, "Stop it, Gale."

Gale could feel the adrenaline pulsing through his body as he decided what to do next, but when he heard Tuck lower her voice and say, *"Please. Gale,"* he twisted Spivey's shirt collar and shoved him once more before letting him drop to the ground. Spivey' face was red and perspiration dotted his forehead. Breathing hard, Spivey said, "I won't forget that you asshole."

Gale could feel his ribs burn from the sudden movement. He stared at Spivey for another moment and then turned to Tuck to say, "Let's go, Katie."

As they walked away, Spivey said, "You leave my kid alone. Understand? Or you'll be in a world of hurt."

Gale and Tuck ignored him and climbed into Gale's pickup. Gale put the truck in drive and drove away from Spivey's house. He pulled over in front of a small park, shaded by a skimpy row of trees. Beyond the park, he could see rigs pumping in the distance and the plains stretched to the horizon.

"Are you okay?" he asked.

Tuck shook her head. "No."

"I'm sorry. He shouldn't have said that about your husband."

"I'm not worried about that. I'm past my grieving. I just know that something terrible is going to happen to a kid I care about, and I'm going to have a hard time not killing that man."

Gale looked over at Tuck who was staring out her side window. "I'm gonna make sure to stay on your good side." When Tuck didn't acknowledge his attempt to lighten the mood, he put the car back in gear. "I'll take you home now, and we'll figure out how to make sure something bad doesn't happen tomorrow."

Seven

Billy Pax had a habit of putting his finger in his ear and sniffing it. He was doing just that as he sat in his McClendon County Sheriff's SUV on the outskirts of Caton. The sun was starting to drop but the thermometer on Pax's dashboard read 97. The AC hummed and Pax poked his index finger into his ear again. He was scanning the road running from town as he mindlessly put his finger under his nose for a lingering whiff.

The patrol vehicle was brand new, thanks to Bart Waters' patronage. The SUV had less than 2,000 miles of wear, and Pax loved the way the new car smell mingled with the pungent odor of ear wax. While he knew he should be more careful about the number of cheeseburgers and donuts he inhaled, despite his growing stomach and an acrimonious divorce, Pax couldn't complain. Amy Lee and her lawyer didn't know about the wads of cash Pax kept under his bed in a musty, thirty-year-old vinyl suitcase or the new ATV he had bought and kept in his buddy's shed on a patch of land outside Caton. By virtue of Pax's elected position, he'd fallen into easy money. All Pax had to do was play dumb and occasionally run interference, like when Myron Bellwether had called him about Dean Spivey's creepy kid. Pax made sure he cut out Caton's municipal police force, a tandem of clowns who spent most of their time in their cruisers scrolling on their phones. While Pax would have enjoyed busting Spivey, with his long hair and surly expression, he knew Johnny was off limits. Just like Clay, Pax knew to keep his mouth shut and not to ask questions about anything that might even come close to involving Bart Waters. A rumor had started that a stray bullet had killed Moorhead and that story was fine with Pax even though he knew it was a crock. He'd been told by the higher ups that they were putting the case on the backburner. That was fine, too.

Pax thought of finding Moorhead splayed on the bass boat's deck in a pool of blood. The flies had been swarming, and Moorhead had smelled like fresh dog turd. Pax shook his head to erase the scene from his memory. He'd never heard of anyone target shooting near Twin Mesa Reservoir, especially in the middle of summer. But as long as the cash kept coming, and he could buy toys like the ATV, he was happy to believe otherwise. While he missed Amy Lee, especially when he slid into bed at night, he took pleasure in the payoffs. The extra money made his meager sheriff's salary a whole lot easier to swallow. He hoped the gravy train would keep coming. As long as he wasn't asked to kill anyone, he would fetch the stick when he was told. That was the way it was done in Caton.

Johnny Spivey swore when he looked into the mirror and saw his mangled lip and swollen eye. It wasn't the first time his father had struck him. One of Johnny's front teeth felt loose, and he pushed on it with his tongue and winced. His father had found Johnny before the football game the evening before smoking weed with friends in a lot behind the elementary school. He'd scared Johnny's buddies off and then flew into a rage, shoving Johnny against his Porsche and slapping him with the back of his hand adorned with a diamond studded Caton High School championship football ring. The ring had split Johnny's lip and chipped his front tooth. As Johnny had begun to flail, Spivey had thrown him onto the pavement. Stunned, Johnny had held his head in his hands while blood dripped from his lip.

"You tell anyone where you found the drugs, and it'll be the last thing you ever do," Spivey warned. "Hear me?"

Johnny nodded, frightened as much by the rage and desperation in his father's eyes as by the threat.

"Because of the stunt you pulled, there are men right now who wouldn't hesitate to kill you or me," Spivey hissed. "When you get home, you tell your mother you got into a fight and some kid you didn't know beat the crap out of you. Understand?"

Johnny grew numb and felt tears streaking down his cheeks.

Then his father, breathing hard, shook his head, climbed into his car, and drove away. Dazed, Johnny had sat on the pavement for a few minutes, trying to understand what had just happened.

Johnny turned from the mirror and slowly climbed onto his bed. He ached all over, and he felt a sharp pain along his jaw. His mother, in tears the night before, had urged him to go to the emergency room, but Johnny had refused. He knew the doctors would pry and ask him questions.

But the real question was why his father had all that shit hidden in the shed? Johnny had shown his two buddies the plastic bag of powder as they sat in the flatbed of a pickup smoking weed. His friends' eyes had grown big, and they'd asked Johnny how he got it. Johnny had flashed a toothy grin and said a source. They'd pressed. Johnny had been coy. He'd wanted to tell them, but something told him he better keep it to himself. Johnny shivered. It was one of the few good decisions Johnny had made. He knew his father hadn't been kidding.

Gale checked his watch and tried to stretch his cramped legs, but the pew in front of him had wedged him in his seat. Earlier in the service, Tilly and the other children had been led away to Sunday school, and now Gale and Marybeth sat in the crowded church listening to the pastor's homily, which had just agonizingly crept past the 20-minute mark. Gale sensed a coolness toward him in Kinney since he'd been coerced into coaching Caton High School. Making matters worse, Gale's successor had presided over a .500 season the year before. People had been civil to Gale but hadn't gone out of their way to be friendly. Only the Olbrecht twins had gotten ugly when Gale had walked into the Pump and Drill Diner the morning after word got out that he'd taken the Caton job. They'd cussed him out, and Gale knew if he went after them, he'd lose. The twins had played for Jack Engle a few years before Gale had started high school and had been trouble then. They bounced from job to job as roughnecks in the oil and gas fields and had the scars to prove it. Billy, the meanest, had served time in his early twenties after holding up a liquor store clerk at gunpoint in Amarillo.

During the service, Gale tried to be attentive, but he kept thinking about Johnny Spivey and how he'd come upon thousands of dollars of narcotics. It didn't take a genius to figure out that either Johnny was connected to some very bad people, or he stumbled upon the drugs. The look on Dean Spivey's face the day before told Gale that Spivey wasn't just a father protecting his son. There was something there. *Bigger. More sinister.* Gale tried to stretch again, and Marybeth shot him a look. "Sit still," she whispered, putting her hand on his knee.

Two rows in front of them, Gale was surprised to see Grayson and Dot Wallace. Wallace hadn't been to church in months. The last time he had come, the pastor, Elijah Prinn, had gone off on a diatribe about the evils of alcohol, and the whole time had seemed to be directing his ire toward offenders in his flock, including Wallace. Wallace was known to have a whiskey before his morning cup of coffee despite the protests of his long-time secretary, who scolded him like he was a wayward schoolboy. It was no secret in Kinney that the things Wallace loved most were whiskey, football, the law, and Dot – possibly in that order. After the service, Wallace had shaken his unruly shock of white hair and had said to Gale in disgust, "Ah, to quote my friend Samuel Clemens, 'Too much of anything is bad, but too much good whiskey is barely enough.'" With that, Wallace hadn't been seen in church for months. Gale wondered why he'd returned.

Prinn leaned closer to the lectern, his voice booming with ferocity when Gale's phone started to vibrate. He'd set the cell face down next to him on the pew, but slowly reached for it and saw a text from Mason Hayes.

You need to come right away. Never seen anything like this. MH

Gale quietly showed Marybeth the text. He whispered, "Can you and Til get a ride home with Grayson and Dot?"

Marybeth nodded; her eyes filled with concern. Gale carefully slid out of the pew and left the church through a side exit. He felt his temples begin to throb and hopped into Marybeth's SUV. As he pulled out of the parking lot, he tried calling Hayes, but the call went to voicemail.

Twenty minutes later Gale stood 300 yards from the house in his Sunday best, dress shirt and slacks, wearing a new Stetson Marybeth had given him on his birthday. The sun was already beating down, and Mason Hayes said, "I've never seen anything this senseless, Gale."

Mateo Santos stood next to Hayes and turned away from the carcass for a moment with a look of disgust. Gale shook his head and felt his stomach turn. One of his cattle had been decapitated and its head had been spiked a few yards away on a fence post. He thought of his confrontation with Spivey and realized that there was no way to prove a thing. After all, the killing of the Longhorn could have been a random act of vandalism and cruelty. *The Olbrecht boys?* Gale had no way of knowing.

"You want me to call the sheriff?" Hayes asked.

Gale nodded.

"What do you want us to do with the carcass?" Santos questioned.

Gale kicked the dirt and said, "It's been out here too long. Otherwise, I'd have Hal Blake process it and give it to the food bank." Blake had created a good business in Kinney as a game processor besides owning a gun shop on the outskirts of town.

Gale said, "We'll bury it. And let's get it done before Marybeth and Tilly get home."

Hayes tugged on his belt and strode toward the large metal storage shed near the barn. Gale took his phone out and snapped a half dozen photos of the Longhorn and the head impaled on the fence while Santos watched with a pained expression. A few minutes later, Hayes and Santos had the headless Longhorn in the bucket of the front loader and were taking the carcass to the dead pit on a remote part of the ranch.

Later, after Marybeth had served Gale, Tilly, Santos, and Hayes chicken salad sandwiches for lunch with watermelon slices for dessert, Marybeth and Gale had walked out to the spot where Hayes had found the dead Longhorn.

"Who do you think did this, Gale?" Marybeth asked.

Gale didn't want to alarm her. He thought it better not to tell her it could have been Spivey or one of his cronies. He had no proof. "It could have been anyone," Gale said.

Marybeth turned to him. "It's Caton, isn't it?"

Marybeth was nobody's fool.

"I don't know," he said, feeling the heat rise off the hardpan.

"But you have a feeling?"

"Maybe."

"Why are they after you? You agreed to coach."

"Who knows. There's some folks not too happy with me here in Kinney too."

"We always find trouble, don't we?" She stared off toward the house. "After San Antonio, I thought we were free and clear."

Gale shook his head and checked his watch. Hayes had said the sheriff would be arriving sometime in the afternoon. A cattle truck had rolled over on Route 385. The Martin County Sheriff's Office had bigger priorities than a beheaded Longhorn.

Gale pulled his hat off and wiped his forehead with his sleeve. "Let's go inside. It's hotter than hell, Marybeth."

She nodded and they walked slowly side by side to the house.

Later in the afternoon, the sheriff pulled up to the barn and parked next to Gale's pickup. After nearly twenty minutes of questioning, he climbed back into his vehicle and drove off.

"Will he find out who did this?" Marybeth asked Gale as they watched the sheriff drive away.

"Doubtful."

"That's what I thought," she said, sighing.

Myron Bellwether's administrative assistant shook her head when Katie Tuck asked if Johnny Spivey had shown up for school. Jaycee McCubbin was up to her elbows in files and yellow sticky notes were stuck randomly on her desk. It was Monday morning, the first day of school. Finally, McCubbin said, "Audrey Spivey called and said he's sick."

"Oh, I bet."

McCubbin rolled her eyes. "If I had a dollar each time that family covered for their kids. Johnny held the record last year for no shows. I'm surprised he passed any of his classes."

Tuck wasn't surprised. Despite a horrendous attendance record and poor grades, Johnny's test scores were off the charts. He was bright, bored, and troubled. A deadly concoction. "Will you tell me if he shows up?" Tuck asked.

McCubbin nodded.

"Jaycee?"

"Yes."

Tuck pointed toward Bellwether's closed office door. "How's Myron?"

McCubbin put her head down for an instant and then looked up with pursed lips. "I pray for that man."

"Tell him I stopped by."

McCubbin said, "He's such a lost little boy. Sometimes I want to wrap him in my arms and tell him things will be okay."

"I know how you feel."

"He's scared of his own shadow."

"That's what bullies do to people."

McCubbin paused. "His little girl was the one who found the cat."

"That's what I heard."

"It was strung up by its tail."

"How awful."

Tuck closed her eyes for a second and turned away.

"Who does that?" McCubbin asked, sighing.

Tuck shook her head. Ever since the confrontation with Spivey, she'd been plagued anew with the thought of her husband riding the Harley with another woman after the two of them spent the afternoon curled up in a motel room. The accident had been horrific. The bike had hit a patch of sand, and they'd slid under an oncoming eighteen-wheeler. They were killed instantly. Tuck hadn't even an inkling that Mark had been cheating on her. She'd sat stunned when the call came from the patrol officer. She wondered how she could have been so blind. No more blindness, she vowed as McCubbin began to jot another message on a sticky note.

Tuck said, "I'll come by later and check on Myron."

McCubbin gave a sad smile. "I'll tell him you came by."

Tuck stepped into the hallway as students brushed past her. She felt an urge to call Gale McClanahan. There was something soothing about him. Steady, reliable, strong, soft spoken. He was a man a woman could depend on. No drama. She'd made some bad choices. Mark was one of them. When McClanahan had pulled over after their confrontation with Spivey and asked if she was alright, she'd wanted him to hold her tight. She hadn't been held in so long. She wanted to cry and cry, but she fought that weakness in a way that she couldn't have before finding out about Mark. McClanahan's presence somehow made her think that everything was going to be alright.

"Mathematically, punting hurts your chances of winning," Gale said in the darkened coaches' room as game film flickered from the overhead projector onto the screen. Lloyd Avery had challenged Gale and was trying to bait him. Over the past couple of weeks, Gale could sense that the team was beginning to grow frustrated with Avery and had begun to side with Gale. Every time Avery called a series of running plays, Gale could sense Eben Daly and the team's frustration. Short of eye rolling, Daly's body language sent a message to Avery that he wasn't buying in anymore. He could tell Avery knew it too, and that it was behind the present goading. Not for the first time Gale resisted the urge to ask how many times the Kinney Lions had beaten Caton during his coaching tenure, but he bit his lip. Best to tiptoe amongst rattlers.

"It makes no sense," Avery snorted. "Hell, you may be some kind of statistical genius, but in Caton we punt and live to fight another day."

"Lloyd's right," Marshall grunted. Gale noticed the other assistants nodding. "People are going to skin you alive if you go for it when a sane coach would punt. Let my boys on D do their jobs."

Gale glanced around the darkened room. He'd stood up to intense criticism before. When he coached the Lone Stars, rarely did the team punt. In the first possession of his professional coaching debut against Philadelphia, on the road and in front of 70,000 fans, he'd gone for it from their own 23-yard line. With Gale's bowels twisting, Jack Engle had called a slant, and Matt Abruzzi had thrown the ball into the slot receiver's hands for a first down. Gale remembered feeling immense relief, but even when the play backfired, he never questioned the decision. It was the same as gambling. If you always play the odds, you win in the long run.

Gale never got over the nervous feeling as the season opener approached. He grew even more concerned because he had no relationship with the coaching staff and no belief that Avery would change his ways. Gale would have relished having a coach he could trust like Jack Engle to take over as offensive coordinator. The problem was that Gale had no leverage over Avery and the other coaches. If he fired them, he imagined Waters would go public about H.W. Owen and Marybeth's mother. Gale grew angry thinking about what Waters' threat had done to Marybeth. She was no nonsense, hardened in ways even Gale didn't fully understand, but the truth about her mother and H.W. Owen had been devastating. Marybeth always yearned for her parents' love and approval, especially her mother's, which her life choices had made it more difficult to gain. It didn't help that Marybeth's older brother was an alcoholic who'd drifted in and out of rehab and hadn't been able to hold a job. Her complicated relationship with her family stood in stark contrast to Gale's relationship with his parents. Gale was an only child, and Tom and Sally McClanahan had circled him with love and respect. Even when Gale had announced that he was going to teach and coach instead of work on the ranch, they'd supported him. Every Friday night during football season, they'd sit in the same seats and proudly watch their son coach the Kinney Lions. By contrast, before moving to Colorado, Marybeth's parents rarely attended a game. Even when Gale had been named head coach of the Lone Stars, Delilah had said, "Marybeth could have been earning that much money long ago if you'd let her go to medical school."

NO HEART TO KILL

Gale knew it was futile to argue with the coaches. He could recite the statistical evidence behind his philosophy about punting again and again, but he might as well be banging his head against a wall. Making matters worse, Gale knew Avery's conservative play calling would make it more difficult to go for it on fourth down. Gale had an uneasy feeling about the opener against Hargrove High School.

Lloyd Avery's thoughts drifted. While the coaches watched film and discussed the upcoming game, Avery found himself growing angrier about Dean Spivey's screw-up and Waters' decision to name McClanahan head coach. There were few people Avery liked. He especially despised lawyers. Years before, playing for Denver, Avery had been cheated by his agent, a hotshot Los Angeles attorney. Avery had discovered that the sumbitch had been siphoning funds from Avery's accounts. As Avery had been a promising center, he had signed a three-year deal with a modest bonus. During training camp, he suffered a career-ending neck injury. With fury, he recalled the day he was told by the team neurosurgeon he'd never play again. A few months later, he returned to Caton with a fresh incision running down his throat only to discover he'd been fleeced.

With an empty bank account and no prospects, he had seen an ad for a salesman at Waters' Motors. He'd wandered into the showroom and Bart Waters had hired him on the spot. Avery had quickly become Waters' top salesman. He had the guile to make a prospective buyer believe the used pickup with faulty brakes and a bad transmission was the deal of a lifetime. Avery knew that Waters valued his ruthlessness as a salesman, so in a way he wasn't surprised that he was the first person Waters had brought into his office when he made the decision to exploit the border country. The extra income had helped him regain all that had been stolen from him and more.

Given how much he'd done for Waters, it was galling that he had given the job to McClanahan. And now, not only had Spivey broken operational protocol, but McClanahan had witnessed Spivey's tirade at Bellwether and showed up with Katie Tuck at Spivey's house looking for Spivey's kid. After Marshall had strung up the cat on a tree outside Bellwether's house, Avery had figured Bellwether would climb back into his hole. No worries there. But McClanahan. Despite what he and Marshall had done to the Longhorn, Avery had a nagging suspicion that their problems with McClanahan were only beginning. Waters seemed to think he could control McClanahan, but from what he had seen of the man, Waters may have bitten off more than he could chew.

Avery looked up at the game tape flickering on the screen and glanced around the dimly lit coaches' room. A few months earlier, everything had been good. Clay Moorhead had been leading the program, no one was asking questions, and Avery figured he had Waters' trust. Avery's fists tightened at the thought of Dean Spivey's kid stumbling upon the fentanyl. McClanahan going for it on fourth down was the least of his worries, but something about that boy scout made him want to mess with the man whenever he could.

Eight

Ephraim Hernandez heard a rustling and slowly opened his eyes. He lay still on his bedroll and made out a shadowy figure creeping across the empty warehouse's concrete floor. The abandoned building stood a few miles outside of Del Rio in a vacant industrial site surrounded by fields. For years the warehouse had been used to store heavy machinery. Now, most of the warehouse's windows were broken and pigeons nested on the rusted steel beams that buttressed the building's porous roof. The building smelled of gasoline and crankcase oil and the heat was stifling. Ephraim heard the steady sound of sleeping men breathing and the intermittent snoring of the old man a few feet away. Ephraim had slept in the warehouse before. It offered shelter and a place to rest after a backbreaking day of work. Earlier in the night, a group of the Hondurans had gotten drunk and began making fun of the Mexicans. Ephraim had kept to himself, too tired after roofing a house in the scalding sun to push back when one of the Hondurans kept drunkenly hurling insults at him. Ephraim had crossed paths with Diego before, and Ephraim had taken a strong disliking to the burly, sour-mouthed, pockmarked-faced *cabron*, who after a few shots of tequila, quickly became a rotten drunk.

As Ephraim's eyes adjusted to the darkness, he realized it was Diego silently moving across the warehouse. In disbelief, Ephraim noticed him kneeling next to each sleeping figure and stealthily going through the man's belongings. Ephraim's anger began to build as he watched Diego crouch next to another sleeping migrant. By nature, Ephraim was gentle. All he hoped for was a quiet life with Maria. They'd struggled to put enough money together to escape to America where they'd been promised assurances of work in Denver. He had cherished the nights they had spent in each other's arms dreaming of a better life. Now he was alone, trying to suppress the rage he felt for the men who stole her from him so he could get through each backbreaking day. He prayed that he would find her alive and unharmed, but where could he even begin to search?

Just as Ephraim was about to shout, Diego slipped out of the warehouse. Livid, Ephraim pulled on his t-shirt, stained jeans, and work boots, and moved out of the fetid warehouse into the warm night. The brightness of the stars that blanketed the cloudless sky allowed Ephraim to see the outline of Diego moving swiftly down the flat stretch of road toward Del Rio. Ephraim started to run after him, causing Diego to stop and turn.

As Ephraim approached and his eyes adjusted to the darkness, he could make out Diego's cruel smile as the thief set his backpack on the ground. "*Pendejo*," Diego said. "Out for a walk?"

Ephraim ignored the insult and moved close enough to smell Diego's sour breath.

Diego casually pulled a knife from a sheaf on his belt. "Go back to bed, *Pendejo*."

"You don't want to get hurt, do you?"

With the image of Maria being ripped from his arms, Ephraim held his ground and said angrily, "Thief."

"Thief?" Diego spit. "There are no thieves. Only the strong and the weak."

"Coward. You sneak about in the night like a *puta*."

"Coward?" Diego asked. Laughing, he sheathed the knife and without warning struck Ephraim in the face with a balled fist. Ephraim felt a flash of pain and jerked backward. Diego knocked him to the ground, pounced, and began pummeling him on the hard-packed dirt that ran along the side of the crumbling pavement of the access road.

Ephraim felt Diego's weight on top of him and the force of his blows as the big Honduran punched him repeatedly in the face. Enraged, he moved his hand to Diego's face and started gouging his eye with his thumb. Ephraim heard Diego cry out and felt a fist strike him in the side of the head. As Ephraim struggled to resist, he felt the handle of Diego's knife. He yanked it out of the sheaf and plunged the long, serrated blade in Diego's back. Diego spun away, and the desperate grip that Ephraim had on the hilt caused the blade to dislodge. For a second, Diego looked at him as if he were pondering the surreal nature of being stabbed, but then he pounced on the arm in which an equally astonished Ephraim still held the blade.

Ephraim fought to hold the knife but Diego twisted, partially rolled away, and finally clutched Ephraim's wrist before he forced the blade toward Ephraim's throat. Ephraim pushed away and flailed, but then felt Diego push the blade deep into the muscle below his collar bone. Ephraim closed his eyes and felt the agony of the knife. The pain caused his eyes to roll back in his head and he thought he was going to faint. As he was starting to accept the inevitable, his thoughts turned to Maria. It was then that he felt Diego crumble on top of him. Through his pain and confusion, it took Ephraim a few moments to realize the *cabron* had stopped breathing. Finally, Ephraim gathered his strength, pushed Diego off and tried to sit up. Each movement brought fresh flashes of intense pain. He sat there a moment focusing on his new reality. He had killed a man. He had been stabbed, and he had killed Diego on a hot night underneath a swath of stars. What would become of him now only God knew.

Katie Tuck checked the absentee list on her laptop. Johnny Spivey still hadn't come to school. Repeated phone calls to the Spiveys had slid to voicemail and texts had gone unanswered. Tuck sighed and looked out her office window. The sun was already beating down. Another hot day.

She snapped her laptop closed and wondered whether she should attend the Panthers' first game of the year. She'd avoided football, and since Mark's death, often spent Friday nights reading or watching one of the myriad of Netflix reality shows. Somehow, she was drawn to trashy TV. She wasn't sure why, but after an exhausting week caring for teenagers, she took special pleasure in not having to participate in the drama that unfolded on the screen.

Tuck heard the bell ring to end class and rose from her chair. She could hear groaning metal doors opening and students bursting out of classrooms. She had a bad feeling about tonight's game. Her instinct told her she'd better attend. She sighed and stepped into the hallway where she was met with smiles as kids rushed past her. It was gratifying to know that over the years, students had grown to trust and confide in her. Parents had grown to rely on her when their children needed help. They recognized a strong woman who would go to extraordinary measures to help a student. Tuck wished she could somehow earn Johnny Spivey's trust. She hated to think about what went on behind the Spiveys' closed doors, especially since the ugly confrontation with Dean Spivey. She hoped Johnny would be in school on Monday. She desperately wanted to speak with him.

Gale's stomach roiled as it always did before a game. For many years, he'd thrown up before kick off. His penchant for vomiting had become a longstanding tradition and family joke that had stopped with the Lone Stars when a game's outcome had become trivial compared to losing his reputation and family. He still felt nerves, but after that realization, he hadn't thrown up once in anticipation of the opening whistle.

Gale studied his players during warmups as fans poured into Clay Moorhead Stadium. As the stadium's lights poured down on the field, Gale's uneasiness grew. He watched Buck Marshall and Lloyd Avery huddled together conversing at midfield with surly expressions.

To make matters worse, upon arriving at the stadium, Gale had locked his keys in his pickup. In his haste, he'd left the truck's keys sitting in plain sight on the bench seat. It wasn't the first time he'd locked himself out of his pickup. Marybeth had gotten the call before from Gale and had found herself having to deliver the extra set of keys. A few times during their marriage, Gale had been driving, and while consumed in thought, had run out of gas. He'd called Marybeth for those moments, too. With a roll of her eyes and a "Gale, what am I going to do with you?", she'd come to his rescue. He was a lucky man.

In the stands, he searched for and found his family. Marybeth held Tilly in her lap as Til munched on popcorn. Gale waved. Marybeth solemnly waved back, and Til shouted, "Daddy!" before shoving another handful of popcorn into her mouth. Gale noticed how worn Marybeth appeared as she held their daughter. Marybeth wore faded jeans and a white T-shirt. Her thick, dark hair was pulled back into a ponytail. Gale's heart lurched with the love he had for both of them.

As Gale turned, he saw Bart Waters standing in Caton's endzone, arms folded, face frozen, watching warmups. Then he searched for Dean Spivey. Spivey was conspicuous in his absence. Gale turned away from Waters and focused on Eben Daly, who'd begun throwing to one of the team's receivers. Gale had recognized early on that Daly could play major college football. He had a live arm, a quick release, and on the rare occasion when he'd had the opportunity to pass, he'd shown composure. Unlike most high school quarterbacks, he didn't flee the pocket at the first sign of pressure. Gale and Avery had collided once again earlier that evening over Daly. Gale had wanted the first play of the game to be a fly pattern to shake things up. Avery had refused, saying the team needed to establish the running game early on. Throwing on first down would play into the opposing team's hands. *What if the ball was picked off?* After a few minutes of disagreement, Gale uncharacteristically let it go and turned away. He didn't want to die on that hill. There were going to be bigger battles to fight with Avery.

Gale scanned the stands searching for Myron Bellwether, but he was nowhere to be seen. When Jack Engle served as Kinney's principal, he always stood in the corner by the endzone to keep an eye on the stands. He made himself a visible presence to deter referee-baiting parents and unruly students. Gale hadn't seen Bellwether since the night his office was vandalized. He felt sorry for the man. He wondered why Bellwether had ever become a school administrator, a tough job even in the best of circumstances. He wished Bellwether had stayed in the classroom to be appreciated and admired by students who shared his passion for music. Instead, Bellwether had put himself in the crosshairs of bullies. Bullies were the one thing in life that Gale couldn't abide.

Gale was about to turn back to the field when he glimpsed Katie Tuck emerging from one of the stadium entrances. For an instant, she hesitated, studying the crowd, searching for a place to sit. Then she turned and caught Gale's eye. She wore a denim shirt, jeans, and hooped earrings. She gave Gale an uncertain smile before disappearing into the stands.

Fifteen minutes later, when warmups had ended, the teams and school band lined up at midfield as a hush fell over the stadium in a moment of remembrance for Clay Moorhead. Bart Waters walked slowly onto the field with a microphone in hand. Gale wondered why Eben Daly's father, Abraham, the team chaplain, wasn't leading the ceremony. The entire stadium fell into silence as Waters began a brief testimonial to Moorhead before moving into prayer. For a moment, Gale looked over at Avery and Marshall, standing side by side, heads down. Then Avery looked up, his head turning, and caught Gale's eye. Avery's face was emotionless, his eyes mirrors of ice. Gale looked away and felt the bile rise in his stomach.

Gale's trepidation proved prescient. He stood motionless on the sideline late in the fourth quarter with Caton up, 7-3, over Hargrove. The packed stadium had been subdued. They had been expecting Hargrove to roll over on an emotional night dedicated to Clay Moorhead's memory in large measure due to their belief that a shiny, new coach, who'd won more state championships than even the legendary Moorhead, and who'd successfully turned around the Lone Stars, would guarantee victory. Despite the feelings of invincibility, the conservative Panthers struggled to move the ball for most of the game. The crowd had shown their displeasure on the handful of times Gale had forgone punting and the team had failed to gain a first down. At halftime, when Gale had caught Avery heading toward the locker room, they'd had sharp words about Avery's play calling. Avery had shaken his head violently and growled, "You let me coach the offense. Understand?" Gale's eyes had locked on Avery's, then in frustration, Gale had stepped away. Now Gale was looking at fourth down and four on his own 37-yard line with just under two minutes to play. His mind raced as he calculated the risk of going for it instead of punting.

Gale gritted his teeth and said into his headset, "Give me 21 red lightning." The play call was a quick slant.

"Punt," Avery hissed. "Hell, you're going to piss it away."

Gale felt his ears grow hot. If the Panthers secured the first down, the game would be over. He heard the crowd chanting, "*Punt, punt, punt!*"

"You heard me," Gale said into his headset. "21 red lightning."

Avery threw his play sheet on the ground and cupped his mic with his hand. Gale could see him speaking to the receiver who was impatiently waiting to give Daly the play. Seconds later, Gale watched the Panthers break the huddle and step into the wrong formation. With no timeouts, Gale watched helplessly as Daly handed the ball to Caton's tailback who was dragged down at the line of scrimmage. Gale kicked the dirt and shouted, "21 red lightning!"

"That's not what I heard," Avery barked over the headset. "Did you hear that, Buck?"

"Hell no," Marshall hissed, tearing his headset off and throwing it onto the field, making sure the entire stadium witnessed his displeasure.

"You've done it now, Coach," Avery chided. "Hargrove better not score, or you're going to get run out of town."

In the game's aftermath, Gale looked up one more time at the scoreboard as catcalls rained down from the emptying stands. 10-7. Hargrove had pulled off an upset. Gale looked straight ahead and walked toward the tunnel to the locker room. He felt his fury grow. Marshall and Avery had set him up. Gale knew if they lied about his play calling with a game on the line, they would lie about anything.

As Gale cut across the field, he spotted Bart Waters approaching with an angry look.

"Son, that was the worst example of coaching I've ever seen."

Gale stopped and stared hard at Waters.

"You pissed the game away."

Gale indulged his standing fantasy of grabbing Waters by the throat and squeezing, but finally he turned away and walked toward the locker room.

Katie Tuck didn't move when the bleachers had emptied. She sat under the glow of the stadium lights and tried to make sense of what had happened. She'd watched the game fall apart at the end and she'd heard the angry shouts and the insults hurled at McClanahan as he left the field.

As she was about to leave, Tuck felt a hand grip her shoulder. Dean Spivey had emerged in the bleacher row above her. He leaned down and put his face near her ear. His breath smelled thick with booze and his sharp eyes drilled into hers as she turned to face him.

"What do you want?" Tuck said, startled.

"You leave Johnny alone," Spivey whispered coldly.

Tuck tried to pull away.

Spivey's grip grew stronger. Stunned, Tuck winced as his fingers dug under her collarbone. "You're in over your head, Ms. Psychologist. No more texts. No more calls. No more upsetting Mrs. Spivey. Understand?"

"You're hurting me." Tuck felt a sharp pain radiate across her shoulder and down her spine.

Spivey smiled thinly. "What did you say? I can't hear you."

"Don't touch me," Tuck cried as Spivey slowly relaxed his grip.

"You're a good-looking woman," Spivey said, still whispering as if he was sharing a secret. "I wouldn't want to see you hurt."

Tuck stared in disbelief.

Spivey suddenly let go, stood up, and shook his head slowly. "Shame about the game tonight. Coach McClanahan's going to be a mighty unpopular man. We don't like losers in Caton."

Then he turned and slowly started to walk down the stadium's aluminum steps.

Stunned, Tuck watched him as she fought back tears of rage. She gritted her teeth. Screw him. She was more determined than ever to speak with Johnny Spivey.

After the stadium parking lot had cleared and the players and coaches had left, Gale went into the coaches' conference room and did what he always did after a game, watch game film. Yet he couldn't shake the image of his players, stunned and angry in a silent locker room, the "told you so" look of the coaches, and the smug expression on Marshall and Avery's faces. Making matters worse, Eben Daly had refused to meet Gale's eye. After a few minutes, Gale closed his laptop. He couldn't concentrate. He needed to go home, try to sleep, and figure out how he was going to deal with Marshall and Avery. Gale vowed he would find a way to run Marshall and Avery off and win back the confidence of the players.

When Gale found his pickup, his heart sank. Someone had smashed the front and driver side windows. Under the dim parking lot lights, Gale noticed his keys still sitting on the seat where he'd left them amidst scattered chunks of glass. One problem had been replaced by another. Gale sighed, reached in and unlocked the door, and with the back of his hand, started carefully brushing the glass off the dashboard and seat. It was going to be a long, hot drive home.

Nine

Ephraim Hernandez's heart raced. His breathing was short and painful, and his shirt was soaked with blood and sweat. He'd ripped part of his t-shirt off after killing Diego the night before, and after nearly passing out, had stuffed the soiled cloth into his wound. After he'd staunched the bleeding, he'd staggered away and found himself in a Union Pacific rail yard where he hid inside one of a long line of empty box cars. As another night approached, Ephraim was desperately thirsty. He felt dizzy and feverish in the stifling air and fought the panic that was consuming him. He didn't want to die in a freight yard in Del Rio, Texas, but he also didn't want to be locked away for life in an American prison. Even though it was self-defense, he was heartsick at the realization that he had killed a man, especially since it might lead to him never seeing Maria again. He felt his eyelids grow heavy and his head spin. He needed help. As he was about to nod off, he heard a diesel engine strike up and growl in a distant area of the yard. A few minutes later as the box car began to inch forward, Ephraim Hernandez was in the hands of God, heading toward the unknown.

The morning after losing to Hargrove, Gale was greeted by a call from Grayson Wallace. Before Gale could say a word, Wallace grunted, "I told you so."

Gale stood a few yards from his house with a mug of coffee in hand, trying to make sense of what happened the night before. He loved the early morning and the way the light played on the land. Gale squinted against the rising sun. He'd risen silently as always, carefully lifting the bed covers, making sure not to wake Marybeth. When he'd left the bedroom, she was sleeping soundly, curled cocoon-like with her thick dark hair mussed on the pillow. Unlike Marybeth, Gale hadn't slept at all, plagued by a deep sense of dread. His eyes swept the horizon, and he said, "Early to be calling me, isn't it Grayson?"

"What happened?"

Gale explained. Wallace grunted and said, "Uneasy lies the head that wears the crown. Which one wants your job? Jealousy, my boy. It's an age-old story."

Gale went silent for a moment before asking, "What do you know about Lloyd Avery and Buck Marshall?"

"Nothing."

Wallace's response surprised Gale. "I thought you knew everyone, Grayson?"

"None of this would have happened if you'd listened to me."

"Listened to you?"

"Yes. I've been telling you for years to punt." Wallace chuckled. He paused. "I still don't understand why you took this job. You're not telling me everything, are you?"

Wallace's intuitiveness didn't surprise Gale. For an instant, Gale watched as a mule deer grazed on a slight hummock beyond the distant fence line. Cattle were scattered along the horizon, feeding on pasture grass. Gale sighed. "I had my reasons."

"Missed the game? Did it for the kids? In the past two years, you've had more coaching offers than anyone in the country. Caton High School calls and you say 'yes'? As your agent –"

Gale interrupted. "You're not my agent, Grayson."

"Who negotiated your settlement with the Lone Stars? Who led you to the promised land?"

"I don't have an agent, and I don't want one."

Wallace laughed. "Sharper than the serpent's tooth is the ingratitude of children."

"And you're not my father either."

"Why Caton?" Wallace asked bluntly.

Gale kicked the dirt and stayed silent.

Wallace said, "No one partners with Bart Waters willingly."

"How seriously do you take attorney client privilege?"

"How dare you ask," Wallace chortled. "Spill it, Gale."

Wallace had been invaluable during Gale's herculean struggle in San Antonio, but this was different. His wife's reputation was at stake. Gale held deep respect for Wallace, but the legendary attorney was simply too fond of his bourbon, and he worried that it could cloud his judgment. Gale hadn't even considered telling Jack Engle, his most trusted confidant. Still, at this moment, Gale desperately needed an ally.

"Waters threatened me."

"Bart's standard business practice."

Gale took a deep breath and told Wallace about the letter and Marybeth's mother's tryst with the state senator. Afterwards, Gale was met with silence, a rare occurrence for Wallace.

"Are you still on the call, Grayson?" Gale asked after a pause.

Wallace finally said, "There were others, Gale."

"Others?"

"Owen wasn't the only one."

It was Gale's turn to be silent.

"Delilah had a long affair with Jake Beckett." Gale had known the Becketts. They'd owned a ranch south of Kinney. Gale remembered Beckett and his wife, Liv, had three children. Several years earlier, they'd divorced, and Liv and the kids had moved to Abilene to be close to family.

"Liv showed up one day in my office in tears and begged to speak with me," Wallace said. "One afternoon, she'd gone to Midland to shop with the kids, and realized halfway there she'd forgotten her purse. She'd turned around to fetch it, saw a strange car parked next to the house, and found Delilah and Jake in the shower. They never heard her."

Gale grimaced.

"You picked a beautiful, loyal bride, Gale. But her mother, a different tale. It took all my negotiating savvy to keep the sordid details from spilling out. Luckily for Beckett and Delilah, Liv didn't want the story to go public. I negotiated a favorable settlement for Liv which was easy enough since she had Jake by the shortest of hairs."

"I told Marybeth about Owen."

"Owen never met a man he didn't want to fleece or a woman he didn't want to undress."

"Marybeth doesn't want her father to find out. Otherwise, why would I coach for a skunk like Bart Waters?" Gale was still trying to shake off this new image of Jake Beckett with Marybeth's mother. He shifted the subject. "Can you make some inquiries about Avery?"

"What do you want to know?"

Gale studied the hazy, early morning sky. "I'm not sure. But there's something going on besides him wanting my job."

"I'll do some digging."

"Careful digging, Grayson."

"I am the very picture of discretion."

Gale rolled his eyes. "And Grayson. . ."

"What, my boy?"

"What I told you about our state senator goes to the grave."

"Of course."

"I mean it."

"I know you do."

"Do you?"

"Why would I add to Marybeth's list of woes? She has to deal with you, Gale. Isn't that enough?"

Gale gave a half smile. "Grayson, how is it that you always manage to get the last word?"

"They're my stock in trade, Brutus."

Mateo Santos, his wife, and two small children were in Santos' double-cab pickup driving north on Route 285, 55 miles south of Fort Stockton. They'd been visiting his parents in Sanderson and had left after attending mass at St. James, where Santos had been an altar boy and received first communion. In Terrell County, Sanderson was near the end of the line for Route 285, which had been branded "Death Highway" for the number of tanker truck accidents occurring each year. The road was a two-lane death trap running through the heart of the Permian Basin. Only three years earlier on the same stretch of road, Tom and Sally McClanahan had been struck head on during a bleak January night.

Santos had worked on the ranch for Tom McClanahan for nine years. McClanahan had given Santos work, a steady paycheck, responsibility, and most importantly, respect. The McClanahans were fair people and treated Santos and his family as if they were kin. When the McClanahans had died, Santos was suddenly without steady work, doing odd jobs to make ends meet. It was a miracle when Gale and Marybeth had been able to secure the ranch from foreclosure. Santos found Gale to be as hard working and as decent as his father and Marybeth to be as kind as Sally McClanahan. Gale's settlement with the Lone Stars had brought a much-needed infusion of capital to the operation, and Santos now had more responsibility, and at times, more headaches and surprises. As a tanker truck sped by in the opposite lane, Santos thought about the killing of the Longhorn and wondered how people could be so cruel.

Santos had seen vandalism on the ranch before. A few years back, he and Hayes had discovered someone had stolen one of the ATVs and had left the vehicle spilled on its side with a broken axle on the ranch's northern boundary. With some digging, they'd found it was a teenager joyriding late one Saturday night. Occasionally, they would find the gut pile of a poached mule deer, or a fence post shot apart. Santos, however, during his time working on the ranch, had witnessed nothing like the beheaded Longhorn. The sight of the decapitated animal had sickened him, and he could tell by McClanahan's expression, the killing hadn't been a random act. Santos couldn't shake the uneasy feeling the incident was a bad omen, a harbinger of more ills to come.

Santos carefully scanned the highway and glanced at his wife, Josephine, who'd fallen asleep in the front seat, and quickly turned to check on Emilio, his 10-year-old, and Freddie, his seven-year-old. The boys were transfixed on Josephine's iPad watching cartoons. Santos marveled at how quickly they were growing and how much they resembled their mother with their thin, straight noses and curly black hair.

As another heavy tractor trailer passed on the opposite lane, Santos' eyes wandered to a long ditch running parallel to the road. Beyond the ditch sat a long line of rigs pumping steadily, like bobbing iron giraffes feeding in a wasteland on burnt silver bluestem grass and baked earth. Santos adjusted his sunglasses and thought he saw a clump, and then what appeared to be a deer carcass on the side of the ditch among cactus and scrub. He focused harder and with alarm, realized it was the body of a man. Santos' heart began to race and for an instant, he thought about ignoring what he'd just seen until he found himself braking to pull over. He turned on the pickup's flashers and felt Josephine's hand touch his shoulder. "What's going on?" she asked drowsily.

"Wait here," he said, opening the door and sliding out of the cab. For a moment, the heat sucked the air out of his lungs as he began to backtrack to the sound of gravel under his feet. As he grew near, he realized the man's shirt was caked in dried blood. Dead, Santos thought, his heart beating hard. An army vet who had served in Iraq during the Surge, Santos was no stranger to seeing the wounded, dying, and dead. He knelt next to the man's body as he felt the rush of an eighteen-wheeler roar by kicking up dust.

Santos studied the young man's sunburnt face, matted hair, and blistered lips. *Madre mia*, Santos whispered. The boy was no more than seventeen or eighteen, Santos thought, noticing the dirty rag stuffed into a puncture wound under the teenager's collar bone. *A knife wound Santos told himself. Trouble.* Santos shook his head and sighed. He was about to cross himself and pray for the boy's soul, when he noticed the teenager's eyes flicker and his hand agonizingly reach out to touch Santos' elbow. Shocked, Santos cursed himself for not checking the boy's pulse.

"*Te llevaré al hospital ahorita*," Santos said as he knelt beside the stricken teenager.

The boy's eyes betrayed his fear. He pleaded in a desperate, choked whisper, "*No. Te lo ruego, por fa.*"

Santos shook his head. "*¿No tienes papeles?*"

The teenager closed his eyes and slowly turned his head. His silence gave Santos the answer. The knife wound opened the door to more questions.

Santos impulsively picked up the boy and slung him over his shoulder as if he were carrying him away from enemy fire. The teenager was surprisingly light, probably starving he thought. A few seconds later, Santos noticed Josephine step out of the cab and start hurrying toward him.

When Josephine grew closer, she asked, her voice rising, "What are you doing?"

Without a word, Santos hurried past her as she turned and followed. When they got to the pickup, Santos pointed at a pile of horse blankets stacked in the truck bed and asked her to spread them.

Josephine climbed onto the flatbed and began to unfold the blankets. As occasional cars and trucks passed oblivious to the unfolding drama, Josephine helped Santos lift the stricken boy onto the flatbed, held the teenager's head up, and gave him water while her boys pressed their faces against the cab window with a mixture of fear, excitement, and curiosity. The teenager tried to drink greedily from the water bottle, but Josephine worked carefully to make sure he took measured sips. A few minutes later, Josephine had produced a bottle of Extra Strength Tylenol from her handbag and had given the boy a dose of the painkiller. Then she pulled a clean t-shirt from her overnight duffel, soaked it from an extra water bottle, and washed the teenager's face.

Soon they headed toward Fort Stockton with a wounded teenager in their truck bed. Santos drove in silence while Josephine pensively looked out the passenger side window. Santos didn't know what to do. He prayed that the drive home would give him the answer.

Gale heard the pickup pull up to the house in a swirl of dust. He looked out the kitchen window and saw Mateo and Josephine Santos slide out of the truck. Josephine quickly went to the back of the pickup, popped open the tailgate, and climbed onto the flatbed while Santos hurriedly walked to the house calling, "Gale? Marybeth?"

Before Gale knew it, Marybeth had met Santos at the door and had quickly followed him down the slate path to the truck. Tilly cautiously followed her mother. Gale knew something wasn't right. He could tell by Santos' expression and the look of alarm written across Josephine's face.

Gale stepped out the kitchen door into the heat and walked across the burned-out patch of lawn toward the truck. Marybeth had climbed onto the pickup bed and was kneeling next to Josephine. For a moment, Gale wondered if Santos had rescued an injured dog until he grew closer and saw a teenager covered in blood lying on a pile of horse blankets. Santos said to Gale, "Undocumented."

"We need to get him to the hospital," Gale said.

Santos said, "He's got a knife wound."

Gale looked closer. The boy's hair was matted with dust, and he had a few whisker tuffs sprouting from his grime covered chin. He was barely shaving, Gale thought. Just a kid. Gale saw the soiled cloth stuffed into a gaping hole under the teenager's collarbone. Fortunately, the bleeding had stopped. Gale said, "I'll call an ambulance."

Gale noticed when he said "ambulance," the teenager's eyes shot open, and he shook his head. "No," he choked.

Santos put his hand on Gale's arm and said firmly, "He's afraid."

Gale shook his head. "Well, we can't treat him here."

Gale turned to Marybeth for confirmation, but she said firmly, "Let's get him inside out of the heat." She gave Gale a meaningful look. "I'll call Ana. You help carry him."

Ana Torres was one of Marybeth's closest friends and the McClanahans' pediatrician. Torres practiced in Midland and had been Marybeth's roommate and sorority sister at TCU. Torres hailed from Odessa, and they'd formed a tight bond when they'd found themselves roommates their freshman year.

Meanwhile, the Santos' boys had climbed out of the pickup and were watching the scene unfold. Tilly chewed a fingernail and stood pensively under a shade tree near the house.

Gale finally said, "We're not going to have a boy die in our home, Marybeth. He needs a hospital -"

"He can't go," Santos interrupted.

"Why not?" Gale asked.

"He can't." Santos looked away for an instant. Gale started to speak, but Santos continued.

"Trust me," Santos said firmly. "He's just a boy." His stare unnerved Gale. "I don't think you understand what will happen to him."

"We'll argue later. Let's get him in the house," Marybeth said impatiently.

Josephine nodded.

Gale stood bewildered. He didn't like what was unfolding. He was about to harbor an undocumented migrant in his home with a potentially fatal knife wound. A host of questions swirled unanswered. The consequences of harboring an illegal with a stab wound made his imagination churn. The newly elected governor's hot-button issue was illegal immigration, and he made it known that Texas wasn't going to look the other way. Gale was about to object again when Marybeth shot him a withering look.

She stared at Gale and snapped, "Didn't you hear Mateo? Now let's get the boy into the house."

Gale shook his head and climbed onto the pickup's bed. Soon, Gale and Santos were carrying the teenager to the guest room. After they placed him carefully on the bed, Gale could hear Marybeth in the hallway speaking with Torres on her cell phone.

A few minutes later, Marybeth stepped into the airy, cream-colored room and watched Josephine wiping the teenager's forehead with a cool washcloth. She turned and looked at Gale, who stood near the door. Gale said, "I don't like this, Marybeth."

Marybeth fixed him with a stare and glanced at Josephine, then at Santos, who stood next to his wife. She turned to Gale. "Go check on the kids," Marybeth barked. "Didn't you hear Mateo? We're *not* taking the boy to the hospital."

Gale recognized the expression on Marybeth's face. He'd seen it before. Her glare left little room for debate. Soon he was scooping ice cream for the kids, waiting anxiously for Ana Torres to arrive. Torres would help Marybeth see sense.

An imposing woman wearing a floral muumuu and large turquoise earrings, who had sharp eyes and frizzy, black, braided hair, Anna Torres once had been arrested in front of the statehouse in Austin for boldly tugging off her bra in the name of women's rights. Torres was as liberal as Marybeth was conservative. Somehow, they not only got along, but agreed on a host of issues. When Torres had finished cleaning and stitching the teenager's shoulder, she stepped into the hallway with Marybeth, and said, "He's lucky. A few inches lower and the knife would have killed him."

Marybeth nodded.

"He's lost a lot of blood, but luckily the blade found muscle," Torres said. "Let's get him on antibiotics and see if we can make him more comfortable."

Marybeth could hear Santos, Josephine, and Gale talking in the living room. Marybeth nodded, then asked, "Ana, what should we do with the boy?"

Torres said, "First, let's get him healed."

"Gale doesn't want him in the house. He's worried we could get in trouble."

"You do know what will happen if you take him to the hospital, don't you?"

"But for all we know, he tried to kill someone."

"I don't think so."

"How come?"

Torres gave a half smile. "It's not exactly scientific, but the boy seems gentle. Besides, he's just a kid."

Marybeth shook her head. "Gale's not going to like that explanation."

"Tell Gale that not everything needs to be explained."

Marybeth rolled her eyes and offered a half smile.

"Marybeth . . ."

Marybeth's eyes focused on Torres.

"I never was here. Understand? I'll come by and check on the boy, but I never set foot in this house to treat an undocumented migrant with a knife wound." Torres' eyes sharpened. "I could lose my medical license."

Marybeth nodded. "We have something at stake here too."

"I know you do. Make sure everyone knows that." Torres pointed toward the living room and broke into an impish grin. "But I'm glad you called. Whenever I can break the rules for a just cause, it makes me happy."

Marybeth knew Gale's concerns were legitimate and that she was placing them in jeopardy, but she kept returning to the thought that caused her to make the decision to bring the boy into her house in the first place: "What would Jesus do?"

"I can't thank you enough, Ana."

"You'd do the same for me."

Marybeth smiled and pulled away.

"Make sure the boy doesn't spike a crazy temperature. If he does, call me."

"Got it."

"I'll be back sometime tomorrow. My schedule's insane." Torres paused. "And Marybeth. Tell Gale it's going to be okay."

"He's a worrier."

"That's one of the reasons you love him."

Marybeth gave Torres a knowing look.

"He's still mad about you."

"You think?"

"I know," Torres said. "He's like a puppy dog around you."

"Now if I could just housebreak him."

Torres broke into a throaty laugh. "Good luck."

Ten

Gale and Marybeth had been up all night with the boy. They'd been alarmed when the teenager started moaning and crying out just after midnight, seemingly caught in a vicious dream. They'd found him soaked in sweat and the blanket thrashed off onto the floor. Marybeth had been able to calm the boy and take his temperature, which revealed a low-grade fever. Nothing to call Ana Torres about, Marybeth thought.

Nevertheless, she'd sat on the edge of the bed and held the boy's hand while he slept in fits and starts. Gale sat in the stuffed chair in the corner and dozed on and off, making sure he stayed close in case there was trouble. Gale had reluctantly gone along with having the teenager remain in the house but told Marybeth he wasn't going to let the boy out of his sight until Mateo Santos arrived in the morning to take his place.

Marybeth studied the boy's face. His forehead and cheeks were heavily sunburned and his lips severely blistered and swollen. He had a blackened eye and an ugly bruise on his cheekbone. One of his ears had been cut, presumably from a knife, and was covered with gauze. She noticed one of his front teeth had been chipped. Despite Josephine and Marybeth trying to clean him with a washcloth, the teenager gave off a stale odor, like dirty socks. He needed a bath.

When the sun finally broke over the hummocks and scrubby plain in soft, yellow tones, and light filtered in through the bedroom windows, Marybeth lifted herself off the edge of the bed while Gale slept in the chair. She needed to get ready for school. It was going to be a long day. She was exhausted and worried. She still didn't know the boy's name. When he'd been in the throes of a nightmare, over and over he had called for someone named Maria. Marybeth vaguely wondered who Maria was. There'd been desperation in his voice.

Before leaving the bedroom, Marybeth glanced at Gale. He'd finally fallen asleep. His chin rested on his chest, and he breathed deeply in long pulls. Marybeth studied her husband. His face was lean and his body still muscled and wiry. She always thought he looked handsome with a day's growth of beard. She thought back to when they'd started dating in high school. They'd been so young, around the same age as the teenager in the bed. Marybeth and Gale had big hopes and dreams. She wondered what dreams the boy had as an undocumented migrant. Now here he was nearly fatally stabbed, alone in a strange place, far away from his family. She felt a renewed surge of empathy.

The boy had drifted off and slept with his head to one side on the soiled pillow. For an instant, Marybeth felt a sense of calm, but the feeling soon ebbed, replaced by a gnawing fear. Still reeling from the discovery of her mother's illicit relationship with Owen, and the revelation the state senator was her biological father, Marybeth couldn't shake the dread that the world would bring more surprises. Then she thought about Bart Waters threatening to reveal her family's secrets and the Longhorn's severed head impaled on a fencepost. Marybeth wondered what kind of omen the boy would bring. Was he a harbinger of better things to come or another in a series of existential threats?

Jaycee McCubbin sat behind her desk and looked up when Katie Tuck entered her office. Without a word, McCubbin picked up a file and handed it to Tuck.

"You're not going to like it," McCubbin said.

With lack of funding and an outdated and unreliable computer system, Tuck wasn't surprised anymore when the high school's electronic recordkeeping failed. Administrators were still sharing manila folders when the rest of the world had gone paperless.

For a moment, Tuck studied the file.

"Dean Spivey sent me a love note this morning," McCubbin said, as she brushed her hair out of her eyes. "I printed the email. It's in the file. He wants all of Johnny's records. He's withdrawing him from school."

"What?" Tuck asked. She stared at McCubbin for a moment and pursed her lips in frustration.

"Dean and Audrey are sending him to Hood Military Academy in Carlsbad."

"I've never heard of it," Tuck said as the morning bell rang. Soon she heard the clamor of students going to first period class.

"I googled it. The school says it serves promising young men."

"In other words, juvenile delinquents," Tuck said.

"Exactly."

"The perfect place to send a kid you don't want around."

McCubbin pointed at Bellwether's closed door. "I told Myron this morning. He breathed a sigh of relief. If he had a happy dance, which I doubt, he'd be doing it behind that door right now."

Tuck studied the folder and frowned. She didn't like giving up on kids, even if they were troubled and had parents like Dean Spivey. While she tried to rationalize that he might be in a safer place at a military school in New Mexico than at home with his father, Tuck knew that Spivey was hiding something. It didn't add up that a teenager would be in possession of thousands of dollars' worth of what could be heroin, fentanyl, meth or a deadly mixture. Tuck could see Johnny peddling weed or prescription meds he stole from his parents. That was for sure. *But thousands of dollars' worth of opiates?*

Something sinister was at hand. Bellwether's trashed office. The mutilated cat swinging from a tree. The ugly marks left from Spivey digging into her shoulder with his sharp fingertips. Tuck tried to tell herself to leave it alone and go about her business at Caton High School. She wondered if her determination to speak with Johnny Spivey came from her hate for his father, and, for that matter, Bart Waters, and the grip they had on the town. But she knew in her heart that it was more than that. She'd always gone the extra mile for students. She refused to give up on them, even when their prospects seemed hopeless. She'd seen enough ruined lives to know that if she could save a teenager from self-destruction, it would make the world better. And drugs unquestionably ruined lives. She simply could not in good conscience close this case even if Johnny had moved on.

Tuck looked at the closed office door. "How's Myron?" she asked.

McCubbin shook her head. "He told me he doesn't want to be disturbed."

"He can't hide forever."

"I suspect he knows that."

Tuck thought about the cat hanging from a tree in front of Bellwether's house and the role Dean Spivey may have played. "How's Myron's little girl?"

McCubbin leaned back in her swivel chair and grimaced. "He says she doesn't want to play in the yard anymore."

"She needs to see someone. She's traumatized."

"She's not the only one," McCubbin said.

Tuck handed back Johnny Spivey's file. "Can you email me the contact at Hood?"

McCubbin looked surprised.

"I need to find out more," Tuck said.

"Looking for trouble?"

Tuck sighed. "I've already found it, Jaycee. Oh, and tell Myron that I'd be happy to talk to his daughter."

In the early afternoon, still listless from his long night standing watch over the boy, Gale prepared to make the drive to Caton for practice. Santos was attending to the teenager in his absence, and Gale had relayed the host of instructions that he'd received that morning from Marybeth before she'd left for school. When Gale had told Mason Hayes about the undocumented teenager, he'd looked away. "It means trouble." Hayes' eyes had hardened. "Mateo might have done better leaving the boy in the ditch."

Gale nodded and climbed wearily into the truck. With a sigh, he put the pickup in gear and made his way down the drive.

Mondays after losing a game always hit Gale hard. Coaching the Lone Stars, Gale had discovered it wasn't only the loss, but the injury report handed to him on a Monday morning. Trying to manage a pro roster was a complex, often daunting task. As a coach, you always worried about losing the players' support, especially after a game where the team had doubts about a coach's judgment and, ultimately, competency. In a way, Gale had plenty of currency. He'd won state championships, been named Coach of the Year in the League, but memories were short. If a coach blundered, it didn't matter if he was the second coming of Vince Lombardi, the whispers would begin, especially with a new team.

Gale's uneasiness grew as he approached Caton. He knew he'd have to deal with Avery and Marshall and carefully navigate the players after the defeat against Hargrove. Eben Daly's refusal to look Gale in the eye after the game spoke volumes. Gale's ears grew hot, and jaw tightened at the thought of Avery and Marshall in cahoots, brazenly lying about Gale's play calling.

When Gale arrived, his heart sank further. He spotted Bart Waters' sparkling black pickup in the stadium parking lot and a silver Porsche pulled up beside the truck. Gale took a deep breath and grabbed his laptop. A few minutes later, he found Waters and Spivey waiting for him in the coaches' conference room. They didn't get up when he entered.

"How's the herd?" Spivey asked, his black eyes slits.

Gale's jaw tightened, but he let the comment pass. Now he knew the Ohlbrecht twins had nothing to do with the beheaded Longhorn.

"Have a seat," Waters gestured, pointing at a swivel chair at the end of the table. Waters sat under the large photo of Clay Moorhead celebrating after winning a state championship.

Gale reluctantly took a chair.

Waters continued. "I hired you to win, Coach McClanahan. Not to pull dumb stunts like you did on Friday night."

Hired? Gale's anger grew. *How about threatened and coerced?*

"Going for it when a punt would have sealed the deal?" Waters asked, leaning back in his chair and turning to Spivey. "Could you imagine Clay doing something like that?"

Spivey shook his head.

"I'm not Clay Moorhead," Gale said.

"That's for sure," Spivey said.

Waters pushed forward in his chair, sat up, and pointed his finger at Gale. "No more going for it on fourth down. No more squabbles with Buck and Lloyd. You hear? We have a lot riding on the season. We got to make the town forget Clay. The sooner, the better. We need to win a state championship. That's what we *hired* you to do, Coach."

"If Avery had called the play I wanted, chances are we would have gotten the first down." Gale suddenly felt lame trying to defend himself. He clamped his mouth shut. He wondered why Waters had said, *We got to make the town forget Clay.*

"I can't have Lloyd and Buck running to me every day," Waters said. "I've told you they're good men, Coach. They know football. They know Caton. They know how to win."

Spivey leaned forward and jabbed his finger at Gale. "You need to apologize."

"For what?"

"For pissing the game away," Spivey said, his eyes focusing on Gale. "For embarrassing the players, the coaches, the town."

"You go into that locker room today and tell the team you screwed up, and it won't happen again. Short of getting on your hands and knees, you say you're sorry and beg forgiveness," Waters said. He raised his large hand and pointed at Gale. "Hell, I'm trying to help you avoid an insurrection, son. Buck and Lloyd don't want anything to do with you. Those players are hurt and angry. Dean and I are trying to save you from yourself." Waters broke into a saccharine smile. "I wouldn't want to have to fire you, would I? You don't want that, do you Coach McClanahan? How would that play?" Waters turned slowly to Spivey. "That wouldn't be good, would it, Dean? Reputations could get ruined."

Spivey smiled knowingly.

Waters sat back in his chair and started twisting his Caton Championship ring with his thumb and forefinger. He looked at the ring in mock puzzlement, then lifted his head. "You do what we tell you and you'll be wearing one of these." He flashed the ring at Gale. "Don't you want that, Coach?" He looked at Spivey. "Hell, Dean, if Coach McClanahan does what we say, he'll be a hero." He turned to Gale. "Don't you want to be a hero, son?"

Gale looked away, kept silent, and lifted himself from his chair.

"You don't want the alternative, Coach," Waters said.

"What's it going to be?" Spivey asked, pointing his finger at Gale, obviously pleased with himself for being the one to call the question. "You wouldn't want a family secret being shared, would you?" Spivey looked at Waters and grinned.

Gale felt his heart start to beat hard. He looked at Waters.

Waters flashed his sharp teeth and gave a thin smile. "Dean is like family to me."

"You son of a bitch."

Waters shook his head. "You can rest assured that Dean can keep a secret as long as you do what we say." Waters turned and looked hard at Spivey. "Isn't that right, Dean?"

"Scout's honor." Spivey's words dripped with sarcasm.

Gale took a deep breath. He felt like he was back with the Lone Stars, all odds stacked against him. But as he walked away, he vowed to himself that he was going to find a way to do exactly what he did in San Antonio, win football games and fight bullies.

"Coach," Waters said after Gale had reached the hallway.

Gale paused.

"Give my best to the beautiful Mrs. McClanahan."

After Gale left, Waters turned on Spivey. "The herd? Family secrets? Hell, Dean."

Spivey held his palms up. "I was just trying to put him in his place, Bart. Make him know where he stands."

"Keep your mouth shut," Waters hissed. "You already screwed up enough."

Spivey's mouth hung open.

"Where's the kid?"

"I took him to Carlsbad yesterday," Spivey said defensively.

"He better not talk." Waters slowly tapped his finger on the hard-wood table.

"He won't. I told the Commandant not to allow any visitors but me and Audrey. They confiscate phones and block the internet. He's got no way to communicate."

Waters looked right through Spivey, who sat across from him. "If I didn't know it, Dean, I'd think you were going rogue on us, trying to move that crap for yourself. That couldn't be, could it?"

Spivey's eyes grew large. "Hell, Bart, I swear to God I just got careless. I'll never do it again."

Waters slowly tapped his finger on the table. "You put me in harm's way, not to mention Lloyd and Buck. Get your head out of your ass. Understand?"

Spivey nodded.

"I'd hate to see anything bad happen to you, Dean, or your boy. I've always valued our friendship."

Fear grew in Spivey's eyes. "He won't talk, Bart. Promise."

"Better not."

"I'll make sure of it."

Waters slid his chair away from the table and snarled. "You wouldn't want to end up like Clay, would you, Dean?"

Music thumped from a speaker as the players dressed for practice, but the energy in the locker room evaporated when Gale entered. Eben Daly didn't even look up. He stared at his phone and scrolled back and forth. Still burning from his confrontation with Spivey and Waters, Gale went over to Daly and said above the music, "Eben, let's go outside."

Daly hesitated briefly then followed Gale into the stadium tunnel's shadows where the afternoon heat felt like a blast furnace against Gale's face.

Gale said, "I want to talk about the game."

"We could have won," Daly said, looking away. He stood in the tunnel wearing shorts and a Caton High School t-shirt and flip flops. His sandy hair was close cropped, and he had a scrape on his cheek from being driven into the turf in the second half.

"We could have, "Gale said. "But we didn't."

Daly looked Gale in the eye. His voice was steady. *The minister's son.* "Coach, I'm not mad that we didn't punt."

"Okay."

"It's the play you called. It gave us no chance. You let me put the ball in the air, and we win."

Gale nodded. He thought back to the end of the game and Marshall and Avery's conspiratorial look.

Daly said without a hint of arrogance, "You let me throw and we'd have won."

Gale wanted to tell the kid the truth but held back. It would be disastrous to reveal a rift in the coaching staff, so he had to figure out a way to circumvent Avery and Marshall.

Gale turned his head for a moment, then said, "You're right, Eben."

Daly looked surprised.

"It won't happen again."

Daly took a step back. "Are you apologizing to me?"

"I am."

A look of confusion crossed Daly's face. "If I'd said anything like that to Coach Moorhead, he would have slapped me."

"Slapped you?"

"He hit kids."

"I'm not hitting anyone, Eben."

Daly's expression relaxed. "Everyone knows you want to win, Coach. But there's a bad vibe."

"I know."

"The coaches hate you."

Gale smiled thinly. "You think?"

"They're out talking to parents, telling them you don't listen and that you're disrespecting Coach Moorhead's legacy."

"You think that?"

Daly looked down for an instant and kicked at the cement walkway. "You want the truth?"

Gale nodded.

Daly hesitated and bit his lip. "I'm glad Coach Moorhead's dead."

Gale took a step back. Stunned.

"My father would kill me if he heard me say that. It's not Christian. But I hated that man for what he did." Daly looked away.

Gale kept silent waiting for Daly to continue. But after a few moments, he realized Daly wasn't going to say anymore.

"Those are strong words," Gale said.

Daly nodded, his eyes burning. He was a big kid, Gale thought. Mature. Confident, but not reckless.

Then an idea struck Gale. "This is what we're going to do, Eben."

"What?"

"You call the play if you don't like the one we gave you," Gale said.

Daly looked surprised. "What?"

"That's right. You don't like a play call, you change it."

Daly's voice rose. "Without Coach Avery's permission or yours?"

"That's what I'm telling you."

"Honest?"

"Honest."

"No coach allows a high school quarterback to do that."

"Most coaches don't have a quarterback as mature and able as you are. I trust you to do the right thing."

A slow smile crept across Daly's face. "What's Coach Avery going to say?"

Gale gripped Daly's shoulder. "It doesn't matter."

"But Coach Avery - " Daly said, a hint of fear in his voice.

"It's okay, Eben," Gale said, cutting his quarterback off. "I got your back. You lead this team and let me worry about Coach Avery."

NO HEART TO KILL

A few minutes later, Gale walked into the locker room. He kn
had to do. He had done it countless times over the years. Wh
weren't going well, Gale would give the players a chance to sp
minds, clear the air. Gale knew the greatest fear any coach had was losing the locker room. Allowing players to vent was essential. Honest conversations led to trust and trust led to a winning culture.

Gale turned to the players sitting in their dressing stalls and milling around the room. No other coaches were present. Gale flipped off the music and called the kids' attention. After a few moments, he said softly but firmly, "I know you're angry about what happened against Hargrove. You have a right to be." Gale paused and swept his eyes across the locker room. "I'm not going to change the way I coach or what I believe. But I know I need to coach better and listen better."

Gale noticed Daly nodding.

"Any player who wants to meet with me, let me know. I have an open door. You can tell me what you believe will make this team better. I won't ever hold it against you. Understand?"

The players started to nod.

Suddenly, Gale heard Lloyd Avery's voice behind him. It was like crunching metal. "An open door, Coach?" Avery grunted. "How about you listen to your coaches? We had that game won."

Gale's face flushed.

"Boys, Coach McClanahan's got a lot to learn. He may have an open door for you, but he don't hear a word the coaches say."

Gale wondered what his chances were taking on Avery and then quickly dismissed the thought. Gale wasn't about to get in a pissing match with a coach in front of his players. He said, "Coach Avery's got a point."

Avery looked surprised. The players looked at each other wondering where Gale was going.

"I'm going to let Coach Avery call the plays and keep my mouth shut." Gale turned to Avery. "Hear that, Coach? I'm done interfering."

Avery's expression turned to confusion.

"It's all on you, Coach," Gale said. "Do it the Caton way."

The players glanced at each other uneasily.

"Looky here, boys," Avery said. "Coach McClanahan has finally seen the light."

Gale looked hard at Avery. "That's right, Coach."

"Wait until I tell Buck."

"You do that," Gale said. As Gale turned to leave, he noticed Eben Daly shoot him a look.

Their eyes met, and Daly broke into a knowing smile.

Eleven

The head prefect, a senior named Stolich, eyed Johnny Spivey. Stolich stood close to 6-5 with a carrot-top buzz cut, a cleft chin, and meaty hands. Spivey stood at attention in issued white boxers at the foot of his cast iron cot and tried to stop his lip from quivering. A few minutes earlier, he had caught a glimpse of himself in the latrine mirror and hated what he saw. The school barber had shaved his head, and his scalp looked pasty white with a thin coating of black bristles.

The day before, his mother had broken down in tears, and his father had barely spoken to him except to lean in close and warn him yet again to keep his mouth shut. Johnny stood in a stark barrack-style dormitory with a handful of other ragged plebes waiting to get the crap kicked out of him by a dude named Stolich, who eyed him up and down like he wanted to shove a baseball bat up his ass. Or worse.

Stolich looked at Johnny in disgust. "What happened to your face, Asswipe?" Stolich barked.

Since his father had attacked him, Johnny's face still looked like he had plastered on concrete. While the swelling had subsided, the bruises and cuts hadn't healed, so he had the misfortune of entering a military school with the appearance of someone who gets his butt whipped. A week earlier, Johnny had been hanging out with friends, sleeping late, getting high, doing anything he wanted. Then while smoking weed one afternoon with Melanie Sprague, a girl he'd been hooking up with, he'd found the stash in the garden shed behind a bag of fertilizer and all hell had broken loose. Now here he was in this shithole military school, where once your parents left, they screamed at you, kicked you in the ass, took your clothes, and shaved your head so you looked like you were on chemo.

As Stolich continued to inspect him, Johnny looked down to hide the tears forming in the corners of his eyes. Immediately, Stolich, wearing a starched khaki shirt with his name badge above his right pocket and olive-green trousers with razor sharp creases, pushed his baton into the soft flesh under Johnny's chin.

"You look me in the eye, Asswipe. Hear?"

Johnny couldn't stop his hands from trembling or the tears from escaping.

"I heard you're the biggest douchebag we got. Is that right?"

Johnny tried to avert his eyes again, but once more felt the baton push into his throat.

Stolich looked left and right at the handful of plebes who stood at attention in their skivvies. "I want everyone to know that Asswipe isn't going to make it. Are you hearing me?"

The line of plebes belted out, "Yes, sir!"

"I can't hear you!"

In unison, the plebes shouted louder, "Sir, yes, sir!"

Stolich turned back to Johnny. "You're going to wish you never set foot on this sacred ground." Then he leaned in and said, "I'm going to personally make every second of your day hell. I heard you're a stoner and a loser. You won't leave this place alive."

Stolich sneered and pushed the baton harder into the flesh under Johnny's chin. Stolich leaned in again and said, "No more Mommy and Daddy to protect you."

Stolich lowered the baton and glowered at him before moving down the line.

Johnny wiped away his tears, but nothing was going to erase the image of Stolich's demonic eyes.

Gale walked off the practice field and noticed Katie Tuck standing to the side by the parking lot entrance. She gave him a half wave and stepped toward him carrying a knapsack and wearing a white T-shirt and jeans.

"Do you have a second?" she asked, tugging her knapsack up on her shoulder.

Gale nodded and noticed her eyes. Deep blue and penetrating.

"It's about Johnny Spivey," Tuck said. "Dean and Audrey sent him to a military school in Carlsbad. I need to speak with him. It's essential. I tried calling the school's counselor today. They don't have one. I tried to speak with the Assistant Commandant. I guess that's what they call the Vice Principal."

Gale listened.

"They wouldn't speak with me. They said they don't share information on new cadets."

Gale fought off exhaustion. It had been a long day with little sleep the night before. "Why not let it go? Johnny might be in a better place away from his father."

Tuck's eyes hardened. "That's what Myron told me this afternoon. He didn't want me making any calls. He wants the whole thing to go away."

"Maybe he's right?"

Gale noticed a speck of perspiration on her upper lip.

"I don't give up on students," she said.

"How about former students?"

Tuck placed her hands on her hips and stepped back. "I have a bad feeling about Johnny Spivey. There's more to the story. It doesn't take much to understand that."

Gale nodded.

"I want to know why he had the drugs. I want to know if any other kids are in danger."

"And," Gale prompted.

Tuck's eyes grew fierce. "I want to bring Dean Spivey down."

She slid her t-shirt away from her shoulder and showed Gale the red and bruised marks. She explained what had happened at the game. Gale's jaw tightened.

"Will you go with me to Carlsbad tomorrow? I'm taking a personal day."

Gale thought about Dean Spivey's threat to reveal Marybeth's family secret. The smug look on his blunt face. "I thought they wouldn't let you speak with Johnny?"

"We'll figure it out," she said resolutely. "We'll make it up as we go. We can leave early and be back in time for your practice. It's only a couple hours' drive."

Gale thought about the undocumented teenager with a knife wound in his guest room, Marybeth having to teach, Mateo Santos and Mason Hayes needing to get things done on the ranch. Gale would be leaving all of them at a bad time to drive to New Mexico to try to speak with Dean Spivey's misfit kid.

Tuck's voice became plaintive. "I don't want to go alone."

Gale thought about Spivey threatening Tuck and the marks he made on her shoulder. He looked away for an instant. "Okay," he said.

A hint of a smile crossed Tuck's face. "Thank you."

"If we stop for lunch, no vegan food. Promise?"

Twelve

An unmarked refrigeration truck sat in a basin next to an abandoned mine in the Sierra Del Carmen. Dark, wispy clouds swept past a quarter moon and the air was dry and hot. Two men sat silently on the back of the open trailer waiting with their legs dangling above the scrub and hardpan. They were big men with large forearms and scarred hands, dressed in jeans and plain t-shirts. They were men who had a capacity for violence. One of them sat with a rifle resting on his lap as he scanned the dim horizon, his eyes adjusting to the night.

Lloyd Avery checked the luminescent dial on his Rolex. Early morning practices had thrown off the timing of the operation. McClanahan was already making his life more difficult. When it was just running drugs, he and Buck could easily get back in time for a few hours of sleep before practice. But with the illegals, all bets were off.

He looked up the narrow trail again hoping he would see one of the coyotes emerge from the darkness. No luck. When Waters had given Avery the news he was passing him over for the head coaching job, he had taken it in silent fury. What else could he do? Waters wanted a big name to keep people from asking questions about Clay, a choirboy. Well, he got one alright, and now he wouldn't even support him when the choirboy had moved practices to 6 a.m. Waters had shrugged and said, "It's only for a few weeks until school starts. Make it work." Well, that was easy for Waters to say. Avery was exhausted. He looked at his watch again and cursed.

Finally, he saw the outline of people bridging a rise before the final descent. Avery pushed himself off the truck bed and gripped his rifle. "Here we go," he said to Buck Marshall. "Game time."

Gale had left the ranch early in the morning after two mugs of coffee and a bowl of oatmeal sprinkled with raisins. The teenager had had another rough night, embroiled in bad dreams and calling out for the girl, Maria. Marybeth had sat vigil next to the boy's bed holding his hand while he broke into sweats and kicked his covers to the floor. Despite her fatigue, when Gale had entered the room and had looked at Marybeth, he realized again how much he loved her. She was no nonsense, a tough woman from the oil patch, but unlike her mother, Marybeth gave people the benefit of the doubt and refrained from judgment. She worked hard to see the best in others. Without being demonstrative about her faith, she was the most Christian woman he knew.

For most of the previous day, the boy had slept until Ana Torres came by to check on him. She'd made him sit up in bed. His eyelids had been heavy and his face drained. He hadn't uttered a word but wore the look of a deer in the headlights. When the teenager was asked his name, he looked away. Mateo Santos and Torres had tried to assure the teenager that he wasn't going to be handed over to the authorities, but he seemed intent on not trusting anyone. The boy grimaced as Torres examined the knife wound and changed his bandage, but thus far, no infection.

The night before, when Gale had told Marybeth about Johnny Spivey and driving to Carlsbad with Katie Tuck, she had quickly snapped, "Don't we have enough on our plate?" Then she'd immediately softened her tone. "I'm sorry," she'd said. "Are you worried about this kid?"

"Something's going on, Marybeth." Gale had told Marybeth about Spivey threatening Tuck and hurting her.

"Sometimes I want to find a faraway island. Just me, you, and Tilly," Marybeth had said wistfully. "Everywhere we turn we seem to find trouble."

"We do."

"Some fine day . . ." her voice had drifted off. "But I'm grateful to have you, Gale."

Gale broke into a soft smile. "I'll be home after practice."

"Okay. I'll hold down the fort. Josephine Santos is coming over today to look after the boy."

"You need to get some sleep." Gale had noticed deep circles under Marybeth's eyes.

Marybeth had studied Gale's face. "I'm not the only one."

"Would the island have a king-size bed?" Gale had asked.

"Absolutely."

"Soft pillows?"

"Yes."

"A beautiful woman beside me?"

"Yours truly."

"Let's sell the ranch. I'm on board."

Marybeth had rolled her eyes. "I wish."

NO HEART TO KILL

    Hood Military Academy rested eight miles from the city of Carlsbad and a few miles from Carlsbad Caverns National Park. The Academy rose out of the sand and stood stark and ominous in the mid-morning sun. The main administration building, built in adobe style, was flanked by a half a dozen stone buildings, including two rectangular barracks with ugly flat roofs. On the far side of campus, playing fields stretched and Gale spotted a line of cadets with their heads shaved jogging in unison as part of their morning PT.

    Gale and Tuck pulled up to the gatehouse and a sentry, a cadet with an acne-cluttered chin and a service cap pulled low, stepped out in front of Gale's pickup, which the day before had received a new windshield and driver-side window. Gale could barely see the teenager's eyes beneath the brim of his cap. Gale rolled down his window. The heat instantly filled the truck's cab, and the cadet came around with a clipboard in his hand. "Can I help you?" he asked.

    Tuck leaned over. "We're here to see the Commandant."

    "Do you have an appointment?"

    Gale glanced at Tuck. Without missing a beat, she said, "He expects us."

    "Your names?" The cadet raised his clipboard and pulled a pen out of his front pocket.

    Tuck hesitated. "Audrey and Dean Spivey. We're here to see our son, Johnny."

    The cadet frowned. "I don't see you on the visitor list."

    "A family emergency," Tuck said. "It's urgent."

    The sentry appeared puzzled and said, "A moment please."

    The cadet entered the guard house and Gale could see him reaching for the phone. Gale turned to Tuck and raised his eyebrows. "Audrey and Dean Spivey?"

    "You have a better idea?"

    "They'll throw us in the brig."

    "What's that?"

    "Jail."

    Tuck shook her head. "Sometimes you have to tell a few fibs to get to the truth."

    Gale was about to reply when the cadet put the phone down and walked back outside. "Do you have an ID?"

    "ID?" Tuck burst out. "Are you kidding me? We just dropped our son off the other day, and you want ID?"

    "It's policy, ma'am."

    "We pay $50,000 a year in tuition, and you won't let us see our son?" Tuck shook her head. "I'm going to report you."

    The cadet stepped back and stuttered, "For what?"

    "Being rude and insolent."

"Rude?" the sentry asked, nervously.

Tuck pulled her phone from her purse and snapped a picture of the teenager. She started typing on her cell as she spelled the name above his breast pocket aloud. "H.E.N.R.Y. B.I.N.G.H.A.M.T.O.N."

The cadet started to object, but Gale noticed fear growing in his eyes.

When Tuck finished typing, she said with steel in her voice, "You have a choice. Either let us through or I'll tell the Commandant how *difficult* you've been."

Blood drained from the cadet's face. He shrugged and said, "Okay, okay. The main administration building is straight ahead."

As Gale pulled away, he looked in his rear-view mirror and could see the teenager shaking his head as he entered the gate house.

"I thought you liked kids?" Gale asked.

"I do," Tuck said, putting her phone in her purse.

"Then what was that?"

"Oh, he'll get over it. Tonight, he'll be telling his buddies about the asshole mother he met."

Gale paused. "What now?"

Tuck looked straight ahead toward the administration building. "Can't you see, Coach McClanahan? We're making things up as we go."

The Commandant's administrative assistant wore cat glasses, the kind women wore on old black and white television shows now looping on TV Land. Overweight and officious, she had a mole above her lip, beehive hair, and the most powerful job short of Commandant at Hood Military Academy. She was gatekeeper and took her responsibilities seriously. She eyed Gale and Tuck suspiciously when they entered the Commandant's suite, which was adorned with Navajo carpets and hickory furniture. Light filtered in from two large windows facing the parade ground. She sat behind her hardwood desk underneath a portrait of General MacArthur. On another wall was an epic nineteenth-century painting depicting cavalry giving chase to a band of Native Americans riding bareback through a rose-colored canyon.

"Impossible," she said. "The Commandant only sees visitors by appointment, and no one just walks in and meets with our cadets. We have rules and regulations." She thumped the table with her palm. "And we make *no* exceptions."

"This is important," Tuck said.

"Important?"

"We're concerned about Johnny Spivey."

The woman leaned back in her chair. Her eyes were frigid behind her thick retro glasses. "How so?"

Tuck hesitated. "He's got substance abuse issues."

"Not here," the administrative assistant snapped. "Cadets aren't allowed off campus. Personal items are regularly searched. We have drug sniffing dogs come through the barracks every night, and if we find out a cadet has illegal substances or paraphernalia, they are in deep," she paused, "you know what. We don't mess around. If Johnny Spivey had a drug problem, he doesn't anymore because he's at Hood Military Academy."

"What if I told you other kids might be in danger?"

"Here?"

"In Caton."

"Not our problem."

"He was caught with thousands of dollars' worth of narcotics."

"Honey," the woman said, shaking her head, "I'm not at liberty to discuss the cadets, but let's just say that Johnny is not the only boy with a past at this school. They come in troubled, and we make men out of them."

"Am I correct that you don't have a school psychologist?"

"Nope. And never will. Hood Military Academy doesn't believe in psychotherapy. We specialize in discipline."

Gale could tell Tuck was growing exasperated.

"Isn't there anybody we can talk to about seeing Johnny? All we need is fifteen minutes."

"Sorry." The woman grunted and started shuffling papers on her desk. "You can leave now."

"That's it?" Tuck questioned.

The woman looked up. Her glasses rested on the tip of her nose and her eyes were pools of ice. "You heard me."

Tuck shook her head. "What a shithole."

Gale took a step back. Surprised.

"Call it what you want," the woman snapped. "The door," she said, imperiously pointing her finger.

"We're not done yet."

"Oh, yes, we are. We have former MPs running security detail. They'd enjoy showing you off campus."

"I bet."

The woman smiled thinly and said in a raspy voice, "Young lady, make my day." When she reached for the phone, Gale grabbed Tuck by the arm and led her out.

When Gale and Tuck left the Commandant's suite, the administrative assistant slid off her chair and knocked on the Commandant's door. She heard him bark "what is it?" and pushed the door open with a firm hand.

With a face like carved granite, the Commandant sat behind a large mahogany desk, reviewing a stack of papers, wearing a heavily starched khaki shirt and tie. "What, Ms. Mack?" he asked without looking at her, annoyed by the interruption. Glenda Mack didn't care. She'd survived six Commandants in fifteen years and would survive this one.

Staring her boss in the eye, Mack said, "It's about the new cadet, Johnny Spivey."

The Commandant looked up. "Spivey?"

"Yes. The school counselor from Caton was here and said it was urgent. She said she needed to speak with him."

"And?"

"I told her to leave."

The Commandant considered her words. "Call the father."

"The father?"

"Tell him his son had visitors."

Mack nodded.

"And Ms. Mack," the Commandant said. "Good work."

"Thank you, sir," Mack said crisply. "I know my job."

Johnny Spivey fell to his knees and threw up on the gleaming turf football field. He had felt his knees weaken and his stomach churn halfway through a three-mile run in 90-degree heat and had the misfortune of vomiting on the Hood Military Academy logo. Johnny had hit the bullseye. When he lifted his head, he noticed the other plebes jogging in place with loathing written across their faces and Stolich bearing down on him like a cruise missile. Johnny was about to throw up again when Stolich kicked him in the ass, then squatted beside him and with menacing black eyes, the senior prefect pointed at the vomit-stained turf and said, "Eat it, Asswipe."

At the thought, Johnny felt another wave of nausea, and before he could turn, Stolich was struck in the face with a projectile of vomit. Johnny could hear the collective groan of the plebes and a grunt of disgust coming from Stolich. Johnny was about to shut his eyes, waiting for the inevitable blow, when he spotted Ms. Tuck and the new football coach walking side by side in the parking lot next to the administration building. While he had avoided Tuck like the plague at school, he wanted to cry out, yell for help, and have her rescue his sorry ass from this nightmare. But his father's warning raced through his mind, and despite the agonizing fear he felt, and the beating he knew he was about to take, he kept his mouth shut. For a split second, Johnny helplessly watched Tuck and the football coach climb into the pickup before Stolich's fist struck him between the eyes.

Gale and Tuck rode back to Caton in near silence. Gale noticed Tuck's pensive expression and wondered what she was thinking as she gazed out the passenger door window with her chin resting on her hand and both feet casually propped on the dash.

Gale understood her obsession with Johnny Spivey. In his experience, school counselors wanted to save the world. They were often overworked and underappreciated. They had a unique fervor for not giving up on a student. Marybeth had shown the same resolve. On three occasions, Marybeth had been named Teacher of the Year at the local elementary school. Gale was always amazed at how much time and attention Marybeth devoted to her students. While Tuck was obviously driven to save Johnny, find his source, and protect kids from the crap he had been peddling, Gale knew that part of the reason they were in the car right now was their shared hatred of Dean Spivey. Gale smiled and, not for the first time, wondered how Tuck's husband could have brazenly cheated on her. She was attractive, bright, complicated, and had uncommon resolve. Gale liked smart, complex women. He had married one.

When they stopped at a truck stop near Hobbs, Gale purchased two bottled waters and handed one to Tuck when she appeared from the restroom. "I need sugar," she said, eyeing a candy bar.

"It's on me," Gale said, grabbing the candy and walking back with her to the cash register.

"I'm sorry about today," she sighed.

"Don't be."

"I wasted your time, Gale."

"At least we got onto campus."

Tuck shrugged. "But no cigar."

"The school's going to call Spivey, you know."

"I know," she said, shaking her head. "And all hell's going to break loose."

An hour and a half later, when Gale and Tuck pulled into the Caton High School parking lot, Billy Pax sat in his McLendon County Sheriff's SUV waiting for them. He slowly climbed out of his vehicle after Gale and Tuck had parked and shuffled toward them with one hand resting on his leather holster. He had a ketchup stain on the front of his uniform.

Gale and Tuck stood beside Gale's pickup watching the Sheriff.

"It seems you two have been causing trouble," Pax drawled.

Gale studied Pax. Pax's gut hung over his belt, and he seemed out of breath from the short walk across the parking lot.

Pax stared at Tuck, and as he drew closer, he sighed. "You've royally pissed off Dean Spivey, know that Ms. Tuck? You and Coach McClanahan have sure stepped in it. I was minding to business when I get a call that you'd gone joyriding to New Mexico." He paused. "Ain't that outta your way?"

Gale said, "What's it to you?"

Pax threw his head back and guffawed. "What's it to me? Now that's a very good question." Pax stuck his finger in his ear and dug in as he considered his next words. He turned to Tuck. "Dean told me you're harassing and stalking his boy."

"Not true," Tuck shot back.

"Oh, contrary, as the man says." Pax smiled.

"Whatever Spivey told you is bullshit," Tuck said.

"Okay. We'll start with the fact that Mr. Spivey asked you to leave his son alone. What'd ya do? You and Coach McClanahan crashed the pearly gates of Hood Military Academy pretending to be Johnny's parents. Do I got that right?"

Tuck said, "Johnny had thousands of dollars' worth of narcotics. Myron Bellwether said you laughed it off. Myron's office gets trashed, and the opiods disappear, and you do nothing. Do I got *that* right?"

"I'm a fair man," Pax said. "I consider all sides." He flashed a thin smile. "Dean wants me to slap a restraining order on both of you." He shook his head. "But I'm charitable, and I don't think a restraining order is going to play for Coach McClanahan." Pax laughed. "He's got enough troubles after his bonehead coaching cost us the Hargrove game. And Ms. Tuck, how's it gonna look that the school counselor got slapped with a court order?" Pax pushed off against the truck and moved closer. He stuck his stubby finger in Tuck's face. "Not good."

Gale took a deep breath. He realized what Pax was saying was true. He could only imagine what Grayson Wallace would say. *A restraining order, Brutus? Not only a traitor, my boy, but a stalker?*

Pax continued to eye Tuck. "As I said, I'm a fair, honorable man. And because of it, I'm going to give you a warning. But you bother Dean, Audrey, or Johnny Spivey anymore, and I can assure you a world of hurt."

Pax turned to Gale. "And one more thing . . ."

Gale kept silent.

"Punt, Coach."

Thirteen

Sandington sat 35 miles east of Midland and became infamous thirty years earlier when a group of paramilitary fanatics held off a swarm of law enforcement officers five miles outside of the town in one of the biggest shootouts in Texas history. A handful of officers had died and nearly the entire group of militants perished after law enforcement swarmed the encampment. Like so many tragedies which once captured the public's attention, the killing field at Sandington was largely forgotten. Only a simple historic road marker pointed to the spot where the carnage had taken place.

Gale knew about Sandington's history when he stepped off the bus to play the team's first road game. During the trip from Caton, Gale had sat behind the driver and felt growing anxiety as the game approached. The week of practice had been relatively quiet. Avery and Marshall had kept to themselves, and Gale had done his best to run efficient practices and let the players sort out their emotions after the Hargrove game. Quietly, Gale had spoken with Eben Daly about different defensive scenarios Sandington would throw at the senior quarterback and how he might counter them with his audibles.

At home, the injured teenager had shown improvement. The knife wound was healing, and the day before, he'd slept through the night. He was starting to eat. Mateo and Josephine Santos had spent time with him trying to allay his fears of being handed to the authorities and deported. But when they had asked him what had happened, the boy would look away in fearful silence. As usual, Marybeth showed her ability to juggle a million things at once, and Gale had finally conceded that the boy posed no threat. Tilly seemed fascinated with the teenager, so she had taken it upon herself to be a "big girl" and deliver him tea and meals, and the evening before, had brought freshly baked chocolate chip cookies that she'd help make.

Gale stood at the foot of the bus and watched as the coaches and players stepped past him toward Sandington's gym. Avery hung back and emerged after everyone had exited and snapped, "Remember, leave it to us, Coach."

Remaining silent, Gale let Avery slide away toward the visitors' locker room before making the short walk to the football field. The stadium lights had already been flipped on and Gale stood in the end zone and surveyed the scene as the sun lowered in the late summer sky. Over the years, he'd coached against Sandington and found them to be tough and disciplined. He knew Caton would be in for a fight. When Gale turned to walk to the locker room, he spotted Bart Waters speaking with Avery and Marshall by the entrance. As he walked past them, he was met with a stony silence.

Eben Daly thundered past Gale before being dragged down on the team's first possession on his own 29-yard line. Gale found himself three minutes into the first quarter with the scenario he dreaded. Ordinarily, he wouldn't have given it much thought. Armed with his belief in punting's detrimental effect on winning, Gale would have gone for it. But he felt a creeping doubt, knowing that the coaches, most of the players, and the entire town of Caton wanted him to play the game by a dated philosophy. It was Daly who decided the course of action when, after he bounced up from where he was tackled, he caught Gale's eye, clapped his hands, and barked, "Let's go for it." Daly's support gave him a sudden calm. Gale turned toward Avery, and said, "We're going for it."

Avery raised his hands in disgust and said, "Hell, no."

"Call the play, Lloyd," Gale said, gritting his teeth.

Avery eyed Buck Marshall and shook his head. "You're a fool, McClanahan."

"You heard me," Gale said.

"Oh, I heard you." Avery spit and pulled the receiver toward him who'd be running in the play. "12 Blast Red Knight." Gale heard the play call loud and clear on his headset. The running play was doomed. Avery was setting Gale up. A few seconds later, after the receiver raced to the huddle and whispered the play in Daly's ear, Daly eyed Gale and shook his head. Gale nodded and knew his quarterback was changing the call.

When Caton broke huddle and stepped to the line of scrimmage, Gale glanced at Avery, who looked confused. Gale heard Avery yell into his headset, "That's not the formation I called. Hell."

Avery was about to yell for a timeout when Daly took a quick snap, dropped back, and threw a strike for a first down to Marcus Jones, a skinny sophomore slot receiver. Daly stuck his fist into the air and then Gale heard Avery shout into his headset, "Get Daly out of there." Suddenly, one of the assistants pushed Caton's backup quarterback onto the field as Avery began screaming at Daly. Without hesitation, Gale spotted the sideline judge and called timeout.

NO HEART TO KILL

Gale's heart beat fast as he strode toward Avery. Gale could feel his chest about to explode as he shouted, "Leave Daly alone."

Avery flashed his sharp teeth as he ripped his headset off. "He's out, McClanahan. No quarterback I coach pulls that crap."

"Get out of here," Gale yelled.

"What?" Avery said.

"You heard me. Get off the sideline." Gale jabbed his finger in Avery's face as his insides boiled.

Avery stepped toward Gale and seemed ready to come to blows, then hesitated, and turned toward the bleachers behind Caton's bench. Gale had braced himself for a fight, so he was surprised at Avery's reaction. Something was holding Avery back. Then Gale saw Bart Waters standing a few rows up from the Caton bench and realized something unsaid had passed between Avery and Waters. Waters must have called his dog off.

Avery slowly tugged his headset on and said into the mic to the other coaches, including Marshall who stood a few yards down the sideline, "Coach McClanahan lives another day. First down. Lucky him."

Three quarters later, Caton had its first win, 17-6. As Gale walked off the field, he watched Eben Daly high five his teammates as he threaded his way to the locker room. Gale was about to follow when he felt a hand on his shoulder. He turned. It was Daly's father.

Abraham Daly stood as tall as his son, but unlike Eben, he had the look of a man who had shared many sorrows. He wore a tie with white shirt and slacks, and his hair was cut short and graying at the temples. As the team chaplain, Gale wondered why Daly hadn't been a presence during the young season by giving the pre-game prayer. He hadn't stepped foot in the Panthers' locker room.

"Thank you," Daly said.

"For what?"

"For making the game fun for Eben."

Gale nodded.

"Eben's life hasn't been easy. My wife died when he was fifteen. God took Mary. Cervical cancer. She was 40 years old. It's just been me, Eben, and," Daly hesitated as if he wanted to offer something more, but fell silent.

"I'm sorry," Gale said, stumbling for words.

"God's will," Daly said, shaking his head. "We'll find a way."

"Eben's a good kid," Gale said.

Daly gave a sad smile. "He is."

"It's been a pleasure to coach him."

Daly hesitated, then his eyes turned wary, and he said, "I've been praying for you. I know you've probably regretted taking this job. Following Clay Moorhead, you probably feel like you're in the town's bullseye."

Gale stood silent under the stadium lights as players and fans made their way across the field.

Daly added, "Caton's an unforgiving place. God's work needs to be done."

Gale considered Daly's words. "Why haven't you been involved with the team?"

Daly remained silent.

"I'd like you to give the pre-game prayer."

Daly shook his head and looked away for an instant. "Thank you for helping my boy."

Gale floundered in the wake of Daly's unwillingness to respond to his offer. All he could do was echo himself weakly. "He's a good kid."

Abraham Daly slowly nodded and moved off into the crowd.

For a moment, Gale stood alone at midfield. He thought about Abraham Daly's words. *God's work needs to be done.* Gale needed God on his side and hoped Abraham Daly would deliver. Despite the win over Sandington, Gale felt empty and tried to avoid thinking about the rest of the season ahead. The elation he had always felt after winning was missing. He couldn't shake the emptiness and foreboding he'd felt as he watched his assistants after the game. They had gathered and headed for the locker room without him with Avery and Marshall leading the way. Waters was nowhere to be seen.

Gale took a deep breath and headed toward the gym. He would congratulate his players, tell them there was still much work to be done, and climb on the bus for the ride back to Caton. Then he would slide into his pickup and drive home. He hoped Marybeth would still be awake. He wanted to talk with her and feel her against him.

Gale longed for the life he had before Bart Waters and Dean Spivey had crashed his world. With an exercise of will he turned his thoughts back to Eben Daly trotting off the field celebrating with teammates after the win. Gale fixated on that image. He hoped it would bring him a glimmer of joy.

Ephraim Hernandez opened his eyes and found the little girl sitting in a chair near the door. She stared at him with intense curiosity as if she were watching an exotic animal. She reminded him of his five-year-old sister, Isabella. Ephraim felt a sudden pang of sadness. He hadn't seen his sister in months. He wondered if she missed him.

The girl had brought Ephraim hot tea and meals the last couple of days. She would put the tray by the side of his bed and retreat to the chair and watch him with interest. Ephraim didn't feel interesting. His shoulder still throbbed, and his body ached. Despite the reassurances from the couple who called themselves Josephine and Mateo, and the kindness with which he was treated, Ephraim couldn't tamp down the fear of being handed over to

Immigration, or worse, the police. They would discover his wound, put the pieces of the puzzle together, and charge Ephraim with murder.

Ephraim managed a faint smile when the little girl shifted in her chair. For a moment, he looked around the bedroom. He'd never slept in such a beautiful house. The bedroom's plush furniture, the cream-colored walls, the large windows and lace curtains, the soft sheets and pillows, and the rich carpet that covered the entire space, made Ephraim feel as if he were in a dream. The carpeting stood in sharp contrast to where he grew up, where the floor was a concrete slab and walls were painted in waves of grimy stucco and adorned by an unframed family photograph and a crucifix. Maria would have adored this house, Ephraim thought. It was her dream to live in America and have a clean home and running water. He closed his eyes for a few moments, and when he opened them, the little girl was gone.

When he tried to sit up, Ephraim winced from a sharp pain under his collarbone. The thought of Maria made his heart ache and the knowledge that he had killed a man filled him with fear and guilt. He knew he should flee, but the knife wound left him barely able to walk. He put his head back on the pillow and closed his eyes. For now, he was at the mercy of these people.

Katie Tuck stepped out of the shower and began to towel off when she heard the crunch of gravel from a car pulling into her driveway. She quickly reached for her robe hanging on the back of the bathroom door and swirled her towel in a turban to cover and dry her wet hair. It was late and it was a Friday night, and to make matters worse, a full moon, which always meant trouble. The lunar pull's full weight made people do stupid things, which meant teenagers acting impulsively and recklessly.

When she parted the kitchen curtains, she noticed the headlights of a small compact car. In the darkened house, she checked the kitchen door to make sure it was locked and went into the living room and made certain the front door was bolted. Under normal circumstances, she wouldn't feel threatened. There'd been other times over the years when late at night she had received a knock on her door. Usually, it was a student in crisis, or a parent overcome with worry about their child. But with Dean Spivey's threats, Tuck's heart raced.

Someone was coming up the walkway. Through the living room window, she could make out the figure of a man and braced for what was to come. She quickly went over to the coat closet and grabbed one of her husband's golf clubs. Since Mark's death, they'd sat in the corner of the closet collecting dust.

She turned away from the closet when the doorbell rang and shattered the house's stillness. Tuck froze. She didn't know whether to turn on the lights and open the door or remain hidden in the shadows. A few seconds passed when she heard a man's high-pitched voice call out, "Katie. It's me, Myron. Open the door."

Tuck relaxed her grip on the five iron and flipped on the living room light. She unlocked the door and found an agitated Bellwether standing on her step.

She beckoned him in. "Myron," Tuck said, "what's going on?"

Bellwether stepped into the house and Tuck shut the door and locked it. She felt absurd greeting him in her robe with a towel wrapped around her head holding a golf club.

"It's not good. Not good at all, Katie," Bellwether sputtered. "I tried calling you."

Tuck had made the decision earlier in the evening to power down her phone. She'd felt like she'd earned some me time. "Sit down."

Bellwether nervously sat on her couch, and she slid into a chair across from him. His eye began twitching uncontrollably.

"Two kids," Bellwether said.

"What happened?"

"They're in critical condition in Midland." Bellwether turned away. "Fentanyl."

Tuck leaned back and for a moment closed her eyes. "Who are they?"

Bellwether took a deep breath. His eye fluttered like a piston. "Two of Johnny Spivey's friends. Martin Keller and Sam Lowe."

Tuck knew the boys. They were as alienated as Johnny. They hung out in the shadows and spent most of their time finding ways to get high during school. Tuck understood the potential devastating effects of a fentanyl overdose. Kidney and liver failure. Loss of bodily functions. Neurological damage and coma. Paralysis. It could mean a quick death or months, even years recovering.

"Are you sure it was fentanyl, not something else? Heroin? Another narcotic?"

"That's what the doctor said."

"Do we know the source?"

Bellwether's hands shook more violently. "The parents are blaming me. They said they heard that a student had been dealing and that I didn't do anything about it."

"You reported it."

"The Sheriff's denying I notified him."

"You have phone records. Your office was trashed."

Bellwether put his head down and started to rub his trembling hands together. His voice grew higher. "I tried to do the right thing, Katie. I tried. No one listened. Now two students are in critical condition, and they're going to make me take the blame."

Tuck sat back in her chair and studied Bellwether. She reached over and touched his knee. "Myron, any sane person knows you wouldn't ever intentionally harm a student. You're the gentlest person I know."

Bellwether ignored her.

"My wife is beside herself. My daughter won't go outside to play. I have these terrible men hovering over me, making my life miserable." He looked up and declared, "We're leaving."

"What do you mean you're leaving?"

Bellwether stammered. "I'm quitting. We've already packed up our minivan, and we're going back to Missouri in the morning. The movers will get the rest of our belongings."

"What about your house?"

"It's not our house. We rented it."

"You can't leave," Tuck said. "Who's going to be the principal?"

Bellwether stared at her. His eye hammered up and down. "You."

"Me?"

"Yes."

"I don't want to be principal, Myron." Tuck's voice grew cold.

"I'm appointing you. We haven't had a superintendent in two years. I can do what I want." His voice was suddenly defiant. "The School Board can . . ."

Bellwether paused and handed Tuck a manila envelope. "It's all here. Bogus contracts, rigged bids. I may be a coward, but I'm not stupid. Waters has been stealing from the school district and town for years." He put his head down.

"You can't make me principal, Myron. Waters and Spivey will never have it. Besides, I don't want the job."

Bellwether leaned closer. His voice was full of resignation. "People think I'm a minion for Waters and Spivey. . ." His voice faded. "And I might as well be. But you're the strongest person I know. You're a fighter. If anyone can take this job on, it's you. When parents discover that you were named principal, they'll cheer. The kids love you. The parents are looking for someone in this town . . ." his voice drifted off. "Waters and Spivey will have a hard time undoing what I've done."

Tuck sat back. Her face turned pale. "What have you done, Myron?"

"I already sent the email."

"What?"

"I sent an email to the whole community thirty minutes ago announcing my resignation and that you'll be my replacement."

"Are you kidding me?"

Bellwether's eye stopped fluttering, and he sat up. "It's the first time in my life I showed *ba. . .* " he stopped. *"Courage."*

"Myron."

"You'll be a great principal, Katie." He pulled office keys out of his pocket, handed them to her, and rose off the couch. "I know it."

"I won't accept."

"Yes, you will," he said.

"No, I won't."

Bellwether suddenly looked serene as if a great wave of relief had washed over him and landed him on dry ground. "You'll do it because you love the kids."

"*Myron . . .*"

"You're everything I'm not," he said, opening the front door and giving a half wave. "You've got this."

It was past midnight and Gale was still on the road home from Caton. Twice, Gale had to swerve to avoid hitting a mule deer as if the pavement on the two-lane state road had suddenly become a suitable place to graze. After the game against Sandington, the team bus had been nearly empty. Only a few players had remained. The others had ridden back to Caton with family. Marshall and Avery had ditched the bus trip home after taking off their coaching attire and putting on t-shirts, jeans, and boots, like roughnecks headed to the oil and gas fields. Gale had wondered why they'd changed clothes and if they'd hitched a ride with Waters. Gale rode back with the remaining assistants, who except for a few formalities, had acted as if he didn't exist. He'd noticed halfway to Caton that the other coaches, sitting a few rows away, were pointing to their phones. Gale had heard one of them say, "Bellwether," and they'd all started to laugh.

Gale had turned to hear more when his phone began to chime. When he'd heard Katie Tuck's voice, he had leaned forward to keep others from hearing. She'd told Gale about the two hospitalized students, Bellwether's abrupt resignation, and her "appointment" as principal. After the conversation with Tuck, he knew one thing. She was more determined than ever to find Johnny Spivey's fentanyl source.

Now, as exhaustion crept over him, Gale caught himself drifting into the middle of the road. He rolled down the windows in his pickup to keep himself awake. One thing was sure. He wasn't upset to leave Caton in his rearview mirror.

On Saturday morning after Caton's triumph over Sandington, Billy Pax sat at the table across from Bart Waters, Lloyd Avery, and Buck Marshall. Dean Spivey sat at the far end and had the look of a bleeding elk about to be torn apart by wolves. Spivey's jaw was locked with tension. Pax noticed Waters' angry eyes and read the disgust on Avery and Marshall's tired faces.

Lloyd and Buck had pulled an all-nighter, returning from a pickup 25 miles south of McCarney.

Pax settled in waiting for the shit to fly. He'd come into the car dealership through the back door, hadn't had nearly enough coffee, and felt a dull throb behind his eyes from the beer he'd guzzled the night before. He had been off duty, kicking back, when the call had come about the two kids overdosing. He had done what he always did when the crap hit the fan. Deny. Deniability was his go-to play. Unless that skinny geek Bellwether had taped the conversation, Pax was in the clear.

Pax dug into his ear with his index finger and took a quick sniff before anyone noticed. Then he settled into his swivel chair for the fun. He hated Dean Spivey. Always had. Spivey was a few years older and had tried to bully Pax in high school. The only thing Billy liked about Spivey was his wife, Audrey. She was in his class in school and Billy would fantasize about her sometimes. Just the other day he'd been parked in his Sheriff's SUV and watched her saunter down Main Street. He liked the way she wiggled in her tight designer jeans and the way all that dyed blonde hair cascaded onto her shoulders in soft curls.

Waters settled back in his chair and tapped his finger on the laminated conference table. He'd chosen one of the windowless sales conference rooms for the meeting, which meant all hell was going to break loose, Pax thought. Pax stared at a poster of the latest shiny sedan on the wall and a framed inscription hanging beside it that read *Waters' Motors: Great Deals for over 35 Years*. He'd seen Waters angry before. It wasn't pretty. Avery was even worse. Lloyd had a violent temper, and Pax had been called a few times over the years to Avery's house when Lloyd and his ex had fought.

Besides Waters' displeasure with Spivey, Pax knew Waters was enraged about Tuck and McClanahan. He didn't like the two of them poking around, putting their noses where they didn't belong. Pax could feel something bad was going to happen, but for the moment, he was relishing the prospect of Waters tearing Spivey apart.

Waters broke the silence. "When we started this little venture, we agreed that we wouldn't shit where we eat. Isn't that right, Dean?"

Pax saw Spivey give an uncertain nod and caught Avery and Marshall glowering.

"Now look what we got. Two high school kids about to bite the dust, parents asking questions, and Myron Bellwether *appointing* Katie Tuck principal. I woke up to an inbox stuffed with emails from families endorsing her. The only sunshine I got is that we beat Sandington last night. Hell, Dean, explain all this? One moment we're running a tidy business, the next because of your carelessness, your kid thinks he's Tony Montana."

Waters swept his eyes across the room. Then he settled his stare again on Spivey. "If I didn't know better, I'd think you were hoping to take a cut of profit without us knowing. You wouldn't do that to us, would you, Dean?"

Spivey shook his head vigorously and opened his mouth to protest when Waters cut him off.

"Haven't I been a fair and generous man?" Waters pointed at Marshall. "Buck here bought himself a hunting camp in the Pecos and built a new house for himself and that lovely of his. Ain't that right, Buck? How big is that man cave?" He turned to Avery. "And, Lloyd, hell, I don't know what you've done with your money since your wife and kids up and left, but I know you aren't missing any alimony payments. And the last time I drove by your house, the driveway looked like one of my car lots."

Waters banged his fist on the table. His eyes bore into all of them as if they could bite the hand that fed them. "The hell. I give you all a generous cut. And what do I get? Nothin' but heartache. Two kids dying in a hospital, a horde of families wanting Katie Tuck, *Katie Tuck* to be principal, and the real possibility that some desk jockey in the States Attorney's office might be itching to take a closer look at Caton, Texas. Hell, I've done everything I can to keep some government law enforcement bureaucrat from probing into Clay's death, and I don't even know who killed Clay. But I know one thing." He swept his eyes across the room. "Clay may have had it coming, but if one of you shot him, I'm not going to save your sorry ass."

Waters suddenly turned to Pax, who felt his anus pucker. "What have you got to say, Billy? I keep you fat and happy. I pay for all those cheeseburgers and hot dogs you snarf and those toys you got hidden from your ex outside of town. Don't you worry, I know all about that ATV, the new fishing gear, and the wad of cash you hide under your mattress. Don't forget that. You have one job. You make sure no one comes sniffing up our ass. Understand?"

Waters paused and shook his head. He turned back to Spivey. "You were a stray dog, trying to make a living when I let you be my accountant. Now look at you. You're a big shot. CFO of Waters' Motors, live in a big house, pretty wife, hundreds of thousands of dollars in an offshore account. I'll be damned if I don't think you're trying to screw me over."

Silence fell over the room. Pax felt his bowels churn.

"Hell, Dean, you didn't even play football," Waters grunted.

Avery glanced at the championship ring on Spivey's finger and snorted.

Waters turned away for an instant. He paused. "What we got here is a big ole problem. If we're lucky, those two boys in Midland die before they can tell where they got the fentanyl. If they don't," Waters shot Spivey a look, "you're on your own, Dean. Get that? All by your lonesome. You may end up thinking Clay was a lucky man."

NO HEART TO KILL

Spivey's face turned white, and he sat back in his chair.

Pax raised his hand to speak as if he were in elementary school. He was about to open his mouth when Waters said, "Shut up, Billy."

Pax went silent. It wasn't the first time Waters disrespected him. Pax didn't like it one bit. He imagined pulling his Sig Sauer from its holster and putting a slug between Waters' eyes.

Avery leaned forward. "What about Johnny?" He stared hard at Dean Spivey.

"That's right," Marshall said. "What about Dean's kid?"

Pax could tell that Spivey was tensing.

Waters strummed his fingers on the laminated table and stared at Spivey. "Dean tells me Johnny won't talk. Isn't that right, Dean?"

Spivey nodded.

"Dean tells me everything's good with the boy. Isn't that correct, Dean?"

Spivey nodded again.

"Dean tells me Johnny knows where his bread is buttered. He tells me he trusts a 16-year-old boy to keep his mouth shut."

Pax watched as Avery and Marshall exchanged glances.

Waters said sarcastically, "I sleep better at night knowing that Johnny will never say a word." He shook his head at Spivey and acted as if he were a disappointed parent. The room fell silent.

"What about Tuck?" Marshall asked, shifting the subject. Pax watched as Spivey took a deep breath.

Everyone looked at Waters. "We make sure she doesn't take the job," he replied.

"If she does?" Avery asked.

"It won't happen. We can't have a woman who hates football running the school and messing us up. Hell, this is Caton, Texas, not some snowflake town where kids play soccer."

Pax held back a smile.

"What about McClanahan?" Avery asked. His lips were pressed together.

Of all the men in the room, Pax was most fearful of Avery. If anyone could kill Clay Moorhead, it was Lloyd Avery, Pax thought. It was no secret he'd wanted Clay's job for years and had the balls to pull the trigger.

After a moment, Waters said to everyone, "We make sure McClanahan stays in his lane."

"That ship has sailed," Avery said.

Marshall nodded. Spivey kept to himself, but Pax noticed Spivey's fists were clenched.

Avery continued. "McClanahan is dangerous, Bart. And he'll be even more dangerous now that the principal has balls. He's been nothing but trouble."

"I wanted him because he's a choirboy. We needed people to forget Clay." Waters' face hardened. "He wins, too, Lloyd. We'd be 2-0 if you and Buck hadn't crossed him up. Don't think I don't know. I saw what happened against Hargrove."

"He's an idiot," Avery said. "What coach doesn't punt?"

"Last time I checked, he was Coach of the Year in the League. He's won more state championships than Clay." Waters leaned forward and looked hard at Avery, Marshall, and Spivey. "He's smarter than you think. He outmaneuvered Vernon Voss, and from what I hear, has the Commissioner of The League by the shorthairs. Tell me that happened because he's an idiot, Llyod?"

Avery sat back and looked away. "Have it your way. But don't you think that makes him dangerous?"

"Every man's vulnerable, boys," Waters said, smiling thinly. "Especially when it comes to his wife and kids."

"What are you thinking about, Bart?" Marshall asked.

Waters scratched his chin and paused. "First things first. We got to take care of Katie Tuck."

"Okay," Avery said. "Then?"

"If our boy from Kinney decides to be an Eagle Scout, we pay another visit to his ranch."

Avery and Marshall caught each other's eye and broke into cruel smiles. Pax felt his pulse accelerating as Waters pushed away from the table and began to rise. More than ever, Pax knew he needed to stay on Waters' good side. He shivered about the prospect of Avery and Marshall coming after him.

It wouldn't be pretty.

Fourteen

That morning, Katie Tuck found Martin Keller and Sam Lowe's parents in the fluorescent lit hallway outside the ICU in Midland Memorial Hospital. Both couples stood apart, keeping their distance from one another. A few nurses and doctors brushed past as Tuck walked down the corridor toward the stricken boys' parents. Lowe's mother and father had been divorced for years and had put Sam through an epic custody battle. Sam's father worked in the oil and gas fields and had a protruding jaw and thick shoulders. The boy's mother had rebounded by having a series of boyfriends who helped make Sam's childhood a rollercoaster ride of misery. She had flinty looks, a stripe of blue hair, and a smoker's cough.

Keller's father worked as a supervisor at a small construction company and his mother as a bank clerk. They both had weathered looks and worry stitched across their faces. They had five children and always seemed overwhelmed, Tuck thought. Tuck classified them as pleasers. She'd called them in the past about her concerns, and they'd assured her that Martin's surly behavior would stop. It never did. Now he was in critical condition.

During the drive to Midland, Tuck had become even more resolute about rejecting the position. Myron Bellwether had acted impulsively, and Tuck knew her life would change irrevocably if she accepted. She imagined Bart Waters and Dean Spivey wouldn't let it happen anyway, but if they did, that might be even more worrying.

All four adults turned their heads at once when Tuck approached. Tuck noticed the immediate look of contempt on Bet Lowe's face as she broke into a hacking cough.

"I'm sorry," Tuck said to them.

"You ought to be," Lowe's mother spat.

"Shut up, Bet," her ex said.

"You shut up," she snapped. "If they'd been doin' their job at the school, my boy wouldn't be dying in this hospital."

Lowe's ex, Donny, looked at Tuck. "She blames everyone but herself."

Tuck knew not to say anything. The truth was that some parents expected schools to do all the dirty work of parenting. The expectations were overwhelming, especially from the parents who led irresponsible lives and dragged their kids through a trail of dysfunction. Lowe's mother was no different. Besides Bet Lowe's multiple partners, she'd been in and out of rehab, and because of it, couldn't hold a job. It was all too familiar, Tuck thought. But the mess Sam Lowe's mother had made of her life didn't stop her from finger pointing.

"They knew. They knew," Lowe's mother repeated. "Johnny Spivey was sellin' that shit. Bellwether never told no one. They kept it to themselves so that people didn't know they weren't doin' their jobs."

Tuck frowned after hearing Lowe's mother say Johnny's name.

Kellers' parents stepped back. Martin's mother began to sob and buried her face into her husband's chest.

Lowe's mother continued her rant. "You let kids deal drugs and don't do nothing about it."

Donny Lowe turned to Tuck. "Don't listen to her. She's sick in the head."

"Sick in the head?" Lowe's mother shot back. Her face grew red, and she nervously brushed a wisp of lanky hair from her eyes.

She was about to open her mouth again when Keller's mother pulled away from her husband and said between sobs, "Will you be quiet for God's sake? My boy is dying."

Lowe's mother barked, "So what makes you so special?"

Keller's mother started to cry harder and slumped into an orange plastic chair a few feet away. Her husband sat beside her and put his arm around her.

Tuck knew she had to take control of the situation before Lowe's mother went any further.

"I came to say how sorry I was," Tuck said. "Not to make anyone more upset."

"Well, you failed," Lowe's mother answered.

"Shut it," Donny Lowe said.

Tuck ignored them. She lowered her voice. It was the first rule of diffusing a pissing match. "If I can do anything for you or your sons, please let me know."

Lowe's mother said, "You coulda kept Johnny Spivey from dealing fentanyl. Everyone knows he was peddlin' that shit. But no one did nothin' because you're afraid of Dean and Audrey Spivey." Her eyes bore into Tuck's. "Ain't that right?"

Tuck's eyes settled on Lowe's mother. "Like I said, I'm here to lend support, not get into an argument."

Lowe's father pointed his finger at Sam's mother. "Can't you see what she's sayin'?"

"It ain't going to make my boy better."

There was nothing more to say, Tuck thought. Her presence was like throwing gas on an angry fire. She'd tried to show compassion and knew it was time to leave. Tuck said, "If I can do anything for you, please let me know."

"Anything?" Lowe's mother asked, breaking into a phlegmy cough. "How about savin' my boy?"

Tuck approached the hospital entrance and was about to step into the harsh sunlight when she heard, "Ms. Tuck . . ."

She turned to find Martin Keller's father moving toward her across the lobby. Tuck braced herself, wondering if Keller's father was going to explode. Instead, he avoided an elderly couple moving slowly toward the elevator. Keller looked sorrowful and shook his head mournfully when he approached Tuck. "I'm sorry Sam's mother gave you hell."

Tuck shrugged. "I'm no stranger to angry parents."

"It was uncalled for."

"I'm sorry about Martin."

"I know you are, but I didn't follow you out of the hospital to talk about my son." Keller's eyes welled, but his voice was resolute. "I read the email from Mr. Bellwether. If there's anyone who can clean up that high school, it's you."

Tuck felt a chill move up her spine. His words hit her hard. She had awoken from a fitful sleep to find over two dozen congratulatory emails and texts from families thrilled that she would be taking charge. The outpouring surprised her. She thought about the manila envelope Bellwether had given her. The evidence was as filthy as Bellwether had promised. Tuck knew she could make a difference, but Waters and Spivey would make her life hell. She knew that.

Keller said, "You kept warning us about Martin, and we never did anything. It's not your fault what happened. It's ours."

"It's no one's fault."

Keller's eyes welled. "We kept hoping Martin would grow out of it. Instead, he's in the ICU hanging onto life. We may not be able to save Martin, but as principal, you can make sure something like this never happens again."

Tuck gave a subtle nod.

"Mrs. Keller and I have faith in you, Ms. Tuck. We'll help in any way we can." He turned to the elevator, and a few seconds later, was gone.

Tuck slowly slung her handbag over her shoulder and started toward the door. She stopped when she saw the tall figure of Abraham Daly entering the hospital, wearing a light-colored shirt, tie, and black trousers. Daly's skin was pale, and he looked haggard. He was a quiet, reflective man, but since his wife's death, Daly had grown more reserved. He was clearly having trouble reconciling his losses, Tuck thought. Tuck knew that Daly's daughter, Alexa, had fallen in with the wrong crowd and suspected Alexa's poor choices had alienated her from Abraham. Tuck hadn't seen Alexa since graduation the spring before. She had disappeared.

When Daly saw Tuck, he shook his head slowly and gave her a brief hug. "How are the boys, Katie?"

"Hanging on, apparently," Tuck said.

"The parents?"

Tuck looked away for an instant. "Not good."

"I've been praying for them."

"Watch out. Sam Lowe's mother's spitting fire."

Daly nodded. "The others?"

"Devastated."

Daly's eyes settled on Tuck. "I saw the announcement from Mr. Bellwether."

"It was a shock, to say the least," Tuck answered.

"It's God's work."

"I'm not sure I'm up to the task, Abraham."

"You are. I've prayed on it and can see that God sent you. But be careful, Katie." Daly's eyes darkened.

Tuck held back. She had been about to tell Daly she didn't want the job, but suddenly felt like she didn't want to disappoint his faith in her. She thought about Keller saying, *Don't let us down.* She decided to be noncommittal. "I'd be stepping into a minefield."

Daly nodded. "Myron spoke with me often. I prayed for that man, but he wasn't cut out for the job. You are."

"I'm glad he could confide in you."

"He told me what happened to his daughter's pet and about Johnny Spivey."

Tuck stared. How many people had Bellwether told? The rumor about Johnny dealing had to start somewhere. She had thought it had been the boys themselves, but now she wasn't so sure.

"These are dangerous people, Katie. But you are smarter than they are, and you have God and all of the good people of Caton on your side. Use your strengths, and you'll prevail."

Before Tuck could press him, Daly stepped toward the elevator. He took long strides and walked with his hands clasped behind his back and his head down. A moment later, he disappeared behind the elevator door.

Tuck stood in the lobby while people bustled past. She replayed her conversation with Daly. Then she turned toward the hospital entrance wondering if she had the courage to take the next step.

As Tuck drove back to Caton, Martin Keller's father's words kept playing over and over in her mind. Since Mark's death, she'd lost faith in herself. She had thought of herself as a confident person, but his infidelity had shaken her badly and had made her feel less than whole. She'd retreated into her counseling work and tried to make that enough, but she had to admit that her life had fallen short of her expectations. Here she was, single and lonely in the middle of the oil patch with nothing to show for it. The thought of becoming principal terrified her, but Daly's faith and Martin Keller's father's words struck a chord. She could make a difference. Maybe it was time she made her world large again.

The call from Bart Waters came early in the afternoon. Tuck had pulled into her driveway after the drive from Midland. She heard Waters' heavy drawl on Bluetooth, closed her eyes for a moment, took a deep breath, and leaned back against the car's headrest.

"You aren't thinking of taking that job, are you?" Waters asked, his voice hard and sharp.

Tuck stayed silent.

"If you are, don't. You write up a nice little email telling parents you're declining. Hear?"

Tuck could feel her hands tighten on the steering wheel.

"What if I don't?"

"Then we have a problem."

"Which is?"

Waters grunted. "There's only one person in this town who decides who the principal's going to be. And it isn't you or Myron Bellwether."

"What if my nice little email tells parents the truth?"

"The truth, Ms. Tuck?"

"Two boys are in ICU hanging onto life because of Johnny Spivey."

"Not true."

"Or how Dean Spivey threatened me at a football game?"

"Don't be silly."

"Or the folder I have with bogus school and municipal contracts?"

Tuck heard Waters grunt and take a breath. "Nonsense," he finally spat. "A fabrication. You think anyone is fool enough to believe you?"

Tuck's jaw tightened. She thought of Martin Keller's father's words. "You think you can tell me to write a 'nice little email'? You think you can keep manipulating people so you can control the town?" She clenched her teeth. "I wasn't going to take the job. The last thing I wanted was to be principal. But not now. You and Dean Spivey changed all that. Matter of fact, I'm going to send a 'nice little email' to parents telling them I'm honored and excited to be the next principal. For many of them, it's going to be great news that you aren't the one dictating who does what in this town. How does that sound?"

"You don't want to go down this road, Ms. Tuck. It's fraught with peril."

"If the press gets what I have, we'll see who's in peril."

"That would be a fatal error."

"Is that a threat?"

"Take it any way you want."

Tuck ended the call. She hung up on Bart Waters. She felt giddy.

A few moments later, Tuck climbed out of her car into the afternoon heat. The giddiness was gone and the metallic taste of fear now hung in her throat. She shivered and took an uncertain step. When she entered her house, she made sure to lock the door. Her world had suddenly changed. Waters had her in his bullseye. She figured it was only a matter of time before he struck.

She sat down with her laptop and took a deep breath. She thought of Mark's betrayal and her own shattered confidence. She looked around the living room. There were no sounds of children playing or a loving husband meeting her at the door. The house was empty. She realized she had nothing to lose. She would make a difference or go down trying.

Tuck's email was short, gracious, and to the point. When she hit send, she realized there was no return. She'd "accepted" the principal's job and thanked parents for their support and said how much she appreciated the "confidence" of the School Board. She knew there would be a reckoning, but it didn't matter. Caton High School was hers, at least for now, for better or worse. Screw Bart Waters.

That afternoon, after Gale had returned home from running a short workout and film session for the players in the aftermath of the Sandington game, Hayes and Gale had taken Gale's pickup on the beaten dirt tracks that snaked along the ranch's flats and hummocks to survey the herd. The heat had been scorching, and the drought was now in its third year. Frowning, Hayes with his sunburned face and clear eyes, had pointed to the desiccated grass and shrunken watering holes, then proposed thinning the herd to save on feed and hay. Gale knew that ranchers across West Texas were facing the same dilemma.

Gale had long heard the predictions about heat extremes caused by global warming. But he was accustomed to heat and lack of rain in the summer, so he figured he'd wait to see if all the hullabaloo over climate change impacted the conditions for raising cattle. For now, Gale and Hayes had agreed to leave the herd intact and hoped that fall would bring rain.

When Gale and Hayes had entered the house through the kitchen door, Gale was surprised to see the teenager at the kitchen table with his arm in a sling, a sweating glass of lemonade resting in front of him, and Til sitting across from the boy studying him closely. Marybeth leaned against the counter by the stainless-steel refrigerator smiling.

"Ana called and said it was time we got our friend out of bed," Marybeth explained. She and Torres had been talking daily. "There were a few grunts and groans, but we made it to the kitchen."

Marybeth smiled at the teenager.

Gale studied the boy. After a week, the teenager was beginning to show signs of improvement. The cuts on his face were healing and his cheeks were losing their hollow look. His complexion appeared healthier.

When Hayes spotted the teenager, without a word, he went back outside. Gale caught Marybeth's eye and shrugged. Gale left the house and followed Hayes to the large storage shed, where they kept the front loader, tractor, and ATVs.

"Mason," Gale called.

Hayes turned and stood in the sun with one hand on his hip.

"You shouldn't a done it, Gale," Hayes said as Gale approached.

"Done what?"

"Took him in. That Mexican is trouble."

Gale shook his head.

"They find that boy, and they'll shut down the ranch. In this climate, no one's turning a blind eye to illegals. You could serve time. And if he killed someone . . .," Hayes' voice drifted.

Gale knew it was true.

"Put that boy in your truck and take him south. Get him out of here."

"Soon."

"Now." Hayes' expression hardened.

Gale was surprised. He'd never seen Hayes so adamant.

"He's threatening the ranch and our livelihood."

"Soon," Gale repeated firmly.

"Have it your way, but don't say I didn't warn you."

"Warning taken," Gale said.

"Just remember. The road to hell is paved with good intention."

Gale nodded and turned toward the house. He knew Hayes was right.

That night, Gale couldn't sleep, so he lay in bed studying Marybeth's silhouette. She slept deeply, and he could see her breasts rise with each breath. He wanted to wake her and explain his growing worry. Not only did he have his hands full with Caton, but he was sheltering a boy who could ruin his business and reputation and land him in jail. He thought about Mason Hayes saying, *"If he killed someone"* and wondered again how the teenager had ended up with a gaping knife wound.

But how to handle it? Even with the language barrier, Gale realized Marybeth had grown fond of the boy. Marybeth had always wanted a big family and a son. For years they had tried to have children and had even seen specialists in Dallas. When Marybeth had discovered she was pregnant with Tilly, it had been a miracle. After Til was born, they failed to have another child. Gale knew Hayes was right. But just how attached was Marybeth at this point, and how much of a fight was he going to have on his hands if he did what he knew he should?

Gale closed his eyes, but given the hyperactivity of his mind, he knew that sleep was likely to elude him. What he wanted was to feel Marybeth under him. He wanted to be inside her and feel the physical exhaustion it would bring. Instead, he rolled over on his side and began to think about Katie Tuck. Gale knew she too was in the crosshairs. He knew it wouldn't be long before there'd be a reckoning. It was clear that Moorhead's death was the tip of the iceberg. Caton was malignant, and unfortunately, it looked like he and Tuck were cast in the role of surgeons who had to cut out the cancer. Best not to think about what lay ahead. He sighed and closed his eyes. Maybe sleep would come.

Setting her Caton Panthers' coffee mug on her desk, Jaycee McCubbin pointed at Bellwether's office and said to Tuck, "It's yours now."

"For better or worse," Tuck answered, looking warily at the office door.

"What have you gotten yourself into, girl?" McCubbin took a sip of coffee. The majority of students hadn't arrived yet, and the main hallway outside the principal's office was silent. "Myron didn't leave a thing. It's as if he never existed."

Tuck nodded. She knew her first day as principal was going to be hard. She'd planned an assembly to address the two boys lying in an ICU and offer support to students and teachers. The kids and faculty were upset, and she knew her day was going to be spent in the hallways and classrooms. "So where do I start, Jaycee?"

"With the student in your office."

"Student?"

"Melanie Sprague. She's waiting for you."

Tuck gave a surprised look. Of all the students she didn't expect to be camped in her office, Sprague was near the top of the list. A sophomore,

Sprague hung in the shadows. Since entering high school, Sprague had been on Tuck's radar. Her ninth-grade year, she began piercing her lips, eyebrows, and nose. She followed with multiple tattoos stenciled on her arms and neck and wore her bleached hair in a bristled cut. Sprague's father had disappeared a few years earlier after being convicted of armed robbery. Itchy, in the grasp of a nasty heroin addiction, he had walked into a pawn shop with a sawed-off shotgun a few minutes before closing. After holding up the clerk, it wasn't long before Midland County Sheriffs ran him down outside of Odessa. The clerk had gotten the make and plate number of his pickup.

Sprague's mother worked off and on at the cash register at Dollar General, and she and Sprague lived in a moldy trailer on the outskirts of town. Sprague didn't have a chance. It broke Tuck's heart.

Sprague didn't get up when Tuck entered her new office. Jaycee McCubbin was right. Bellwether had left no trace. The cinderblock space was barren but for a metal desk, an empty bookshelf, a couple of folding chairs, and a dead potted plant in the corner. A singularly unimpressive space, Tuck thought. Outside the window, she could see the gleaming hulk of Clay Moorhead Stadium glowing in the soft morning light. Tuck placed her laptop and handbag on the desk and sat down across from Sprague, who nervously chewed on a long, purple fingernail.

"This office sucks," Sprague said.

Tuck smiled. She was always amazed by kids' honesty. "Not exactly a palace," she agreed.

"I'd shoot myself if I had to work here."

Tuck's smile evaporated. "What's going on Melanie? What's up?"

Sprague chewed on her fingernail and leaned forward in her chair. "I got secrets."

Tuck leaned back. "Secrets?"

"Yup."

"Are you going to share?"

"It depends."

"On what?"

"If you keep me out of it."

"How so?"

"I don't want to get in trouble. Okay?"

"I can't keep secrets if you or anyone else isn't safe."

Sprague turned to look into her eyes. "That's why I came. People ain't safe."

Tuck had a feeling from her tone that Melanie was going to talk. She had to make sure she didn't get in the way. "It takes courage for you to be here. I get that."

Sprague considered Tuck's words. "Promise I won't get in trouble?" Sprague's eyes welled. She wiped away a tear. "If I'd known that shit would kill someone, I never would have let Johnny deal it."

Tuck asked softly, "What happened, Melanie? Where'd Johnny get the fentanyl?"

"Please, Ms. Tuck. Don't tell anyone I told you."

Tuck nodded.

Sprague shifted uncomfortably in her chair and wiped another tear from her cheek. "Johnny and I were hooking up. No one was at Johnny's house. After we did it, we went to his father's shed to smoke weed. We didn't want to smoke in the house. I was digging around the shed and found a cardboard box behind some garden equipment. We opened it. We couldn't believe how much shit there was."

Tuck's eyes narrowed. She felt her pulse race. *Fentanyl in the Spivey's shed.* "Then what?"

"Johnny took it. It was so stupid," she said, shaking her head. "He showed Sam and Martin and sold them some."

"Did he sell to anyone else?"

"Not that I know of."

Tuck leaned forward in her chair and eyed the girl. "Do you have any idea why there was a stash in the Spivey's garden shed?"

Sprague averted Tuck's stare.

"What, Melanie?"

"Please."

"Tell me."

Sprague looked down at the floor and put her head in her hands. "I asked Johnny."

"And?"

Sprague hesitated then looked up. "He said he thought his dad was involved in some kind of drug operation."

Tuck sat back. "What made him think that?"

"Johnny said he was messing around one day on his dad's computer and found a weird email about a delivery."

"Delivery?"

"That's what it said. It was from the guy who owns the car dealership."

"Bart Waters?"

Sprague nodded and rubbed her eyes. A hint of relief spread across the girl's face. She hesitated. "There's something else."

"What?"

"He broke one of Johnny's teeth." Sprague started to bite her nail.

Tuck felt her anger rise. She knew she'd have to call Child Protective Services about Johnny. Like so many calls that she'd made over the years, she wondered if her report would go anywhere. A wave of sadness hit her. "Oh, Melanie, I'm sorry."

Sprague looked blankly at the cinderblock wall. "I don't think I would have told you if Johnny's dad hadn't hurt him. Johnny texted me never to tell no one." For an instant, Sprague averted Tuck's eyes. "But I don't want anyone else to get hurt. I know how that feels."

"You've been brave in coming to speak with me."

A hint of a smile crossed Sprague's face. "You mean I'm not in trouble?"

"Not at all. You've been courageous."

"You mean that?"

"I do."

The first period bell rang sharply, and Sprague leaned over to pick up her book bag. Tuck noticed blood oozing from Sprague's finger where she'd been chewing her nail.

"If you need anything, you come see me. Understand?" Tuck said.

Sprague nodded.

"Please keep this conversation to yourself."

Sprague nodded again.

"And Melanie –"

"What?" Sprague said, lifting herself off the chair.

"Can you do me one more favor?"

"What's that?"

"No more drugs. No more hooking up. Be good to yourself. You deserve it."

Tuck thought she could detect the hint of a smile cross Sprague's face as she got up to go. "I'll try, Ms. Tuck."

Sprague stepped away from Ms. Tuck's office thinking how nice it would be to have a mom like her instead of the screwed-up bitch she had. She was happy she told about the stash and had for a moment even thought about telling Tuck about what Johnny called "the ledger." After his dad had beaten him up, Johnny wanted to get back at him, so he hacked his safe and found a large spiral notebook with names, dates, types of drugs, and codewords. He took pictures of the pages and sent them to her in case he ever needed it to get him out of trouble. He called it his "magic bullet." He made her swear on her life not to show it to anyone until he told her to. But since his dad sent him to that military prison, she hadn't heard a word from Johnny. It was nice knowing that she had something on the bigshots in town. Melanie figured she would wait to hear from Johnny unless some other major shit went down.

Fifteen

Ephraim Hernandez woke up to find Ana Torres peering over him. She frowned, checked his pulse, and placed a digital thermometer against his forehead. Mateo Santos stood by the bedroom door watching Torres examine him. The house was quiet.

When Torres checked the thermometer, Ephraim noticed her frowning. He had chills during the night and had broken into sweats. He'd felt dizzy and sick to his stomach when he'd gotten up to go to the bathroom. He'd been feeling stronger, so it worried him that these symptoms had returned.

Torres turned to Santos and said, "Let's see how the wound's healing."

She peeled off Ephraim's dressing and studied the row of stitches running under his collarbone. She carefully probed around the wound with her fingers. She turned and said to Santos in English, "It's infected." Santos came over to see. She ran her forefinger parallel to Ephraim's stitches. "See the red streaks?"

Ephraim could tell by the tone of her voice and look on her face that something was wrong. He felt his heart begin to beat harder. Torres brushed away a few wisps of Ephraim's hair, and for a moment, rested the back of her hand on his forehead. "He's got a fever," she said to Santos again in English. "Let's hope not sepsis."

Ephraim tried to understand their conversation. He recognized the words "antibiotic" and "hospital" and began to feel a chill move down his spine. He started to shake his head after the word "hospital" and lift himself out of the bed.

Santos placed a hand on Ephraim's good shoulder and said, "no."

Torres broke into Spanish. "You've got a high temperature and an infection. I'm going to give you a stronger antibiotic."

"If it doesn't work?" Ephraim asked.

Torres quickly glanced at Santos and then focused her eyes on Ephraim. "It should work. And if it doesn't, we'll figure something out."

"No hospital."

Torres didn't respond.

"Please..."

"Mateo," Torres said, switching back to English. "I'm going to call in a prescription. Can you pick it up?"

Santos nodded. Ephraim tried to follow the conversation.

"Make sure the boy doesn't move around. Keep him still."

"Okay."

"I thought we were good," Torres said to herself, shaking her head, and then to Santos, "I hope he won't need an antibiotic drip. If he does, we'll have to take him to Midland Memorial."

"I never should have brought him here," Santos said between pressed lips.

"What do you mean?" Torres asked.

"I don't like it, Ana. This is a bad omen."

"It's an infection, Mateo."

"It's more than that."

"Why?"

Ephraim tried to follow. He watched Santos' eyes darken. He felt lonely and hollow and wished he were with Maria. He didn't like the doctor and the ranch hand speaking English. It was as if they were building another wall to lock him out.

Santos said, "The boy did something bad. I know it now."

"How so?" Torres asked.

Santos clasped the small, silver-plated cross attached to the pendant around his neck. "God's angry."

"It's an infection, Mateo," she repeated. "It has nothing to do with God."

Ephraim watched Santos shake his head and turn away. Ephraim felt feverish and his body had a dull ache. He heard Santos sigh before the ranch hand started for the door and say words in English he didn't understand but knew weren't good. Santos said, "Mason Hayes was right. I never should have pulled him from that ditch."

After Santos spoke, Ephraim closed his eyes and tried pushing away the fear. He wanted to be with Maria, but she was gone.

Billy Pax had been given explicit instructions. Lloyd Avery had walked him carefully through the plan and had left Pax feeling angry and uneasy when he'd said, "Don't screw it up, Billy."

Pax didn't like the idea of riding around in his Sheriff's SUV with heroin. He didn't like Avery and Marshall's tone or the anger in Waters' eyes when they had met two days before at the car dealership. They kept changing the rules on him. Pax wasn't just being asked anymore to play dumb. He was becoming enmeshed in something that wasn't worth Waters' meager payouts. Sure, he could buy toys like the ATV and top-of-the-line fishing gear, even hide extra cash from his ex, but doing Bart Waters' dirty work wasn't worth the possibility of being sent to prison. Judges hated filthy cops. Sentencing would be harsh. With his flabby belly, soft, pudgy hands, and fleshy chin, Pax knew he'd be dead meat in prison.

The plan was simple enough, though. New car models had locking cylinders that prevented the Slim Jim from working but this car was old. Piece of cake.

Regardless, Pax hated the escalation of his role with Waters, and the way that Waters ordered him around. He sat behind his cluttered desk in his dingy McClendon County Sheriff's office and listened to the HVAC unit rattle in the ceiling. It was brutally hot, and it was already past Labor Day.

After this, he hoped they would leave him alone, but he knew the opposite was more likely to be true. Every time he worked for them, he was digging himself a deeper hole.

Gale pulled up to the house and parked his pickup. Mason Hayes climbed out of the cab, went around to the flatbed, and retrieved a cardboard box containing parts for a broken generator. Gale slid out, put his Stetson on, and started for the house when Santos popped out of the kitchen door and said, "the boy."

Gale gave him a puzzled look. Hayes set the box full of parts back on the flatbed and stared at Santos.

Santos said, "He's got a bad infection."

"Where's Ana?" Gale asked.

"She just left."

"What did she say to do?"

"She called in a new prescription."

"Antibiotic?"

Santos nodded.

Hayes said, "I thought he was doing better. Hell, the boy was sitting in the kitchen two days ago."

Gale began to worry. If they were forced to bring the teenager to the hospital, there'd be questions. They'd ask who treated the boy and stitched him up. They'd dig for answers, and it wouldn't be long before they would know Gale and Marybeth had harbored an undocumented migrant with a knife wound and Ana Torres had knowingly treated the teenager in violation of the law. If the boy had indeed been involved in a crime there'd be serious consequences. Gale's thoughts were broken when Hayes said, "Get him out of here now."

"We can't do that Mason," Gale said.

"Get him his medicine and take him to the border."

Santos looked hard at Hayes. "He could die."

"I don't care," Hayes answered. "Take him to Del Rio. There are people who'll take care of him."

"We're not going to do that," Gale said. "We're going to see this through."

"You're risking it all, Gale," Hayes warned. He turned to retrieve the generator parts out of the flatbed and began walking toward the storage shed.

Gale turned to Santos. "How's the boy doing now?"

"Fever and chills. It's not good."

"Go get the antibiotics. I'll watch him," Gale said.

Santos looked down for a moment and kicked the dirt with his boot. "I'm sorry, Gale."

"For what?"

"I never should have brought him here."

"Let's just get him healed."

"I couldn't leave a boy to die."

Gale reached out and put his hand on Santos' shoulder. "It's okay, Mateo. I wouldn't have left him either."

Gale left Santos standing in the heat and walked toward the kitchen door. Gale felt apprehensive, but tried to tell himself the teenager would be okay. The new antibiotic would kick in and the boy's fever would subside and then they could get him off the ranch. Ana Torres would make sure the boy came out alright. She was a good doctor and cared and wouldn't let the boy's condition worsen. There'd be no reason to have to take the teenager to the hospital. Then he remembered a college teammate who had knee surgery after tearing his ACL against Oklahoma State. A kid from Port Arthur, he went into surgery the next day, and two days later a staph infection killed him. Gale and his teammates were stunned. No one died because of knee surgery. It was the moment that Gale first understood the fragility of life.

Gale was reaching for the kitchen door when he heard his phone ping. He pulled his cell out of his back pocket and saw a text from Katie Tuck. It read:

It was Spivey.

In the mid-afternoon, Gale pulled into an empty space in front of Caton High School. Classes had ended for the day, and students were pouring out of the building and piling into a row of grimy school buses. Others were headed toward the student parking lot to their cars.

Earlier, Gale had spent the day tending to the teenager until Josephine Santos had arrived. The boy had been racked by fever until a Tylenol and Motrin concoction had brought down his soaring temperature. While Gale was driving to Caton, he talked to Marybeth, who'd left work early and was on her way home. There was alarm in her voice. "Ana thinks it may be sepsis," Marybeth had said. "I thought everything was good, Gale."

It wasn't. Things were getting worse on all fronts.

Gale cut past the packs of students and headed into the high school. He dodged kids with back packs and found the principal's office. Jaycee McCubbin sat behind her desk and said, "She's waiting for you, Coach. Be nice. She's had a tough first day on the job."

Gale nodded and tapped on Katie Tuck's office door.

He found Tuck staring out the window, looking beyond Clay Moorhead Stadium. The sun beat down on the hulking structure and the large asphalt parking lot sitting in front of the football complex sat nearly empty. Tuck turned when she heard Gale enter.

"You might want to put a few pictures on the wall," Gale said with a thin smile studying the barren office. "Maybe a diploma or two. Did Myron leave you anything?"

"Only a dead plant and problems," Tuck replied without irony. She had circles under her eyes. "Spivey's running a drug operation with Waters."

Gale sat down across from her desk in one of the folding chairs.

Tuck recounted her conversation with Melanie Sprague. "Dean beat up Johnny, too."

"Does it surprise you?"

"Nothing Dean Spivey does surprises me."

"Is the student credible? The sheriff didn't believe Bellwether about the drugs. Why should he believe a kid?"

Tuck turned away for an instant and fell silent for a moment. "I've thought about calling the State's Attorney office."

"What's the downside?"

"My guess is that they will see this as a case for the local authorities." Tuck then told Gale about the manila envelope Bellwether had given her and the conversation she'd had with Waters.

Gale thought about Marybeth's mother and H.W. Owen and wondered how deep corruption ran in West Texas. It was possible that the State's Attorney would shrug off pursuing small-town drug peddlers and tell Tuck to work with local law enforcement, a non-starter in this case. Still, it was worth exploring with Wallace. One thing was sure, no local authority was going to act. Caton was rotten. Waters had bought everyone off.

Wallace had been uncharacteristically silent. Gale wondered when Wallace was going to get back to him about Lloyd Avery.

"What do we do?" Tuck asked.

"Nothing for now."

"Here's what I don't understand. Why would Waters be involved in drugs anyway? He makes enough money selling cars and stealing from the town. Plus, I heard he's got oil and gas leases."

"Greed. Power. Testosterone." And friends like H.W. Owen to run interference for you, Gale thought.

Tuck sighed. "No offense, but sometimes I hate men."

"No offense taken."

"But I like you, Gale." She gave him a tired smile.

"Everything but the testosterone?"

She laughed. "I bet you have plenty of that."

"I guess." Gale shrugged.

"What do we do?"

Gale thought about the teenager on his ranch and Waters, Avery, and Marshall circling. He had enough trouble. "We wait. We watch. Hopefully, those boys in the hospital pull through and can confirm they got the drugs from Johnny. Maybe they know more."

Tuck sighed. "It doesn't look good for them."

Gale nodded. "No, it doesn't."

"Do you ever wish you had it in you to run like Myron? Ditch everything and leave?"

Gale thought about Marybeth's island paradise. "Sometimes. How about you?"

Tuck turned her back to Gale and looked out the window. Her lithe figure was silhouetted in the light. After a few moments, she turned to him and said wistfully, "All the time. The problem is, I have nowhere to go."

After the final sprint in the early evening light, Gale blew the whistle to end practice. The players moved slowly toward him, trying to catch their breath after a series of shuttle runs. Gale waited for the players to circle up. Unlike the other kids, Eben Daly trotted to midfield, unfazed by the conditioning drills. Gale noticed the coaches standing off to the side like cattle clumped around a watering hole. He looked more closely and searched for Avery and Marshall, but they must have cut out during the shuttle runs, Gale thought.

He wondered why they were in a hurry to leave. Then he realized he didn't care. The less of Avery and Marshall, the better.

The teenager's temperature hit 105 before sunrise. Marybeth held the icepack on the boy's forehead to keep him from thrashing it off. The bed sheets were soaked with sweat and the bedroom smelled of bile from the boy vomiting into a trash can. The teenager moaned softly and fell in and out of consciousness.

When Gale came back into the room after calling Torres, Marybeth looked at him with pursed lips and asked, "What did she say?"

"She's going to meet us at the hospital."

"Jesus, Gale."

"She said he's got sepsis, and it could kill him."

Marybeth shook her head. "I can't believe this is happening."

Gale couldn't help but think about what Mason Hayes had said. *The road to hell is paved with good intention.* There'd be serious consequences. At the hospital, Marybeth and Gale would be hit by a flurry of questions and soon those questions would turn into accusations. Ana Torres' medical license would be placed in jeopardy. Gale tried not to think of the laws that they'd broken. He knew himself and Marybeth. They'd tell the truth. They'd come clean. That's who they were. Guilty as charged.

Gale watched the boy. The teenager moaned and arched his back as if he were tied to a bed of nails. He tried to swivel his head from side to side, but Marybeth held the ice pack firmly on his forehead. Fear was stitched across her face.

"I'll put the seats down in the SUV," Gale said, "and come back to get him."

"Why not an ambulance?"

"By the time they get out here, we'll have lost an hour."

"We can't leave Tilly."

"You stay. I'll take him."

Marybeth frowned. "You're not going alone."

"Til?"

"I'll get her up."

"But what if he dies, Marybeth?" Marybeth froze and fixed him with a stare. Gale looked down again at the boy and was beset by a wave of empathy as he thought about the poor kid alone, racked with fever, amidst strangers. "I'll get the car."

"I'll have Til ready in a second."

Sixteen

Sixty miles southwest of McCarney under a quarter moon, the Mexican whore bit him when she'd realized she was being dropped in the middle of nowhere. After she stopped swinging and kicking, she'd sat on her ass and refused to budge from the truck. When Avery started cursing and dragging her out, she'd clamped onto his arm and ripped through to the bone.

When Avery had finally broken loose, he pushed her off the truck. Then when the other migrants had started to come after them, Marshall had stood over the woman and put the tip of his rifle barrel a few inches from her temple. The migrants had backed off.

As they drove away, Avery stripped off his shirt and tied it off around the gash. Blood had splattered on his jeans, the dashboard, the passenger door, and seat. It wasn't the first time he'd had a whore bite him as he unloaded the truck, but she'd gotten him good.

Looking straight ahead, with his face half-lit by the dashboard, Marshall asked, "Stitches?"

"Hell, yes."

Marshall nodded as he navigated the refrigerator truck on the dirt track. "Where?"

"We got to get away from here. Get to Midland."

"What are you going to say?"

"Dog bite," Avery said. He gritted his teeth. His arm was starting to throb.

"You think they'll buy it?"

"Maybe."

Marshall drove the truck up a slight rise. An armadillo broke from the narrow track after being spooked by the headlights.

"Who cares if they don't," Avery added.

"I should have killed that woman."

For a moment, Avery stared out the passenger window and then turned to Marshall. "Don't you think we got enough trouble?"

Through the haze, Ephraim reached out and tried to touch Maria's hand. She smiled and told him she loved him, and he tried to touch her again but she vanished. He felt the gurney move and the blinding lights in his eyes and the rancher's pretty wife side by side with the gurney moving down a wide white corridor and the doctor they called Ana with a haggard look on her face say something to the man pushing the gurney. Maria appeared again and told Ephraim she loved him. When he tried to touch her, she left him again. He closed his eyes and broke into a cold sweat. His joints ached and chills swept through him, and he felt sicker than he'd ever felt in his life.

He'd been in a curtained off room for what seemed like hours. In his delirium, he'd tried to rip out the thing they put in his arm and then they'd given him a shot and Maria had come and stood over him with her smile, but he couldn't touch her. She'd moved away into the light and now he was being pushed down another corridor.

He tried to find Maria, but she'd gone. The rancher's wife took hold of his hand and the doctor they called Ana pointed to a door at the end of the hallway. Nurses and doctors moved past him, then an old woman in a hospital gown slowly being wheeled by an orderly. Then Maria smiled and he reached for her just as she disappeared. He tried to find her again and then he saw the man with the wide jaw, narrow black eyes, and scar running along his throat coming down the corridor in a bloody shirt and baseball cap pulled low. He was holding his arm. Ephraim felt his heart explode when the man drew close. "Maria," the teenager cried and started thrashing. But they were holding him down and his eyes rolled back in his head.

As soon as Gale had pulled away from the hospital parking lot, Tilly had fallen asleep in the SUV's back seat. It was close to noon and the temperature had soared to 100 degrees. For nearly two hours, a sheriff from the Midland Criminal Investigation Office had questioned Gale about the teenager while Tilly had played in the corner with her mother's iPad. Marybeth and Ana had stayed with the teenager.

Gale knew he was in trouble. The sheriff, a tall Black man with a withering stare and forearms like two by fours, had sat across from Gale with a look of disbelief as Gale answered questions. When the sheriff had finished, and had finally let him go, Gale knew Grayson Wallace would scold him for speaking without legal representation. The sheriff had shaken his head and said, "I know you thought you were trying to do the right thing, but I could arrest you now and that wouldn't be good for a famous football coach." Before Gale had been allowed to leave the hospital, the sheriff's eyes had narrowed and he'd said in a low voice, "You better hope that boy lives."

Before Gale had left, outside the teenager's room, Marybeth had told him about the boy screaming and trying to rip himself out of the gurney.

Marybeth had looked puzzled and had said, "It was a man, Gale. He was smeared with blood and held a compress on his wrist. He blew past us, and the boy went crazy."

"Why?" Gale had asked.

"I don't know. But I feel like I've seen that man before. Somewhere. He was going quickly, and when the boy screamed and tried to pull himself off the gurney, Ana and I were trying to hold him down and keep him from tearing out his IV. He was wearing a baseball cap. I didn't get a good look."

"Was it the kid's fever?"

"I don't know. But it freaked me out."

"How's Ana doing?" Gale asked, changing subjects.

"Ana told me the hospital's CEO is furious, and the sheriff wants to meet with her. She thinks they're going to suspend her until this mess is resolved."

"It keeps getting better," he muttered wryly. "When is the sheriff meeting with you?"

"I told him I wasn't leaving the boy. I told him he could wait."

"What did he say?"

"He muttered something and walked out of the hospital room."

Gale gave a half smile. Marybeth was tough. The sheriff could probably see she was no one to mess with. Smart man.

Gale glanced over his shoulder to check on Til. She slept peacefully holding her stuffed rabbit, Elmer. She'd hugged Elmer so often that patches of the stuffed animal's fur were rubbed off.

Gale turned and set his eyes on the road. As he drove, the sinking feeling grew worse. He knew he needed to call Wallace but dreaded the conversation. Besides being a traitor, he was now under criminal investigation by the Midland County Sheriff's Department. He wondered what Shakespeare Grayson was going to hit him with now.

He vaguely thought back to what Marybeth had said about the teenager's reaction to the man in the hospital. But the boy must have been delirious, Gale thought. Out of his mind.

Just before noon, after Gale had dropped Tilly off at school, he called Grayson Wallace from the Kinney Elementary School parking lot. A few minutes later, Wallace grunted and said, "An undocumented migrant, Gale? I thought this was going to be a garden variety illegal immigration case until you sprinkled in the knife wound and a doctor denying proper medical care. Oh, and let's toss in a new governor who ran on prosecuting migrants and those who aided and abetted them. Our governor friend in Austin would relish making a famous football coach into a headline and a felon."

"Ana's a great doctor, Grayson," Gale shot back. "That boy got better care than he would have anywhere else. He had round-the-clock nursing."

"Don't care. If I were on the other side of the aisle, I'd go for her throat, your's and Marybeth's. I'd paint you as reckless, egotistical, and nefarious for hiding a teenager from the law."

Gale's mind raced at the implications. "But you're not on the other side. You're my lawyer."

"True. And you're a veritable comedy of errors."

"Now that you've scolded me with Shakespeare, where do we go from here?"

There was silence. Gale imagined Wallace sipping whiskey in his dark paneled office above Main Street with a clutter of legal journals and files scattered across his desk. Wallace started drinking early and finished late, but Gale rarely saw Kinney's finest attorney sloppy.

"They gave you a mulligan by not arresting you," Wallace said. "I'll call the DA and see if I can buy you time."

"Okay."

"In a case like this, we need to prove good intent."

"Our intentions were good." Gale thought about how naive he sounded.

"If the kid dies, that won't matter."

"If he lives?"

"We put him on the stand. We show everyone how he refused to go to the hospital. Mostly, we demonstrate how your good will was betrayed by this manipulative scoundrel. Especially if we discover the boy was trying to kill someone, or worse, and got stabbed in a brawl."

"He didn't murder anyone," Gale said.

"You don't know that."

Despite Gale's feelings to the contrary, he knew Wallace had a valid point. *They didn't know. They didn't even know the boy's name. He had no ID. They were presuming innocence on gut instinct.*

"You're suggesting we put everything on the kid. We make out we were conned?"

"Exactly."

"We can't do that, Grayson."

"Do you want the book thrown at you?"

"No."

"Is there another angle besides you, Marybeth, and Ana Torres being duped?"

Gale met the question with silence.

"None of this matters if he dies."

"What are you suggesting?"

"Ah, Gale. If you're all lucky, probation and community service hours. Torres might escape with a suspended license."

"And if the boy comes clean?"

"You have a shot to all walk away, particularly if what he says begs sympathy."

Gale looked over at the school playground. Children were beginning to pile out of the building for recess. Gale squinted to see if he could spot Til. He reminded himself he needed glasses, but given all that was happening, his nearsightedness was far down the priority list.

"Did you ever find anything on Lloyd Avery?" Gale asked.

Wallace paused. "A domestic assault charge that was dropped. He was sued by his ex-wife for child support. He also beat up a guy in a bar. That suit didn't go anywhere either."

"Sounds like Avery."

Wallace shifted. "How are those two kids doing, the ones who overdosed? I heard about it the other day. It's all over Kinney."

"Not good."

Gale brought up Tuck's question about the fentanyl and bogus contracts. Wallace agreed the State's Attorney office would shrug off the narcotics case to local law enforcement. As for Waters siphoning off funds from municipal and school contracts, Wallace said, "She's right, Gale. The State's Attorney office will most likely turn a blind eye, especially since it seems likely Waters would have the sense to have someone on his payroll in that office. And now that you've harbored a migrant, you don't have a shred of credibility."

Gale sighed.

"You have a lot going on, my boy."

"My troubles are legion. Is that Shakespeare?"

"No," Wallace said. "When sorrows come, they come not in single spies, but in battalions."

"OK, then that."

"You should never have allowed that kid onto your ranch."

"Too late now."

"As you know, I'm a skilled and deft attorney, but you're challenging my talents."

"Are you drinking?"

Wallace grunted. "Yes. And after my conversation with you, I'll need to drink more. Keep myself sharp."

Gale hoped football practice would prove to be a distraction from his growing troubles. Marybeth had called him on his way to Caton and told him the boy's condition hadn't changed and doctors were pumping him full of a hefty combination of ampicillin and sulbactam, giving him ice baths, and plenty of fluid to keep him from falling into septic shock. Gale knew he needed to tell Katie Tuck about the teenager. He didn't want her to be blindsided by having the school's football coach arrested.

Gale thought about his conversation with Wallace. Wallace usually brimmed with bombastic self-confidence and legal invincibility, but not today. Gale blamed himself for putting his family and Ana Torres in a bad situation. Hayes was right. He should have put his foot down and told Mateo Santos to take the boy to a hospital. If he had, he would have saved himself, Marybeth, and Torres from trouble. He hoped Wallace could resolve their legal woes, but realized that if they came before a jury, they'd be at its mercy. Then there was the boy. Gale felt his heart sink and said a quiet prayer. *Please God, don't let him die.*

The sun hung low in an angry yellow haze as Gale stepped onto the practice field. Players were milling around before practice, while Eben Daly was making soft throws, warming up on the sidelines. Friday night they would play Henderson. Gale needed to focus on getting the Panthers prepared. But he also realized that shutting out the distractions was nearly impossible.

The assistant coaches stood at midfield and turned away when they saw him appear. He didn't see Avery or Marshall. There were a few parents at the far end of the field watching practice. Gale turned and glanced at the other end of the field and spotted the crane-like figure of Abraham Daly standing alone, watching his son loft tight spirals to a teammate.

Gale was about to blow the whistle when Avery and Marshall appeared. They walked slowly and silently toward the middle of the field holding laminated practice sheets and permanent scowls. Gale started moving toward the fifty-yard line and began to raise his whistle when he noticed the large bandage on Avery's wrist. Gale's heart began to pound.

"What happened?" Gale asked, approaching Avery and pointing at Avery's arm, trying to keep his voice flat.

"None of your business," Avery snapped.

"Looks like you ran into a chainsaw."

Avery glared at Gale. "More like a dog bite."

"Pitbull?"

Avery spat and brushed past him. Gale watched him. Avery walked with a slight limp but retained the vestiges of a center breaking huddle and moving to the line of scrimmage. Gale wondered how many eyes Avery had gouged and knees he had destroyed with cut blocks. Offensive linemen were smart and mean. Guards, tackles, and centers often scored high on the Wonderlic, which was the test employed by the League before the draft to determine aptitude. Gale had scored in the upper echelon. It was one of the reasons Atlanta had signed him as an undrafted free agent.

"You need to be more careful, Coach," Gale said. "Dog bites are nasty."

Gale's words were met with a scornful silence. He wondered if it was a coincidence. Marybeth had said she hadn't gotten a good look at the man holding a compress on his wrist. Gale stared into the distance for a moment then tried to focus on the task at hand. But he couldn't shake the feeling that something was falling into place.

Gale started to raise his whistle when he noticed the players trotting toward him. He didn't need to blow it. They were beginning to be familiar with his mannerisms and style. They knew practice was about to start. Gale lowered the whistle and waited for the team to circle up. That one gesture helped set aside his troubles and turn his attention to what he loved – coaching football.

Katie Tuck glanced across the high school's chipped and cracked asphalt parking lot at the practice football field. She could see the players standing in a circle at midfield and Gale McLanahan in the center addressing them.

When she had entered her office that morning, Jaycee McCubbin had handed her a sealed envelope from the School Board. When Tuck had opened it, she found a principal's contract with Bart Water's signature sprawled across the bottom. She had taken an apprehensive breath. Then her eyes had gone to the salary figure. The School Board had given her a nice raise. In ordinary circumstances, she would have been gratified. She'd have a few more dollars. Maybe she'd take a vacation, or more practically, fix the leak in her roof and buy a sorely needed new washer and dryer.

However, like everything else in Caton, something didn't smell right. The contract had materialized too easily. She knew the last thing Bart Waters wanted was for her to serve as principal. He'd threatened her. Nevertheless, after a few minutes, she'd taken a determined breath and signed the agreement, made a photocopy, sealed the contract in an ivory-colored envelope, and handed the document to McCubbin.

Since signing the contract, the pit in Tuck's stomach had grown. The uneasy reality of being responsible for the High School had struck her but the prospect of Waters looming in the background made her even more apprehensive and suspicious.

Tuck pushed the unlock button on her car fob, swung open the passenger door, and placed her handbag on the seat. As usual, the Camry's cab was oppressively hot. She closed the door, went around to the other side of the car, opened the driver side door, and pulled the large, foiled sunshade from the windshield, folded it, and tossed it in back. She wondered why she even used it. How much hotter could a car get? Then she gingerly climbed into the steaming car and pushed the key into the ignition. When she tried to start the

Camry, she heard a stream of clicks followed by silence. She attempted to start the engine again. Nothing.

Tuck sighed and climbed out of the car. She looked over at the practice field as players stretched in the late afternoon heat. Tuck pulled out her phone and went into her contacts. She'd had car trouble before. When you drove a 10-year-old sedan with 160,000 miles, you had to expect problems, she thought. She wondered if her raise might be better spent on a new automobile. She punched up the number for the only auto repair shop in Caton not owned by Waters.

Thirty minutes later one of her former students pulled up in a tow truck and popped open the Camry's hood. Covered in grease and sporting a thick beard and a faded John Deere baseball cap, Richie Williams was in his mid-twenties. He had been one of her favorite students. He was one of those kids who never had a bad day. He was a mechanical whizz who rebuilt a 1988 Impala in shop class his senior year. Williams shook his head and said, "Ms. Tuck, you got a dead starter motor."

He leaned against her car and folded his arms. ""I'll need to tow your car to the garage."

"You can't fix it here, Richie?" Tuck asked.

"Nope. Sorry about that."

Tuck looked across the parking lot to where Jaycee McCubbin parked. McCubbin's spot was vacant. She sighed. She wasn't catching a lift home with McCubbin. She turned and looked out at the football field. Gale had the players running drills. Tuck decided she'd go back to her office and do paperwork until practice finished and catch a ride home with McClanahan. She needed to catch up with him anyway.

Tuck said, "I guess you better take the car."

Williams nodded.

"When can I pick it up?"

"After school tomorrow. I might have to replace the part."

In the morning, Tuck would need a lift to school. She made a mental note to text McCubbin for a ride. "Okay. Is it going to be expensive?"

Williams smiled. "Maybe it's time to buy a new car, Ms. Tuck. This one's seen a lotta road."

"I know."

"I heard Waters' Motors has some good deals."

Tuck shook her head. "That's what they'd like you to think."

Williams looked puzzled.

"I'll see you tomorrow afternoon. And Richie?"

"Yes."

"How much would I get in a trade-in?"

"Not much. This car has seen better days."

While he drove, Tuck noticed Gale's weathered hands. They were like vise grips, but oddly gentle appearing. He held the pickup's steering wheel as they pulled out of the high school parking lot. Before she could tell him her news, Gale told her about the migrant boy in the hospital with a knife wound and soaring fever. She stared at him in disbelief as he recounted his conversations with the sheriff and with a lawyer he knew. So now there were three teenagers clinging to life in the ICU, she thought. It made her sick to think about.

While she was processing, "Starter motor?" Gale questioned pulling out of the Caton High School parking lot to give Tuck a lift home.

"Yes."

"Have you ever had trouble with the starter before?"

"No."

"That's strange. Usually there are warning signs."

"Warning signs?"

"Usually. Over time, the engine gets harder and harder to start."

"What are you suggesting?"

Gale turned to her. "Nothing really."

"You sound suspicious."

"That's what coaching Caton High School football will do to you, I guess."

Tuck glanced out the passenger window and nodded as they crossed the Rock Island Railroad tracks and headed toward town. In the evening light, the plains stretched out in muted tones. Grime covered the edges of the pickup's windshield where the arc of the wipers had missed.

"There's a good chance I'm going to be charged," Gale said.

"I know," Tuck answered, turning to him. "I should suspend you for being under investigation. That's what a good principal would do."

"I'm sorry to bring you more problems, Katie."

"Do you have a good lawyer?" Tuck asked.

"Grayson Wallace."

"Never heard of him."

"He'd be shocked."

"Why?"

"Grayson has an ego."

"Bull in a china shop?"

Tuck saw Gale give a half smile. "Not quite how I'd describe him, but he certainly has some bull in him."

Tuck thought about Richie Williams, covered in grease, leaning over her car engine with the hood popped open. "What did you say again about my car?"

Gale paused. "Starters usually show signs of trouble before giving out."

"Now you've got me thinking," Tuck said, leaning back in her seat.

The call from Gale startled Marybeth. She'd started to fall asleep in the recliner next to the teenager's bed. The boy had been sedated and his breathing took on a jagged rhythm. The hospital room was dimly lit but for the monitor showing the boy's vitals. Marybeth glanced at the teenager. Even in the poorly lit room, she noticed the dark rings under the boy's eyes, his gaunt cheeks and ghostly complexion. The boy's lip quivered as he slept. *A bad dream?* Lifting herself out of the chair and going into the corridor, Marybeth answered the call. As she stood by the nurse's station, she listened as Gale told her about Avery.

"It could have been him, Gale," she said, "but I've only seen him from the stands during a football game. Not exactly ideal. And as I said, he was wearing a baseball cap, so I didn't get a great look at his face.'"

"I'm going to text you a photo I found on the internet."

Marybeth closed her eyes. Her body ached with exhaustion. She'd missed a day of school, and she was in trouble with the law. The boy wasn't showing any signs of improvement. Now Gale wanted her to identify the man she'd seen storm past her in the hospital. All day, she'd tried to stay focused on the boy. She'd tried to shut out the fear of the teenager dying, the possibility of her and Gale being arrested, and Ana's medical career ruined because Marybeth begged a misguided favor. Marybeth wanted to go home and climb into bed and pretend the whole mess was a nightmare to wake from.

Gale interrupted her thoughts. "Okay, the picture is on the way."

Marybeth checked her phone. She saw Gale's text and clicked on the photo. She studied the picture. The man stood next to Clay Moorhead and was holding the state title trophy at Texas Stadium. He had narrow eyes and a lantern jaw. Then her pulse started to race. She noticed a scar running down the man's Adam's apple. She thought back to the man in the hospital corridor. His hat had been pulled low and he'd been moving fast, but she'd seen the purple scar running like a stain down his throat.

"It's him, Gale," Marybeth said, her voice beginning to tremble. "Avery."

"Are you sure?"

"Yes. I'm sure."

"I'll bet anything he did something to the boy," Gale said, his voice tightening.

"Jesus, Gale . . ."

"That sumbitch."

"Please don't do anything that'll get you hurt. We already have enough trouble."

Gale went silent for a beat. "You know me, Marybeth. I need to find out what happened. It'll eat me up if I don't."

"Why not tell the authorities? Let them figure it out."

"Why would they believe us? We have zero credibility, right? We're lucky we haven't been locked up."

"What are you going to do?"

"I don't know. But I'll think of something."

"Gale, please don't make this whole thing any worse."

"That's not my intention, but we're in too deep to turn a blind eye," Gale said before asking, "is the boy getting any better?"

"No."

"The poor kid."

"I can't pray enough."

"How's Ana doing?"

"Trying to weather the storm."

"I spoke with Grayson."

Marybeth turned away from a nurse striding down the corridor. "What did he say?"

"He said if he was opposing counsel, he'd go for our throat."

"I would, too."

"Grayson was drinking."

"I feel like having a drink myself."

"You?"

Marybeth shook her head. "I hate alcohol, but it might make me feel better."

"It would make you feel worse."

Marybeth sighed and closed her eyes. "How can I feel worse, Gale? I'm watching a teenager die."

When the call with Marybeth ended, Gale stepped outside into the warm night. The cicadas buzzed incessantly like electricity running through a high-tension wire. The storage shed and barn were silhouetted in the moonlight. Beyond the outbuildings, he noticed the horses clumped together in the pasture. Mateo Santos had put them out for the night. Gale wondered if Avery had been the man who had knifed the teenager. As he thought about Avery's wrist he suddenly remembered during pre-season practice the scratches on Avery's face and the gash on his hand. There had to be an explanation for Avery and Marshall arriving late and cutting out early from practices, for their having changed clothes and bolted after the Sandington game.

Gale heard one of the horses snort and shake its mane. The others followed. He scanned the moonlit horizon for coyotes. They would sometimes slip into the pasture and spook the horses. When Gale was a boy, coyotes had once packed in the middle of the night and tried to take down a foal, but Gale's father, awakened by the coyotes' high-pitched, yipping sound and whinnying of the horses, had driven them off.

Avery was a predator, Gale thought. He had a capacity for violence lurking behind his dead-eyed stare. Avery could easily have killed Clay Moorhead and plunged a knife into the boy.

After a few moments, the horses quieted down. The night was silent again but for the buzz of cicadas. Gale stared up at the moon, which hung in a thinly veiled orange haze. It seemed to him that the walls of his life were closing in on him. He needed to act. There'd be no telling what the future would bring, but his gut told him to pursue Avery. If Gale wanted truth, Avery was his man.

Seventeen

Tuck gasped and shot upright in bed. She choked, trying to catch her breath. It was as if an eighteen-wheeler had been dumped on her chest. She had dreamt that Richie Williams had pulled a newborn baby out from under her car's hood. He'd held the wailing, grease-stained infant by the leg and cursed. "No wonder your car wouldn't start," he'd said, shaking his head.

Tuck looked wildly around the pitch-black bedroom and fought to breathe. After a few moments of terror, she realized she'd been dreaming. There was no Richie Williams and no grime-covered, crying baby. *My God, she thought. How could I have dreamt something so awful?*

She caught her breath, lifted herself out of bed, and pulled open the shade. In the feint moonlight, she could see the outline of her driveway and her neighbor's home across the street. She glanced at the red glow of her digital bedside clock. It was just after 2 a.m.

What Gale had said earlier about her car's starter bothered her. In twenty-four hours, Waters had threatened her, then a contract had floated onto her desk with a nice raise, then she had a dead engine. Coincidence or causality? Like Gale had said, working in Caton made you suspicious.

She turned from the window. She reminded herself that things weren't always what they seemed. As a school counselor and assistant principal, she'd seen a sea of smiling kids posing for selfies on social media and realized that some of those smiles hid stark truths: broken homes, depression, abuse, and addiction. In the world of Instagram, you were supposed to be happy and carefree. A ruse. Behind those winsome smiles misery festered.

But cars broke down all the time. Especially a decade-old Camry with 160,000 miles. Tuck looked over at the outline of her bed. She thought how nice it would be to get back under the sheets and drift off to sleep. She took a step toward the bed and felt a shiver. Then she turned, snapped on the light, changed into black leggings and a gray t-shirt, put her hair in a ponytail, grabbed her extra car keys, and a few minutes later stepped outside into the empty carport.

Resting against the house sat Mark's bicycle. Tuck hadn't touched it since his death. She recalled all the moments Mark had casually told her he was going for a long workout, only to wonder later if the *ride* he took was inside another woman. She tried to shake-off the thought as she walked the bike away from the carport. When Mark had purchased the road bike, Tuck had been stung by how much he'd spent. The Bianchi was tall for her, but after a few wobbles, soon she was moving smoothly through the warm night toward town.

At 3 a.m., Caton was deserted. Storefronts were shuttered, and the only light came from a scattering of streetlights. Tuck made sure to bypass Main Street until she neared the rear entrance of the auto shop which stood next to Panther Liquor Store. Only in Caton would a liquor store use the name of the school mascot to peddle booze, Tuck thought. The exploitation disgusted her. She slowed, braked, and slipped off the bike. She rested it against a wall behind the garage next to a couple of foul-smelling grease drums and started searching for her car amidst the vehicles crammed around the building. Under a dim streetlight, she found her car wedged in between a pickup and an SUV. For a moment she studied the Camry. She felt foolish. What was she looking for? She'd ridden three miles in the middle of the night on her dead husband's bike for what? Even if there was something wrong with the car, foul play, she'd have no clue how to identify it beyond what Richie Williams had told her.

Tuck studied the Camry and pulled out her spare keys. She was about to open the door when the sound of an approaching car caused her to duck behind the Camry to avoid being caught by the headlights. She could feel her temples pound when she realized the vehicle wasn't moving past the auto shop but turning toward her and pulling into the parking lot. Tuck slid away from her car and, bending at the waist, maneuvered between a row of vehicles before taking position behind a dumpster off to the side of the garage.

Tuck heard the crunch of gravel as a McClendon County Sheriff SUV slowly pulled in and came to a stop in front of the Camry. The driver killed the engine and headlights and slid out of the vehicle. Tuck could make out the figure of Billy Pax and watched with growing confusion as Pax approached the Camry and began to slide a flat metal bar between the driver side window and door. After fumbling for a few seconds, Pax grunted and pulled the door open. He was silhouetted by the car's cab light as Tuck watched him reach into her car. Moments later, she heard a click, and the pop of the trunk opening. She watched with growing anger as Pax turned, walked back to the SUV, and after a few seconds of rummaging in the back seat, pulled out a small package then brought it over and left it in Tuck's trunk.

NO HEART TO KILL

After Pax had pulled out of the parking lot, Tuck waited until the sound of his SUV had drifted off. When she felt safe, she walked quickly to her car, opened the door, and popped the trunk. She pulled back the tire well cover and started digging for the package. She finally found what she was looking for wedged into the tire well, and after closing the trunk, she sat in her car and carefully unwrapped the package. She knew immediately what she held was a bag of heroin. She was about to open the container when she heard another car approaching. With a racing heart, she shut the door quietly and ducked her head below the dash. The approaching car's headlights lit the Camry's cab and then to her relief, the vehicle slid past into the night.

After throwing the heroin in the dumpster next to the garage, Tuck pedaled hard, her fury growing with each spin of the tire. They'd tried to set her up. Pin a drug charge on her. It was an easy way to destroy her career and reputation. Now she realized how deep the corruption ran. Billy Pax was as filthy as the others.

She rode furiously past darkened store fronts and vacant lots toward the edge of town. The street was empty in the early morning hours but for a couple stray cats darting away when they heard Tuck's bike approach.

Tuck's mind raced. She tried to calm herself as she pedaled in the night. But it was impossible. As she approached Waters' Motors and spotted the dealership's gaudy neon sign, she felt her anger boil over into pure loathing.

When she rode onto the lot, she braked hard and came to a stop. She knew there were security cameras capturing her shadowy movements, but she didn't care. They'd know who did it. She wanted them to know. She climbed off the bike and started hunting around behind the poorly lit dealership until she found what she was searching for. A sledgehammer leaned against the cinder block wall next to a garage bay. Along with the sledgehammer, there were a couple of tire irons in a plastic bucket, a broken shovel, a grungy trash barrel, and a stack of worn tires. Tuck grabbed the sledgehammer. It was heavy and awkward, but her adrenaline was running hard. A few moments later, she faced the large plate glass showroom window holding the sledgehammer in her hands. Inside, she could see the latest model cars and trucks lit dimly by a few overhead track lights. She began to feel tears well. She didn't care anymore. She hated these men. She detested them. *You bastards* she said to herself lifting the sledgehammer over her shoulder and swinging it as hard as she could.

To Tuck's astonishment, the glass buckled but it didn't break. She stepped back and wiped tears away with her t-shirt and caught her breath. Determined, she took a few steps forward, lifted the sledgehammer again, and slammed it into the showroom window.

Glass exploded. Shards flew into the building and scattered across the tile floor. The violence of the act amazed her. After a few seconds, she dropped the sledgehammer. *Fuck you,* she said under her breath. *Fuck you, fuck you, fuck you.*

A few moments later, Tuck was pedaling hard through town. The exhilaration of shattering the window was beginning to fade. She yearned to feel a sense of satisfaction, but instead felt only growing dread. They'd come after her like never before.

With the muted whine of a shop vac sucking up glass in the showroom as background noise, Billy Pax sat slumped in Bart Waters' office as Waters, red-faced and seething, pointed his finger at him. Lloyd Avery and Buck Marshall sat off to the side as if they were watching a hog about to be devoured by a lion. Dean Spivey was nowhere to be seen.

Waters leaned forward, his eyes turning to slits. "We give you a simple task, and you screw it up. Tell me, how does Tuck figure out in the middle of the night that there's drugs in her car?"

Pax shrugged and bit his lip. His bowels churned, and he felt the nervous urge to plunge his finger into his ear and dig around. A good whiff might settle his nerves. "Hell, Bart, I don't know."

Waters glared. "You must have tipped your hand somehow."

Pax averted his eyes just as Waters turned to Avery and Marshall. "What now?"

Pax felt a wave of relief. He prayed Waters was moving on. Pax had no idea how Tuck had figured it out. He'd been extra careful. He'd waited until the middle of the night when he knew folks would be sleeping.

"There are other ways to make her quit," Avery finally said.

Waters rubbed his chin. "I don't like it. But I like what she knows even less. Use your imagination, boys. It needs to be an accident."

Pax suddenly felt sick to his stomach. Everything was amping up. Now he could be an accessory to murder.

"Does the punishment fit the crime?" Pax asked meekly.

"What are you saying?" Avery shot back.

Waters turned on Pax. "Don't you go soft on me, Billy. I won't have it."

Pax paled. He realized what Waters was telling him.

Waters turned back to Avery and said, "Do what you need to do, but don't screw it up. Hear me? I don't want a shitshow like with Clay."

Avery and Marshall glanced at each other and nodded.

"And Billy," Waters said.

"What, Bart?"

"I'm not done with you yet."

Pax thought he was going to shit. "*But Bart . . .*" Pax pleaded.

Waters looked at Avery and Marshall. "You boys can leave now unless you want to see Billy get skinned alive."

Avery and Marshall smiled like jackals as they stood to go.

Waters' jaw tightened. "We're going to have a little chat. Aren't we, Billy?"

Gale placed his father's 12-gauge Benelli in its sheepskin-lined leather case underneath the pickup's seat and a box of Federal 00 buckshot in the truck's glove box. He could still smell the gun oil on his hands. After Katie Tuck had told him what occurred the previous night, Gale was taking no chances. Gale hadn't told Marybeth about the Benelli. If he had, there'd have been hell to pay. And even riding around with the gun made him feel like a fraud. The only time he used it was shooting cracker shells to scare off predators. He hoped like hell the shotgun wouldn't come into play. He had no desire to kill.

Climbing into his truck, Gale struggled to put together the pieces of what seemed like an intricate puzzle. Dean Spivey's involvement in the drug trade, the teenager's violent reaction to Avery in the hospital, and Waters' grip on the town. He remembered the frustrated looks of Avery and Marshall when he had announced early morning pre-season practices. Had he interrupted a drug operation? Gale wondered if the boy had been stabbed in a drug deal gone wrong. Were Avery and Marshall working with Spivey? If so, where did Waters fit in? Was he the kingpin? Caton's version of the Godfather? Was Clay Moorhead involved and why a high-powered rifle round to his chest?

Gale didn't have all the answers, but he knew he'd better find them. Time was running out. Although he and Marybeth hadn't yet been charged for harboring the boy, the Midland County Sheriff's Department was circling. Grayson Wallace had been pushing back against the Midland County district attorney to keep the authorities at arm's length. Katie Tuck was in the middle of a bullseye, too. Given everything that was going on, Gale decided he needed to follow his instinct. He'd rather play offense than defense.

Against Marybeth's wishes, Gale had decided to tail Avery and Marshall. The last few weeks, Avery and Marshall had left practice before it was finished. In ordinary circumstances, Gale would have protested, but not coaching Caton High School, where the absence of his two assistant coaches was a source of relief. He didn't like the idea of playing amateur cop any more than Marybeth did, but waiting around to see what Waters was going to do to him and Tuck was out of the question.

A few minutes later, Gale turned off the ranch and headed south toward Caton. Gale thought of Marybeth standing vigil in the boy's hospital room. The boy hadn't shown any improvement. They'd pumped him full of drugs, and he was still burning with fever. In less than an hour, Josephine Santos would be picking up Tilly from school. Marybeth had told her principal about the boy and missed another day of teaching. She'd expected to be suspended, but her principal, a longtime friend and Kinney High School graduate, had instead been supportive. Despite the general sentiment against migrants, Gale knew how valuable Marybeth was to the school, so that didn't entirely surprise him.

During practice as the sun lowered in the sky, Caton's defensive end, a cattle rancher's kid who was being recruited hard by Arizona State, tripped and tumbled onto Eben Daly. Daly swore and picked himself off the turf clutching the wrist on his throwing hand. "I think it's broken, Coach," Daly said, gritting his teeth.

Gale's heart sank.

Soon Daly was being escorted off the field by the athletic trainer, and Gale knew it was time to end practice. The team would play Henderson in two days and, likely, Gale would have to play his backup quarterback, a quirky sophomore with attention deficit issues.

After Daly had left the field, Lloyd Avery had smirked and said, "I guess we'll be running the ball against Henderson, Coach. It's back to the Caton way."

Forty minutes later, after addressing the team and attending to Daly, who was headed with his father, Abraham, to the hospital for x-rays, Gale walked from underneath the stadium. He assumed he had missed Avery and Marshall but was surprised to see them climbing into Avery's truck. On occasion, after practice, Avery with his scarred throat and meaty hands, and Marshall, with his shaved head and hollow cheeks, would hang out in the coaches' conference room drinking longnecks with the other assistants. While Gale would never have allowed alcohol in the coaches' room at Kinney High School because it set a bad example, at Caton, the battles were endless. A couple of six packs in the conference room refrigerator was the least of his worries.

As Avery and Marshall were leaving the parking lot, Gale noticed Katie Tuck walking briskly across the pavement from the high school. Before leaving for practice, Gale had called Tuck to let her know his plan. Despite Gale's objections, Tuck had been adamant about joining him. When she approached, she said, "I'm going with you."

Gale shook his head. "Not a chance."

Tuck said, pointing, "You can shake your head all you want, but we'll lose them," and proceeded to sit on the hood.

"Let's go," he said grudgingly, keeping his eye fixed on Avery's truck.

Gale and Tuck parked down the street from a small, grimy convenience store with a gas pump in front after Avery and Marshall stopped on their way out of town. Nearly 10 minutes later, the two coaches walked out of the store carrying plastic bags and bottled water. Soon they pulled out and less than a quarter mile later turned into Waters' Motors. They parked Avery's pickup to one side of the dealership and disappeared into the building. Gale had kept a safe distance and pulled his truck into a strip mall lot across the street. He noticed a large sheet of plywood covering the showroom window where Tuck had shattered the glass.

"How'd you break it?" Gale asked, turning to Tuck.

"A sledgehammer."

"You weren't messing around."

She gave a half smile. "It took me two swings."

Gale frowned at her. "You shouldn't have come."

"The stakes are as big for me as they are for you. In fact, bigger."

"There could be trouble."

"I can handle myself," she said.

"Not if it gets dicey."

"Dicey?" Tuck asked, taking off her sunglasses and folding them in her hands. Her eyes narrowed. She was wearing jeans, a faded green T-shirt, and boots. She must have changed clothes after school, Gale thought.

"I thought we're just following them, seeing what they're up to."

Gale shrugged. "I can't promise that. If we stumble into something they don't want us to see, we could find ourselves in hot water."

"What's the plan for that?"

"There's a 12 gauge under the seat."

"Good," she said resolutely. "I'd like to be the one to pull the trigger."

"You think?"

She set her jaw. She paused for a moment and said, "I know where I'll be aiming. It won't be pretty."

"Have you ever fired a weapon?"

"When we were dating, Mark once took me to a shooting range. I fired a pistol at a cardboard man."

"Your aim?"

"Shaky at first, but it got better."

Gale reached over and opened the dust-covered glove compartment. The pickup had gone all summer without a wash. "Well, I pray you don't get that chance, but here are shells in case we need them." He grabbed the box of ammo and showed Tuck before returning them and snapping shut the glove box door.

"What do you think we're going to find?" Tuck asked.

Gale shrugged. "Nothing good."

Tuck slid down in the seat, and said, "Here they come."

They watched Avery and Marshall emerge from the car dealership. Avery was stuffing a half-eaten sandwich in his mouth. "They've changed clothes. They've put on their Sunday finest, " Tuck commented.

Avery and Marshall had shed their coaching attire and now wore grungy jeans, t-shirts, and boots. Gale turned to Tuck, smiled thinly, and said, "You match."

Tuck looked down at her t-shirt and faded jeans and said, "I'd like to think I pull it off better than they do."

Gale wore Caton High School gym shorts and a gray Lone Star t-shirt. He kicked himself for not changing after practice, but he thought Avery would already be gone. Foolishly, he was wearing light colored cross-trainers.

Gale started up the truck as Avery and Marshall climbed into Avery's pickup.

"Let's go," Gale said.

"Don't follow too closely."

"I won't."

Tuck took a deep breath. "I don't really want to fire that shotgun."

An hour later, Avery and Marshall had turned south on Rt. 285, Death Highway. Gale wasn't surprised the two men were headed toward the border. Ahead lay Sanderson and Dryden, and Gale wondered if the cut off would be before they hugged the Rio Grande toward Del Rio. Gale thought about the time his truck had broken down years before south of Dryden. He was headed to Del Rio to pick up an engine part for his father. With a Nokia phone in his hand and no cell service, Gale had sat on the hood of his pickup on a warm spring afternoon and waited for help. Finally, a rancher had stopped and given him a ride to town.

As the hazy sky turned to dusk, they rode through the heart of the Permian Basin. Ahead, Avery and Marshall kept a steady pace. Gale was glad the growing dark would make it harder to identify his truck, but he found himself fighting a deep-seated sadness. He hated this road. When he passed the spot where his parents had died, Gale felt heartsick. He fought the growing lump in his throat. All his emotions were hitting him at once.

"You okay?" Tuck asked, sensing his melancholy.

Gale nodded and looked ahead.

Tuck wasn't buying it. "Something's up, something more than what we're doing now. You've changed."

Gale shrugged but didn't trust himself to speak.

"My husband kept everything bottled up. He led this secret life where he refused to let me in. Why do men do that?" She paused. "Do you share your feelings with Marybeth?"

"Sometimes."

Tuck sounded every bit the school psychologist, Gale thought.

"Would you tell her what's bothering you now?" Tuck asked.

"She'd know."

"Intuition?"

Gale turned to Tuck. He said quietly, "We just passed the spot where my parents were killed. Head on collision."

The color drained from Tuck's face. "I'm so sorry. I shouldn't have pried. Professional hazard."

"Hell. There's no need to apologize."

Tuck asked him softly, "How did it happen?"

"A tanker truck. The driver fell asleep."

Tuck turned and stared out the passenger window. After a while, she murmured, "I should have left Caton after Mark died."

Gale noticed Tuck's pensive expression. While he was thinking how to respond, she asked, "Why'd you quit coaching San Antonio? You were Coach of the Year. Famous. Who walks away from that?"

"I love my wife and daughter. I didn't want to lose them."

"Yeah, I guess that sort of life could be hard on a marriage, but that reminds me, you've never told me why you took the Caton job."

Gale tapped his finger on the steering wheel. His face was lit by an oncoming car. Night was coming, and Gale strained to follow the taillights of Avery's pickup ahead. He was reminded again he should have listened to Marybeth and had gotten his eyes checked. The side of the highway was lined with rigs, floodlit under the darkening sky. The light pollution made it more difficult to follow the outline of the road. "Waters didn't give me a choice."

"What, did he have something on you, Gale?"

Gale thought for a moment. He sighed. "A family secret."

"Blackmail?"

Gale nodded. He felt the urge to tell Tuck everything. He trusted her. Waters had hurt her, too. Her vulnerability mirrored his own. She'd understand. But just then, he noticed the directional signal flashing on Avery's pickup. Soon Avery and Marshall pulled off Death Highway and were headed along a gravel road. Gale drove past the road and pulled off onto the shoulder. Looking back, he could see the flare stacks of a brightly lit oil and gas facility and noticed Avery's truck pulling into a dirt parking lot next to a chain link fence, a construction trailer, and a handful of heavy-duty vehicles. Avery parked next to a nondescript white paneled van. A few seconds later, Gale and Tuck watched Avery and Marshall climb into the van and pull out of the parking area toward the highway. Tuck and Gale ducked in their seats as the vehicle passed. Then Gale put the pickup in gear and followed.

Eighteen

Pumpville, Texas sat 17 miles from the Rio Grande. In the time of steam locomotives, Pumpville provided water for the Southern Pacific Railroad. When the need for water was replaced in the 1920s by Diesel-fired engines, railroad executives sent their people elsewhere, and Pumpville became a ghost town. The only hint left of past prosperity was the Baptist church, with its stone façade and dying congregation.

Gale was confused when the van pulled off Highway 90 and headed north under a vast, star-lit sky. He'd never gone off the highway to Pumpville. There was no need. There was little there. He and Tuck hung back and watched the taillights of Avery and Marshall's truck fade. Gale wanted to make sure he gave them plenty of distance. But why head north?

Gale killed the pickup's lights and inched along, slowly trailing as Avery and Marshall's van pulled off the narrow paved road a few hundred yards ahead and parked in a dirt lot next to a dilapidated wooden structure amidst the scrub and cactus. Gale spotted a dirt track, turned off and crept along about the length of a football field and killed the engine. He turned to Tuck and said, "Let's try to get a closer look."

She nodded, and without a word, opened the glove box door, pulled out the box of shotgun shells, and handed them to Gale in the darkened cab.

"Looking for trouble?" he asked with a half smile.

"Just in case," she answered.

Gale reached under the bench seat and pulled out the 12 gauge. He climbed quietly out of the unlit cab, unzipped the leather case, and gripped the shotgun. He carefully placed the case in the truck and quietly slipped five shells into the chamber. Even loading the shotgun made him uneasy. It was one thing to shoot cracker shells to scare off a mangy coyote. Using it on something, a man no less, was something else entirely. He tried to put the thought aside.

He and Tuck kept low under a sky brimming with a million pinpricks of light and moved in the shadows across the rugged terrain toward Avery and

Marshall. Avery had killed the engine, and the van sat in the dark a few hundred yards ahead. Once again, Gale cursed himself for not changing into jeans before he left Caton. He nearly yelped when he stepped on a cactus and the searing, needle-like barbs pierced his ankle.

Gale grimaced and kept moving. Besides the pain in his leg, Gale's damaged ribs ached. Are they warning me, Gale wondered? Tuck followed closely and at one point reached out for Gale's hand as they stepped across a dry, overgrown irrigation ditch. Her skin felt soft and warm, and it reminded Gale of how much he wished he were home with Marybeth, curled in bed, secure in her arms.

As they grew near to the parked van, they made out the figures of Avery and Marshall standing near the vehicle. Gale and Tuck moved forward a few more yards and settled behind a limestone outcropping. Gale could hear Avery and Marshall conversing but couldn't make out their words. The only distinct sound was Tuck's breathing as she knelt beside him. As they watched, a coyote yipped and was followed by others joining in chorus. At the sound, Tuck reached out and grabbed Gale's forearm, startling him with the strength of her grip.

Gale turned and tightened his hold on the 12 gauge when he saw the lights of a vehicle approaching. The headlights grew larger as the vehicle sped toward them. When the vehicle pulled into the dirt lot, Gale squinted and saw that it was an oversized border patrol pickup with light bars on top. With the engine still running and the headlights illuminating Avery and Marshall, two men climbed out of the pickup wearing border patrol uniforms. Without a word, Avery went to the pickup's flatbed and pulled open the tailgate, while Marshall began to untie the lashing which secured the canvas covering the load. The two border patrol agents watched with their hands on their hips, as if they'd done this repeatedly before. Show up in the middle of nowhere, deliver the goods in the dead of night, and step out of the way, as if they didn't want to get their hands any dirtier.

Gale shook his head as Avery and Marshall each lifted a half dozen medium sized boxes and placed them in the back of the van. It was all coming together. This is what's going on, Gale thought with disgust. This was what Avery and Marshall were cutting out of practice for. It all seemed to fit. Almost certainly Avery and Marshall were handling hundreds of thousands of dollars' worth of narcotics. But now he knew the corruption ran even deeper than he'd supposed. Waters controlled the McClendon County Sheriff's office and border patrol agents. How far did the corruption run up the ladder? Who else did he have under his thumb?

Gale recalled reading about corruption in a town near Laredo. One family had controlled nearly all the municipal and school district contracts and over a quarter century had stolen millions of dollars. On a more sinister scale, Gale read with fascination about Whitey Bulger, the infamous organized crime boss who ruled Boston. In the 1970s and 80s, Bulger and his cronies had the entire Boston FBI office on the take. Even more astonishing, Bulger had a friend in an even higher place. His brother, Billy, was President of the Massachusetts State Senate and allegedly made sure Whitey got what he wanted. If corruption could run that deep in a town near Laredo, or a city like Boston, why not in a dust bowl like West Texas, where there were millions to be made in drug trafficking? It was all coming together: Waters and the state senator, H.W. Owen, were best of friends. Behind the facade of selling cars and buying oil and gas rights, Waters and his cronies were free to control Caton with an iron fist, stealing from town coffers. But that wasn't enough for Waters. Like Bulger, he had used his connections to corrupt law enforcement to become complicit in his operations, which clearly included drug smuggling. But why in the world would they be hiding fentanyl in Spivey's garden shed? It made no sense unless Spivey had a side hustle that Johnny stumbled on.

What Gale and Tuck were witnessing, however, didn't explain the teenager's reaction when he saw Avery at the hospital. It didn't explain the cut on Avery's arm or the earlier wound on Avery's hand and scratches on Avery's face. The exchange between the border agents and Avery and Marshall seemed casual and commonplace.

Gale was about to give Tuck the signal to move back toward his pickup when Tuck gave a muffled cry, and he felt something cool and leathery brush his elbow where he had propped himself on the outcropping. He froze. He knew rattlers rarely hunted after sundown. He resisted the urge to panic and held his breath as the shadowy outline of a snake slithered across the limestone in front of him. Gale realized it was a night snake. Mildly venomous, the reptile posed no threat to humans. Gale shot Tuck a look. She had covered her mouth with her hand. Gale glanced toward Avery and Marshall and the two border agents as the snake disappeared in the brush. They'd turned and were looking in their direction. Gale tightened his grip on the shotgun and braced himself. The men started moving toward them when suddenly coyotes struck up again, their lonely cries echoing across the plain.

At the sound of coyotes, the men stopped and stared into the night. They listened as the shrill cries pierced the darkness. After a few moments, to Gale's relief, they turned and walked back toward their vehicles.

Soon they were gone.

When Gale and Tuck climbed into Gale's pickup, Tuck said, "I almost got us killed."

"The coyotes' timing was impeccable."

"Thank God."

"Remind me not to run coyotes off my ranch for a while. I owe them one."

Tuck's phone lit up. Tuck turned her attention to her cell. "Who's texting me at 1 a.m.?"

Gale watched Tuck read the text. She closed her eyes and put her head down.

"What happened?" Gale asked.

Tuck hung her head. "Abraham Daly texted me. Martin Keller died."

Gale leaned back. "I'm sorry, Katie."

After a moment, she slowly looked up and stared straight ahead. She paused. "We have to call the DEA. We have to tell someone," she said angrily.

In theory, Gale knew Tuck was right. The reality was different. They had no concrete proof that a drug exchange had taken place with border patrol agents. For all Gale knew, those boxes in the border agents' pickup could have contained anything. It was Gale and Tuck's word against the words of Waters and his cronies. Anyway, if the corruption ran as deep as Gale imagined, Gale and Tuck's complaint would fall on deaf ears. Surely Waters would orchestrate a smear campaign that would have everyone asking, "What was the principal of Caton High School doing in the middle of the night in Pumpville, Texas with Gale McClanahan?" It would only get worse when the news of the criminal charges looming over him came to light.

Gale thought about Martin Keller's parents. The idea of losing Tilly made him wince. He couldn't imagine their devastation. While Tuck was right about getting help from the authorities, Gale knew they needed more evidence. He also recognized that he was so far over his head that proceeding any further without Wallace's counsel could have disastrous effects for him, but more importantly, for his family. If the teenager's violent reaction to Avery originated from some earlier interaction, Gale needed to know why.

Ephraim would never forget the man's face and the scar running down his throat. Ephraim had fought, but the man had gripped Ephraim's neck like a vice and had lifted him off the ground and hurled him into the brush. Ephraim had tried to get up, but the man had stood over him, kicking him viciously in the ribs. As Ephraim had curled into a ball to shield himself from the blows, the sharp toe of the man's boot had found a kidney, and the boy had shrieked in pain. One of the migrants, a kind man Ephraim and Maria had called Jose, who had offered them food and water during the night, had charged the man and leaped onto his back, but the other gringo, nearly as big as the one with the scar, had struck him on the head with the butt of his gun. Jose had fallen like a stone and lay crumpled on the ground. Then the man with the gun had pointed the barrel at the group of migrants, driving them back, while the man who had kicked Ephraim slammed shut the refrigerator truck's doors. "Maria," Ephraim had screamed as the men climbed quickly into the truck. Seconds later, under a canopy of cold stars, the vehicle had groaned as it bounced away on the hard-packed dirt track, its taillights fading in the distance.

Marybeth woke in the darkened room when she heard the boy cry out and begin to moan. He moved his head from side to side. His hair was damp, and his pallid face was clouded with pain. She lifted herself from the recliner, carefully sat on the edge of the bed, and put her hand on his forehead. The poor thing, she said to herself. Get better. Please get better. Then Marybeth heard the teenager cry out for Maria. She'd heard him call for her before. Who was Maria? Who was this boy? She didn't even know his name. Marybeth bit her lip. Please don't die. Dear God, please let him live, she begged before settling back into the recliner and falling asleep.

When Marybeth awoke, a nurse was bent over the teenager. His chest was moving peacefully up and down. Then Marybeth heard the young Filipino nurse say, "98.6," as she put her digital thermometer on the metal tray next to the bed and broke into a smile. Marybeth smiled, too, then opened the drapes as a soft yellow light filtered into the room.

"What is the saying?" the nurse asked. "We gave him everything but the kitchen, and it worked."

"Kitchen sink," Marybeth corrected.

The nurse laughed. "The doctors will be very, very pleased."

"Yes." Marybeth felt a wave of relief. Later in the morning, she was to meet with the Midland County Sheriff. The day before, Ana Torres had told Marybeth there could be manslaughter charges filed if the teenager died. *Denying appropriate medical care, Torres had said. Felony manslaughter.* Marybeth hadn't told Gale. She didn't want to burden him any further. She had been tempted to call Grayson Wallace but decided against it. Why go down that rat hole of fear?

"You think he's out of the woods?" Marybeth asked the nurse, who was replacing an empty IV bag. She couldn't remember ever feeling as tired and emotionally drawn.

The nurse shrugged. "Sepsis is funny. But I think he's going to be okay."

Marybeth nodded. She wanted to close her eyes and sleep. Instead, she softly patted the boy's arm and went to the hospital's cafeteria to fetch coffee and call Gale.

After Gale learned the good news about the boy and told Marybeth what he and Tuck had seen the night before, he found Mateo Santos carrying a hay bale over each shoulder to the horse pasture. "The boy's fever broke," Gale said to Santos. One of the mares, pretty with a patch of white on her forehead, was nudging along the fence wanting to be fed.

Santos said, "Thank goodness," and crossed himself.

Gale briefly filled Santos in on what had occurred with Avery. Santos rested the hay bales on the ground and kicked at the dirt as Gale spoke.

"I need to know more, Mateo," Gale said, his eyes narrowing. "I need to know why the teenager went crazy when he saw Lloyd Avery."

Santos eyed him.

"I need you to come to the hospital with me and find out what's going on. Would you do that?"

Santos took a step back. "I've tried, Gale. The boy doesn't want to talk. I don't think he's involved with a drug ring. He doesn't seem like a criminal at all."

Gale looked past Santos. A turkey vulture was circling a few hundred yards away. The sky was a sharp blue. There wasn't a wisp of clouds. "I don't think so either, but we need the truth. My life, Marybeth's, and Ana's all depend on knowing."

"What if he refuses?"

"You'll get him to talk."

Santos' face darkened. "I'll speak to him, but I don't see why he'd be any more willing to talk now."

"I need to know." Gale felt a growing frustration. "Just remember, your living may depend on it, too. If I end up in prison, you may end up unemployed."

"When do you want to go? Now?"

Gale nodded. "Yeah, I got no time. The Midland County Sheriff would like to throw the book at me."

"What about the horses?"

"Text Mason and tell him to leave what he's doing." Hayes was working the fence lines, making sure they were holding up.

"I need to tell Josephine that I'm going to Midland."

"You do that."

"He's a kid, Gale," Santos said, pulling his phone from his back pocket. "He's no criminal."

"Let's go," Gale said impatiently. "The clock's ticking."

Johnny Spivey was sitting in a hard-backed hickory chair in the Commandant's office waiting for what fresh hell waited for him. His stomach roiled, and under the arms of his Hood Military Academy uniform, he sopped with sweat. Johnny's escape plan had been ill-fated from the start. He had crept out of the barrack with a knapsack slung over his shoulder as the other cadets slept, only to find Stolich sneaking a smoke behind one of the dumpsters resting next to the dormitory. Stolich had dropped his cigarette, and after realizing who had startled him, had walked slowly toward Johnny in the darkness. Johnny had started to bolt, but he knew he stood no chance. Stolich was bigger and faster, would run Johnny down, and give Stolich reason to pummel him again. After two or three strides, Johnny froze and thrust his hands in the air like a prisoner of war. Then as Stolich, smiling as if he had trapped a rat, had grabbed Johnny by the scruff of the neck and had shoved him toward the barrack.

He'd had it loosely worked out. Get to Carlsbad, then hitch a ride west before he was found AWOL. His fantasy was to somehow get to LA. He would change his name, smoke weed, and hang out in a cool place like Malibu. There'd be girls like Melanie Sprague to hook up with, and best of all, he'd never have to see Hood Military Academy, dickhead Stolich, or the Commandant again. No more towel whipping in the showers and douchebags kicking in the toilet stall door when he was taking a dump. No more reveille at 5 a.m., crappy food, and three-mile runs wearing tactical boots in 90-degree heat. And best of all, he would be able to settle the score with his father for imprisoning him in this hellhole. At first he'd thought only of turning him in to the cops, but once the plan formed to start a life in LA, he realized he could blackmail the old bastard for all he was worth.

When the door to the Commandant's office swung open, Johnny knew he was screwed. The Commandant was followed by Stolich. The Commandant's cold eyes burned a hole through Johnny, but it was Stolich's presence that made Johnny shrink. Johnny had thought about ratting out Stolich and telling the Commandant that the prefect was smoking a butt, but he knew snitching would lead to a world of hurt, so he kept his mouth shut. The Commandant walked around to his desk. Stolich stood at attention, but something about his face terrified Johnny. It was nearly the same sadistic look his father had when he struck him.

After the Commandant sat, to Johnny's horror, he turned to Stolich, and said in a gravelly voice, "We need to teach Cadet Spivey a lesson, Captain Stolich."

Stolich straightened his already rigid frame and asked, "Teach him a lesson, Sir?"

The Commandant nodded and leaned back in his high-backed swivel chair. He looked at Johnny. "Clearly you need to learn how we do things at Hood."

Johnny stared blankly at the Commandant.

"I believe in leadership. Pure and simple. The more ownership cadets demonstrate, the more we empower outstanding young men." The Commandant's gaze turned to Stolich. " Isn't that right, Captain Stolich?"

"Yes, sir."

The Commandant tapped his forefinger on his sprawling oak desk. "This is what we're going to do, Cadet Spivey. I'm going to ask Captain Stolich to take charge of your discipline. I'm sure he'll be measured and appropriate." The Commandant looked at Stolich and asked, "Right, Captain?"

"Yes, sir." Stolich gave a crisp salute.

"Captain Stolich's going to make a man out of you," the Commandant said, pointing his finger at Johnny.

Johnny's mouth opened but no words came out.

Stolich saluted again.

"You're both dismissed. And Cadet Spivey," the Commandant said. "You do what Captain Stolich tells you. I don't want to see you in this office again."

"He'll learn his lesson," Stolich said, still at attention. "I'll make sure of it, sir."

A hot breeze rolled across the parking lot as Santos slowly followed Gale into the hospital. Santos' reluctance to be a willing partner in questioning the teenager bothered Gale, all the more so because he had only a few hours' sleep the night before. Gale knew there was an unwritten code among Latino citizens. Mateo Santos had gone to extraordinary measures to save the teenager from dying in a ditch. Of course, he wanted to protect him. Mateo Santos was a proud, loyal man, an expert horseman, a superb ranch hand, and a decorated veteran, and Gale held great respect for his employee, but at this point Gale's search for truth overrode any blind loyalty to the boy or to Santos. It was time he looked after his family and himself.

When he got to the hospital entrance, he realized that Santos had stopped ten yards behind him. He turned fully around and snapped, "All I'm asking you to do is translate, Mateo."

"You can find another person to do that. This is Texas. There's no shortage of Spanish speakers."

Gale pulled off his Stetson and wiped his forehead with his sleeve. "The boy trusts you."

"You want me to interrogate, not translate."

"Maybe. But I'm not looking to hang the kid."

"You may not be, but they're plenty of people who will."

"What the teenager says stays with us. Promise." Gale realized how disingenuous he sounded. Santos was no fool.

Santos and Gale stepped away from the hospital entrance when an older couple exited the building. They appeared tired and sad and didn't acknowledge Gale or Santos. Heavily stooped, the man needed the woman's help to navigate the stainless-steel revolving door. When the couple was out of earshot, Santos said, his olive skin reddening, "I get all the problems the boy has brought. And I delivered him to your doorstep. But I'm not going to help you be the kid's executioner."

"You've made that clear, Mateo."

"But you're not hearing me. You're pushing me and it feels like you're going to push the boy."

Gale threw up his arms. "My ass is on the line, not to mention Marybeth and Ana's. Considering that no one listened to me in the first place, I'm showing considerable restraint."

"Just remember what you knew when you brought him into your house, that he's a hurt and terribly frightened boy all alone in a strange country. Can you do that?"

Marybeth stood in the corner of the hospital room while Gale and Santos pulled chairs up close to the boy's bed. The teenager had been conscious earlier and had sipped water before falling back to sleep. Gale gently shook the boy's arm, and the teenager's eyes shot open, and he looked at Gale and Mateo with a mixture of confusion and alarm. Gale noticed the burst blood vessels around the boy's irises, the hollowness of his face, and his fetid breath. Gale felt a pang of guilt. He thought about Santos' words, but too much was at stake. Unfortunately, Clay Moorhead's grisly murder had flung open a pandora's box of questions, and Gale felt sure that the boy had answers that could be key to solving the mystery.

There was no turning back.

"Ask him about the man with the scar on his throat he saw in the hospital. See if he remembers, Mateo."

As Santos asked the boy about Avery, Gale could see a transformation in the teenager's face, but then the boy turned his head toward the pillow, averting his eyes from both of them.

A few seconds passed.

"Ask him again," Gale said, his voice hardening. Tell him we need to know so that we can help him."

Santos stared at Gale. Reluctantly, he repeated the question. The boy avoided eye contact and remained silent.

Gale felt his frustration grow. Clearly the boy recognized Avery. He reached over and took the boy's jaw in his hand and gently shifted the teenager's head so he was facing Gale. "Ask him now, Mateo," Gale said, gripping the boy's jaw while the teenager's eyes grew wide with fear.

Santos said, "I don't like this."

"Again," Gale snapped.

"Gale," Marybeth said, alarmed.

Gale said, "Now, Mateo."

Marybeth stepped forward and put her hand on Gale's arm, gently but insistently pulling his hand away from the boy's face. She gave Gale a hard look and pointed her head to the chair to direct him away from the bed altogether. She said softly to Santos, "Mateo, ask him about Maria."

When Marybeth said the girl's name, the boy's mouth opened in surprise.

"Maria?" Santos asked the boy.

The boy's eyes started to well. Marybeth brushed a wisp of hair away from the teenager's eyes.

"Who's Maria?" Santos repeated in Spanish. "Your sister?"

The boy shook his head.

"Who is she?" Santos asked.

Gale studied the boy's expression. The teenager was fighting back tears.

"We want to help you," Marybeth said. "Tell him that, Mateo."

Santos nodded. Although Marybeth was exhausted and about to meet with a Midland County sheriff, Gale could see how serene she was in stark contrast to his exasperation.

"Maria?" Santos asked once more. "*Novia?*"

A tear rolled down the boy's cheek. He turned his gaze to Marybeth and slowly nodded.

"Where is she?" Santos asked.

The boy coughed. Marybeth gave him a sip of water from a plastic cup resting on the bedside table.

"I don't know," the boy whispered in Spanish.

Santos leaned back in his chair and glanced at Marybeth. He turned to the teenager. "When did you see her last?" Santos asked.

The teenager closed his eyes. "When they abandoned us. That's all I remember."

"Where did you cross?"

"The del Carmen."

Santos translated, then he and Gale exchanged knowing glances. A crossing was nearly impossible in that part of the borderlands, south of Sanderson. An undocumented immigrant faced a series of severe obstacles to enter. Gale had spent little time in the borderlands, but he knew Santos had grown up in Sanderson and knew the territory. The area was marked by a gauntlet of canyons, jagged mountains, and 2,000-foot cliffs.

The teenager wiped the tears away with the back of his hand. Marybeth pulled the rolling stand for the IV drip closer to the bed so the boy wouldn't tear away the port.

"*Que pasa?*" Santos asked, leaning closer, suddenly taking the lead.

The boy hesitated.

"You can tell us," Santos continued in Spanish. Santos gave Gale a look of warning before turning back to the boy. "There's no need to fear us."

Gale backed away from the bed.

Marybeth took the teenager's hand and gently squeezed it.

"What happened?" Santos repeated.

The teenager turned his head and looked away as if he were trying to formulate what he was about to say. Gale watched him closely.

"Tell us," Santos said.

The boy started to speak, never making eye contact. His voice trembled as Santos carefully translated.

Several minutes later, after recounting how Maria had been torn from him by the man with the scar on his throat, how the man named Diego had knifed him after stealing migrants' money, and the blur of his desperate escape from Del Rio, the teenager finished. Gale glanced at Santos, but he was staring at the floor. Marybeth turned to Gale and said sharply, "Avery, that son of a bitch."

Before he left the room, Santos leaned forward in his chair and asked the boy, "What's your name?"

The boy hesitated. His lips were slightly parted. He whispered, "Ephraim," as he stared blankly at the bone-white hospital room wall. "Ephraim Hernandez."

Gale drifted around the hospital trying to find cell reception. He finally turned to an overweight orderly pushing a mop near the cafeteria and said, "I can't get a bar." Gale's head hurt, and he was fighting to stay alert.

The man shook his head. "The walls are too thick. Too much concrete and steel." He pointed outdoors to a small courtyard surrounded by glass.

Gale stepped out into the empty courtyard and blinked in the blinding sunlight. It was early afternoon and the day had brought no relief from the heat. Wrought iron benches circled a small, trickling fountain depicting an elaborate angel of mercy pouring water into a cement bowl. Along the edges of the courtyard ran a bed of pink and purple petunias arching toward the sun.

Gale pulled out his phone, and a few seconds later, Grayson Wallace answered.

Wallace asked, "What gives, Brutus?"

Gale felt a bead of sweat run down the small of his back. He wished he wasn't wearing new jeans. The Wranglers felt hot and sweaty, and the stiff denim rubbed painfully against the cactus scratches on his ankle. He told Wallace about the exchange he and Tuck had witnessed the night before and what the boy had recounted about Lloyd Avery.

Gale was met with silence. A rarity for Wallace.

"Are you still there, Grayson?" Gale asked, wondering if Wallace had been cut off.

"Still here, my boy."

"Where do we go from here?"

"You said border agents?"

"Yes."

"And the McClendon County Sheriff is on Waters' payroll?"

"That's right."

"Sounds like Bart isn't as small a swindler as I thought. Running narcotics and smuggling undocumented migrants. Then again, he was best friends with that cretin H.W. Owen, so perhaps I shouldn't be surprised."

"Toss in kidnapping," Gale reminded. Gale didn't want to think about what Avery had done with the teenager's girl.

"I could make some calls . . ." Wallace's voice drifted away.

"But?" Gale asked.

"It's your word against theirs."

"So?"

"Not 'so.' You've harbored an illegal immigrant, and you've allegedly withheld appropriate medical care. You have very little credibility. I've told you that. Bart is seen as a pillar of the Caton community. A bastion of good citizenship."

"Really?"

"Perceptions, Brutus. Don't underestimate perceptions. I've learned in forty years of practicing law, that even a toad can be seen as a prince."

"What are you saying?"

"We can call the DEA and every other law enforcement agency in West Texas. Without evidence, there will be little sympathy, even for a famous coach, given your present circumstances."

"What about the bogus contracts? Bid rigging? The boy? What about his story?"

"It could be seen as just that. A story. He's not credible. He's in this country illegally. He could be a thief and a liar. Maybe a murderer. As for the bogus contracts, if Waters' corruption runs that deep, the chances of obstruction are good. Likely he's not the only one dipping into the cesspool."

"But the boy's story adds up. Why else would he go crazy when he saw Avery in the hospital?"

"Delirium."

Gale grunted. "You're telling me it's a dead end."

"Not entirely. You have some pieces, but you need more. Other than the contracts, you have only circumstantial evidence and hearsay."

Gale's jaw tightened. "But why not call the DA and tell him what you know? At least see if he'll act?"

Wallace gave a sardonic laugh. "He despises me. I trounced him in court too many times, but don't underestimate the heroic efforts I'm putting forth to prevent you, Marybeth, and that doctor friend of yours from being charged. Bottom line, we need more credible evidence largely because you, Marybeth, and the boy are sorely lacking in credibility. Anything you say right now will seem as though you're trying to save yourselves from your own legal difficulties."

Gale felt perspiration beading below where the sweat-stained leather band of his Stetson pressed against his forehead. He felt alone and powerless. He could hear Wallace wheezing. He gritted his teeth and said, "I got to get off the phone, Grayson."

"Don't do anything rash, Brutus."

"Seems like you're leaving me no other option."

"Not so, my boy. There are always options. As you grow older you will learn that there is a lot of wisdom in the adage, 'Slow and steady wins the race.' In the past, I recall rashness as being your guiding principle. And it hasn't always worked well for you. You wanted my counsel and there it is."

"When are you coming to Midland?" Gale asked. Later that afternoon, Marybeth was scheduled to meet with the Midland County Sheriff.

"Soon. Tell Marybeth not to say a word until I arrive."

"Okay."

"And Gale. I suppose I should tell you this now. I don't want you to hear it from anyone else."

"What?"

"If the boy had died, they would have charged you with manslaughter."

"Manslaughter?"

"Yes. As bleak as your present situation may appear, it could have been bleaker."

Gale said nothing.

"Consider yourself fortunate."

"Fortunate is not what I'm feeling right now, Grayson," Gale said.

Wallace paused and sighed. "Value the silver linings in everything, my boy. Even a hot mess like this. And remember, slow and steady."

Santos met Gale in the hospital lobby. As they stepped outside and walked to Gale's pickup, Gale turned and asked as he and Santos neared his truck. "Where do you think Avery and Marshall are picking up the migrants?"

Santos shook his head. He'd grown up in Sanderson and understood the borderland's challenges. "It could be anywhere. It's brutal country. Most of it has to be covered by foot, maybe an ATV. Horses are the best bet. I've ridden into Big Bend and into the del Carmen."

"Where would you bring a truck to load migrants?"

Santos looked down for a moment, thinking. "Maybe northwest of Dryden Crossing."

"Are there roads in there?"

Santos smiled thinly. "I wouldn't call them roads."

"It has to be a place where a truck can get access."

Santos paused. "There are very few places where that can happen. But I know one."

"Where is it, Mateo?"

"There's an abandoned mercury mine. My father told me about it when I was a kid. Most of the mining is done south of Alpine in Brewster and Presidio counties, but they tried mining for it in the mountains south of Sanderson."

"Could we get in there without being noticed?"

"There's only one way in and one way out. Doubtful."

"What about horses?"

Santos wiped his brow. The sun beat down on them. Cooler weather couldn't come fast enough, Gale thought. Santos said warily to Gale as they neared Gale's pickup, "What are you thinking?"

"I'm not sure. But I may need to take matters into my own hands. Waters has bought nearly everyone off. We need to catch them in the act."

Santos frowned. "We?"

"You want Avery and Marshall to smuggle more people? Take more girls?"

"It's rough country."

"You ride better than anyone I know."

Santos broke into a half smile. "I'm not worried about me."

"Hell, Mateo, I rode the junior rodeo circuit."

"100 years ago. No offense, but now you're a football coach and a gentleman rancher."

"Gentleman rancher?"

Santos slowly broke into a grin. Santos' good-natured dig told Gale that he hadn't lost Santos over the boy.

"We'd have to trailer the horses, then possibly ride in at night. Dangerous as hell for a lot of reasons."

"What are the chances we find Avery and Marshall?"

Santos shrugged and said to Gale, "Not knowing the time or place?"

"A needle in a haystack?"

Santos nodded as they reached Gale's pickup.

"We have to try something," Gale said. "Are you in?"

Santos' eyes thinned. "Only if I get to kill the sons of bitches."

Santos' ferocity surprised Gale. "Remember, it's not Iraq."

"We'll see," Santos said, looking away. "The borderland is lawless. Men die. Some are never found."

"What are you saying?"

Santos stared at Gale. "Those *cabrons* deserve to die."

"Maybe, but Waters won't be with them, and so the problem would remain for the migrants and for me."

Santos nodded. "I'm in," he said, "but you need to prepare yourself for anything in that country. Are you sure you're up for this?"

Gale opened the door to his truck taking in what Santos had said. He checked his watch. He needed to get to Caton. There was no way he could be late to practice. The Panthers played Henderson the next evening, and Gale needed to put thoughts of killing, or being killed, aside.

"You have a good guess for where, what about when?" Gale asked, climbing into his truck as his mind began to race about what lay ahead.

"If I was trafficking, I'd be running migrants the next few nights," Santos said. "There's no moon, Gale. Perfect conditions."

Nineteen

Eben Daly stood next to Gale in street clothes and watched practice. Daly's injured wrist was only a sprain, so it was taped. Daly's face was filled with pained exasperation watching his replacement bungle play after play. When his substitute at quarterback turned the wrong way on a handoff and collided with the tailback, Lloyd Avery slapped his laminated practice sheet against his thigh in anger and yelled, "Run it again." Buck Marshall swore at the offense and asked, "Hell, how can I get my defense prepared if you can't run a play?"

After the teenager had shared the story of Avery's brutality the night he was separated from Maria, Gale's hatred for his assistant coaches was even harder to dissemble. The idea that the gang of four, Avery, Waters, Marshall, and Spivey, would escape justice, was inconceivable. Martin Keller had died, another boy was clinging to life, the teenager's girl had been kidnapped, and Katie Tuck had nearly had a drug charge pinned on her. And now he was certain that Clay Moorhead's killing fit into this equation somehow. What was next? Gale wasn't going to wait to find out.

Gale turned to Daly and glanced at his wrist. "Any chance you can play tomorrow night?"

Daly raised his arm and flexed his wrist back and forth. "I think I better try."

Gale thought about Avery running the ball play after play and shook his head. Even with Daly's wrist injured, it probably didn't matter if he couldn't throw, but Gale wasn't going to put an injured player on the field. Gale asked Daly, "Can you put the ball in the air?"

Daly shrugged. "A bit."

Gale turned back to the offense breaking huddle. He hoped the sophomore would run the play right. He was tired of Avery beating up on the kid. Soon he would have to step in. He thought of what Santos had said in the hospital parking lot, and Gale imagined Avery and Marshall bleeding out in the del Carmen. He tried to put his grisly thoughts aside and focus on practice, but he couldn't. If Santos had his way, Gale thought, Gale's two assistant coaches would be in the crosshairs. Santos' words stuck in Gale's mind. *Men die along the border. Some are never found.*

After practice, Gale entered the house and met Marybeth in the kitchen. Tilly sat at the breakfast nook eating a small bowl of ice cream before bedtime. When Gale entered, he kissed his daughter on the top of her head and gave Marybeth a peck on the lips. Gale felt a pang. He realized how much he'd missed the three of them together. Since leaving the Lone Stars, he loved having dinner with his wife and daughter and the routine that followed until bedtime. Coaching Caton had disrupted their household rhythms and bringing the teenager into their home had brought chaos. Now it was only the three of them, and for a few moments, Gale tried to put the mess they were in aside. Despite his bone-deep tiredness from his foray near the border with Katie Tuck, he relished the moment. He went to the refrigerator and pulled a carton of chocolate ice cream from the freezer, and after generously filling his bowl, he plopped down next to his daughter. They ate in glorious silence as Gale tried to forget the tumult around him.

Later on, after Gale had read to Tilly and put her to bed, he found Marybeth in the living room.

Marybeth was sitting on the stylish white sofa, placed her hands on her lap, and pressed her knees together. Gale sat across from her in one of the cushy chairs she'd purchased when they'd remodeled the house. He was struck by how different they lived since receiving millions of dollars from the League. The furniture they had owned in the old house had been worn and outdated except for the couch they had splurged for at the Midland Park Mall. At the time, the cost of the couch had made Gale wince.

"How's the teenager?" he asked.

"Better," Marybeth said. "When I left the hospital, he was eating ice chips."

Gale nodded in approval. "The meeting with the sheriff?"

"Grayson was a pit bull," she said.

"No surprise."

"The sheriff was exasperated."

"How did it end?"

As Marybeth answered, he could hear the exhaustion in her voice and see the deep rings under her eyes. He noticed a strand of gray hair he hadn't seen before. "Let's just say the sheriff left frustrated and angry."

"What did Grayson say?"

"He thought he bought us more time."

Gale raised an eyebrow. "By pissing off the Midland County Sheriff's Department?"

"Who knows?" she sighed.

Gale leaned forward. "I need to tell you something."

Marybeth furrowed her brow.

"Mateo and I are going into the borderlands. The del Carmen."

"My God, Gale, will it ever end?" Her voice grew sharp.

"Grayson said we need evidence, Marybeth. We need to catch Avery and Marshall in the act. It's one thing to watch them load boxes into the back of a truck with border agents looking on, it's another to catch them smuggling migrants. Anything could have been in those boxes, but human trafficking is a different ballgame."

Marybeth put her head down in dismay and then looked up. "Even if you catch them, who's going to believe you? You said Waters has everyone bought off."

Gale considered her question. He didn't have an answer. "I guess we'll have to leave that to Grayson," he said vaguely.

"This doesn't sound like a plan. It sounds like a Hail Mary. Besides, the del Carmen? It's vast and dangerous. You'll never find them."

"It's all I got, Marybeth."

"What you're saying is, you'll probably be wasting your time, but if you're lucky, you'll be putting Mateo and you in danger. I don't like it."

"I don't either, but I can't think of an alternative. Grayson may be running interference now, but he can't do it forever. Sooner or later, we're going to face charges. I'd rather take my chances breaking up a smuggling ring and plea bargaining our way out of trouble than waiting for the Midland County Sheriff's Department to throw the book at us."

"But even if you do find evidence against them, there's no reason the sheriff can't still charge us."

Gale sat back. "Look at it this way. If the boy's telling the truth, we can't let what happened to his girlfriend happen to anyone else."

Marybeth shook her head sadly. "Maria."

"That's right. God knows what happened to her and where she is right now. She's just a teenager, Marybeth."

Marybeth lifted herself off the couch. "I know, but I still don't like this, Gale. How are you going to track them down?"

"On horses."

"Horses?" She rolled her eyes at Gale and shook her head.

"Mateo says it's the only way in to where he thinks they might be bringing the migrants."

"In that country? Mateo maybe, but not you." Marybeth paused. "You're a football coach, Gale. You're not a horseman."

Gale grinned. "That's what Mateo said. He called me a gentleman rancher."

Marybeth smiled thinly. "Well, he's right. If anyone should go with Mateo, it's me. If it weren't for Waters blackmailing us, we wouldn't be in this mess. I have a score to settle."

Marybeth had been a barrel racing champion in high school and relished riding her beloved mare, Eula, as often as she could between juggling work and the demands of being a wife and mother.

Gale said to her, "That's not going to happen."

Marybeth's eyes started to burn. "Why not?"

"You could get hurt."

"So could you. Besides, I can handle myself," she said resolutely, pointing her finger at him. "Don't sell me short, Gale. I can shoot and ride better than you can. I'd be of more use out there than a gentleman rancher." She got up and walked out of the room.

Gale slowly lifted himself out of the chair. To his dismay, his problems were multiplying.

Katie Tuck pulled into her driveway, switched off the ignition, and rested her forehead against the steering wheel. She'd picked up her car from the garage late in the afternoon before returning to her office to work. Now darkness had settled, and she had to fight off the urge to close her eyes during the drive home. What a terrible day, she thought. She and the faculty and staff had been caring for upset students in the aftermath of the news about Martin Keller. Then there had been the condolence call to Keller's mother. An awful day.

But throughout the day, the shadow of the night before followed her, and she dreaded what was sure to be a backlash for having thwarted the plan to set her up, not to mention shattering Waters' dealership window.

Exhausted from the drive the night before, and still processing what she and Gale had witnessed, Tuck finally lifted her head, retrieved her leather satchel on the passenger seat floor, and slid out of the car.

Tuck's legs felt like granite blocks. All she yearned for was to kick her shoes off and collapse in bed.

She followed the dark walkway to the kitchen entrance and pulled her keys out of her purse. Before she opened the door, she glanced over her shoulder when she heard a car slowly driving by on the narrow street, barely lit by a single streetlight on the corner of her small, mid-century development of tired single-story ranches. She breathed relief when she recognized it was her neighbor, an eccentric, frail woman in her eighties who wore a tiara, saddled herself with glittery costume jewelry, and dressed in garish housecoats.

A moment later, after fumbling with her keys in the dark, Tuck stepped warily across the threshold into the kitchen. She was about to snap on the lights when she noticed how warm the house was and was overwhelmed by an odd, lingering odor. The smell was sulfuric, like rotten eggs. Then it struck her. Gas. Startled, she pulled her hand away from the wall. Tuck realized that all it took to set off a gas explosion was a spark, a single tiny burst of electrical discharge from an outlet. She stood frozen in fear and heard an almost imperceptible hiss behind the stove. Somehow, the gas line had been severed. The hair rose on the back of her neck. Had she flipped the light switch, in all probability, she would have immolated herself.

Stunned, she struggled to comprehend her situation. They had tried to set her up. Now they were trying to kill her. *My God, she thought, these people will stop at nothing.*

Waters Motors' neon sign blinked in the night as Bart Waters took a sip of Seagram's from his low-cut crystal glass. He had his back to the room and was staring out the window at the road leading away from Caton, which was empty this time of night.

Dean Spivey felt his stomach knot as he sat on the couch, waiting anxiously for Waters to speak. Waters hadn't said a word or offered him a drink. When Spivey had arrived, Waters had coldly gestured for him to sit. When he'd been summoned by Waters, Spivey had tried to put away the fear and brace himself for what was to come. He knew Waters was capable of anything, but Spivey was hoping to buy more time, especially since the Keller kid died and he'd heard there wasn't much hope for the other one. He hoped for a reprieve, especially since he was able to assure Waters that there was no chance of Johnny shooting his mouth off and making things worse. Sending his son to Hood Military Academy was like exiling him to Siberia. Hopefully, Spivey thought, the school was hammering sense into his jackass son. Spivey cursed. If Johnny hadn't discovered the fentanyl, he'd still be running his little drug operation on the side, and Waters wouldn't have a single whiff of suspicion.

A year earlier, Spivey had begun skimming a box here and a box there from the rundown hangar they used at an old airstrip. Since Spivey oversaw the accounting, his thievery was too easy. His last transaction, five pounds of what the Mexicans called Black Goat, had brought him a windfall of nearly $50,000. Spivey had been careful. He knew Waters scrutinized his offshore accounts in the Caymans. Instead, Spivey would wire the money from the stolen drugs to a hidden account in Belize. Soon he would make use of it. Unknown to his wife Audrey, Spivey had been hooking up with a realtor in Odessa, a married woman with a snotty eleven-year-old. They'd met on a flight to Vegas, and Norma and Spivey had dreams of escaping together to a Central American paradise like Belize or Costa Rica with hundreds of thousands of dollars of illicit funds to lavish on themselves.

Because of his idiot, pot smoking, mouthy son, Spivey had a bullseye on his forehead and Waters, growing angry and desperate, had gone so far as ordering Avery and Marshall to kill Tuck. Spivey could have cared less about the Caton High School administrator, but to his horror, he realized that he could be next.

"You're lucky," Waters said finally, turning to Spivey.

Spivey kept his mouth shut.

"One down, Dean."

Spivey knew he was referencing the kid, Martin Keller.

"But that's not the only problem we have. Buck and Lloyd think you've been stealing from me." Waters allowed his words to linger as he took a sip of whiskey, his eyes boring into Spivey's. "Is that true?"

"Hell no, Bart."

"You've always carried a chip, Dean. Always wanted to show people how big you are. Always wanted more," Waters said.

Spivey thought Waters could be describing himself, but his growing fear curtailed any analysis of his boss. "I've always done what you asked. I've been loyal."

Waters' eyes darkened and transformed into narrow slits. "Why don't I trust you?"

"Honest, Bart." Spivey felt his pulse race and raised his palms in the air.

Waters stared at Spivey and broke into a half smile. "Tell me about your cutie in Odessa."

Spivey felt his stomach in his throat. He felt his temples begin to throb. "What cutie?" he stammered.

"Maybe I need to refresh your memory," Waters reached across the desk, picked up his phone, and tapped it. Seconds later, he handed the iPhone to Spivey.

After scrolling through a dozen photos, Spivey thought he was going to throw up. A series of pictures showed Spivey and Norma kissing in his car, entering and exiting a hotel in Amarillo, and embracing at a rest area west of Monahans. At the rest area, Norma wore a tank top with a bare midriff and tight denim shorts as her hand clutched Spivey's ass.

Spivey's hand began to shake as he placed the phone on the desk.

"I'd hate for Audrey to see those photos, Dean. I'm sure she's broke up enough about Johnny."

Spivey's body felt numb.

Waters went on, "Hell, there's nothing wrong with getting a little on the side. But lying to me, Dean?" He tapped his finger on the desk. "It shows a lack of loyalty."

"What are you going to do with those photos, Bart?" Spivey asked nervously.

Waters took a sip of whiskey. For a moment, he considered Spivey's question, clasping his fingers together and bringing them to his chin as if he were praying. "Whatever you stole from me, you have one day to wire the money into my offshore account. Understand? You do that, Dean, and I'll forgive you. We go on with our lives like nothing happened. I know a man occasionally falls prey to greed. I'll write it off as temporary insanity. All will be forgiven."

Spivey knew whether he wired the money or not to Waters, he was a dead man. "What about the photos?"

"Oh, I'll delete them in twenty-four hours. You can be sure of that." Waters lifted himself from his chair and rested his black eyes on Spivey. Spivey felt his stomach turn. "I'm a man of honor. That wife of yours is a good woman. I wouldn't want her to know her husband has been diddling on the side."

"I appreciate that, Bart," Spivey sputtered, trying to keep from hyperventilating, realizing how little time he had.

Reaching for his whiskey glass, Waters flashed his sharp teeth. "Remember Dean. One day. Hear me?"

Spivey reached his car and vomited. He retched and retched, wiped his mouth with the corner of his shirt sleeve, and climbed into his Porsche. His mind was spinning. He had close to $550,000 in his hidden Belize account and over two million sitting in Grand Cayman. Plus, he had stocks and bonds that he and Audrey had invested as a nest egg worth close to another couple of million that he could liquidate and wire to himself. It was more than enough to set up a comfortable lifestyle in Belize or Costa Rica, or if need be, Ecuador, which Spivey had heard was inexpensive and beautiful if you could put up with a dangerous criminal element.

He pulled the burner he used to communicate with Norma out of his pocket and began to text. They would need to drop everything and drive to Dallas. From there, they'd catch a flight to Belize City or Liberia, which sat on the Pacific coast of Costa Rica. Hopefully, Waters wouldn't put good money after bad. He would write off Spivey as bad debt and forget about him. Spivey was almost sure of it. Still, they'd lie low for a while.

Spivey had barely twenty-four hours before he needed to be in the air. His thoughts spun as he tried to work out a plan. He thought about Tuck and McClanahan with burning hatred. Thoughts of revenge swirled in his head. He started his Porsche and pulled out of the dealership. He would go home and start packing. He would tell Audrey he was going on a business trip. He'd be vague. She'd press. He'd lie. It was nothing new. During their marriage, he'd gotten good at it. The trickier part was going to be getting the money together and convincing Norma to be on board with his plan. But regardless, one thing was certain. He had seen the last of Caton.

The hotel room Katie Tuck found outside of Midland smelled like cigarette smoke. When she'd checked in, she had asked for a toothbrush and toothpaste. The clerk had eyed her suspiciously, as if she had needed the room for a spur of the moment rendezvous, or perhaps, because she was fleeing an abusive partner. After she'd discovered the gas leak, she'd left the kitchen door open, circled around the house, and shut off the gas valve in the carport. For a few minutes, she'd been torn about what to do, but then decided that if Waters was trying to kill her, she shouldn't hang around waiting for one of his henchmen to return. While she had carefully checked her rearview mirror as she drove, she couldn't shake the worry that one of Waters' goons could be watching her now, ready to launch plan B. Leaving the kitchen door as it was, she had fled. After all, who was she going to call, Billy Pax?

Tuck looked around the motel room. She would never enter a motel again without thinking about Mark and that woman together, kissing and groping in a rented room while she went about her daily life oblivious to their deceit. She shook her head trying to erase the image. The foul hint of smoke and upholstery cleaner in the air made her even angrier and more upset. Normally, she would have gone to the lobby to complain, but there was no thought of that now in the darkness. She had already dragged a butcher block chair to brace against the bolted door. It was time to plan her next move. Gas lines leaked all the time. Even if she could find an honest cop, an investigation likely would reveal nothing. It was clear to her now how insidious Waters was and how cunning. Nothing he had done could be traced back to him.

Tuck picked up her phone and discovered her battery nearly out of charge. Her heart sank. Where was her head? She'd left her charger in her car. She turned off her phone to save what little charge she had left. A shower was non-negotiable, so she slipped her blouse over her head, unsnapped her bra, and slid out of her jeans and panties. Soon she felt warm water coursing over her body and smelled the scent of bath soap. She hoped to relax, but instead fear started to rise in her chest. They really tried to kill her. They'd tried to detonate her house and murder her in a conflagration of fire. Despite the warm water, Tuck shivered involuntarily. She turned off the water and quickly drew the curtains aside. She had to have a plan for the morning. She couldn't live like this. She wouldn't.

Marybeth had been serious. The morning sun rose above the hillocks and Gale watched Mateo Santos and Mason Hayes hitch the horse trailer to

Santos' Silverado. Santos had placed the saddles, panniers, and horse blankets in the back of his pick-up before sliding his Mossberg tactical rifle, Gale's 12-gauge Benelli, and a .22 caliber Ruger in scabbards and fitting them under the double cab's back seat.

Gale had bitten his lip when he saw Santos placing the Ruger in the truck. He thought back to the conversation he'd had with Marybeth in the kitchen before she'd gone to the hospital to check on the boy and Gale had taken Tilly to school. He thought with a night's sleep, Marybeth would have better sense and drop her demand to ride with Gale and Santos into the del Carmen. The opposite had occurred. She'd become even more resolute. When she got like this, she overwhelmed Gale. Worse, he knew he didn't have a good argument to stop her. She was a better rider and a better shot. Hell, Gale had never gotten over the elk, so how was he going to pull the trigger on a man, even ones he hated like he did Avery and Marshall?

They'd sat across from one another in a rare moment of solitude. Marybeth, wearing her white terrycloth robe, her hair still mussed from sleep, had set her coffee mug on the kitchen table and had put up her hand when Gale had started to object. Gale knew it was a lost cause when her eyes had started to bore into his and her face reddened. He'd been with her long enough to know he was entering the danger zone, where even if he had reason on his side, he was no match for her will.

Reluctantly, Gale had picked out the Ruger for Marybeth. He figured she could handle the .22 if there was trouble, but he couldn't help imagining a worst-case scenario. It was strange that neither of them had brought up Tilly. Instead, Marybeth had said she trusted Santos. If Santos could survive his experience in Iraq, he could lead Gale and Marybeth safely on horseback to Avery and Marshall. She made it that simple.

Besides, she had a score to settle, Gale knew. Waters had blackmailed Gale with a dark family secret. His threat to reveal Marybeth's illegitimacy after Clay Moorhead's death had endangered them and set off a mind-blowing revelation that shattered every assumption Marybeth had made about her mother, her father, and herself. She had a husband who loved her, a beautiful daughter, money in the bank, but she was H.W. Owen's child, and the thought of her tainted blood made her question the very foundation of her existence.

Finally, there was the boy and his girl. God only knew what Avery and Marshall did to Maria. Gale realized that Marybeth had attached herself to the teenager. He'd noted the range of emotions she'd experienced since the boy had landed on their doorstep, but now Gail realized something much bigger was at stake. Her care for the boy had clearly passed over into the maternal. As much as Gale wanted to see Waters, Avery, Marshall, and

Spivey go down, Marybeth's thirst for justice, and possibly revenge, ran deep into her very core.

As Gale watched Santos and Hayes start leading the horses, two of the mares and Marybeth's horse, Eula, to the trailer, Gale was still surprised that Marybeth had told him she had called Grayson Wallace the previous evening after Gale had collapsed into bed.

After cupping her slender fingers around her coffee mug, Marybeth had taken a sip and said, "I told Grayson about my mother and Owen."

"Why?" Gale asked, surprised.

"He needed to know the whole story, and I wanted to make sure he understood what we were about to do."

Gale nodded slowly, feeling a pang of guilt.

"But Grayson already knew about Delilah," she said, her eyes probing Gale's. She pulled her robe to her neck and set her mug down.

"I had to tell him, Marybeth," Gale said, fessing up.

Marybeth shook her head. "No, Gale. Grayson knew years before you told him. My mother came to Grayson after she found out she was pregnant with me and wanted to talk about divorcing my father. Seems she saw better prospects with Owen. Grayson talked her out of it. A few weeks before, another young woman with an infant in her arms, desperate for support, told Grayson the baby was Owens'. After my mother heard that, she reconsidered. Grayson said that later the other woman disappeared."

Gale looked away for an instant, lost in thought.

Now Gale wondered about the day ahead as Santos finished loading the pickup. After the game, Marybeth and Gale would meet Santos southwest of Sanderson at a staging area Santos had chosen leading toward the border. From there they would ride through the night where the Rio Grande made a great deflection to the south and hope to arrive at the abandoned mercury mine before sunset the following day. Then they would wait and see if this was the site and Saturday night, with its new moon, the place. There was no guarantee they'd find Avery and Marshall, but it was the best chance they could think of. Gale didn't like the thought of riding at night, considering they would be traveling through deep limestone canyons and navigating mountain ranges to avoid the only two track leading into the mine, which Santos had rejected because the horses' droppings and tracks would likely give them away. Gale tried to take solace that Santos knew the country. In the days of Judge Roy Bean and Billy the Kid, Big Bend had harbored many outlaws, and cattle had been smuggled across the Rio Grande at fords and other crossings. Those days seemed quaint compared to what was occurring now, Gale thought. Deadly drug smuggling and human trafficking had replaced cattle as the commodities of choice.

On a Friday during football season, Gale would have been consumed by the upcoming game. He would have been watching film and making last minute adjustments. He would have been ulcerating about Eben Daly's wrist. It all seemed trivial now compared to what lay ahead. While he hoped Daly would be able to play, Gale would grudgingly make do with his senior quarterback's replacement. But the thought of standing on the sideline with Avery and Marshall made Gale's fists tighten and his pulse quicken. Despite the loathing he felt, Gale would play his cards carefully, like Wallace advised, and with a stroke of luck, be able to witness Avery and Marshall in the act of smuggling immigrants. After Gale, Marybeth, and Santos secured photographs and video, they would head to the Midland County Sheriff's Office, where Wallace would join them. They would make their case, and if what they told law enforcement fell on deaf ears, they would go to the media. They would do their best to bring Waters and his cronies down one way or another, and hopefully, catch a break from any charges pressed against them for harboring the teenager.

Gale was about to turn and walk back to the house when he thought about what Marybeth had said about the young woman clutching the infant and meeting with Wallace years before. The thought continued to nag him. But nothing clicked, so he decided he needed to text Eben Daly. He hoped Daly's wrist was better. He needed his senior quarterback to play.

After a fitful sleep and a cup of thin motel lobby coffee, Katie Tuck gritted her teeth and returned to her house after dawn had broken and the sun was inching above the horizon. She found the kitchen door still slung open. Reasoning that she was safe during broad daylight, Tuck entered the house, and was relieved when she determined that the rotten egg odor had mostly dissipated. After she grabbed Mark's golf club out of the coat closet, she went carefully from room to room opening windows as a cautionary measure.

She entered her bedroom, checked her closet, and locked the door. She slipped her clothes off, changed into fresh underwear, and put on a pair of gray linen slacks and a white blouse. After dressing, she went into the bathroom. She was reaching to turn on the spigot to wash her face when she looked up and felt as though the air was being sucked from her lungs. She began to choke and sank to her knees holding her head in her hands while the water swirled in the sink.

Taped on the mirror was a glossy black and white Texas Highway Patrol photo of twisted metal and two mangled bodies resting in pools of blood under a jack-knifed tractor trailer. One of the corpses was nearly sheared in two and the other was beheaded. A charred Harley Davidson rested on its side, crushed under the truck's weight.

NO HEART TO KILL

Tuck gasped for air, feeling as though she were suffocating. She'd avoided imagining the grisly details of how Mark and the woman had perished. Now, they were indelibly seared into her mind.

Tuck's terror grew. They'd broken into her home, punctured the gas line, and presumably had then come back when they realized she had avoided the fate they had planned for her. Why? Just to mess with her head? She fought the urge to panic and slowly lifted herself off the tile floor, trying to calm her breathing and somehow plan her next step. She knew the high school would be the safest place to go. They wouldn't try to hurt her amidst students and faculty. *Would they?* She inched toward the bathroom door and scanned the empty hallway. She listened for a moment for footsteps. *Nothing.* Then she bolted.

Dean Spivey was nearly out of his mind. Norma hadn't texted him back or returned his frantic calls. Upstairs, he heard Audrey in the bathroom, the loud whine of her hair dryer echoing down the grand stairway into the lavishly decorated living room which was punctuated by an elaborate fireplace and Travertine mantel. Since Spivey had sent Johnny away to Hood Military Academy, Audrey and Spivey had become empty nesters. Their daughter had left at the end of August for her senior year at a small, private, and obscenely expensive college in Vermont, and now it was Audrey and Spivey alone in their 8,000 square foot Austin stone home with a marble terraced pool perched at the end of a cul de sac.

Spivey wanted to explode. After he had arrived home the night before and Audrey had finished pestering him about his sudden business trip, he had run into a series of time-consuming hurdles trying to liquidate stocks from his online brokerage account and set up the wire to his bank in Belize. Before he'd left, he had shredded the offline accounting ledger he'd hidden and put together for Waters, making sure to meticulously cover up his duplicity. Along with the ledger, he'd destroyed several documents that would have made juicy evidence. When he arrived at the airport, he would transfer his Cayman account. Since Waters had access to that account, he'd wait until the last minute to keep his transaction off Waters' radar.

Spivey paced back and forth. Soon he would need to decide. Should he drive to Odessa and coax Norma out of her real estate office, or leave her behind? The thought of an empty bed in Costa Rica depressed him but paled in comparison to the fear of what Waters would do if he caught him fleeing. Time was running out. He'd booked two seats on an evening American Airlines flight from DFW. The drive to Dallas would take much of the afternoon. He closed his eyes for an instant and tried to find comfort in the thought of the two of them safely aboard the plane, with a cocktail in hand, headed toward the safety of a Central American paradise. Spivey's image was interrupted when he heard Audrey's hair dryer stop. A few seconds later, she stood at the top of the stairway and began asking once more why he had to go so suddenly to St. Louis.

Spivey's fists clenched as he looked up at Audrey. She was wearing her $1,000 Dolce & Gabbana jeans and a Linden sequined blouse that cost nearly as much. Her blonde hair was perfectly coiffed, her eyebrows immaculately plucked, and her makeup highlighted her cheekbones and crystal blue eyes. Despite the slight bulge around her abdomen that hours of fitness classes couldn't erase, men saw a striking middle-aged woman. Spivey saw a wife he'd grown sick of. She was nosy, she raised two spoiled brats, and she drained his bank account. He took a deep breath and tried to tamp down his growing desperation. Without a word, he picked up his leather briefcase and Samsonite suitcase and left the house. He was going to start over. Start fresh. Leave all traces of his life in Caton, Texas behind and live off the spoils of his stolen riches.

Standing in the kitchen, Gale heard a car door shut. Through the window above the sink, he watched Josephine Santos hurry toward the metal storage shed. She would be caring for Tilly and her sons while they were gone. She wore a worried expression and carried a small duffel. She met her husband near the horse trailer, which rested in the shade underneath a scarred live oak. When she reached him, she shook her head and buried her face in Santos' chest.

Gale could see Mason Hayes, standing in one of the paddocks, watching the scene unfold. Hayes stood in the blinding sun, his Stetson shielding his eyes, frozen under a blue, cloudless sky. Gale turned away from the window when his cell dinged and checked his phone. There was a message from Katie Tuck. *Please call me*, she texted.

His apprehension grew. But he had to take one thing at a time. He needed to finish loading what they would need for the borderlands so that everything would be ready to go when Marybeth got home. There could be no mistakes. He would call Tuck from the road to Caton on his way to the game. He had to hope her news could wait.

Marybeth drove away from Midland Hospital after seeing the boy. Her stomach hurt. The cramps moved across her abdomen in painful waves, and she thought about pulling into a gas station to use the restroom. Almost surely, the upset stemmed from jangled nerves. She'd begun to question her decision to ride with Gale and Santos. Strangely, she felt little fear for herself, only growing anxiety about leaving Tilly. She tried to dismiss the thought. She'd allowed other people to control her life for too long. She'd been the good wife, the dutiful elementary school teacher, and for so many years, the needy daughter. She was tired of taking a backseat. And yes, tired of being a woman in a world where men called the shots. She ached to take control of her own destiny.

Still, the thought of leaving Tilly tugged hard against her. Marybeth had always seen herself as responsible and trustworthy. As a child, when her father traveled selling rig equipment across the oil and gas patch, Marybeth had often cleaned up the mess after her mother drank late into the night. The morning after, while Delilah slept in a haze of alcohol, Marybeth would throw away the drained bottles and scoop up the dirty highball glasses. She'd clean the dishes in the sink, and on occasions replaced the tipped over furniture and scrubbed the wine stains from the upholstery.

With this thought, Marybeth had to concede that Gale was right. She had to stay behind. The idea of Tilly falling into the hands of her mother was inconceivable. As Marybeth neared Kinney, she knew she'd never ride into the del Carmen. She'd never be the one to bring justice. But the basic unfairness of the world had her fighting angry tears the rest of the ride home.

Twenty

Billy Pax sat in his Sheriff's SUV eating an egg and bacon biscuit sandwich he'd bought at the Valero on the edge of town. When Katie Tuck's home didn't burst into a ball of flame the evening before, Lloyd Avery had told Pax to go into the house and tape the photo to the bathroom mirror. He guessed that the plan was to keep the pressure on so that she'd realize that her only course was to disappear. As usual, Pax did as he was told, but he didn't like it. Not one bit. Things were getting out of control.

Pax took a bite of his biscuit sandwich and a gulp of coffee from the large Styrofoam cup. He tried to calm his growing anxiety. Waters had ordered him to go with Avery and Marshall the next night to pick up a larger than usual load of illegals. Pax had never been asked to join them before. He didn't like that either. The idea of having to ride in a truck cab with Avery and Marshall made his skin crawl. If Waters wanted Tuck out of the picture, why not Pax? Waters had ripped him a new one after he'd accused Pax of botching the drug set up and Tuck had smashed the dealership window. And Pax knew too much. Maybe Avery and Marshall would try to kill him somewhere near the Rio Grande and leave his carcass in the desert for the turkey vultures and coyotes. Pax tried to dismiss the thought. Killing a county sheriff would be a bad move for Waters, Pax reassured himself as he bit off a chunk of biscuit. Waters wouldn't go that far, would he? Most likely not, but Pax wasn't going to turn his back on Avery and Waters. That was for certain. He'd bring his service Sig Sauer. If they made a move, Billy Pax wouldn't go down easily. He was a law enforcement officer after all. Trained and ready. No one was going to put a bullet in his back. Billy Pax would make sure of that.

Dean Spivey pulled into the empty strip mall on the outskirts of Odessa and parked in front of Crane Realty. Sandwiched between a dry cleaner and a drab Mexican restaurant, the realty office was dark and vacant and the sign hanging on the inside of the glass door said *Closed*. Spivey swore under his breath and checked his Rolex. It was edging toward noon and still Spivey had heard nothing from Norma. It was unlike her not to respond.

Spivey wondered if Norma had seen his texts and gotten cold feet. For the past six months she'd talked a big game, but when push came to shove, maybe leaving her husband and child on the spur of the moment was too much. Still, when they'd discussed running off together in the past, she'd never expressed hesitation. Norma wanted out of her marriage, showed no remorse about leaving her kid, and vowed to be the partner Spivey had always craved. Spivey thought again about what a stroke of luck it had been when she'd picked the seat next to him on the Southwest flight to Vegas. She'd worn sexy jeans and a silk blouse unbuttoned to reveal her slightly freckled cleavage. Her auburn hair spilled around her shoulders and Spivey could detect a faint whiff of sweet rose. She'd been traveling for a girls' weekend with her sorority sisters. For three straight nights, they'd hooked up in her hotel room as the Bellagio's gaudy fountain intermittently burst into the neon sky and the rest was history. He quickly discovered that Norma's capacity for giving pleasure far exceeded his wife's. Over the years, Audrey had shown an increasing reluctance to do the kind of things she'd done when they had first dated. Not only that, but she'd made a habit of sliding out of bed to shower as soon as he finished as if Spivey was some john in a cheap motel.

Spivey knew he needed to focus. The window was closing. His instinct told him to put the car in gear and bolt for Dallas, but his desire paralyzed him by reminding him of the curve of her breasts and the way her hips moved when she rode him. Then there was the faint smell of perfume on the nape of her neck and her full, blood red lips pressed against his.

Spivey closed his eyes to gather his thoughts. The idea that had been in the back of his mind all morning came tumbling forth. Waters couldn't have already gotten to her, could he? He was about to open his eyes when he was startled by a tap on the driver-side window. He almost screamed as he turned to see Lloyd Avery standing next to the car holding a pink burner phone and wearing a shit-eating grin. Spivey was about to hit reverse when Buck Marshall appeared in front of the Porsche pulling Spivey's mistress by the wrist. Her eyes were bloodshot, and her mascara was smeared across her cheeks.

Avery's smile disappeared, and he made a motion for Spivey to roll down his window. Spivey could feel his hand moving to the stick shift. All he had to do was click into reverse, drill down on the accelerator, and back out hard before fishtailing out of the lot. He was about to depress the clutch when Avery wagged his meaty finger back and forth. Then Spivey understood. Marshall had a handgun aimed at his face.

Avery again made the motion for Spivey to lower his window. Spivey's lips began to turn numb, and he could feel a warm stream of piss dampening his crotch. As if in slow motion, Spivey reached for the switch to put down the window. Seconds later, Avery had grabbed him by the throat. As he struggled to breathe, the last words he heard before he passed out were, "Nice piece, Dean. But the fun's over."

As Gale pulled onto the state highway for the drive to Caton, he listened to Katie Tuck on speaker phone recount the gas leak at her home, her night spent in a foul-smelling motel in Midland, and the photograph taped on the bathroom mirror. She was in her office and Gale could tell she was pressing hard to be calm and collected. She was tough alright, but she had to be frantic with fear.

Gale told her about his plan to ride into the borderlands. Tuck went silent, then, after a few moments said, ""I'm going to the game tonight."

"Is that smart?"

"The more people I'm around the better."

"Then what?"

"I don't know."

"Do you have family?"

She hesitated and said flatly, "My mother lives in St. Angelo."

Gale sensed St. Angelo wasn't an option. "Find another motel. Hopefully, we'll have the proof we need that Waters is trafficking drugs and people and then this whole nightmare will be over."

"But what if that doesn't work?"

Gale fell into silence as a large, dirt-covered pickup with an oversized American flag mounted on the cab roared by on the way to Kinney. Gale wasn't sure he liked the look. Even though he was ever the patriot, flags flapping on the back of pickups reminded him of Middle Eastern jihadists with tattered banners and machine guns mounted on flatbeds.

"I hate to say it, but it sounds like a longshot, Gale," Tuck added with a sigh.

"Maybe. But it's all I got."

"Any updates from the sheriff's office in Midland?"

"Our attorney keeps fending them off. But it won't be long before they press charges."

"Would it be shameful to tell you I'm scared shitless?"

"Not at all."

"Are you?" she asked.

"Yes."

"You never show it."

"Neither do you."

"You really think you're going to find Avery and Marshall?"

"I hope so." Gale gazed out the pickup window as the empty road ahead shimmered in the heat and hoped Santos' guess was right about the abandoned mine.

"I can't live like this much longer, Gale," Tuck said finally. "I feel like a hunted animal."

Gale was surprised to see Abraham Daly step onto the field before the game and under the stadium lights lead the prayer and moment of silence for Martin Keller. Daly had shown an odd reluctance to be anything more than the respectful father of the star quarterback, even though he was officially team chaplain, but now he was standing at midfield in front of a microphone mournfully reciting the 23 Psalm as nearly everyone packed into Clay Moorhead Stadium followed in unison.

Daly then led a moment of silence for Keller, and as the crowd hushed, Gale could hear a barking dog and then the distant sound of a car alarm bleating in the night. Out of the corner of his eye, he noticed Avery and Marshall gazing straight ahead while everyone else bowed their heads. Avery wore a sullen look, while Marshall's expression was vacant. They appeared as exhausted as he felt. Gale had seen Bart Waters standing alone near the end zone with his arms crossed on his chest during warmups and wondered why his lapdog, Dean Spivey, hadn't been beside him.

When earlier, with a shake of her head, Marybeth had told Gale she wasn't going with him and Santos, Gale had breathed a sigh of relief, and while he realized she'd made the right decision, he knew how much remaining behind had cost her. They had issues to resolve, issues that were in many ways a result of the culture they lived in, and Gale knew working things out would entail more than a conversation at the kitchen table. He had to let Marybeth dictate new terms regarding her place in the marriage.

Gale scanned the stands for Tuck, but she was nowhere to be found. Her absence gnawed at Gale. He kicked himself for not offering to have her stay at the ranch. Gale could have asked Mason Hayes to stand watch. Hayes would have embraced the role. Gale could picture him sitting on the front porch with his rifle resting on his lap peering into the darkness. Gale would try to set that up after the game.

When Abraham Daly stepped away from the microphone, the crowd roared back to life and a group of students dressed in jeans and cowboy hats raced across the field holding a spirit flag while the cheerleaders raised pompoms and spurred on the crowd. The memory of Martin Keller evaporated into the West Texas night with the excitement of a football game. For a moment, Gale studied Eben Daly's father as he walked off the field. There was an infinite sadness about the man. Abraham had only Eben, and soon his son would graduate. For Abraham's sake, Gale hoped Eben would choose a nearby university. Texas Tech had been lavishing Eben with attention, and Gale thought it a good match because Tech needed a top recruit at quarterback.

Somehow the name association reminded Gale of the biblical story of Abraham and Isaac. He couldn't imagine sacrificing a child. Stories like this one were why he had disliked discussing the Old Testament when he taught Sunday School. As a Christian, he was thankful "an eye for an eye" had been replaced by "turn the other cheek," though he kept finding himself in positions where living up to that ideal seemed almost impossible. Gale wasn't going to sacrifice Eben to win and ruin his chances of playing college football. He wanted to protect the kid for his sake and for Abraham's. A wrist injury wasn't anything to take lightly, especially for a quarterback.

Before the game, Gale had conferred with Caton's longtime athletic trainer to make sure Eben was healthy enough to play. The man people called Doc had given Gale a lethargic nod. Doc acted oblivious to everything swirling around Caton, spending most of his time away from the trainer's room smoking cigars and drinking quart bottles of Dr. Pepper in a lawn chair under the stadium. He'd been a fishing buddy of Clay Moorhead's and was nowhere to be seen on the day Moorhead had been murdered.

After the Panther band played the National Anthem, Gale was about to pull on his headset when Avery turned to him.

"I saw you searching the stadium," Avery said with a cruel smile. "Looking for Ms. Principal?"

"What are you talking about?" Gale shot back. He felt a chill and his mind began to churn.

"You had that forlorn look, like you lost your puppy dog."

"Coach the game," Gale snapped.

"Oh, I'll do that. Believe me," Avery said, turning toward the field as the players lined up for the opening kick off. Then he turned back to Gale. "The whole town's here to pay respect for that dead boy, and the person who's in charge of the high school ain't nowhere to be seen. Maybe the job's too much? Maybe she got scared and ran like Bellwether?"

Gale kept silent. He felt his temples begin to throb and his fists involuntarily tighten.

"Ole Bart might have to find another principal. That would be a shame, wouldn't it?"

Gale felt growing alarm.

"Pretty woman, too. Eye candy like your wife, Coach. A looker."

Gale's eyes shot daggers. "Shut your mouth."

Avery shook his head in mock disbelief. "I meant it as a compliment, Coach McClanahan," he snorted. "You've got good taste in women."

NO HEART TO KILL

Gale used all the self-control he could muster and turned his back on Avery. He gazed with steely eyes toward the end zone and noticed that Waters was gone.

Katie Tuck sat stunned in her locked car in the stadium parking lot. She looked at the Instagram post in disbelief. Sam Lowe had died minutes before, and his mother had posted a painful, outraged diatribe blaming Tuck, Caton High School, the town, and seemingly the entire universe for her son's death.

Tuck closed her eyes for an instant and wanted to weep. Soon news of Sam Lowe would spread like wildfire. She knew she needed to go to the game, especially now, but she felt paralyzed, unable to climb out of her car and make the short walk to the stadium. It was as if she were being held down by an invisible hand. Smothered. Then she noticed another Instagram post pop up on her phone. Her heart pounded as she started to read it. Melanie Sprague in a moment of fury and adolescent impulsivity had posted, ***Fuck Dean Spivey. Fuck Bart Waters. They killed Sam and Martin. If they weren't dealing that shit, Johnny never would have found it.***

After a few moments of confusion, Tuck was struck by a photo below Sprague's harangue. It was a snapshot of an accounting ledger, the page packed with names and figures. Below the picture, Sprague had written:

If you don't believe me, I got proof.

Tuck felt the urge to vomit. In one misguided moment, Melanie Sprague had put herself in Bart Waters' sights. The skinny, pierced, tattooed sophomore with a mother as lost and desperate as Sam Lowe's, and a drug-addled father serving time for armed robbery, had joined Tuck as one of the hunted.

Tuck needed to find Melanie Sprague. She needed to make sure she was safe. Tuck could easily imagine what they would do to Sprague if they found her. She was the kind of poverty-ridden, lost, and desperate girl whose disappearance could easily be written off. *Promiscuous. Runaway. Street girl. Drug addict. Prostitute. It all made sense.* Waters would see to it that Sprague vanished without a trace.

Tuck took a deep breath and started her car. She pulled out of the stadium parking lot as the twilight ebbed. Soon the stadium lights began to fade in her rearview mirror. She headed to the Rock Island Trailer Park, a place she dreaded. Ramshackle single wides bunched together on the edge of Caton. Rusting vehicles sitting on cinder blocks, piled debris on postage stamp yards, and feral cats roaming the property. She'd been there before accompanying the truant officer several times over the years. Twice she'd been called to Melanie Sprague's home. No matter whose home she went to, it was always depressing. Poverty. Broken homes. Domestic violence. Addiction. Hunger. It was a longshot that Sprague would be in her home on a Friday night, especially for a girl with no supervision. But Tuck had to start somewhere.

Tuck drove as quickly as she could. She sped through the empty town and headed south. On Friday nights, Caton was shuttered during home football games. Practically the whole town made a pilgrimage to Clay Moorhead Stadium.

Some of the men who grew up in the trailers and beehive apartments scattered around the edges of town drifted to the oil and gas fields as roughnecks. The women worked in convenience stores and Tom Thumb, behind cash registers, stocking shelves, or as cooks and cleaners. Early pregnancies and single mothers were a drain on the town. Waters and his cronies were complicit in all this misery by stealing from the municipal and school coffers. They stole from them any possibility of an education that might free them from this cycle.

Tuck turned into the poorly lit trailer park and drove by some people sitting on stoops smoking, as well as a few men and women stumbling around zombie-like, high. Tuck shook her head in disgust. In the growing darkness, she could make out the sagging rooflines of rotting single wides. She made her way through the park hoping to find Melanie Sprague's trailer by memory. Twice, Tuck pulled onto the wrong street. Finally, she found Sprague's single wide. She pulled up alongside the cracked curb and gazed at the trailer. The only light inside came from a naked bulb hanging from the ceiling above the cramped entryway. Tuck took a deep breath and slid out of her car. She walked carefully across a trash strewn yard and knocked on a broken screen door, which hung precariously by a frail hinge. After a few seconds, she knocked again. She was met by silence until she heard the dog growling behind her. She slowly turned and faced a pit bull ready to pounce. She could make out its bullet head, scarred ears, and collarless neck. The dog panted heavily between snarls. The pit bull's ribs protruded under a mangy hide. Starving, Tuck thought, as she fought the instinct to flee. Tuck tried to breathe slowly and avoid a sudden move. She knew if she showed fear or flinched, the dog would launch.

Avoiding any sudden movements, she reached her hand into her handbag, feeling around for the canister. But before she could pull the pepper spray from her handbag, the dog leaped. As she braced herself for impact, she heard the crack of a gunshot shattering the stillness and a sharp cry followed by a series of whimpers. The pit bull staggered, let out a long burst of flatulence, and collapsed on its side. Dogs instantly struck up across the trailer park, and Tuck could hear doors opening and the murmur of neighbors asking what the hell had just happened.

NO HEART TO KILL

A man carrying a rifle emerged from the shadows. He was stooped and lame and Tuck could make out a shock of white hair in the night.

"They ain't here," the man said in a low, hoarse voice. "The girl's gone. The mother, too."

Tuck tried to fathom the scene. The man had killed a dog a few feet from her. Fired a bullet that could have struck her if he'd missed. It wasn't the first time in West Texas she'd heard of a man solving a problem with a rifle. Now he had the gun slung over one shoulder and was speaking casually, as if killing a dog in a trailer park was a normal occurrence.

"That girl is trouble," the man added. "But not as much trouble as her mother."

Tuck nodded slowly. Her legs felt weak as she glanced at the lifeless dog. "Where'd they go?" she asked, trying to compose herself.

"They?"

"Yes."

"Don't know. The mother ain't been home in over a week and the girl cut out before you got here."

"Did someone pick her up?"

"Bebo."

Bebo made a slim living shuttling old people, those too poor to own a car, and drunks when the handful of bars around town closed. He drove a battered mini-van with torn upholstery and worn brakes, wore the same soiled clothes, rarely showered, and chain-smoked cigarettes.

"What direction?"

"Toward town, I think."

"Whose dog?" Tuck asked, unable to take her eyes off the dead pit bull.

"Don't know. But it's been scaring people. There's enough to worry about living here. We don't need a mangy stray harassing no one."

Tuck shifted and stepped away from the trailer. "If Melanie comes back, will you tell her Ms. Tuck needs to see her. It's important."

"She ain't coming back," the old man said.

"How do you know?"

"I asked her where she was going."

Tuck gazed toward the man in the shadows. "What did she say?"

"That she was never coming back."

"What else?"

"She said something about finding a boy."

Tuck's thoughts started to churn. She nodded ever so slightly and stepped around the dog. "Please pass along the message that I'm looking for her if you see her."

The old man stood silent.

Tuck said, "Thank you."

"For what?"

"The dog."

The old man grunted. "No choice. You would've been ripped apart."

Tuck nodded and moved quickly toward her car. There was no time to lose. The bus stop in front of Valero was on the other side of town. There was no doubt in Tuck's mind that Melanie Sprague was headed to New Mexico to find Johnny Spivey.

Tuck opened her car door when the old man added, "You aren't the only one looking for the girl."

Tuck turned. "What do you mean?"

"The sheriff."

"Pax?"

"That's the one. He was here in that fancy cruiser."

"Did he tell you why?"

"Said she was in big trouble. Said she was responsible for two boys dying. I figure that's why she lit out."

The referee threw the flag with 23 seconds remaining in the half. Gale looked on with disbelief as the game official signaled a pass interference call against the Panthers, which would move the ball down to the four-yard line. The crowd groaned and Gale feared a change in momentum.

Seconds later, Henderson scored on a crossing pattern to the tight end and the Panthers found themselves losing, 14-7. As Gale made his way to the locker room, he heard catcalls. One fan kept shouting at him to go back to Kinney. Another eyed him as he neared the dressing room tunnel and shouted, "If Lloyd Avery were coaching, we'd be up by 30."

Gale ignored them and stood under the stands as the players filed into the locker room. He wanted the kids settled down before he addressed the team.

His phone buzzed. Under normal circumstances, he wouldn't answer his cell phone during a game. But with his life in turmoil, he figured he'd better check who was calling. Tuck's absence from the game was weighing heavily on him, especially after Avery's taunts.

But it was Grayson Wallace.

"Why aren't you watching Kinney play?" Gale asked, knowing Wallace rarely missed a game.

"I am. We're losing, Brutus. Everyone's asking me why you're coaching Caton. Tempers are rising. They want their hometown boy calling the shots."

"Calling me during a game, Grayson?"

"I figured it was halftime."

"What's going on?"

"Not good news for you."

Gale's heart sank.

"The Midland County Sheriff has had enough of me. He's going to charge you. They want you to surrender in person."
"When?"
"He was coy. He didn't say. Maybe tomorrow, maybe the next day."
"Marybeth?"
"They're sparing Marybeth and her doctor friend for now. They want the former Coach of the Year."
Gale shook his head. "That's not going to happen."
"You'll be a wanted man."
Gale paused. "You never got a hold of me, Grayson."
"Say again, Brutus?"
"I never got this call."
"Ignorance, my boy?"
"Yes," Gale said, peering toward the locker room door.
"It'll never stand up in court."
"Bad cell reception."
Wallace grunted. "They'll have a phone record."
"I need twenty-four hours. Hear me?"
"An eternity," Wallace sighed.
"Twenty-four hours, Grayson. I'm going to get your evidence."

Billy Pax was pissed. He had been standing on the sidelines before the Caton game checking out the female action in the stands. Despite his gut, he felt impressive in his uniform, a catch for the right *señorita*. He loved to hobnob with the fans, flash the championship ring from his senior year, and lie about how he'd made the crucial block on the touchdown that gave them the title. He loved Friday nights and the pageantry of the games. Now he was in the parking lot of the feed store across from the Valero station, watching some girl sling her backpack over her shoulder. Why did Waters suddenly want to pin the boys' deaths on this skinny piece of trailer trash? It was bad enough that he would be up all night in the borderlands, but he had to miss the game too? He'd had just about enough.

Pax picked his ear and sniffed. When the girl entered the store, he slid out of the SUV and ambled across the street. The station was empty except for the girl and the geezer working the cash register. He'd grab the girl, then deliver her to Waters. He felt a pang of remorse as he thought about what Waters might do to her, but if things went without a hitch, perhaps he would be able to catch the second half.

Tuck raced toward the Valero station and slammed on her brakes when she spotted the McClendon County Sheriff SUV parked across the street from the gas station. Her mind swirled. Waters already had Sprague in his sights. Then she spotted Pax climb out of the SUV and start walking across the street toward the gas station. When he entered the building, Tuck put the car in gear and drove quickly past the Valero and parked behind a shuttered hardware store. The once family-owned business, like scores of small-town stores, had died when Lowe's and Walmart built centers between Caton and Midland.

Tuck slipped out of her car and crept toward the Valero. Making sure to stay in the shadows, she caught sight of Pax through the plate glass windows wandering inside the store. Tuck could see the top of Pax's head as he walked between store shelves hunting for Sprague. Then Pax disappeared. Tuck figured he'd gone into the restrooms to check for the girl. Finally, he reappeared and approached the store clerk. Tuck could tell Pax was perplexed. He must have been barking at the guy because the clerk raised his hands with the palms up and shook them in an exaggerated show of ignorance. Pax scoured the station once more before walking out. For a few moments, he stood near the gas pumps scratching his head until the headlights of a Great Western bus approached. Tuck watched as Pax studied the bus coming toward him. He rooted in his ear for a moment, then moved out of the way as the bus pulled into the station. No one got off the bus and no one got on. Seconds later, the Great Western pulled away and disappeared into the night.

Pax circled the building again and reappeared by the gas pumps. He shook his head and went back into the station for another look. A few minutes later, Tuck watched him emerge devouring a hot dog and slurping a soda. He crossed the street shaking his head, climbed into his SUV, and drove off.

Tuck slipped out of the shadows and entered the brightly lit station. She nodded at the clerk and cut up and down the aisles and then checked both restrooms. In a small storage area tucked near the bathrooms, she noticed a stack of empty cardboard boxes that had blocked an exit had spilled over. Without hesitation, she stepped through the rear door into the night. An empty field stretched behind the gas station. As her eyes adjusted to the darkness, Tuck searched for the girl, repeatedly calling Sprague's name, but after a few fruitless minutes of beckoning, finally walked back to her car.

Tuck was as perplexed as Pax. Sprague had vanished into the night. The only thing she could figure was that Sprague had spotted Pax, smelled danger, hid her tiny frame behind the stack of boxes, and when Pax had left, took off into the darkness.

Tuck sighed and slid into her car. She was about to start the engine when she felt a tap on her shoulder. Her heart nearly exploded as she whipped around to see Melanie Sprague leaning forward in the back seat.

In a wispy teenage voice, as if she were requesting a hallway pass to use the bathroom, Sprague asked, "Will you give me a lift to Carlsbad, Ms. Tuck? I got to see Johnny."

Twenty-One

Given all that was going on, Gale found it easy to ignore the shouts from angry fans. In the last minutes of the game, Henderson had driven the ball 83 yards to beat the Panthers, 28-21. Caton players milled about the field, dazed and angry. He spotted Abraham Daly consoling Eben near the end zone. Gale felt vulnerable and alone. His mind swirled as he walked to the stadium tunnel. He needed to let Marybeth know what Grayson Wallace had told him. He needed to make sure Katie Tuck was okay. He needed to catch Avery and Marshall, both of whom had immediately disappeared after the game, in the act. It was a longshot, but it was his only shot.

An hour later, after telling his dispirited team that Saturday's workout was canceled, Gale drove down Death Highway toward the border. He'd just finished reciting to Marybeth what Wallace had said. She'd responded with a sigh. After the call, he punched up Katie Tuck's number. A few rings later, he heard Tuck's tense voice. She told him about Melanie Sprague.

A tanker truck blasting its high beams nearly blinded Gale as it roared toward him in the night. Gale shielded his eyes from the oncoming tractor trailer.

Tuck said, "We're trying to find a motel. Somewhere safe. Melanie's in the gas station using the bathroom."

"What about Melanie's mother?" Gale asked as the truck sped past. "Have you spoken with her?"

Tuck sighed. "What mother?"

"Go to my ranch," Gale said.

"The ranch?"

"I should have offered it earlier. You'll be as safe there as anywhere."

"What about Marybeth? I don't want to bring harm to your family."

"She'll be thankful to have you."

"How's the girl?"

"She's a handful. Since I refused to take her to Carlsbad to find Johnny, she's upset with me."

"Marybeth loves kids. Why else would we be in this mess?" Gale asked, thinking about the migrant boy called Ephraim and the trouble he brought. Gale made a mental note to call Marybeth to tell her about Tuck and the girl before he dropped out of cell phone range.

For a few moments, Tuck fell into silence. Finally, she said, "I can't believe they tried to kill me, Gale."

"You'll be safe with Marybeth. I'll have Mason stand watch over all of you. He's a good man."

"What happens if your plan doesn't work?"

Gale shrugged as he drove south. "I'm not sure. But I know it won't be good. Go to the ranch. I'm calling Marybeth now. I'll be in touch as soon as I'm able."

It was well past midnight when Gale reached the rendezvous point and found Mateo Santos asleep in his pickup. The horses were tethered to an old cattle fence, constructed with wire and anchored by wooden posts running sentry-like along the dirt track which followed a dried-up creek bed. To Gale's surprise, Santos had brought Eula. He'd thought with Marybeth remaining at the ranch, her horse would stay behind. Eula snorted and whinnied when Gale climbed out of his pickup and approached the mare. Gale quickly realized having an extra horse was a smart move, even though he was uneasy at the possibility of Marybeth's beloved mare getting hurt. Gale could make out the panniers strapped to Eula's side. From the rise, Gale could see the distant thread of highway because of the occasional headlamps from vehicles driving toward Del Rio or headed west to Alpine.

As Santos climbed groggily out of his truck, Gale checked his cell for bars from the glow of his phone but found there was no reception. He and Santos were on their own, about to ride into the del Carmen. Gale was relieved he'd had the opportunity to tell Marybeth about Tuck and the girl. He figured they'd be alright, especially since Mason Hayes was going to stand watch while he was gone.

Santos raised the fob in his hand and locked his truck. He walked over to the gray mare and swung himself onto the saddle. Gale followed, climbing onto the horse Tilly had named Bumpkin. Gale knew from hard experience that Bumpkin had a stubborn streak. Once on the saddle, Gale turned to Santos as his eyes adjusted to the darkness. "Lead the way, Mateo."

Santos nodded and gripped his reins with Eula tethered behind. "There's something you should know."

"What?"

"I forgot the night vision goggles."

"Nothing to do about it now," Gale said with a shrug.

"Yeah, but we have enough disadvantages as it is."

"You think we'll have any chance of finding them?"

"Maybe," Santos said, digging his heels into the flanks of his horse and steering the mare and Eula away from the track. "But the odds aren't good."

Gale nodded and prodded Bumpkin with a light slap on her flank. For an instant, he felt a sharp pain in his side. Gale gritted his teeth until the pain passed. There was nothing to do about it. The doctor had warned him that his ribs might never heal.

Gale settled in for the long, grueling ride ahead and followed Santos up the trail.

"Hell, Billy, what do you mean you lost her?" Bart Waters asked, leaning forward and pointing his finger at McClendon County's finest. Waters stood behind his desk as Pax squirmed and Avery and Marshall's eyes turned to slits.

"She disappeared, Bart," Pax stammered. "I searched every inch of the Valero and the surrounding property."

"You sure she didn't get on the bus?"

"Positive."

Avery grunted and shook his head. "You're a dumbass, Billy."

"What?" Pax protested. "I'm telling you the girl just vanished. I searched the entire store three times. I watched the bus and the door never even opened. Hell, it was only in the lot for five seconds."

"What now?" Marshall's voice betrayed his disgust.

Waters turned and looked out his office window. His face was lit by the glow of the Waters' Motors sign blinking in the night. "I want the girl, and I want her phone before she can do any more damage." Waters turned to Avery and Marshall. "How the hell did she get photos of Dean's ledger? Tell me that? I told that sumbitch to guard those files like they were the Crown Jewels. So what happens? A little brat has us by the short hairs."

Waters took a deep breath. He said to Avery, "Did you find anything at Dean's house? In his office?"

Avery shook his head. "Nothing. Audrey told me that before Dean left for his 'business trip', she heard him running the shredder hard."

"What did Dean tell you?"

"After he quit hyperventilating, the same thing. He destroyed all the files."

Waters paused. His eyes narrowed. "I don't like it. But this is what it'll have to be. Billy and I hunt down the girl." He pointed at Avery and Marshall. "You two keep to the plan."

"You sure? Marshall asked.

"It's the biggest load of migrants we've seen," Waters said, turning away from the window. "We call it off, and we're going to have trouble with our Mexican friends. So, yeah, I'm sure as long as you two can manage."

"Buck and I can handle it," Avery said.

Waters turned to Pax. "Besides, Billy here is going to come through for us this time. Ain't that right?"

Pax shifted uncomfortably. He said unconvincingly, "We'll find her, Bart. She's got nowhere to go."

"As much as I don't like it, we'll stick to the plan," Waters said. He glanced again at Pax and shook his head. "You'd better bring your A game, Billy. I'm about out of patience."

Pax took a deep breath. Against his better judgment, he blurted, "Where's Dean?"

"He's on vacation, Billy," Waters said. "And if we don't find the girl and get her phone, you may well be joining him."

Gale was amazed at how the temperature fell as he and Santos followed an empty stream bed running toward the Sierra Del Carmen. The desert always cooled at night, but it still surprised Gale, who hadn't felt a chill in the air for months. Underneath a blanket of stars and a moonless sky, Gale reached into his saddlebag and fumbled for his phone to check for reception. Up ahead, Santos' face was lit by his handheld GPS.

"In an hour or so we move into the canyons," Santos said, looking over his shoulder, as he led his horse and Eula. "There'll be no room for error."

Gale nodded and checked his phone. No bars. He looked forward to dawn when the sky would lighten, and they'd be able to see the trail.

"There's always trouble this time of year."

"What kind of trouble?" Gale asked.

"Bears, for one."

Instinctively, Gale reached back and partially unzipped the scabbard attached to his pannier. He ran his hand across the Benelli's stock.

"In the basins, the areas are rich in mesquite beans. For a bear, it's like candy. They've had to shut down parts of the Park because of activity. Happens every year."

"Any maulings?" Gale asked, shifting in his saddle, his butt and haunches beginning to grow stiff and sore.

"A few. Hikers stumble into trouble. Next thing they know they've got a bear charging them."

"What other trouble?"

"Besides drug smuggling and human trafficking, cats."

"Cats?" Gale thought of the mountain lion he'd recently seen standing atop a hillock on the ranch.

"You'd be surprised. Seems like every year, a big cat decides a hiker's going to be its next meal."

"Great." Gale reached down once more and felt for the reassuring feel of his shotgun.

"Biggest danger is people. Always has been, always will be." Santos slipped the GPS into his saddlebag. "Big Bend's a million square miles of beauty and trouble."

Gale nodded as he listened. He couldn't help thinking that Santos was in his element. He could imagine Santos going from building to building in Mosul as an Army Ranger.

'At this pace, what time will we get to the mine?" Gale asked.

"If a horse doesn't drop a shoe or ride off a cliff, we should be there before the sun sets tomorrow."

"That long?"

Santos looked back over his shoulder. "Like I said, canyons are up ahead. Then the del Carmen."

Gale thought about the migrants picking their way across the mountains. "Aren't there easier ways for migrants to get into the country?" After he spoke, he suddenly felt naïve. Gale could make out Santos shaking his head.

"Easier ways?" Santos repeated. "There's nothing easy about being a migrant. Ask the boy. Hell, ask Maria. That's if she's still alive."

An hour later, Gale sensed the stream bed curling away and the angle of his saddle shift as they started to climb. The distant del Carmen were lit only by millions and millions of stars burning like embers in the absence of a moon. Soon they found themselves dipping into another dried creek bed lined by the shadow of mesquite and buttressed by sheer limestone walls rising on either side. Eerily, the canyon narrowed, and Gale felt as though he were riding into a dark tunnel as the overhang of limestone partially blocked the stars. The effect unsettled him.

After a few miles in the canyon, Gale felt a slight breeze on his face and then smelled the smoke. He was about to warn Santos when he saw his ranch hand rein in his mare and look over his shoulder at Gale. Santos raised his finger to his lips.

The smell of burning mesquite grew stronger and reminded Gale of a BBQ smoker simmering meat. Santos dismounted and Gale followed, dropping silently off Bumpkin.

"Wait here," Santos said, handing him the reins to his horse and Eula. He broke away from Gale and disappeared. Gale's heart pounded, and he broke into a sweat. Finally, he made out the outline of Santos bent over, moving quickly toward him. When he reached Gale, he whispered, "They're muling, Gale. There are five of them about 75 yards up the canyon."

"Armed?"

Santos nodded. "Yes, and sleeping."

"Horses? ATVs?"

Santos shook his head. "Hoofing it with rucksacks."

Gale glanced at the steep canyon walls. "Is there another route?"

Santos shook his head again. "If we double back, we'll lose hours."

Gale stared numbly at Santos.

"The canyon widens up ahead. We'll try to slip by them. It's our only choice."

Gale nodded and took a deep breath.

In the darkness, Santos took his horse's reins from Gale, slowly unzipped his scabbard, and unsheathed his rifle. Gale followed and held his shotgun close by his side. He followed Santos as they carefully walked the horses through the canyon, making sure to find whatever scant cover was available by hugging the steep limestone wall and patches of mesquite dotting the banks of the stream bed. When they turned a corner, Gale was able to make out the glowing embers from a dying fire and patches of smoke wafting skyward from the burning mesquite. Around the fire, he made out the lumps of men, curled in bedrolls and what appeared to be a couple of empty liquor bottles scattered near the fire. Next to them rested large backpacks, and Gale could make out a handful of rifles leaning up against the rucksacks.

Gale felt his heart pump as he gripped his shotgun. He knew that if they woke the smugglers, there'd be shooting.

Santos put his hand up and halted. In the silence, Gale heard the nocturnal song of a poorwill and felt a breeze tunneling through the canyon, lightly rustling the leaves. Gale could tell Santos was weighing the odds, trying to determine when they would move ahead. After a few minutes of careful watching, Santos waved them on.

Gale gritted his teeth. Every sound the horses made, a slight whinny, a snort, a hoof dropping onto the granular surface of the canyon floor, sounded like the clash of cymbals. Every noise was distorted, and Gale kept trying not to imagine what would happen if the men woke. Would Gale and Santos try to reason with them, or shoot their way out?

Gale had heard stories of innocents stumbling upon drug traffickers and being murdered. Gale imagined Santos aiming his tactical rifle at the first man to stir. Gale would be forced to follow. It was surreal. Gale was a rancher and football coach. Now he'd gone from overseeing his family's ranch to wandering in the night under a cold, starlit sky through one of the most desolate and rugged places in North America. He felt he'd been dropped into a scene from a century and a half ago.

As they approached the campsite, sticking along the canyon wall in the deep shadows of mesquite, Gale realized the sleeping men couldn't be more than 20 yards away. Gale could hear one of the men snoring beside the small fire's dying embers. Suddenly, Eula gave out a loud snort, startling Gale. He knew Marybeth's mare was intuitive, so he looked back to the campsite. Gale saw one of the men pick his head up in a stupor and stare his way. The man slowly propped himself up on his elbow and cocked his head. Next to him, Santos slowly aimed his rifle at the smuggler.

The man behaved as if in a dream, his movements those of someone under water. With maddening languor, he scratched his head, rubbed his eyes with his fists, and pulled himself out of his bedroll. Gale braced for the crack of Santos' rifle, but then the man turned his back and staggered toward the opposite wall of the canyon. Soon, the man was facing away, urinating into a patch of bushes. Gale remained motionless, bracing for him to turn and spot the horses. When he finished and zipped up, he belched and walked unsteadily to the fire. After gazing emptily one more time in their direction, he climbed into his bedroll.

Gale shot a quick glance at Santos. After a few moments, Santos lowered his rifle and motioned for Gale to move. Soon, they found themselves past the men, and when they glanced over their shoulders, could see the faint embers of the burning fire slowly disappear.

When they were out of earshot, Santos whispered, "We got lucky. He must have been drunk."

Gale nodded and could feel the tension ebbing from his neck and his grip on the Benelli ease. "That was close."

"He'll wake up and tell everyone about his dream. Two men with horses. And a rifle aimed his way. When they find the tracks, they'll know he wasn't dreaming."

Gale said, "You would have killed him."

Santos nodded. He slid his rifle into the scabbard and mounted his horse. Gale followed. As they moved out of the canyon onto higher ground, Santos pointed at the dark looming outline of the high ranges. He said with a sigh, "The del Carmen. The locals call it Sierra del Caballo Muerto. *Dead Horse Range*. A trafficker's paradise."

Gale shook his head and gazed to the east. To his dismay, there was no sign of the coming dawn.

After picking their way along an elevated trail leading to a switchback, the horses clumped around a small spring and drank the cool water. In the early afternoon heat, shimmering across the horizon, Santos pointed to the west where Avery and Marshall would find one of the few dirt tracks to transport migrants – that is, if they were transporting from the abandoned mine. Gale wondered if Santos could possibly be right. While the horses drank, Gale looked around. From his vantage point, Gale could see miles and miles of desert and just below, the rose-colored canyons and cliffs melding into the base of the del Carmen.

NO HEART TO KILL

Gale felt his heart sink. Avery and Marshall could be trafficking anywhere in this desolate border country. Gale glanced at Santos who was chewing on a Power Bar and sitting on his haunches studying the GPS. Gale was about to take a swig of water from his canteen when he heard the noise. He noticed Santos lift his chin and look into the cloudless sky.

Gale said, "Sounds like a swarm of bees."

Santos cupped his ear and stood. He turned to Gale. "A drone."

Gale looked at Santos quizzically.

"Could be the DEA or traffickers. Maybe border patrol. They want to know who's out here."

The buzzing sound grew louder and without a word, Santos put the GPS in his pannier and motioned toward the horses. They led the mares a few yards so that they were under a rocky overhang where they stood in the shadows and listened as the buzz grew louder.

"If the DEA or Border Patrol spot us, they'll wonder what we're up to." Santos paused as the buzz grew louder. "If it's smugglers, all bets are off."

As the drone grew louder, Gale pressed against the limestone wall and pulled Bumpkin closer.

"Most of the drones out here probably only relay video. Hopefully, it doesn't have heat signature capacity."

"If it does?"

Santos shook his head and scratched his neck. "Depends on who's operating it and whether they see us as a threat."

Santos turned away and gazed out as the drone's buzz bounced off the limestone walls like a swarm of angry hornets. The horses began to snort and fidget as the sound grew louder. Gale rested his hand on his mare's flank to calm her.

Santos said, "Just in case, don't let the camera see your face. I'd shoot it, but then we'd most likely have company. "

Gale spotted the drone winging toward them and shivered. Before he turned away, he noticed the drone had four rotors and was no larger than a trash can lid. It looked like one of those drones you could purchase off the shelf at Walmart.

At eye level, the drone swiftly approached and then stopped and hovered no more than 30 feet from the overhang. It hung in the air and inched closer. The sound of the rotors agitated the horses, prompting them to stomp and whinny as Gale and Santos tried to hold them still and hide from the drone's video feed.

Gale wondered how long the drone would hover when it suddenly flew at them like an angry hawk, stopping no more than 10 feet away. Gale felt Bumpkin rear up and as he turned to gain a tighter hold on the reins, he found himself staring at the drone. A few seconds later, the drone broke away and buzzed toward the horizon.

After Gale and Santos calmed the horses and led them away from the overhang, Gale lamented, "I might as well have been posing for a mug shot."

Santos nodded and put one foot on his horse's stirrup.

"Who are they?" Gale asked.

"Like I said, could be the DEA or Border Patrol, but most likely smugglers trying to scare us off," Santos said, wiping his brow before slinging himself onto his saddle. "And if so, then they won't be happy when they see that we're not turning back."

Billy Pax was mopping his own sweat as he stood under the late afternoon sun next to Melanie Sprague's trailer. He'd searched everywhere for Sprague and had made calls to the bus lines and even to Amtrak, trying to hunt her down. He was trying to convince himself she hadn't strayed too far and was hiding right under his nose. She must have seen him the night before at the Valero and slithered away before he could catch her.

Usually, Pax would have called in for help. He and his kid deputy, who'd graduated from Caton High School a few years before and had greasy hair and pimples erupting all over his chin, would have split up to scour the area, but Pax didn't want questions. Pax was waiting at the trailer park because he couldn't think of anything else to do. He figured either she or her mother, who Pax had tried to find at Dollar General, would return.

For the past hour, Pax had ignored two calls and an angry text from Waters. He had nothing to report, and until he did, he didn't relish a conversation. All he knew was that he didn't want to go on vacation with Spivey.

Pax noticed a scraggly tree behind the trailer. He decided to get out of the sun while he collected his scrambled thoughts. He walked around the dilapidated single wide and nearly choked. At his feet was a dead dog, bloated and stinking next to a heap of trash. A swarm of flies buzzed around the carcass. The pit bull had a bullet hole in its swollen flank. It looked like it had been dragged and left to rot behind the trailer.

Pax gagged and nearly threw up.

It was a bad omen. And he didn't like it one bit.

Katie Tuck tried not to let Melanie Sprague out of her sight. Since arriving at the McClanahan's ranch, Melanie had spent most of her time leaning against a paddock fence smoking cigarettes. She seemed fascinated by the horses and stroked a gelding who kept nudging her. Tuck had given up nagging Sprague about smoking.

Tuck sat with Marybeth on the veranda in a wicker chair and drank sweet tea. She was struck by Marybeth's warmth and beauty. Gale's wife had high cheekbones, hazel eyes. and thick dark hair. The McClanahan's daughter sat with her knees to her chin on a chair beside her mother and never took her eyes off Sprague, seemingly fascinated by the girl. Tuck guessed that Tilly hadn't occasion to see too many girls with bleached hair, arms and neck laced with tattoos, and piercings protruding from her eyebrows, nose, and lips.

When Tuck and Sprague had arrived the night before, she'd worried about how she and Sprague would be greeted. They were in Bart Waters' deadly sights, which she had made sure to explain clearly, and she wouldn't have blamed Marybeth for turning them away. But without hesitation, Marybeth had warmly shown Tuck and Sprague their rooms and the adjacent bathroom adorned with soft towels and fresh lavender soap. Tuck had noticed Sprague's eyes grow moist as she peered into Tilly's bedroom where she would be sleeping. Tilly was going to sleep with her mother. The walls were painted a soft yellow and Tilly's bed was piled high with stuffed animals. A dollhouse sat in the corner. From her expression, Tuck had guessed that Melanie was reflecting on her own lost childhood. In her ramshackle trailer, there were no frilly lace curtains or finely scented bath soaps. No dollhouses or stuffed animals piled high.

Tuck gazed toward the herd. Longhorns were scattered across the hillocks milling under the late afternoon sun. When she turned, she was startled to see a man emerge from the barn carrying a rifle. Tuck cocked an eyebrow at Marybeth.

Marybeth said, "That's Mason."

"Gale told me about him."

"He's taking the threat seriously."

"That's reassuring."

Marybeth nodded and put her hand on Tuck's. "If there's anyone who'd like to shoot a bad guy, it's Mason Hayes."

"Let's hope it doesn't come to that."

"Let's hope," Marybeth agreed. But something about the way she said it made Tuck do a double take.

Twenty-Two

Lloyd Avery and Buck Marshall eyed the unmarked tractor trailer and cursed. Avery circled the vehicle with Marshall following and kept shaking his head. About a quarter mile away from the vacant warehouse facility, vehicles sped along Death Highway in the late afternoon. Avery didn't like it.

"You think we can drive on a two-track with this monster?" Marshall asked Avery as they stood under a broiling sun.

Avery spit and said, "No choice."

"Even at night, they're going to cook in this thing."

Unlike the refrigeration truck, the semi's trailer had no air conditioning. "We may lose a few before we ditch them," Avery said.

Marshall didn't blink. "How many we got?"

"Our friends on the other side of the border said over a hundred."

"The hell. Can we fit 'em all in?"

Avery studied the eighteen-wheeler and slowly nodded. "Oh, we'll fit 'em in. But it'll be tight."

"This whole thing is screwed up."

Avery grunted and said, "I don't like it either, Buck. As soon as we squeeze them all in, they're going to realize we've packed 'em in an oven. They'll be raising hell to get out. Besides, that two-track can barely hold a pick-up, much less a semi."

"Like I said." Marshall looked grim.

Avery nodded and pulled a canister from a nylon rucksack he had slung over his shoulder. It looked like a metal water bottle.

"What the hell is that?" Marshall asked.

"Flashbang. A stun grenade."

Marshall stepped back.

"In case our migrant friends don't like their transportation."

"How many you got?"

Avery gave him a crooked grin. "Enough."

Marshall hesitated, then reached out and took the flashbang from Avery. "Sweet Jesus."

"That's what those migrants will be saying if they cross us."

"They won't be saying nothing if this thing explodes."

Avery lifted his head and snorted. "Let's go. I want to be on that two-track by the time the sun sets."

"And our friends?" Marshall asked. He turned and glanced at the plain white van they had driven from Caton.

"Toss 'em in the trailer."

"They might suffocate."

Avery shrugged.

"It'll save us from having to shoot 'em."

The two of them stood on the narrow trail in silence. It had been a few hours since they'd spotted the drone, and the only signs of life were turkey vultures circling above. They were resting the horses. Gale squinted as he gazed toward the limestone cliffs. He was nursing his ribs which were now officially killing him. Gale and Santos were elevated well above the desert floor, and Gale noticed scattered pinyon trees on the mountainside. Gale looked straight up the trail and saw that the path appeared to drop again. From his vantage point, he couldn't understand how a two-track could thread its way among the canyons, steep rises, and desert below. The sun still sat above the horizon, but in an hour or so, it would begin its full descent as they neared the basin where the mine sat.

An hour earlier, he'd spotted a black bear plodding along a canyon bed. He was relieved that they were high on the trail and away from the animal, but since he'd never seen one before, he looked on in fascination. It was a nice interlude from the gnawing in his stomach that hadn't left since he had been spotted by the drone.

Gale and Santos had sketched out a rough plan. They'd arrive at the mine at sunset and find a good vantage point. Santos was confident that his new iPhone would capture the scene, even on a moonless night. With a reassuring smile, Santos swore that the phone's Night mode made nighttime photos and video appear as if they'd been taken in broad daylight. Gale hoped it was true. If their hunch had been correct, they'd get the make and model of the vehicle and video of the trafficking. Despite the long odds against them, Gale indulged in fantasies of seeing Avery and Marshall locked up in some hellish federal prison.

If all went according to plan, Gale and Santos would ride out in the morning using the two track and beeline to Midland, where they hoped the DEA and Border Patrol would be on the up and up, and not on Waters' payroll. If their story was met with deaf ears, Gale had another plan. He'd take the story to *The Dallas Morning News*. He thought of it as the nuclear option.

Gale wondered if the Midland County Sheriff had shown up at the ranch looking to charge him. He hoped Marybeth wasn't having to deal with that too. With any luck, Grayson Wallace was working his magic.

Santos motioned for them to get moving. Gale hoisted himself onto Bumpkin and winced when he hit the saddle. Not only were his ribs making a martyr out of him, but despite how much he had ridden in his youth, he had no idea how badly saddle sores could hurt. He was now well aware why Santos and Marybeth had been skeptical about his ability to endure this journey. When this was over, he was going to embrace the role of gentleman rancher without complaint.

Billy Pax was growing desperate. There was still no sign of the girl or her mother, and since he could no longer ignore Waters' texts and calls, he had texted Waters that he was getting close to finding the girl. But for all he knew, she could have hitchhiked to Albuquerque or Lubbock. Hell, she could be in Timbuktu.

Pax's phone buzzed. It was Waters again. Pax stuck his finger in his ear and sniffed as he ignored the call. He had to do something. He was about to put the SUV in gear when he spotted a beat-up pickup pull in front of Sprague's trailer. A thin woman with sunken, pockmarked cheeks, long stringy hair, tattoos covering her arms and neck, and a cigarette dangling from her mouth climbed out of the truck and walked toward the trailer before disappearing inside.

Pax slapped the dashboard and grinned. "Here we go, Billy Boy," he said to himself as he slid out of the cruiser and approached the trailer.

A few minutes later, Pax walked out of the single wide with Melanie Sprague's cell phone number. He was relieved to get out of there. The trailer stunk like rotting food and cigarettes. The kitchen trash can was overflowing with grease smeared paper plates and a mold-covered chicken carcass. At first, Sprague's mother had told him to screw himself when he'd demanded to know where her daughter was.

When Sprague's mother had refused to unlock her phone, Pax had threatened to tell her he'd call protective services for neglecting her daughter. She'd laughed at him. She'd told him he could call all he wanted. It wouldn't be the first time and wouldn't be the last. The agency never did anything anyway. Finally, Pax snatched her cheap handbag off the table and began to rifle through it despite her curses. He found a pipe and a hefty block of meth in a zip lock bag. He held it up and dangled it in front of her and told her he'd put her in the county jail and throw the key away. She gave in after a few choice words. A couple of minutes after discovering her mother's phone didn't have a tracking device to pinpoint her daughter's whereabouts, Pax had to settle for Melanie Sprague's cell number.

Now all he needed was Krystal, the central dispatcher in McClendon County, to use Sprague's number to help him pinpoint the nearest cell tower. Pax had no idea how something like hunting down a cell phone location worked, but he'd done it before. The problem was that Krystal was still angry at him for ditching her one night at a honky-tonk and leaving with her best friend. She'd given him hell the next day. They'd barely talked since.

As Pax sat in his cruiser, he waited impatiently for Krystal to answer his call. The phone rang and rang. Pax pounded the steering wheel in frustration. But suddenly he straightened himself and smiled. Krystal would help him alright.

Marybeth stood outside the house as the blood-red sun began setting beneath the horizon. Ana Torres had called five minutes earlier to tell her she'd heard that Ephraim had eaten his first meal since he'd been rushed to the hospital. Marybeth was relieved. She'd spent the morning with the boy and had noticed marked improvement. Color was returning to his cheeks, and the dark circles under his eyes were fading. His eyes were still tinged with fear and sadness, but through his simple gestures and occasional smile, she could tell he was beginning to trust her.

Marybeth looked at the dirt road leading to her house then turned her head and gazed at the rose-colored plains. She and Gale had chosen to retreat to the ranch after the Lone Stars. She thought they had managed to settle into a nice, quiet life. But all it had taken was a bullet to Clay Moorhead's chest and a boy dying in a ditch to upend their lives.

She turned again and looked at the road leading up to the house. She couldn't shake the thought of the sheriff arriving to charge Gale, or worse, far worse, Waters or his henchmen coming for Tuck and the girl. Her thoughts were broken when she spotted Mason Hayes walking toward her with a hitch in his step in the twilight. He had a rifle in one hand and an unlit flashlight in the other.

He moved toward her and said, "I'm going to block the ranch entrance with the flatbed."

"Okay," she said.

"I don't want to make it easy for someone to drive onto the property tonight."

"Do you want me to follow you?"

Hayes shook his head. "I'll walk back. You stay here."

Marybeth nodded and asked, "You think Gale and Mateo are going to be alright?"

"I'd trust my life with Mateo. And Gale, he's smart enough to follow orders." Hayes paused and said reassuringly, "They'll be okay, Marybeth."

She stepped toward Hayes and buried her head in his chest. It surprised her how much she needed to hear those words. She'd known Mason Hayes for years. He grew up in West Texas north of Ozona and had the clearest eyes she'd ever seen. His skin was burnt from years spent outdoors, and he'd never married. His life was the ranch. Now that Gale's dad had died and hers was in Colorado, Hayes was like a father to them both. She'd remembered him at her wedding giving her a fatherly embrace and telling her Gale was the luckiest man alive. She felt a sudden wave of gratitude for this good man who would help them stay safe.

"Be careful," she said.

Hayes smiled in the half-light. "Oh, I'll be okay."

"Promise?" Marybeth asked, pulling away and looking hard into his eyes.

"Promise."

"Mason," she said as he was about to turn and walk to the flatbed.

"What?"

"I want a gun, too."

"What for?"

Marybeth took a deep breath. "Insurance."

In the fading twilight, Gale could still make out the shadowy figures of coyotes when he and Santos neared the Casa Grande Basin. About an hour before sundown, the pack had picked up the horses' scent and begun following them close enough to put Gale on edge. Gale knew coyotes rarely attacked humans, but with night descending and the narrow trail plunging into an abyss, their presence made Gale feel even more exposed and vulnerable.

While there had been no more drones and no human sightings since the smugglers the night before, Gale's uneasiness grew as they approached the mine. While they had made the decision to ride to the mine after hearing the boy's description, he fought the feeling that he and Santos were on a ride to nowhere. The borderlands' eerie combination of beauty and desolation was clearly working on his perceptions, but he did know one thing. If either of them were seriously hurt, the chances of getting immediate medical attention were nil. In that sense, they were, indeed, very much on their own.

In the dim light, Gale spotted a coyote shoot across the trail in front of them. Gale grew alert and held Bumpkin's reins tight. Gale looked ahead and tried to focus. He was tired and jittery. He tried to tamp down his fears when suddenly, Santos looked over his shoulder and pointed. "Down there," he said in a whisper.

Gale followed his gaze down the steep slope. He could just make out the basin below and spotted a collapsed roofline, a rickety wooden platform, and a sunken shaft carved into the limestone mountainside. A two-track carved into the basin's floor long ago provided access to the mine.

Santos managed a thin smile and said softly, "*Ahora está en las manos de Dios.*"

Gale nodded. He stared down at the ruined mine and could feel his heart pound. He lifted his head, sighed, and gazed upward as the first stars were emerging across the heavens.

It was pitch black but for the truck's headlamps shooting ahead to expose the jagged mountainside and flimsy dirt track. Avery cursed and downshifted the tractor trailer. The desert floor had long given way to a sharp rise in elevation so that the dirt track narrowed until the wall of limestone nearly scraped the semi's side. One wrong move with the wheel and Avery feared the vehicle would slide off the track and plunge down the mountain. It was one thing to bring the smaller refrigerator truck into the del Carmen, it was another to navigate an eighteen-wheeler. Avery swore again and renewed his worries about how he and Marshall were going to transport a semi crammed with heat-stricken, panicked migrants out of the mountains. He shook his head in disgust. He didn't know it was going to be a semi. If the truck didn't roll over the side of the mountain, he was going to have words with Waters. It might just be time to walk away.

Avery glanced quickly at Marshall. Marshall had pulled an empty Glock from his rucksack and kept racking the slide back and forth. Marshall impassively rolled a toothpick between his teeth, seemingly impervious to the sharp drop down the mountainside a few feet away or to the two captives tied up in the semi's trailer.

The more Avery thought, the more he liked the idea of dumping illegals as soon as possible. Why risk transporting them to the usual spot when he could get rid of them in the mountains? It made sense and brought a moment of calm. Spivey and the woman were another question. He and Marshall would face that when they arrived at the rendezvous point.

Avery rubbed his nose with the back of his hand and scowled. The track had narrowed even more. He imagined again the tires slipping and the truck hurtling down the mountain. As sweat beaded on his forehead, he gripped the steering wheel even tighter and focused on the track ahead.

They'd tethered the horses on the trail a few hundred yards north of the mercury mine. Gale and Santos had gingerly hiked down into the basin, making sure to avoid loose rocks and earth, not wanting to slip on the steep grade and plunge down the mountainside.

As Gale sidestepped down the incline, he clung to his shotgun and felt the shell pouch press against his hip. A hundred feet from the basin, Santos skidded and caught himself on a clump of sage. A few rocks broke loose and cascaded down. Gale reached for Santos' hand and pulled him to his feet. He nearly yelped at the stabbing pain in his side.

Soon they stood near the mine shaft on flat ground surveying the tire marks on the basin floor. Santos shone his flashlight at a large tire track and said, "Someone's bringing trucks in here. That's a good sign for us."

Gale nodded as Santos snapped off the light. He could feel his heart pump as he stared at the two track leading into the basin. He imagined the grind of a truck and the steady beam of headlights as the vehicle approached.

Santos, sensing Gale's unease, waved his hand and moved toward the safety of a clump of boulders near the mine shaft. When they settled in among the rocks, they had an unobstructed view of the basin floor. Santos rested his rifle against a limestone slab and pulled off his rucksack. He opened the flap and dug into the nylon bag that contained his iPhone.

As the cell booted up, Gale could see Santos' intense expression in the glow of the screen. A few seconds later, after holding the phone upright and panning the basin, Santos showed Gale the video. Gale shook his head. The world had come a long way. He thought about when he was a boy, and his parents would dust off the Polaroid instant camera to use on special occasions. Usually, Christmas and birthdays. Despite the miraculous video, Gale longed for simpler times. Being around kids in schools for most of his adult life, he couldn't help but see how negatively phones and social media were affecting their lives. Give him Polaroid cameras and Kodak film. Yet, on this night, he was grateful for Santos' iPhone. The test video footage was as vivid and clear as if the video were taken in daylight. Gale could see a smile forming on Santos' face as he carefully powered down the cell and placed the phone back into his rucksack.

"I sure hope Avery and Marshall show up," Gale whispered.

"That's the plan."

"I hurt way too bad for this to have been for nothing," Gale added.

Santos looked at him and grinned. "Is the gentleman farmer feeling it?"

Gale grunted. "You have no idea."

"I know one thing," Santos said.

"What?"

"We have a clear field of fire."

Gale eyed his ranch hand.

Santos reached for his rifle. "If push comes to shove, I won't miss."

Marybeth stared into the darkness waiting for Mason Hayes to return. He'd been gone for nearly an hour, and she found herself panicking. She tried to steady herself by taking a handful of deep breaths. Behind her, she heard the bellow of a Longhorn and then a sharp high-pitched coyote yip. She glanced at the house, and through the large double-hung living room windows, could see Tilly and Melanie Sprague together on the couch watching Tilly's favorite movie, *Moana*.

Marybeth was about to return to the house when she heard footsteps behind her. For an instant, she thought her heart would explode.

"He's still not back?" Tuck asked, emerging from the shadows.

"You scared me."

"I'm sorry. I guess on a night like this, I shouldn't be walking up behind anyone."

Marybeth nodded and began to relax her shoulders.

"I got restless. I went out the kitchen door and went over to the paddocks. If I wasn't so tired and nervous, I'd be enchanted. It's a beautiful night." Tuck gazed up at the smattering of stars blinking coldly above them.

"Seems like Melanie has settled down. She's become Tilly's best friend."

Tuck managed a smile. "I heard the poor girl crying in the bathroom. I asked her if she was okay, and she said she'd never seen bath salts before."

Marybeth could feel her heart sink. "Several years ago, I had a child in my class who came to school every day wearing the same clothes. Smelled to high heaven, like urine." Marybeth sighed. "Social services finally removed her from the home, and she stayed with us until they thought they could place her. At the time, Gale and I didn't think we could have children, so we talked about adoption. Then the mother came back into the picture. God only knows where that girl is now. It broke my heart."

Tuck nodded.

"I guess you've seen your fair share of kid tragedies too," Marybeth said.

"A few . . ." Tuck's voice drifted off.

Marybeth glanced again at the outline of the long dirt road leading out of the ranch and decided she was officially worried. "Mason should have been back by now. He's not one to mess around."

"Maybe we should go into the house."

"That's what I'm thinking."

As they turned to go inside, Tuck hesitated, then said, "I'm sorry Melanie and I've brought more trouble."

"It's okay," Marybeth said. Without taking her eye from the road, she gave Tuck a hug and added, "I wouldn't have it any other way. One thing you'll discover about the McClanahans, if there's trouble, it'll find us."

Twenty-Three

The text Billy Pax had sent had done the trick. Pax had threatened to reveal Krystal's little secret. Not long after Pax's ex, Amy Lee, had walked out after filing for divorce, Krystal had brought Pax back to her place for some fun. Pax had looked around her one-bedroom apartment above one of the bars in Caton and noticed an unwrapped assortment of women's cosmetics: makeup, eyeliner, lipstick, lotions, and other personal beauty products.

In bed, Krystal had given Pax a coy smile, and when he'd pressed, she'd told him about her little hobby and made him promise not to tell. On her days off, she enjoyed driving to Odessa and Midland to steal from stores in the shopping plazas. She had piously told him she'd never used the products herself – they were too fancy – but had sold them on eBay for a tidy profit. Pax didn't care. As long as Krystal gave Pax what he'd wanted, he didn't care if she'd stolen from Fort Knox.

Pax's text must have grabbed her attention because within minutes she sent him the most recent cell tower location for Melanie Sprague. The cell tower sat on the county road outside of Kinney. Using his phone, Pax had dug into property records and when he found the deed, he'd broken into a lopsided grin. He was back in Waters' good graces.

Marybeth's heart leapt when she heard the knocking. But when she glanced through the kitchen window and saw Mason Hayes standing under the porch light, she felt a wave of relief.

"I was worried sick about you," Marybeth said, scolding the seasoned ranch hand when he entered the house.

Hayes shook his head, placed his rifle on the kitchen table, and took off his Stetson. "I got out to the entrance and found a couple of teenagers had a blown tire on their pickup. After I made sure they weren't raising hell, I helped them swap out the spare."

Marybeth took a deep breath. "Thank goodness that's all it was."

Hayes said, "If anyone's coming to do harm, they'll wait. It's too early."

Marybeth noticed Hayes' hardened jaw.

"You think they'll come?" Marybeth asked.

"Hard to tell. It'll take some figuring to discover the girl and Ms. Tuck are here."

Marybeth nodded. She put her hand on Hayes' shoulder and gave him a hard stare. "I want a weapon, Mason."

Hayes turned to avoid Marybeth's gaze. "That's not a good idea."

"Why not?"

"It might put you in harm's way. I told Gale I'd take care of you. I intend to do so."

Marybeth felt a new wave of anger. Her mother's indiscretions and Waters' blackmail were unquestionably at the heart of it, but not being allowed to fend for herself was the tipping point.

Marybeth repeated flatly, "Get me a gun."

Hayes didn't respond.

"Now."

Hayes swallowed hard and turned toward the door. "Okay. I'll fetch the pistol from the barn."

"I'm taking no chances."

"I see that," Hayes said. "Let's hope you don't have to use it. But just in case, I'll give you a few pointers."

Sitting among the boulders, Gale fought to keep his eyes open. The ride the previous night had taken its toll and left him haggard. A couple of times, his chin fell to his chest, and he had to shake his head to keep from nodding off. Santos was another story. He seemed wide awake as he leaned against a large, flat slab of limestone, alert to any signs of trouble.

They'd arrived at the basin two hours before and were in the wait-and-see game. Gale hated it. He wanted the whole mess to be over. He wanted things resolved and to be home in bed with Marybeth to sleep for a week. The ache in his ribs was still a sharp, radiating pain. He tried to put the discomfort aside by thinking of Marybeth and Tilly, but that proved to be a mistake. What was he thinking when he invited Tuck and the girl to the ranch? To help protect a friend, he'd put his whole life at risk. If anything happened to his wife and daughter, his life would be over. Wallace was right. He was too often guided by impulse.

But he knew he had to dismiss thoughts of Marybeth and Tilly in danger. He had to stay present. He scanned the basin. He could hear the occasional distant cry of a coyote and the trill of a western screech owl. He rubbed his eyes and fought against his exhaustion. He was bone tired. More tired than he'd ever been.

Gale felt a violent shake and his eyes shot open. Santos was in a crouch staring toward the basin's entrance. Shaking off the cobwebs of sleep, Gale looked in the direction of the two track and heard a truck laboring in the darkness. Seconds later, he glimpsed the beam of headlamps illuminating the basin and ducked his head behind one of the boulders.

The wait was over. Their long ride into the del Carmen wasn't for naught. Gale felt a wave of relief, followed immediately by apprehension at what a confrontation could bring. He noticed Santos carefully pull the iPhone from his rucksack, switch the cell on, and grab his Mossburg tactical rifle as the truck emerged onto the basin floor. Gale followed. He reached for his shotgun, switched off the safety, and rested the 12 gauge against the boulder in front of him.

The semi entered the basin and drove to the far end. Then the truck began backing, attempting to turn around in the narrow confines. After a few minutes of maneuvering, the truck finally came to rest barely thirty yards from Gale and Santos. The driver killed the lights, then the engine, and without hesitation, hopped out of the semi. Seconds later, Gale heard the passenger side door open and saw a man come around the front of the truck. He heard him say, "I got to take a piss," and instantly recognized Buck Marshall's voice. The other man said, "You're not the only one," and Gale knew it was Lloyd Avery. Gale squinted. Marshall carried a rifle and Avery held a pistol at his side. They moved in opposite directions to relieve themselves in the brush.

Gale glanced at Santos and gave him a thumbs up. Santos' expression was taut, and he placed one hand on his rifle. Gale slowly reached for his shotgun and pulled the 12-gauge close, resting it in the crook of his arm.

After the men relieved themselves, they walked to the back of the semi and slung open the trailer doors. Gale heard them talking, then could make out Avery hoisting himself into the trailer. Seconds later, Marshall followed.

Gale watched as Avery and Marshall struggled to lift two long, heavy objects that looked like rolled up carpets from inside the trailer and drop them on the ground. Without the night vision goggles, he couldn't see well enough to make out what they were. He could see Marshall hopping off the trailer bed. Then he saw Avery follow. He glanced at Santos, who had quickly switched on his iPhone and was capturing the scene.

Avery paused and finally said to Marshall, pointing, "Let's put 'em in the mine. No way they last another day. I don't want to shoot 'em and scare the migrants off."

"Got it," Marshall said.

Marshall lifted one object and began carrying it. With a grunt, Avery picked up the other with his frying pan hands as if he were in a deadlift and slung it over his thick shoulder. Gale shivered. He turned to Santos and whispered, "Those are people." Santos nodded. Gale's mind raced. But no. It couldn't be Tuck and the girl. Whoever it was much bigger. Gale kept a tight hold of his shotgun and settled in to wait.

After dumping their loads in the entrance to the mine, Avery and Marshall quickly emerged from the shaft and started to walk toward the semi. Seconds later, Gale heard a murmur and realized migrants were beginning to congregate at the bottom of the trail. Avery and Marshall heard them, too, and started to walk toward the cluster of illegals. Santos, while continuing to film the scene, whispered to Gale, "We need to get a photo of the truck's plate number."

Gale stared at Santos. He glanced at the semi and the open space between where they hid and the tractor trailer. Even at night, the chances of moving across the open basin undetected were dicey.

"You couldn't get it with the video?" Gale asked.

"I don't think so. The headlights were facing toward me, and when it turned, I never got a shot at the rear plate. I don't think the lens would have been able to pick it up."

"The more evidence the better," Gale said in a whisper.

"Exactly."

Gale was pondering how they were going to snap a photo unobserved. In the darkness, he could make out a large group of people. The migrants spoke in hushed tones and sidestepped down the mountainside.

Gale turned to Santos and noticed he was videotaping the scene. "Looks like you already have a job."

Santos nodded and said in a steely whisper, "That's right. But it can be yours."

Gale took a deep breath and pulled his phone out of the back pocket of his jeans and switched on the cell. "No. I got it."

"I got you covered. Stay low. Move fast. Don't creep along like you see in the movies. Okay?"

"Yup."

"Make sure your flash is off when you get the plate number. The iris on the camera will work without it as long as you're on Night mode. You don't want to light up the basin like a paparazzi."

"Okay."

Gale concealed his phone while the cell booted up and glanced again at the large group of migrants coming off the slope. Gale wondered how they would all squeeze into the trailer. A few were already milling at the basin's far end. Gale shot a glance. Avery and Marshall still had their backs turned to the truck. After a moment of confusion, Gale navigated the touch screen and turned off the flash mode.

Seconds later, he could feel his temples throbbing as he grabbed his shotgun in one hand. He whispered, "Wish me luck."

Santos stopped filming and picked up his rifle as Gale carefully wedged himself between the boulders and took off. A jolt of pain stabbed his side, but as a former professional football player, he could still move. He kept his head down and took off toward the semi, heart pounding and adrenaline racing through his body. Moments later, he was crouching near the front of the tractor trailer, shielding himself behind the truck's massive grill. He was nearly out of breath from the adrenalin rush.

Gale rested the shotgun on the ground and pulled his phone from his jeans. He aimed the cell at the license plate and jabbed the touch screen with his index finger. He took a deep breath and tapped the photo button. Suddenly, the whole front of the truck's chrome grill lit as the camera flash exploded in white light.

Astonished, Gale instinctively fell flat. Bile rose in the back of his throat, and he gazed at the phone in disbelief. He cursed himself. Even his six-year-old daughter could turn off the flash mode on a cellphone. His ineptitude was going to cost him and Santos their lives.

Gale recognized Marshall yelling, "What the hell was that, Lloyd?"

"I don't like it," Avery answered.

Gale looked over toward Santos but could only see the shadowed outcropping of boulders. He heard grumblings, then a growing furor from the large group of migrants, who sensed that the tractor trailer, which was supposed to deliver them to freedom, was instead a coffin. A few of the migrants began cursing and another cried out as a growing sense of discontent grew among them. Gale saw Marshall swing his rifle toward a woman who was beginning to scream.

On his stomach, Gale could hear Avery say with a hint of fear, "Let's get out of here, Buck. Take care of Spivey and the woman. Enrique, get your men and start back up the trail. We'll be right behind you."

Avery's heart was beating hard as he watched Marshall start moving toward the mine shaft to finish off Spivey and the woman. Avery was turning toward the truck when he heard one of the migrants scream and whirled around raising the Glock instinctively. Enrique was shouting at a girl who was wailing. Avery felt a flash of anger. He wanted to choke her. Shut her up. Things were out of control.

Enrique kept shouting orders and the other two coyotes started up the basin's slope. Avery turned back to the truck. He needed to grab the satellite phone and his knapsack from the cab. He hated to think about being stuck out here without being able to communicate. Another migrant began cursing and yelling. As Avery turned to see what was going on, he heard a sharp clap and watched Marshall stumble and fall as the sound reverberated against the mountainside and then rolled away into the night like a passing thunderstorm.

At first, Avery was frozen in disbelief, but then he realized he'd caught a muzzle flash out of the corner of his eye from an outcropping of boulders no more than twenty yards away. As the migrants screamed and scrambled back up the slope, Avery grabbed the phone and knapsack from the cab, quickly moved behind the semi and pulled a flashbang out of the knapsack. Then, with the cab still shielding him, he yanked the pin and tossed the cylinder overhand as if he were throwing to a receiver running a fly route. Seconds later, the flashbang exploded in a brilliant burst of white light among the boulders where he'd spotted the muzzle flash. Whoever was behind those rocks was in a world of hurt.

Avery ran in a crouch toward Marshall with the Glock at the ready and the satellite phone in his other hand. He found Marshall moaning and bleeding out. Avery looked down and said, "Sorry, Buck. The fat lady sings." With that, he was about to start toward the trailhead when he heard a voice.

Moments earlier, after the camera flash had gone off, Gale had hit the ground, then taken cover under the semi's cab. He had heard the gunshot and screaming, and then saw what he assumed were Avery's legs on the far side of the cab. Gale had rolled out the other side just as the bouldered area where Santos had hidden exploded in flames. Shocked, Gale lay there for a moment, but then willed himself to his feet and edged down the side of the truck clutching the shotgun. Avery had emerged from the other side and was standing over Marshall. Gale slid closer and then pointed his 12 gauge at Avery who was holding a pistol in one hand and what looked like a phone in the other, and said, "I don't want to shoot you, Lloyd, but I will."

At first Avery's jaw dropped at the sight of Gale, but he quickly gathered himself. He smiled and said, "I won't even ask how the hell you got up here. But there's one thing I do know. You're no killer. Put down that shotgun and walk away, McClanahan."

"Drop the pistol now, Lloyd."

"What are you going to do if I don't? And even if I do, what then? We're in the middle of nowhere."

Gale hesitated. He hadn't thought things through. He needed to find out about Santos and help him if he was still living. How was he going to deal with Avery too?

Avery continued. "Be smart for once, McClanahan. Here's what we do. We both drop our weapons, and you go your way and I go mine. That's the only solution here unless one of us shoots the other. And I just can't see you pulling that trigger."

Gale's mind raced. He thought back to killing the elk all those years ago and realized that as much as he detested Avery, the thought of killing a man ran against everything he knew. While shooting Avery was his best option, his finger remained frozen on the shotgun's trigger. A few seconds later, he watched in disbelief as Avery raised the Glock. Gale was about to tell Avery again to drop the gun when Avery fired.

Seconds later, Gale lay panting, feeling blood ooze from his side, warm and syrupy through his fingers. Avery stood over him and clucked his tongue. "You're screwed, Coach. Before you go, I gotta know. How did you get here?"

Gale rasped, "Horse."

Avery stared. "What the hell for?"

"I needed answers."

"Answers to what?"

"Lots of things." Gale tried to take a deep breath. He choked, "Who killed Clay?"

"How the hell should I know?"

Gale paused and then asked in a whisper, "What did you do with Maria?"

"Maria? What are you talking about?"

"The migrant girl you stole."

"Do you think I ask them their names?" Avery laughed. "Waters was right about one thing. You really are a boy scout. One last thought, Coach. You really do need to learn how to punt."

Gale's mind whirled with the finality of it all.

As Avery started to raise his gun, his chest exploded.

Twenty-Four

Bart Waters swore when they pulled onto the McClanahan ranch and had to park by the entrance because a flatbed truck blocked the road. During the ride to Kinney, Waters had said squat to Pax except for a few grunts threatening Billy if the girl wasn't there. Waters made Pax's skin crawl. As they began their trek to the house, Waters had a Smith & Wesson revolver tucked into his belt, and Pax had his service Sig Sauer holstered and an AR-15 in his hand. He had no plans to use either. He felt ridiculous carrying a semi-automatic to apprehend a pencil-thin teenager. Pax wanted to go home. He'd had enough. He didn't dare ask questions, but he feared what Waters would do to the girl once they took her off the ranch.

When they got within two hundred yards of the house, Waters had told Pax to go to the front and start making noise as a diversion while he made a sweep to the side. As Waters crept silently behind the house, Pax got a sick feeling in his stomach when he spotted a man standing 30 feet away on the front porch. The man was shrouded in shadows. It was a dark enough night already, and after squinting, Pax felt a lump in his throat when he realized the man held a rifle. Pax hesitated, and shouted with false bravado, "Sheriff's Department. I'm looking for the girl. Melanie Sprague."

Pax flinched as the man sighted him with his rifle. Pax said, "The girl's broken the law."

"The hell she has," the man barked.

"You heard me," Pax said.

"That's right. I heard you. You turn around and git. Come back in the day and be ready to show me your warrant," the man shouted.

Pax stared into the darkness. His heartbeat thundered, and his chest felt as though it would split open. In his years as a sheriff, he'd never been in the sight of a rifle. He'd spent most of his time pulling people from car wrecks and dealing with drunks at closing time.

Then in the darkness Pax spotted Waters coming around the other side of the house and aim his revolver at the man. Waters' Smith & Wesson exploded, and Pax saw the man drop on the porch.

Waters yelled, "Get the girl, Billy."

Pax couldn't move his arms and legs. He was frozen until Waters aimed the revolver at him and said, "You hear me?"

Pax nodded weakly. He noticed the lower button of his shirt had popped and saw a roll of pale belly fat pushing through.

Pax pointed his AR-15 at the stricken man and began wobbling toward the house. He felt dizzy and scared. The whole situation was out of control. He started to tremble when he imagined himself rotting in some federal prison. Inmates hated cops. He tried to not think about what they'd do to him in the shower.

Pax crept onto the porch and cursed when he noticed the man writhing and his stomach bleeding. Waters had shot him through the gut. Pax threw the man's rifle away and moved past him. He tried the handle, but the door was locked. He started banging hard on the windowpane as if he were the UPS man delivering a package.

"You idiot," Waters shouted from the corner of the house. "You think they're going to invite you in?"

Pax felt a flash of anger and thought about turning the AR-15 on Waters. Instead, he shrugged and broke the glass with the rifle stock.

He reached through the window for the doorknob and yelped as someone grabbed his wrist. Suddenly, his hand felt like it had been stuck in a woodchipper. He screamed and tried to wrench free, but that brought more pain than he ever thought possible. He looked through the glass and saw that the girl was kneeling on the other side of the door holding a knife that had plunged through his hand. Reaching out with his good hand through the broken glass, he grabbed her by the throat and began to squeeze as hard as he could.

Marybeth had barely slept. Her nerves were on edge, and she'd worried all night about Gale and Santos. She'd fretted about the girl and Katie Tuck and the whole awful predicament they'd found themselves in. At first, she'd thought she was dreaming when she'd heard the voices, but the gunshot sprang her into action. She'd jumped out of bed, grabbed the pistol resting on her nightstand, and crept to the bedroom window. After peering into the darkness, she heard a window break and then a scream.

She dashed toward the darkened living room, lit only by the glow of the TV, peered around the corner and saw Melanie Sprague kneeling by the front door, stabbing a man's hand viciously with a kitchen knife. For an instant, Marybeth froze before pointing the pistol at the door. She felt her hands shake and realized if she missed, she'd kill Sprague. She heard more screams and curses and then a hand dart through the broken pane and grab Sprague by the throat. Marybeth could hear Sprague gasp, then start struggling to breathe, so she ran across the living room to change her sight line, aimed the 9mm that Hayes had given her, steadied her heartbeat, and pulled the trigger.

The shot shook the sheetrock and reverberated throughout the house. Marybeth could smell the acrid odor of propellant. Sprague had dropped to the floor and whoever had tried to choke her had crashed wailing onto the porch outside.

Marybeth shook her head in disbelief. She'd shot someone. Where was Mason? Was he dead or alive? The idea that he was dead and she alone to deal with this situation caused a wave of dread to wash over her. Just then, she noticed Katie Tuck, wearing a terry cloth robe, was frozen behind her with her hands covering her mouth.

Marybeth followed Tuck's eyes to the door just as it broke open. Now she too was frozen, listening to the rhythmic pounding of her own heart as Bart Waters, silhouetted in the bright glow of the television, stood ten feet away pointing a gun at her face. He was breathing hard, and behind him, she could see a man lying on the porch wearing a sheriff's uniform holding his arm with a blood smeared hand crying for a doctor.

Waters' narrow eyes shifted from Marybeth to Tuck and Sprague. Sprague was off to Waters' right, rubbing her throat and trying to catch her breath. Her t-shirt and arms were splattered in blood. With her spiky, bleached hair, piercings, and tattoos, she resembled a punk vampire.

"Put the gun down," Waters said.

Marybeth let the pistol fall to the floor. She felt chills rippling up and down her spine.

"Now look what you've done," Waters said, shaking his head. "All I wanted was the girl and her phone. Now I got to reckon with all of you. Especially you, Ms. Tuck."

"You don't want to do this," Tuck said. "Why don't you leave before someone else gets hurt?"

"It's not that easy." Waters turned to Tuck. "All you had to do was mind your own business and none of this would have happened. But you couldn't give it up, could you? Ever the school marm. Had to go chasing Johnny Spivey and drum up trouble.

"Right. It's me you want. Leave everyone else alone." Tuck wavered a bit and then added, "You can't think that you're going to be able to walk from this."

For an instant, Waters seemed to ponder the situation. He paused before saying, "Every good salesman is a storyteller. Here's mine. I accompanied Sheriff Pax to arrest the girl for manslaughter and clear my good name. She and Johnny Spivey killed those two boys. Sold them the drugs that she stole from her degenerate mother. She tried to blame me and Dean. As a concerned citizen, I accompanied Sheriff Pax this evening to arrest her and, unprovoked, we were threatened with bodily harm. We took you down in a hail of gunfire trying to protect ourselves. Sheriff Pax was doing his duty, and in trying to help him uphold the law, I acted in self-defense."

Tuck snorted. "Total B.S. You can't think anyone will believe that garbage?"

Sprague scowled and slowly climbed onto her hands and knees. Marybeth glanced at the floor to make sure she knew exactly where the pistol lay. It was clear that she was going to have to act. Certainly, she wasn't simply going to allow all of them to be slaughtered like sheep. As she watched for an opportunity, she issued a silent prayer willing Tilly to sleep through the whole ordeal. Waters was a monster, but he wouldn't hurt a child who couldn't even identify him, would he?

Waters shook his head. "No, it won't be hard to convince people." He smiled thinly. "It's one of my gifts."

"You're going to kill us, aren't you?" Marybeth asked.

Waters nodded. "It's a shame. Gives me pause, but . . ."

Sprague said under her breath, "Asshole."

Marybeth knew she had to act, but there was no way she could reach for her gun without Waters killing her.

Then Waters swung the revolver at Sprague and said, "Now give me that cell phone."

"Go piss off," Sprague snarled.

Waters looked at Sprague and said dismissively, "You're nothing but trailer trash."

"Shame on you," Tuck said. "Don't talk to a child that way."

"Like I said, ever the school marm," Waters answered, swinging the gun toward Tuck.

"Spare the girl," Tuck begged. "She's done no harm."

"Oh, very much the opposite."

"She's just a kid," Marybeth said.

"She's a little monster," Waters replied as he glanced quickly toward the open door. The whimpering sheriff had curled into a ball.

Waters kept the revolver pointed in the direction of Tuck and Marybeth as he eased back toward the door. "Better to use Sheriff Pax's gun for the forensic report." He turned his head for an instant and said sarcastically to the stricken sheriff, "You won't mind, will you, Billy?"

As he bent to pick up the Sig Sauer, Melanie Sprague leapt like a cat, grabbed Waters by the ankle, and bit him. Marybeth heard Waters grunt as Sprague knocked him off balance. Enraged, Waters swung his pistol and struck Sprague on the side of the head. As he did so, three things happened at once. Tuck cursed and charged Waters, Marybeth reached for her pistol, and Sprague fell to the floor. Just before Tuck reached Waters, a shot rang out and Tuck fell at his feet. But that was followed quickly by a second shot, this one striking Waters in the sternum and sending him back through the door where he lay spread-eagled beside the still writhing Sheriff.

Stunned, Marybeth's hands tingled, her ears rang, and her temples pounded. She looked around the room in horror. Seeing Katie Tuck lying on the bloodstained carpet with her head resting at a grotesque angle was too much for Marybeth. She fell to her knees. But then she realized that she had no time to grieve. Marybeth had to act, and as Sprague was in the process of picking herself off the floor, the first thing she needed to do was to find out what happened to Mason Hayes.

Twenty-Five

Through the fog that had settled behind his eyes, Santos lifted himself up and moved toward Gale and the man he'd just shot. He'd raised his head to see one of the smugglers standing over Gale and had instinctively sighted his rifle and fired. The man was dead weight when he hit the ground. Now, as he worked his way to Gale, he did a quick body inventory. There was a sharp pain in his jaw from where he struck the limestone as he dove to avoid the worst of the blast, he'd bitten his tongue badly, and he thought that he might have a busted ear drum. When he got to the men, he glanced at Avery to confirm that he was no threat, and then he knelt next to Gale. Santos was no stranger to gunshot wounds and from the large splotch of blood on Gale's t-shirt, he knew Gale was in danger of bleeding out. He kicked himself. The med kit was in one of the panniers with the horses. Through clenched teeth, Gale said, "Nice shot. I thought you were dead."

"I nearly was. Now let's stop the bleeding. Sorry, but this isn't going to feel good."

With no dressings, Santos tugged off his own shirt and compressed the wound, stuffing the cloth into the bullet hole in Gale's side. Gale groaned. In Iraq, Santos could call a medevac, but here he was on his own. The idea of trying to drive a tractor trailer for the first time on a two track, banged up as he was, terrified him, and, even if he could manage it without killing them both, he doubted that Gale could survive long enough for him to find help. Santos took a deep breath and tried to clear his head. He was getting ahead of himself. The first thing to do was stabilize Gale as best he could.

"I'm going to go get the horses and the med kit. Hold on, and I'll patch you up. Then we'll figure out what to do from there."

Gale nodded before asking in a choked whisper, "What was in Avery's other hand?"

Epilogue

Three months later, Gale walked gingerly out of the house on a cool, clear January afternoon. Mason Hayes sat in a wicker chair with a wool blanket wrapped around him. He was still recovering from his stomach wound, but he was crotchety as ever, stubbornly carrying on. "Remember what I told you, Gale."

"What's that?"

"The road to hell is paved with good intention."

Gale smiled ruefully, looked toward the paddock, and lost himself in thought.

Mateo Santos was teaching the McClanahan's newest ranch hand how to ride. Gale watched Ephraim Hernandez nervously holding Bumpkin's reins. The teenager had settled in, living in the small bunkhouse attached to the barn and learning English from one of Marybeth's school colleagues. Gale had taken Ephraim's silence about Maria as an indication that he had accepted that she was gone forever. Occasionally, however, Gale would see Ephraim leaning against the paddock fence, staring blankly toward the hillocks, lost in thought.

When the story had broken about Waters' drug smuggling and human trafficking operation, any legal threat faced by Gale and Marybeth for harboring the teenager had evaporated when state and federal authorities discovered the astonishing level of corruption in their agencies. Billy Pax had spilled everything for a lesser sentence and Dean Spivey, after barely surviving being hogtied, gagged, and nearly murdered, had tried to plea bargain but found himself facing a fire-spitting prosecutor who wanted nothing less than Spivey to serve a life sentence for the deaths of Martin Keller and Sam Lowe. Johnny Spivey was more fortunate. Prosecutors saw him as a victim of his father's abuse and sentenced him to three years' probation, counseling, and two hundred and fifty hours of community service. Johnny's testimony had caused the New Mexico Attorney General to open an investigation into the Hood Military Academy's "educational" practices.

Unsurprisingly, Grayson Wallace had done a stellar job of leveraging the entire fiasco to secure a green card for the teenager and a clean personnel file for Anna Torres. Of course, he took special delight in reminding Gale of his brilliant legal work but no longer called him Brutus, now that he had left Caton in the rearview mirror. His new nickname for Gale was more Zane Gray than Shakespeare. He now referred to him as "Quick Draw." Gale preferred Brutus.

Tragically, Katie Tuck wasn't so lucky. The county coroner ruled her death instantaneous from the bullet entering her left temple. Gale had held a weeping Marybeth close during Tuck's memorial service. Nearly the entire community had packed Clay Moorhead Stadium. During Abraham Daly's homily, Gale, who had insisted on being there despite still convalescing from his wounds, had recalled the fierce expression on Tuck's face when they were on their way to confront Spivey. Gale knew she'd been one of the bravest people he'd known. A few months after her death, the town voted to build a new school and strip Clay Moorhead Stadium of its name. Katie Tuck Memorial High School was born.

The Texas University Interscholastic League hadn't been kind to Caton High School. After discovering the sordid truth about the football program, the Executive Director had suspended the season and banned the assistant coaches for life from serving in any educational capacity in the state of Texas. Sadly, the players had paid the price. Even if the season hadn't been curtailed, Gale had been in no condition to coach. The bullet wound had barely missed his spleen as it tore through his ribs. Three months later, he still felt the effects of being shot. He chided himself for walking like an old man and bristled at not being able to do physical labor. As Marybeth knew from his days playing in the League, he was a lousy patient. If Mateo Santos hadn't discovered Avery's satellite phone and called in a medevac from the hospital in Alpine, Gale would have died.

Gale watched Santos instruct the teenager as Hayes sat in silence. Along with the emptiness Gale felt, he worried about Marybeth. While his wife had expressed no regret over the killing of Bart Waters, Katie Tuck's death had left her deeply troubled, and the surreal nature of nearly having been murdered had brought her moments of panic and nightmares so intense that she'd stopped recounting them to Gale. With Anna Torres' help, Marybeth had been seeing a therapist in Midland. Gale hoped the sessions would bring back her easy smile and the intimacy they had shared.

Gale turned and saw Tilly and Melanie Sprague sitting in the shade under a live oak. Melanie was braiding Til's hair. Tilly had taken it upon herself to be Gale's devoted caregiver, fetching whatever he needed during his convalescence. She had even declared to Marybeth and Gale her firm intention to be a doctor. Gale knew the irony wasn't lost on Marybeth.

Melanie Sprague's presence had a positive effect on the entire McClanahan family. Since agreeing to temporarily provide foster care for Sprague after her mother was incarcerated on yet another drug charge, Gale and Marybeth had provided Sprague with a home and as much love as they could possibly give. While Sprague sneaked the occasional cigarette, she lived mostly by house rules and grew into the older sister Tilly never had. They had become inseparable. Sprague rejoiced over fresh laundered clothes and a full stomach. She was losing her hard edges. It broke Gale and Marybeth's hearts to think that a court order could easily take her away. They asked Grayson Wallace to begin adoption proceedings. When Marybeth and Gale told Sprague about their plans, she burst into tears and hugged them.

The house was a different story. Although contractors had physically erased evidence of blood and mayhem, Marybeth still refused to sit in the living room. Gale knew it would be months, maybe years before his wife would be able to occupy that part of the house. Gale had even considered razing the entire home and building a new one. For now, though, they sat in the den to watch TV and spent most of their time in the kitchen, sitting at the breakfast nook, working on their laptops.

While his family had survived, Gale couldn't shake the gnawing sense that things weren't resolved. He glanced once more at Tilly and Melanie Sprague under the oak as Sprague carefully fixed Til's hair. Gale knew the women in his life were the most cherished part of his world.

Gale turned to Hayes. "You were right about intentions, Mason."

"I was and I wasn't." Hayes nodded out toward Ephraim Hernandez.

"You think Mateo will make a rider out of him?"

"I think so," Hayes said, breaking into a smile. "He'll make a good hand."

"Does this mean you've come around?"

Hayes lifted his head and settled his gaze on Gale. "I reckon we can use the help."

Gale nodded and said before he went back into the house, "I'm sorry for the price you had to pay for our good intentions."

On a winter afternoon that threatened to finally give them some rain, Gale noticed a white sedan pull up to the metal shed and was surprised to see Abraham Daly, wearing his customary tie and dress shirt beneath a raincoat, emerge from the vehicle. Gale was alone. Santos and Ephraim were on the northern boundary of the ranch repairing fences, Mason Hayes was at home resting, and Marybeth, Tilly, and Melanie Sprague had gone to Midland.

Approaching Gale, Daly gave him a cautious look and said softly, "Eben signed with Tech."

"I heard. Great news."

"By God's good grace, he'll be near. Perhaps I'll be able to see him play."

Gale nodded. "Of course, you will." Gale shook Daly's hand and stood with the preacher under a pale sky. They stood facing one another until Daly finally broke the silence.

"Well, that depends."

"How so?"

"On what I came to speak with you about," Daly said, his voice resolute.

Gale looked quizzically at the preacher.

"I'm sorry for all that you and your family have been through. I'm deeply regretful for it and have prayed for you."

Gale nodded.

"I have something to tell you, Coach McClanahan. It's not easy. In fact, I'm putting myself at your mercy. I'm already at the mercy of the Lord."

"We all are."

"True," Daly said, pursing his lips. "But not all of us are murderers."

Gale took a step back and looked hard into Daly's face, but Daly was looking down at his shoes.

"It's taken too long to get up my courage, but when I heard what happened to you and your family, and most awfully to Katie Tuck, I knew there'd be a day of reckoning. And today is the day." Daly took a deep breath then raised his head and looked Gale squarely in the eye. "I killed Clay Moorhead."

Gale gaped. "You picked up a high-powered rifle on a summer day and shot him?"

Daly nodded and shrugged. "My father was an outfitter in Montana. We were raised hardscrabble. He taught me early on to fish and hunt."

"Why'd you do it, Abraham?"

Daly looked away. His voice cracked. "Clay impregnated my daughter, Alexa, two months shy of her eighteenth birthday. He promised her alcohol and drugs for sex, and she wanted both bad enough to comply with a 58-year-old man. When she found out she was pregnant, she went to see him. He denied everything. What kind of man does that?"

"So you killed him?" Gale thought about Moorhead calling Wallace before his death. Now Gale understood.

"That's right."

"How do you feel about that?"

"You mean as a man of the cloth?"

"No. As a father."

"Vindicated. I felt like I'd cleansed Caton. Or at least started to. You did the rest."

"Where's your daughter now?"

"In a group home for unwed mothers in Denton."

Gale sighed. "Why are you telling me?"

Daly shrugged again and turned to Gale. "I don't regret killing the man. But I regret what's been done to my family and yours. And I'll never forgive myself for what happened to Katie Tuck."

Gale nodded.

"Would you have killed Clay?" Daly asked.

"You mean if he'd violated my daughter?"

"That's what I mean."

Gale stared at the minister and noticed how haggard Daly appeared. "I don't know. I had an opportunity to shoot a man I despised before he shot me, and I hesitated, so maybe I'm not the right man to ask. "

"No one knows what's in a man's heart, do they?" Daly's voice drifted off. "I wasn't thinking clearly. I only knew one thing. I wanted Clay dead."

"How'd you think you'd get away with it?"

Daly bit his lip and laughed bitterly. "I didn't. I figured they'd charge me the day I killed him, but no one banged on my door. When I heard rumors that Clay was shot by a target shooter, I knew the county sheriff wasn't going to pursue it."

"So here we are," Gale said.

Daly took a deep breath. "What now? I'm in your hands. I will abide by whatever course you set me."

Gale looked hard at Daly and shrugged. "Clay had it coming."

Daly held Gale's eyes a moment then looked away. "You think God will forgive me, Coach McClanahan?"

"That's between you and Him."

"I suppose you're right. I have work to do to square myself away with my Maker. But what about you, Coach McClanahan? My sins have affected your family. Can you forgive me for that?"

Gale looked away toward the plains, vast and empty, stretching under an overcast January sky. He turned again to Abraham Daly. "You did what you had to do. You acted as a father. I forgive you."

Daly said, "Thank you."

Without another word, Daly turned and walked slowly to his car. After he drove away, Gale stood with his head down, closed his eyes, and said a prayer for Daly. Gale hoped doing so would help put Caton behind him. He'd had enough.

Gale turned, and as he began walking to the paddock, it started to rain. He looked over and saw Eula nudging toward him along the fence. Gale met

Marybeth's mare and found himself holding out the palm of his hand as the horse approached. He felt oddly comforted by Eula's presence. Before he'd ridden into the borderlands, they'd called him a gentleman rancher, and maybe they were right. But he took solace in the fact that, like Daly, he did what he felt he had to do to keep his family safe.

Gale would forgive Abraham Daly. The world was better off without men like Clay Moorhead, not to mention Waters and Avery. Predators like them were best forgotten. Gale felt Eula nudge his hand and thought about Katie Tuck. He gazed out toward the empty plain and vowed that as long as he lived, he'd honor her memory.

The rain started coming down in soft patters against the hard, baked earth. Let it pour, Gale thought. Let it cleanse the land. He turned to go back into the house when his phone began to chime. Gale pulled his cell out of his back pocket and sighed. It was Grayson Wallace. He thought about telling Wallace about Daly's confession but dismissed the impulse. Besides, he wouldn't be shocked if somehow Wallace already knew.

Gale was about to take the call when he stopped dead in his tracks and shivered. He let Wallace's call slide to voicemail. He needed to think through his premonition that Wallace's call meant more trouble ahead. He supposed the trouble would find him eventually, but for now Gale needed to take comfort in all he had, and all he had kept from losing.

Acknowledgements

I'm deeply grateful for the following people who have championed my writing and provided valuable insight: Annie Britton, Jen Britton, Kevin Colby, Wyatt Colby, Brian Fidler, Tom Helming, Arnie Holtberg, and Eddie Scannell.

As always, I am indebted to my friend and superb editor, Wright Abbot, who has devoted untold hours to *No Heart to Kill* and supported and guided me through the ups and downs of writing three novels, and to Dan Edwards of Creative Texts, who gave me a chance.

I am fortunate to have a loving family who supports my writing obsession: thanks to Annie, Kyle, Trevor, and Jen, whose love and encouragement have been amazing.

About the Author

C.W. Wells began his professional life as an award-winning newspaper reporter before turning to a career in education. He coached high school football in Texas and grew up in a small town. No Heart to Kill is his third novel. He can be contacted at cwwells97@gmail.com.

About the Publisher

Creative Texts is a boutique independent publishing house devoted to high quality content that readers enjoy. We publish best-selling authors such as Jerry D. Young, N.C. Reed, Sean Liscom, Jared McVay, Laurence Dahners, and many more. Our audiobook performers are among the best in the business including Hollywood legends like Barry Corbin and top talent like Christopher Lane, Alyssa Bresnaham, Erin Moon and Graham Hallstead.

Whether its post-apocalyptic or dystopian fiction, biography, history, true crime science fiction, thrillers, or even classic westerns, our goal is to produce highly rated customer preferred content. If there is anything we can do to enhance your reader experience, please contact us directly at info@creativetexts.com. As always, we do appreciate your reviews on your book seller's website.

Finally, if you would like to find more great books like this one, please search for us by name in your favorite search engine or on your bookseller's website to see books by all Creative Texts authors. Thank you for reading.

Made in United States
North Haven, CT
13 February 2024

48705773R00134